JUST REWARDS

Barbara Taylor Bradford was born in Leeds, and by the age of twenty was an editor and columnist on Fleet Street. Her first novel, *A Woman of Substance*, became an enduring bestseller and was followed by nineteen others, most recently *Unexpected Blessings* which reached number 4 in the *Sunday Times* bestseller list. Her books have sold more than seventy-five million copies worldwide in more than ninety countries and forty languages, and ten of her books have been made into mini-series and television movies. She lives in New York with her husband, producer Robert Bradford. Visit her website www.barbarataylorbradford.com for more information.

Visit www.AuthorTracker.co.uk for exclusive information on your favourite HarperCollins authors.

D1151569

By the same author:

Barbara Taylor Bradford

Just Rewards

HarperCollins*Publishers*

This novel is entirely a work of fiction.
The names, characters and incidents portrayed in it are
the work of the author's imagination. Any resemblance to
actual persons, living or dead, events or localities is
entirely coincidental.

HarperCollins*Publishers*
77–85 Fulham Palace Road,
Hammersmith, London W6 8JB

www.harpercollins.co.uk

This paperback edition 2006
1

First published in Great Britain by
HarperCollins*Publishers* 2005

ISBN-13 978 0 00 786971 8

Typeset in Sabon by Palimpsest Book Production Limited,
Polmont, Stirlingshire

Printed and bound in Great Britain by
Clays Ltd, St Ives plc

For Bob, with my love

THE THREE CLANS

The Hartes shown in line of descent

Emma Harte: Matriarch: Founder of the dynasty and business empire

HER CHILDREN

Edwina: Dowager Countess of Dunvale. Emma's daughter by Edwin Fairley (illegitimate). First-born

Christopher 'Kit' Lowther: Emma's son by her first husband Joe Lowther. Second-born

Robin Ainsley: Emma's son by her second husband Arthur Ainsley. Third-born

Elizabeth Ainsley Deboyne: Emma's daughter by her second husband Arthur Ainsley. Robin's twin. Third-born

Daisy Ainsley: Emma's daughter by Paul McGill (illegitimate). Fourth-born

HER GRANDCHILDREN
Shown in line of descent

Anthony Standish: Earl of Dunvale. Son of Edwina and Jeremy Standish, Earl and Countess of Dunvale

Sarah Lowther Pascal: Daughter of Kit and June Lowther

Owen Hughes: Son of Robin Ainsley and Glynnis Hughes (illegitimate)

Jonathan Ainsley: Son of Robin and Valerie Ainsley

Paula McGill Harte Amory Fairley O'Neill: Daughter of Daisy and David Amory

Philip McGill Harte Amory: Son of Daisy and David Amory. Brother of Paula

Alexander Barkstone: Son of Elizabeth Ainsley and Tony Barkstone. Brother of Emily, Amanda and Francesca. (Deceased)

Emily Barkstone Harte: Daughter of Elizabeth Ainsley and Tony Barkstone. Half-sister of Amanda and Francesca

Amanda Linde: Daughter of Elizabeth and her second husband Derek Linde. Twin of Francesca, half-sister of Emily

Francesca Linde Weston: Daughter of Elizabeth and her second husband Derek Linde. Twin of Amanda, half-sister of Emily

EMMA'S GREAT-GRANDCHILDREN

Tessa Fairley Longden: Daughter of Paula and Jim Fairley (Paula's first husband)

Lorne Fairley: Son of Paula and Jim Fairley. Twin of Tessa

Lord Jeremy Standish: Son of Anthony and Sally Standish, Earl and Countess of Dunvale. Brother of Giles and India

Toby Harte: Son of Emily and Winston Harte II. Brother of Gideon and Natalie

Gideon Harte: Son of Emily and Winston Harte II. Brother of Toby and Natalie

Natalie Harte: Daughter of Emily and Winston Harte II. Sister of Toby and Gideon

Hon. Giles Standish: Son of Anthony and Sally Standish, Earl and Countess of Dunvale. Brother of Jeremy and India

Lady India Standish: Daughter of Anthony Standish and Sally Harte, Earl and Countess of Dunvale. Sister of Jeremy and Giles

Patrick O'Neill: Son of Paula and Shane O'Neill (Paula's second husband). Brother of Linnet, Emsie and Desmond. (Deceased)

Linnet O'Neill: Daughter of Paula and Shane O'Neill. (Paula's second husband). Half-sister of Tessa and Lorne. Sister of Emsie and Desmond

Chloe Pascal: Daughter of Sarah Lowther Pascal and Yves Pascal

Fiona McGill Amory: Daughter of Philip McGill Amory and the late Madelana O'Shea Amory

Emsie O'Neill: Daughter of Paula and Shane O'Neill. Sister of Linnet and Desmond. Half-sister of Tessa and Lorne

Desmond O'Neill: Son of Paula and Shane O'Neill. Brother of Linnet and Emsie. Half-brother of Tessa and Lorne

Evan Hughes: Daughter of Owen and Marietta Hughes

THE HARTES continued

Winston Harte: Emma's older brother and business partner

Randolph Harte: Son of Winston and Charlotte Harte

Winston Harte II: Son of Randolph and Georgina Harte

Sally Harte Standish: Countess of Dunvale. Daughter of Randolph and Georgina Harte. Sister of Winston II and Vivienne

Vivienne Harte Leslie: Daughter of Randolph and Georgina. Sister of Winston Harte II and Sally Harte Standish

Toby Harte: Son of Winston Harte II and Emily Harte. Brother of Gideon and Natalie

Gideon Harte: Son of Winston Harte II and Emily Harte. Brother of Toby and Natalie

Natalie Harte: Daughter of Winston Harte II and Emily Harte. Sister of Toby and Gideon

Frank Harte: Emma's younger brother

Rosamunde Harte: Daughter of Frank and Natalie Harte

Simon Harte: Son of Frank and Natalie Harte. Brother of Rosamunde

THE O'NEILLS

Shane Patrick Desmond 'Blackie' O'Neill: Founding father of the dynasty and business empire

Bryan O'Neill: Son of Blackie and Laura Spencer O'Neill

Shane O'Neill: Son of Bryan and Geraldine O'Neill

Miranda O'Neill James: Daughter of Bryan and Geraldine O'Neill. Sister of Shane and Laura

Laura O'Neill Nettleton: Daughter of Bryan and Geraldine O'Neill. Sister of Shane and Miranda

Patrick O'Neill: Son of Shane and Paula O'Neill. Brother of Linnet, Emsie and Desmond. (Deceased)

Linnet O'Neill: Daughter of Shane and Paula O'Neill. Sister of Emsie and Desmond

Emsie O'Neill: Daughter of Shane and Paula O'Neill. Sister of Desmond and Linnet

Desmond O'Neill: Son of Shane and Paula O'Neill. Brother of Linnet and Emsie

THE KALLINSKIS

David Kallinski: Founding father of the dynasty and business empire

Sir Ronald Kallinski: Son of David and Rebecca Kallinski

Michael Kallinski: Son of Ronald and Helen 'Posy' Kallinski

Mark Kallinski: Son of Ronald and Helen 'Posy' Kallinski. Brother of Michael

Julian Kallinski: Son of Michael Kallinski and his former wife Valentine Kallinski

Arielle Kallinski: Daughter of Michael Kallinski and his former wife Valentine Kallinski. Sister of Julian

Jessica Kallinski: Daughter of Michael Kallinski and his former wife Valentine Kallinski. Sister of Julian and Arielle

CONTENTS

PROLOGUE

London: 2002

The man stood in the doorway of the shop, huddled in a corner, sheltering from the icy wind. It was freezing on this bitter January morning, and he felt tempted to hurry off to the nearby Hyde Park Hotel for a cooked English breakfast.

Yet he was unable to tear himself away from this doorway, where he had always had a perfect view of the building opposite, one which he had for so long coveted as his own.

Leaning forward, he stared at the grand and impressive edifice across the road. It had been standing there for over eighty years, but it was unscathed, untouched by the passage of time and impregnable. He thought of it as a bastion of prestige, privilege and wealth.

And it should have been his.

Tragically, he had been cheated. It had fallen into the hands of Paula O'Neill, who now thought of it as her own, when in reality it was *his* by rights.

In the mid-1980s he had almost wrested the flagship Knightsbridge emporium and the provincial Harte stores away from her, when she had made a series of mistakes in a deal related to the stores. So flawed was her judgement that she had played right into his waiting hands.

Unfortunately, just as he reached out, had the stores almost in his grasp, he had been betrayed. As a consequence of this unwarranted and unexpected betrayal, Paula O'Neill had managed to outwit him.

She had been his nemesis for years, but it was from this precise moment that he had become her sworn enemy, had vowed to wreak his revenge on her. And soon he would do that; he would finally triumph over her.

Abruptly, the man stepped forward, moving out of the doorway, his attention on two young women who had hurried out of the store and were studying the windows fronting onto Knightsbridge.

One of them was a redhead, and he knew her at once. She was Linnet O'Neill, Paula's daughter; however, she was now a Kallinski, after marrying the Kallinski heir last month. His thoughts settled on the little church in Pennistone village where they had been married. How easily it would have burned to the ground, killing everyone in it, and his problems with the Hartes would have been solved for ever more.

He cursed Mark Longden under his breath for losing his nerve. What a weak-kneed hypocrite *he* had turned out to be; he had been exiled to Australia by Paula O'Neill, and good riddance to bad rubbish.

For a moment the man was baffled, unable to pin-point the other woman's identity. She was bundled up in a loden cape and long scarf, and her face was obscured. But then she turned and he instantly recognized the distinctive chiselled profile.

His chest tightened, and a virulent anger surged through him as he gazed at Evan Hughes. She was his new nemesis, the American woman who had insinuated herself into the family and was about to become a Harte. He muttered an expletive . . . she was already a Harte, thanks in no small measure to his father's long-ago lust. And now she threatened everybody by her very existence, especially himself. She, too, was now a target along with Paula and her redheaded brat.

A smile slid onto his handsome face; he stared hard at the two women for a very long moment before setting out in the direction of the hotel for breakfast.

That self-satisfied smile remained intact as he turned up the collar of his expensive and impeccably-tailored vicuna coat and increased his pace.

As he walked, he considered a plan he had recently formulated . . . one so devilishly clever it might have been devised by Prince Machiavelli himself. How ingenious it was and it would surely help to bring about the fall of the house of Harte. He was convinced of this outcome.

Jonathan Ainsley laughed out loud. They were going to get their just rewards. He would see to that.

PART ONE

Quartet

Envy slays itself by its own arrows.
Medieval saying: Anonymous

CHAPTER ONE

Flurries of silvery snowflakes were blowing in the wind, sticking to the plate-glass windows of Harte's and on the faces of the two pretty young women gazing so intently into those windows.

Evan Hughes brought a gloved hand to her cheek and wiped the dampness away. Then she drew closer to Linnet O'Neill, shivering and hunching into her dark-green loden cape, feeling the sharp bite of the intense cold.

Instantly, Linnet glanced at Evan, and exclaimed, 'I'm so thoughtless, dragging you outside to look at our windows on a day like this! You're freezing. Come on, let's go inside. We've seen enough.'

Linnet took hold of Evan's arm and hurried her towards one of the double doors leading into Harte's.

'I'm all right, honestly,' Evan protested as she was propelled across the floor of the cosmetics department, adding irately, 'I'm not a cream puff, you know, I'm not going to melt away.'

'You've got guts of steel, I'm very well aware of

that!' Linnet shot back. 'It just became frightfully cold all of a sudden, and if you catch a cold, or get sick, Gideon will have my guts for garters.'

Evan burst out laughing, as usual amused by Linnet's penchant for quaint, rather odd sayings; she was frequently startled by the other girl's bluntness, as well as her pithiness, which could be quite stringent at times. Evan considered her recently-discovered cousin to be unique. She had never met anyone quite like her, and in this past year of working together they had become close, the very best of friends.

Moving through the eye-catching, glamorous displays of cosmetics and perfumes, Evan felt her icy limbs beginning to thaw in the warmth of the store, and she loosened her scarf, opened her cape. Smoothing her hand over her huge, bulging stomach, she confided, 'I feel like an enormous beached whale, Linny. I can't wait to give birth.'

Linnet's expression was sympathetic. 'I know. But just imagine, Evan, you're about to have twins. TWINS! You've certainly given Tessa, India and me pause for thought. We forgot that twins run in this family, that they're quite the norm. Grandy had twins, and so did Mummy the first time around, when she was married to Jim Fairley. It's only just struck *us* that we also might be candidates, have the same fate as you.' Linnet smiled engagingly. 'What do *you* think?'

'We share a lot of the same genes, I guess, so you're probably right.'

'Julian's hoping so, and actually so am I. It

4

makes life easier, having twins. Two children born together . . . an instant family and less time off work!'

'Very well put,' Evan responded softly, laughter filling her eyes. She couldn't help thinking that Linnet's inborn pragmatism inevitably came to the fore, but she admired her for being so down to earth.

By now the two women had arrived at a bank of elevators, and they stepped into one as soon as its doors slid open. Falling silent, they rode up to the management offices and hurried down the long corridor.

When they reached the alcove in the centre, where the famous portrait of Emma Harte hung, the two of them automatically came to a standstill, looked at each other, smiled, and then briskly saluted their great-grandmother and moved on. It had become something of a ritual with them of late, whether they were together or alone. It signified their pride in being her progeny and of working in the renowned store she had founded.

A few minutes later, settled comfortably in Evan's office, Linnet said, 'So, give me your opinion about the windows.'

'I have to agree with you, they *are* a bit outdated. Oh, they're beautiful, Linnet, of course. So well dressed. And they do evoke the kind of image we want for Harte's, but they could be a bit . . . *fresher.*'

'Not enough pizazz, perhaps?' Linnet suggested.

5

'Not pizazz, that's not quite right for Harte's, is it?'

'I suppose not,' Linnet agreed, sitting back in the chair, her eyes on Evan, whose opinion she valued.

Evan bit her lip, then shook her head. 'I think the word I'm looking for is ... *glamorous*. I'm talking about the fashion windows *per se*, Linnet, and they ought to be just a tad more eye-catching and inviting. Listen, they should say something to the customer ... they should say *come in, try me on, buy me.*'

Linnet nodded, her face lighting up. 'That's true. You've put your finger on it.'

Evan said, 'You've only recently come back from New York, and you've seen the store windows there. I believe you're now finding our windows somewhat flat.' Evan's grey eyes rested on Linnet thoughtfully. When Linnet made no response, she asked, 'Am I not correct?'

'I think you are ... but I'm not sure Mummy would agree.'

'Have you discussed the windows with Paula?' Evan probed, sounding anxious.

'No, I haven't had a chance, and she and Dad are staying in Yorkshire this week, recovering from Christmas, the New Year and all of their entertaining. Anyway, they're taking a week off from work, and they just want to stay put, potter around at Pennistone Royal. They enjoy being at home with each other, doing what they've always done since they were kids growing up together.' Linnet shook her head. 'Anyway, I'm not going to say a word until she's back here at work. Actually, Evan, there are some other things I want to discuss with her, certain changes I believe we should make at the store.'

Evan sat up straighter but said nothing, merely raised a brow quizzically, her eyes full of questions.

'You look surprised,' Linnet exclaimed, eyeing her carefully.

'I am. What kind of changes do you have in mind?'

'I'll get to those in a minute, just let me say this first. As you well know, the fashion retrospective was a big success last summer. We gained lots of new customers, and we did terrifically well, but eventually sales dipped. What we need to do is keep our customers coming in, and we need to garner those important new ones as well. I truly believe we're in a new age of retailing. We have to make shopping a unique experience, and offer other services.'

'Obviously you've studied this carefully, and come up with some fresh ideas,' Evan ventured cautiously, wondering if Paula would permit any changes at the Knightsbridge store.

'I have,' Linnet asserted. 'For example, Harte's ought to have a day spa, a really beautiful spa offering every kind of treatment.'

'That would be great!' Evan was swift to agree, and then thought to ask, 'But where would you put it?'

Linnet grinned, and explained, 'I think one of those boring departments such as *mattresses* would have to go. But seriously, we could carve out space. I know this store inside out and we *could* do it.'

'I guess it doesn't have to be a huge spa, just unique.'

'That's it exactly. Evan, listen, don't you think we ought to have more places to eat? Snack bars, for instance. Especially on the ground floor near the food halls. We could feature shellfish, pizza, hot dogs, deli sandwiches, and pastas. The kind of fast food that's actually tasty. I'm sure they'd be successful, and they would appeal to people who work in Knightsbridge and the areas nearby, as well as our customers.'

'That's a great suggestion,' Evan agreed, 'and the bars *would* be popular. I can feel my mouth watering just at the thought. What I wouldn't give for a plate of oysters right now.'

'And ice cream on top, I've no doubt,' Linnet said, grinning at her. 'Isn't that your favourite lunch these days?'

Evan shook her head. 'Not quite, although I have had a few peculiar longings for some very strange food combinations.'

Linnet leaned forward, her expression intense. 'I'd appreciate any ideas *you* might have, Evan, you're always so creative, and I do think we really *have* to revamp the store. A little bit anyway.'

Evan nodded. 'I agree . . .' She paused, hesitating, and then confided, 'I did have an idea a while back. A floor devoted to brides. Called . . . BRIDE. Naturally we would feature bridal gowns, bridesmaids' dresses, page-boy suits, and all those things. But we could also sell bridal shoes, jewellery, gifts for the bridesmaids, and even bridal lingerie. And there's another thing: in the States wedding-planners are very popular, and we could offer that kind of service as well. People would welcome it.'

'Evan, I love it! What a brilliant idea. And what about the Evan Hughes Bridal Collection? You know you'd love to design bridal gowns. How about it?'

Evan considered Linnet's words. 'I think I'd enjoy that. I guess I've been itching to design again.' Evan's enthusiasm was apparent. 'Actually, the store has had inquiries about your wedding gown. There were lots of photographs in the newspapers, and women seemed taken with it.'

'I don't blame them, you created something out of this world. So, let's sell it to them,' Linnet replied in a rush, and at the same pace she continued, 'Also, I think your idea for an entire floor for brides is inspirational. I'd really appreciate it if you could give me something on paper. As soon as possible.'

'I've got a lot of stuff on my computer already. I'll print it out for you before I go to Yorkshire.'

'Thanks. When are you going to Pennistone Royal?'

'In three days. Gideon and I are driving up on Saturday. I'm glad. I'm already a bit panicky to tell you the truth, I feel as if I'm about to give birth at any moment.' She said this lightly, laughing as she spoke, but she was genuinely worried that this actually might happen.

So was Linnet, although she also laughed and

9

tried to reassure Evan. 'You'll be fine, darling. Julian and I will be there for the weekend, so I can help with any last-minute details for your wedding.'

'That's lovely, thanks for offering, but there's not much to do. It's only the family, after all.'

'Your parents are coming over though, aren't they?'

'Oh yes, and my sisters. My mother's already here, she arrived several days ago, and the others will be flying in next week. Robin's being wonderful, very kind, and he's invited my parents and sisters to stay at Lackland Priory.'

'Well, that's nice of him, of course, but don't forget you've given him a new lease of life, Evan. Mummy says he's never looked better. And India tells me that Great-Aunt Edwina is bursting with *joie de vivre*, at the top of her form.'

'So I've heard, but that's surely because India is going to marry Dusty at Clonloughlin this summer. A big fancy wedding is just up Great-Aunt Edwina's alley,' Evan pointed out with a huge grin.

Linnet agreed, then pushed herself to her feet and picked up her coat. 'I'd better go, I've loads of paperwork to catch up with. Thanks for listening, and for your input. It was just what I needed.' She paused at the door, blew a kiss. 'I'll see you later.' Smiling, she was gone.

Evan gazed at the door, her face already clouding over.

She was fully aware that Linnet's nonchalance was assumed, that in fact she was concerned, worried what her mother's reaction would be to her ideas for the Knightsbridge store. Although they were not particularly radical, Evan knew they would fall flat. As a newcomer, she saw Paula O'Neill from an entirely different viewpoint from her daughters and India Standish, Paula's niece. Evan was aware that their boss was a woman who had become a trifle set in her ways. She was also determined to keep Harte's in its traditional mode, to keep its image intact. What Linnet wanted to do wouldn't destroy Harte's image. On the other hand, Paula would be upset. She was Emma Harte's granddaughter and heiress, and she never deviated from the rules set down by Emma. Having run Harte's in exactly the same way for well over thirty years, since before Emma's death, she wasn't likely to make any changes now.

There'll be trouble between them, Evan suddenly thought with a sense of foreboding. Real trouble.

Endeavouring to brush this irrational feeling aside, she turned to her computer, went to her plans for the bridal floor. She hoped to lose herself in her work, but this did not happen. That peculiar sense of uneasiness persisted, and it disturbed her.

CHAPTER TWO

He could see her in the distance, high above him riding on the escalator, obviously heading for the upper floors of the store.

The bright red hair was a fiery halo around her face, impossible to miss, as was the sleek silhouette of her smartly-tailored black suit, austere except for the touches of white at the collar and cuffs.

She was the spitting image of Emma Harte and knew that she was, because everyone had told her this for years. And they had also told her how smart she was and canny, like her great-grandmother, and that she had inherited her intelligence, vivaciousness and drive. But, Jack Figg, head of Security and old family friend, suddenly wondered, had anyone ever told her that she, and only she in the entire family, had been lucky enough to inherit Emma's enormous *glamour* as well. Certainly Linnet was much more glamorous than Paula or her half-sister, Tessa Fairley. In fact, Linnet stole everyone's thunder on that score.

Such a hard thing to define, glamour, Jack thought,

walking towards the escalator. It couldn't be acquired. A person was either born with it or not . . . glamour was innate, something which came from within. It had nothing to do with the length of a woman's hair or its colour, or the beauty of her skin, or her face and figure. Glamour had much more to do with enormous presence and charisma, rather than anything else. And those lucky enough to possess it, be it man or woman, made an impact wherever they went, always caused heads to turn, induced people to make a beeline for them.

A small smile flickered on Jack's face as he stepped onto the escalator, and he acknowledged, somewhat ruefully, that he was prejudiced when it came to Linnet O'Neill. She was his favourite and always had been. To Jack she was the smartest of the younger generation in this family. She and her cousin Gideon Harte were the best and the brightest of the whole bunch. Not that their siblings or cousins were dullards or dimwits – far from it. Very simply put, it was these two who outshone the rest in almost every way. As a whole, though, the family was quite spectacular, with plenty of brain power between them. Hard-working, diligent, loyal and trustworthy, each and every Harte was also extremely good-looking, just like Emma and her two brothers had been.

His thoughts swung to Gideon Harte, who was to marry Evan Hughes in ten days.

Evan Hughes . . . now there was a name to conjure with. The newly-found American relative . . . quite a story that was. Sent to London a year ago by her dying British grandmother Glynnis Hughes, to seek out Emma Harte . . . who Evan quickly found out had been dead for thirty years. Evan stumbling into the midst of the Hartes, meeting Gideon that first day in the store and falling under his spell . . . as he had fallen under hers. *Instantly*. Love at first sight was grand when it happened. Evan impressing Linnet enough to be hired to work at the store . . . eventually causing Paula to wonder about her origins and delve into the past to uncover the truth about Evan's antecedents . . . Paula discovering that Evan was the granddaughter of her uncle, Robin Ainsley, Emma's favourite son.

And then another story had emerged and unravelled. Robin had had a secret liaison with Glynnis during the Second World War. Glynnis had borne Robin a son called Owen, soon after her marriage to her G.I. boyfriend, Richard Hughes, who had brought the boy up as his own. At the end of the war Richard had taken his Welsh bride and the boy to New York, and there she had lived until her death. But there was a much more complex story to the relationship between Robin and Glynnis, Jack knew that now. They all knew it.

Everything was out in the open; there were no more secrets, and with their typical generosity of spirit the entire family had welcomed Evan, made her feel at home amongst them. And later they had welcomed Evan's parents, Owen and Marietta Hughes, brought them into the clan without a murmur or qualm.

And then there was Jonathan Ainsley. He hadn't

welcomed the Hughes family at all. Now there's the rub, Jack thought with a grimace, as he considered Robin's legitimate son, who had been thrown out of the family years ago for double-dealing, disloyalty, and cheating the division of Harte Enterprises which he ran.

Paula, her father David Amory and her cousin Alexander had dispatched him, and *he* had become their sworn enemy. David was long dead, and all of Jonathan's hatred had been focused on Paula for years. He considered her his great nemesis.

Because of his dangerous games, Jack had Ainsley under surveillance at all times wherever he was in the world, as it happened mostly in Paris and Hong Kong. Jack needed to know *what* Ainsley was up to, *when* he was up to it, and most importantly, *where*.

Ainsley was currently in London, and this disturbed Jack. Now that he was once again running Harte's security on a full-time basis, he felt responsible for every member of the family. Ainsley's sudden presence was like a time-bomb ticking.

There was Evan's and Gideon's marriage to think of and it was uppermost in his mind at this moment. It was taking place on Saturday, January 19th, in the little church in the village of Pennistone. Small though the wedding was going to be, most of the immediate family would be present and undoubtedly they offered great temptation to Jonathan Ainsley.

Jack was convinced that Evan and her father were undoubtedly targets now, just as Paula and Linnet were. Linnet's resemblance to Emma must inflame

Ainsley no end, get his hackles up. And he must loathe Owen Hughes, his newly-found half-brother, albeit an illegitimate brother. As for Evan, she was the grandchild Robin had always craved. Jonathan, who had been married and divorced, had never produced any children.

Stepping onto the top floor of the store, Jack glanced around. Linnet, who had been in his line of vision a moment ago, had disappeared.

After walking around the top floor for a few minutes, Jack spotted Linnet in the auditorium. Pushing open the glass doors, he called out, 'Linnet! Good morning.'

Swinging around, a smile struck her face at the sight of Jack; she sped over to him and gave him a hug, then stepped back, and said, 'What a lovely surprise! And how did you know where to find me?'

He grinned. 'I'm good at that, finding people, you know. Actually, I spotted you on the escalator and jumped on behind you. You're a sight for sore eyes, Beauty. I'm glad you're back. How was your honeymoon?'

'Brilliant. Barbados was hot. New York cold. And exciting. We had a great time, enjoyed both places. But it's nice to be home, and to see you.'

Linnet had known Jack Figg all of her life, and he was more like a favourite uncle than a colleague; now she tucked her arm through his in an intimate way, and together they walked across the floor to a grouping of chairs near the stage.

Linnet said, 'I was going to phone you a little later, to talk about Gideon's wedding.'

As they sat down, Jack told her, 'Everything's in place, and the security will be as extensive as it was for your wedding last month. Truly, there's nothing to worry about.'

Linnet nodded and leaned forward. 'Mummy's staying in Yorkshire to have a rest. Ostensibly. But she felt she'd better be there to help Aunt Emily and Uncle Robin with the plans for the reception, since it'll be at Pennistone Royal. Mums could do it by herself, but the others *want* to be involved. Insist, actually. Robin because of Evan, and Emily because Gideon's her favourite child. Nothing's too good for him.'

'Does anyone ever admit to having a favourite?' Jack asked, his blue eyes crinkling at the corners. 'Especially in this family?'

Linnet laughed, amused by his tone. 'No. But they have them. And everyone loves Gid, you know that. He's special.'

Immediately Jack thought of Gideon's brother Toby, whom he found highly competitive when it came to his younger sibling. Toby was jealous. But Jack decided not to comment on this. He merely said, 'True enough,' and continued, 'Your mother gave me Emily's guest list, and I received Gideon's a couple of days ago. It seems to me that family *only* have been invited.'

'Yes, that's right.'

There was a small silence.

Jack broke it finally, his voice grown more serious

when he said, 'There's something I need to tell you, Linnet . . . Jonathan Ainsley's back in London, I wanted you to be aware of that.'

'*He* always manages to show up at the wrong time!' she cried, her voice rising.

'I have everything under control,' Jack reassured her swiftly. 'My people have him under surveillance on a permanent basis, that's how we know he's back here.' Having no wish to upset her unduly, he refrained from telling her that Ainsley had been spotted that very morning watching the store from across the road. And so he went on quietly, his voice as always calm and soothing, 'I'm simply telling you this because I promised to keep you informed about him. I just want you to be *aware* . . . and on your guard, so to speak.'

'I will be. Have you mentioned it to Gideon?'

'Not yet.'

'Shall I say something to Evan?'

'No, don't. It could upset her, and, after all, she's very, very pregnant.'

'She's holding her own, though. And the babies are not due until the last week of March. But it's probably better she doesn't know Ainsley's around. She and Gideon are going to Yorkshire to stay at Pennistone Royal until the wedding. She can take it easy up there, have a rest.'

'And she'll certainly be safe,' he murmured in response. 'That place is like Fort Knox these days.'

'Thanks to you! And no doubt Gid's had you working on Beck House. Installing a security system, I bet.'

'He has indeed,' Jack answered, smiling. 'It's a lovely old house and they're both thrilled it came on the market when it did. Gideon especially, since his father owned it once.'

'With Daddy when they were gay young blades,' Linnet pointed out. 'Gid told me it's almost ready for them to move in.'

'I know. But getting back to the guest lists, do you think there might be any last-minute invitations? To non-family members?'

'I doubt it. You see, Jack, Evan hasn't really made any friends, I mean outside the family. She's been caught up with Gideon most of the time, and with India, Tessa and me. Oh wait a minute, there's that couple who own the hotel . . . George and Arlette Thomas. Her father's friends. I'm sure she would probably invite them, but—'

'She did,' Jack cut in, 'they're on Gideon's list.'

'Then I can't think of anyone else.'

Jack nodded. 'As I said, there'll be plenty of security, but I do need your help with one thing, if you don't mind.'

'Tell me.'

'More than anyone else, *you* know every person who's going to attend the wedding. *You* would spot a stranger in a crowd, and instantly. Far quicker, certainly, than me. Or any of my people. And also, although I'm acquainted with every member of the family, I obviously can't be everywhere at once. So, here's what I want you to do . . . Keep your eyes peeled, make a mental note of everyone who's there, and particularly strangers, and tell me or one of my operatives if you see anyone you don't know. *Immediately*.'

Linnet nodded her head. 'I could wear a wire, or whatever you call it. A mike and an earpiece. Like you did at my wedding.'

Jack burst out laughing, and sat back in the chair, staring at her, amusement reflected in his eyes. There was no one quite like her . . . except for Emma when she was alive. She would have made exactly the same kind of outrageous suggestion as Linnet just had.

'Why are you laughing?' she asked, looking baffled.

'Because only you or your great-grandmother would have said that to me. My God, you're so like her.'

'I'm glad I am, but getting back to the wedding, I *could* wear an earpiece and a mike, couldn't I, Jack? I mean, why not? What's to stop me? Or who?'

'No one really, but don't you think it might alarm some members of the family? Like Great-Aunt Edwina, for instance.'

'Oh come on, Jack, not Edwina! You know better than that. Anyway, if Edwina were to spot me with a mike on my lapel she'd want one, too. You know she's the general in the family, bossing everyone around and taking charge at the drop of a hat. But she's a good egg.'

'Indeed,' he murmured, biting back a smile. There was no denying it, at times Linnet took his breath away, but he had no doubts about her whatsoever. She was brave and determined as well as smart, and one day she would take charge, be the one to run the Harte stores. She was a star.

'Jack, what about it?' she pressed. 'Can I wear a mike?'

'It's not a bad idea at that, Linny,' he replied at last, thinking: But would Paula stand for it? Wouldn't she balk at her daughter being miked-up at a family wedding?

Almost as if she had read his mind, Linnet announced, 'Mummy might object. If she knew. But she doesn't have to know. I'm sure I can hide the mike on my lapel, behind a large flower. And nobody would notice an earpiece. My hair's longer.' As she spoke she fluffed out her auburn bob, staring at him pointedly, her green eyes intense.

'Your hair *is* longer, that's true,' he murmured and stood up, glancing at his watch as he did. 'Listen, I'll get back to you on that idea later in the day. Let me think it through. Basically, I don't believe it will be necessary. It *is* a small wedding, after all.'

As Jack moved away, heading for the door, he turned, and said, 'Oh, there is one other thing. Your mother told me that all of the help at the reception are locals, who've been employed at Pennistone Royal in the past. Just scan them for me on the day, okay?'

She nodded, and rose, walked over to him. 'I'll mention it to Margaret this weekend, make sure they're old hands. And of course I'll keep my eyes open at the reception.'

'Thanks, Beauty.'

Linnet fell in step with him, and just before they reached the door of the auditorium she touched his arm lightly. 'Jack?'

'Yes?' He looked down at her questioningly.

'Do you really think Jonathan Ainsley might try to cause trouble? Do something insane?'

'No, I don't think he will. He's too smart. On the other hand, I like to be one step ahead of the other guys. So I play it safe.'

CHAPTER THREE

Evan picked up a thick, felt-tipped pen and in her bold, flowing handwriting wrote across the manila folder the word BRIDE. Then she pushed the folder to one side of the desk, smiling to herself as she patted it almost lovingly. She had not realized how much work she had already done on the idea of creating an entire floor devoted to brides until she had gone into her computer an hour ago and printed everything out.

After reading all of the pages written weeks ago, she knew she had a workable and comprehensive blueprint for the bridal floor, and she was pleased. She hoped that Linnet would also be pleased. More than likely she would be. But what about Paula O'Neill? Would their boss really let them create a floor catering only to brides at the expense of other departments?

The question hung there in the air for a moment. It was a tantalizing question for which she had no answer. A sense that problems were brewing, a premonition of trouble ahead still lingered in her mind. Very determinedly she tried to push this away, disinclined to ponder problems today. As Linnet would say, in her quaint way, there were better fish to fry.

Rising, Evan walked across the floor to her long work table at the other side of her office. The top of the table was covered with photographs of the house Gideon had bought in Yorkshire, and she had an overwhelming desire to look at the pictures again.

Sitting down at the table, she stared at those which she had laid out days ago. Once more she experienced the now-familiar pleasure and excitement that knowing this would be her home engendered in her, as well as a genuine longing to be there. Such feelings were paramount in her these days, and she could hardly wait to move in.

As she shuffled through photographs of the grounds and the exterior of the house, she thought of that Saturday morning last October, only three months ago, when she had first seen the house.

Gideon had driven her over to the small, picturesque village of West Tanfield, and had explained on the way that he wanted her to look at an old house with him. 'It's a house I've always liked, and it's on the market,' he had said. 'My only worry is that it might be a bit ramshackle and need too much work. But we can walk through it, and see how we feel about it, can't we?'

Evan had immediately agreed, even though she was taken by surprise that he wanted a house in Yorkshire when they both lived and worked in London, especially since they could stay with his parents or at Pennistone Royal whenever they felt the need to escape the city. But then she had suddenly realized that he wanted a place of their own, especially after the twins were born, because his apartment in London, where they were currently living together, would become rather cramped. The idea of a house in the Dales appealed to her.

On the drive over she learned that West Tanfield was halfway between Pennistone Royal, the great stately home which had been Emma's and was now Paula's, and Allington Hall, his parents' family home, which had been inherited from his grandfather, Randolph Harte.

Just before they reached the village Gideon had begun to laugh softly, and had confided that many years earlier his father and Shane O'Neill had actually owned the house they were about to see. Winston and Shane were the same age, the closest of friends since childhood, and had been at Oxford together. They had apparently bought the house originally as a property investment, intending to renovate it and then sell it for a vast profit.

Instead the two young bachelors had become so attached to the house whilst working on it they had finally decided to move in themselves. It became their weekend retreat until Winston married Emily Barkstone, Gideon's mother. Shane had continued to live at Beck House for a year, but in the end he had felt lonely without his old sparring partner, and had finally told Winston he thought they ought to put the house on the market. Winston had agreed they should sell, and the house was snapped up almost immediately. And in the ensuing years it had changed hands only once.

'Dad told me it was on the market,' Gideon had gone on, as he parked outside the house which stood at the bottom of a small hill at the edge of the village. 'He said that whatever its state I shouldn't worry too much, because he and Shane had practically rebuilt it. Anyway, come on, darling, I have the key from the estate agents. Let's go and take a look at what might become our family home.'

He had jumped out of the car and run around to the passenger side to help her alight, and then led her to the black iron gate set in an ancient stone wall. It was quite a high wall with lichen and moss growing between the stones, and many tall trees were visible above it.

'Beck House,' she had read aloud when they finally stood in front of the gate. 'I like the name, Gid.'

He had merely smiled and led her through the gate, along the path to the house. 'It's called Beck House because there's a little stream, a beck, running through the grounds.'

The minute she saw it Evan was instantly enchanted, and she knew whatever its condition she wanted to live there. It was positively beautiful.

Situated in a small dell, it was surrounded by sycamore trees and huge old oaks which encircled the back. Elizabethan in origin, it was a charming house, rather picturesque, low and rambling, made of local stone. It had tall chimneys, leaded windows, and a half-timbered front façade that was Tudor in style.

In her mind's eye Evan had always had an image of what an English country house should look like, an image instilled in her by her grandmother Glynnis Hughes. And on that cool and sunny October Saturday morning, she had seen this image in her mind's eye take shape in reality. And when he put the big old key in the lock of the front door, her excitement knew no bounds; she couldn't wait to step inside.

Evan knew she would never forget how she had felt when she stepped over the threshold and looked around the front hall . . . she filled with a wonderful sense of joy, and she felt, deep within herself, that she was going to live here with Gideon and their children . . . and she knew without any doubt whatsoever that they were going to be happy here. The house had a good feeling, and she was at ease, felt welcomed.

She remembered that morning so well . . . walking through the big empty rooms . . . empty of furniture, but full of atmosphere and sunlight and dust motes rising in the brilliant shimmering air. She thought now of the enormous, old-fashioned kitchen with its dark-wood ceiling beams, mullioned windows and huge stone hearth. It was a family kitchen, the core of the house, the kind every woman loved. To her relief the reception rooms on the ground floor were spacious and well proportioned, while the upstairs bedrooms were cosy and intimate.

'It's the perfect house for a family,' she had told

Gideon without a qualm. 'It's just right for us, and it has family history as well, doesn't it?'

'Indeed it does,' he had replied, his eyes full of laughter as he kissed her cheek, and asked, 'Shall we buy it then?'

'Yes, please,' she had answered him, and then wrinkled her nose. 'If it isn't too ramshackle.'

Gideon had laughed. 'I don't think it's a bit ramshackle, actually, at least not the interiors. The outside woodwork needs a few coats of paint, and the stone wall needs repairing, but otherwise, I think it's rather . . . *a beauty*. Dad said the structure was solid, the bones good, and he was correct.'

And so a decision was made in the middle of what would become their living room before they left, and three weeks later the house was theirs.

Evan picked up some of the pictures and looked through them for the umpteenth time. The interiors had all been repaired and renovated, the walls and doors painted, the floors restored and polished, the chimneys swept by the local chimneysweep, and every window had been washed by the window-cleaner.

Beck House was ready. It awaited them. And next week, whilst they were in Yorkshire getting ready for their wedding, she and Gideon and his mother Emily were going to supervise the hanging of the draperies, the laying of the carpets and rugs, and the placement of the furniture. Many of the wood pieces, which were mostly antiques, had been gifts from Emily and Paula. Both women had hunted through their attics and come up with some really wonderful finds.

Evan had sent computer photographs of the best pieces to her father in New York, and he had sent her an email almost immediately, telling her how good the furniture was, in his opinion. All were Georgian, he was certain of that, he had written, and he had told her he couldn't wait to look them over when he arrived next week.

Evan sat back, reading his latest, very loving email, relieved and happy that their relationship was back on an even keel. Her father was now warm and caring; it was as if there had never been a rift between them.

A light knock on the door brought Evan's head up from the photographs, but before she could utter a word, Ruth Snelling, her new secretary, poked her blonde head around the door.

'Do you need anything, Evan?' she asked in her breezy voice, with a bright smile. As usual, she was showing her concern for her boss, as solicitous of her as she had been from her first day of working at Harte's.

'I'm fine thanks, Ruth. But perhaps you could get me a bottle of water, flat not fizzy, please?'

'No problem. I'll be back in a jiffy.'

'Don't go, Ruth,' Evan exclaimed. 'I have something for Linnet. Do you mind dropping it off in her office?' As she spoke Evan rose, moved slowly across the floor, picked up the manila folder and held it out.

Still smiling, Ruth came and took it from her. 'See you in a minute,' she said as she disappeared, almost running out of the office, intent in her purpose.

Evan smiled to herself. The young woman was extremely eager to please and efficient; nothing was too much trouble for her. Things had been running smoothly since her arrival a few weeks ago, and Evan kept asking herself how she had ever managed without Ruth. *I was always slightly behind the eight ball,* that was the problem, Evan thought now as she sat down in her chair and glanced at her computer, needing to know if she had any emails. There were none so far this morning, which pleased her. Work had begun to pall on her lately, and all she wanted now was to be settled in the peace and quiet of Pennistone Royal.

Paula had insisted she stay there until the wedding in ten days' time, and she was happy to do so. Evan felt at ease in that great house, where she had spent most weekends for the past year. It had been bought in the 1930s by her great-grandmother; she loved being there because she felt the presence and spirit of Emma Harte within its walls. Not only that, it was truly familiar by now and beloved by her. Everyone had made her feel at home, and Margaret, the housekeeper, never stopped fussing over her, was kind, motherly, and also protective of her these days.

Emily hadn't minded that she wasn't going to stay at Allington Hall, and had insisted she had completely understood why Evan would want to be in such a familiar place as Pennistone Royal.

Gideon's mother was one of the sweetest women she had ever met, and hilariously funny at times, frequently a little bit blunt, just as Linnet was.

When Evan had mentioned this to Paula she had laughed and nodded, her violet eyes twinkling. 'They both take after Emma, I'm afraid. She was blunt, too, and Linnet, in particular, has inherited Emma's penchant for genuine pithiness. My grandmother always said what she meant, and so does Linnet.'

'And what you see is what you get,' Evan had replied, and the two of them had laughed.

Winston Harte, Gideon's father, was just as lovely as Emily. Both of them had made her feel really special from the moment she had started going out with Gideon. Like everyone else in the family, they had welcomed her graciously, and had shown their approval of her as a wife for their son. She couldn't have wished for nicer parents-in-law; or for a more lovely sister-in-law than Natalie, now back from Australia. She was pretty, and a charming girl, and they had taken to each other immediately.

The only person who seemed somewhat aloof and in a sense rather removed was Gideon's brother, Toby. Linnet had once confided to her that Toby was inordinately jealous of Gideon, in every possible way. 'And his marriage to the actress faltered almost immediately, so I guess his nose is now out of joint because Gid's got lovely you.'

Not wanting to get into a long discussion about Toby, for fear of seeming disloyal to Gideon, she had merely nodded; luckily, Linnet had suddenly realized she was late for a meeting and had rushed off, much to Evan's relief. The subject matter had never arisen again.

Pushing herself to her feet, Evan went back to the work table where she sat down, and slowly began to look through the numerous photographs Gideon had taken of their wedding presents. Everyone had been extremely generous, had sent extraordinary gifts, which were not only costly but beautiful as well. As Gideon had said, with a chuckle, 'We don't have to put any of these in the attic to be forgotten. We can use everything.' She had agreed, also laughing.

'Hi there! How're you doin'?'

Evan sat up with a jerk, not having heard the door open. But she stared at it now, in disbelief. Standing on the threshold, larger than life, was her twenty-three-year-old sister, Angharad, completely decked out in brilliant red, from her long cashmere muffler to her high-heeled leather boots. Not only that, she had dyed her hair, was now a platinum blonde.

Evan's jaw dropped, so startled was she, and it took her a moment to find her voice. 'Heavens to Betsy!' she said at last. 'What are you doing here? I mean, Mom told me you weren't coming to London 'til next week.'

'I decided to come early. I wanted to mosey around London before heading north.'

Rising, Evan went over to her sister and kissed her cheek; her expression was warm as she went on, 'Well, goodness, don't stand there, come in, come in.'

Angharad did as Evan suggested, her eager and curious brown eyes glancing around the room as she sauntered across the floor. 'This office is *fab*. But then you always do manage to get a nice place to work, nicer than most people.'

Ignoring this hostile jibe, Evan murmured, 'It's warm in here, you'd better hang your coat and scarf in the closet behind you.' Evan padded across her office to the work table, where she began to pick up some of the photographs spread out on it, knowing it would be wiser to put them away before Angharad saw them. She was extremely nosey. But Evan was too late; her sister was heading her way. Turning away from the table, standing in front of it, Evan said, 'Let's sit on the sofa over there, it's comfortable. And would you like something to drink? Tea? Coffee?'

Angharad shook her head, standing stock still in the middle of the room, staring at Evan intently. After a moment, she exclaimed, 'I can't believe your size! It's unbelievable. *You're so huge.*' She began to laugh, the laughter sounding harsh, brittle, and not at all warm. 'You look as if you're about to give birth to baby elephants not twin boys.'

Wincing at these words, Evan did not respond, and in a gesture that was totally involuntary she found herself putting both of her hands on her stomach, almost protectively, as if safeguarding her boys. She hadn't appreciated Angharad's tone; she recognized it only too well. It held that hint of envy which the younger woman had never been able to disguise, not even as a child. It was indicative of

33

her competitiveness, her absolute need to put Evan down whenever she could. She had always been jealous.

Taking a deep breath, Evan now said softly, 'I suppose you're staying at George's hotel with Mom.'

'Yes. And Mom's coming over soon. To meet me here. We thought we could all have lunch together. What do you think?'

'Yes. Yes, of course.' Evan swiftly agreed, although she was annoyed that her mother hadn't seen fit to phone first. She had a lot to do before the end of the day, and lunch had not been on her agenda. She wanted to fulfil her work schedule before taking maternity leave.

Stepping around her, Angharad was suddenly at the work table, looking down at the photographs of Beck House, and within seconds she had zeroed in on the pictures of the furniture.

'This is all Georgian,' she remarked, her voice rising, her eyes scanning everything with total absorption. Picking up one picture, she scrutinized it intently. Then turning to Evan she asked, 'Where did this piece come from?'

'Out of the attics at Pennistone Royal. That's Emma Harte's former home. Now her granddaughter, my boss Paula O'Neill, lives there. Paula gave that sideboard to Gideon and me. It was a discard, found in the attic.'

'*A discard*. Who would ever do that? It's a treasure. Have you had it evaluated?'

'No, we haven't. I was waiting for Dad. I sent him

a set of the pictures, so he could look at them . . . after all, he is one of the great experts on Georgian.'

'I know that. I work with him, don't I? When did you send them?'

'Oh, three or four weeks ago now,' Evan answered, staring at Angharad.

'I wonder why he didn't show them to me.' Angharad frowned, her dark eyes filled with puzzlement, her mouth settling in a tight line. She appeared to be annoyed.

'Maybe he glanced at them and put them away without thinking,' Evan suggested, wondering herself why their father had not shown them to the daughter who worked alongside him in his antiques gallery in Connecticut. The daughter who was actually his protégée.

'Is this the house?' Angharad asked, leaning over the table, peering at the other set of photographs.

'Yes, that's it. Beck House it's called.'

'Very nice. Very nice indeed,' Angharad murmured, without turning around, her interest captured by the pictures of the various rooms, as well as the other snaps of the furniture which Emily and Paula had unearthed at Allington Hall and Pennistone Royal and given to them.

After a while, she straightened, almost angrily, and turned away from the many pictures. With a swift glance at Evan, her eyes bitter, cold, she said, 'Well, you've done all right for yourself, haven't you? But then you usually do land on your feet, Evan. For as long as I can remember. You had everyone wrapped around your little finger when you lived at home. Mom, Grandma Glynnis, and particularly Dad and Grandfather. You were always their favourite. Elayne was second. I came last.'

'But it wasn't like that,' Evan said in a soft tone. 'You weren't last. No one was last . . . and I certainly didn't come first. Dad treated the three of us alike.'

'That's a laugh. It's me you're talking to, Evan. Not Elayne. *Me*. I saw things very clearly. I was adopted and therefore I was not *blood* . . . I didn't have the *Hughes blood* running through my veins. Not like you. Oh no. You were the precious one, the peach darling.'

'Oh Angharad, please, don't be like this. Elayne is adopted, too, and Dad loves you both as much as he loves me,' Evan exclaimed.

'If you believe that I'll sell you a bridge. In Brooklyn.'

Evan shook her head and began to walk to her chair, suddenly feeling sick, needing to sit down. This was an old story, and seemingly one which had not lost any of its colour or drama over the years. Angharad had been repeating it for years, fully convinced that she was the lowest of the low on the family totem pole. It had always annoyed their grandmother, this attitude, this complaining, and whining. Their father had simply ignored it, while their mother had tutted and cooed and embraced Angharad closer than ever, spoiling her in a way that made Elayne, the other adopted child, feel neglected.

'You're his princess!' Angharad cried. 'The best,

the smartest, the brightest, the most beautiful. You were always held up to us as the golden girl. You were the great example. We had to shine like you.'

'You're being really silly,' Evan remonstrated, trying to remain calm. 'It was never like that.' Her protest fell on deaf ears.

'You're *still* the example, even today. But you must know that, by now. Evan the glorious one. The great-granddaughter of the famous Emma Harte. Talented and smart enough to get herself a top position at Harte's. Without blinking an eyelash. So beautiful and bewitching she captures the Prince Charming of the Harte family. The super good-looking, super rich Gideon. And now she's fulfilled Gideon's desire to present his father with an heir. But golly gee whiz, not *one* heir. Oh no, not Evan. She's producing *two*. And his father's equally besotted with the great Evan, who's going to present him with two instant grandsons.'

'Please don't do this,' Evan pleaded, anxiety taking hold, her annoyance with her younger sister making her unexpectedly tense. It seemed to her that her anxiety was suddenly spiralling upwards into a cloud that settled around her.

'*Do what?*' Angharad asked, her voice icy.

'Pick a fight like this. The way you did when we were little. Nobody wins in the end.'

'I'm not doing any such thing,' she shot back, her face flushing darkly with anger. 'I'm telling you the truth is all. And Elayne's as sick as I am of hearing about your damned wedding. Dad never stops talking about walking you down the aisle. Or talking about you. The bride of all brides.'

'So why did you come?' Evan demanded sharply, her indignation flaring. 'If this is the way you feel, why didn't you boycott my marriage to Gideon?'

'Mom wanted us here.'

'Don't do me any favours,' Evan shouted, losing her temper, and took a step backward, one hand groping for the arm of the comfortable typing chair. As her hand touched the arm it rolled away on its casters, and she fell, crashing heavily onto the floor. Evan cried out, and clutched her stomach.

Frightened by what had happened, Angharad remained rooted to the spot, unable to move. Her eyes were wide with shock. Swallowing hard, she asked in a whisper, 'Are you all right? Evan? *Evan?* Are you all right?'

Evan moaned and brought her knees up to curl in a ball, still holding her stomach. Her face was now chalk white and she did not answer.

'Evan, please say something,' Angharad begged, and stepped closer to her. 'Are you hurt?'

'I don't know,' Evan responded faintly. 'Go and look for my secretary . . . Ruth.'

There was no need for Angharad to search for help. At that precise moment Ruth came into the office carrying a glass and a bottle of water, followed by Linnet and Marietta Hughes.

'Oh my God!' Marietta cried out when she saw her daughter sprawled on the floor, and unceremoniously, not heeding the others, she pushed past Ruth and Linnet, hardly looking at them.

'What's happened? My God, what's happened to you, Evan?' Marietta fell to her knees next to Evan, peering at her daughter, alarm racing through her.

'Call my doctor. I can't lose my babies, I can't,' Evan whimpered, tears sliding down her cheeks.

Chapter Four

Gideon Harte pushed open the door of the waiting room at Queen Charlotte's in Chelsea, the hospital where Evan had been taken, and hurried into the room, his expression tense and worried.

Three pairs of female eyes instantly focused on him, and before he could say a word Linnet jumped up and rushed over to him.

'Evan's all right, Gid!' Linnet exclaimed, wanting to reassure him at once. 'She's not hurt,' she added, taking hold of his arm in a proprietary way.

'Thank God,' he answered, a surge of relief rushing through him. 'I've been anxious all the way here.'

Marietta came to join them, and leaning towards Gideon she kissed his cheek. He put his arm around his future mother-in-law, a woman he genuinely liked, and asked, 'What happened to Evan, Marietta? When Linnet rang me at the paper she said you were in Evan's office when she had the accident.'

'I wasn't in the room, Gideon,' Marietta answered

swiftly, shaking her head. 'Evan was already lying on the floor when I arrived. I'd no idea what had happened. I ran to her, of course, and when I was kneeling next to her she said she'd had a fluke accident with the chair. She then asked me to call the doctor. Linnet, who was with me, did so, and then we brought her here to the hospital.'

Gideon was frowning when he asked, 'Did she fall out of the chair? Is that what you mean?'

'Not exactly. Evan told me she had reached behind her with one hand, pulled the chair towards her and then sat down. Somehow the chair rolled away, and down she went on the floor. But she's fine, Gideon, just as Linnet said. The fall *scared* her more than anything else, I think.'

'I understand. The nurse at reception told me the doctor's still with her. Why is that? Do you know, Marietta? Linnet?' He looked from one woman to the other questioningly.

'The doctor gave her a thorough examination when we arrived and came to tell us she was not injured, that all was well. Then he went back to her room.' Marietta shrugged lightly, shaking her head. 'I'm not sure why, he didn't say.'

'I hope he won't be too long,' Gideon responded, and then glanced across at the silent, blonde young woman who was sitting in a corner. She was dressed entirely in red, which he thought somewhat flamboyant. He wondered who she was. He had never seen her before.

Marietta, noticing his sudden curious glance across the room, exclaimed, 'How rude I'm being, I must

41

introduce you to my youngest daughter Angharad. Evan's sister.'

On hearing her name Angharad immediately jumped to her feet. Thrusting out her hand she said, 'Hello, Gideon. It sure is great to meet *you*.'

Gideon took an instant dislike to her, discovered he had no desire to go anywhere near her. Unfortunately, he had no choice but to take hold of the outstretched hand. It was unnaturally cold, icy, in fact, and he dropped it after giving it a swift shake.

'How do you do?' he said in a most formal voice, his manner reserved and coolly indifferent.

She stared at him, looking him up and down in a brazen way.

He stared back, rapidly taking everything in. There was no question that she was pretty, with finely-wrought features, perfect complexion, and large, dark brown eyes. And yet Gideon found her curiously repellent; he took a step backward. His guard went up and his gut instinct kicked in, warning him to be wary of this one. Danger signals went off in his head. She's trouble, he thought.

It struck him that the platinum blonde hair did nothing to lighten the darkness he sensed lived deep within her, and suddenly, in a flash of cold clarity, he saw her in his mind's eye as she really was . . . a small, dark, furtive creature, hiding in corners, peering through keyholes, spying on people, eavesdropping, forever seeking her own advantage. Momentarily, he was startled by these curious thoughts, and yet he was convinced he was accurate in his assessment of Angharad Hughes. He sensed that wickedness dwelt there.

Moving away from her, anxious to put distance between them, he strode across the floor, then turned, glanced at Linnet, his hand on the door knob. 'I'm going to talk to the nurse at reception. I must see Evan, and right away.' As he jerked open the door, he found himself staring into the face of Charles Addney, Evan's obstetrician.

The doctor, who had been about to enter the room, exclaimed, 'There you are, Mr Harte! I was just coming to fetch you. Let's go and see Miss Hughes, shall we?'

Gideon nodded and stepped out into the corridor, closing the door behind him. 'I understand she's all right. She *is*, isn't she?'

'Absolutely. Except for a bruised coccyx. That's the tail bone at the end of the spine. She went down rather hard, I'm afraid. But there's no real damage, and the babies are perfectly fine.'

Gideon heaved a sigh of relief, then asked, 'So I can take her home, can't I?'

The doctor paused in the corridor and turned to face Gideon. 'There's no reason why you can't, but she must have bed rest for the remainder of the day. I've done a thorough examination, and no harm's been done, but I do think she should start her maternity leave from her job. Immediately.'

'I couldn't agree more,' Gideon responded as they began to walk along the corridor again. 'I've been trying to persuade her to do that for several weeks now. We're going up to Yorkshire on Saturday, but perhaps we ought to leave tomorrow. Her problem is that she's a workaholic . . .' His voice trailed off.

'I know that, and I've just had a long talk with her about her work. I told her to put it on hold for the moment. I think you'll find she's now most amenable about leaving for Yorkshire tomorrow.' Dr Addney chuckled. 'Although she did say she was going to take her laptop with her.'

'Naturally,' Gideon exclaimed, and laughed with him.

'Well, here we are,' the doctor said, pausing at one of the doors. 'Let's go in, shall we?' A moment later he was ushering Gideon into Evan's room.

Gideon hurried over to the bed, relieved that Evan looked exactly the same as she had this morning, except that she was somewhat paler than usual. She was sitting up in the bed, surrounded by pillows, quite obviously none the worse for the fall.

'Gideon!' she exclaimed the moment she saw him. 'Don't look so upset! I'm all right.' She beamed at him, her smile warm and welcoming, her large expressive grey-blue eyes full of love for him.

'I've been so worried,' he whispered as he bent over her, put his arms around her, kissed her cheek, then stroked her dark head. 'Actually, I was quite beside myself. I couldn't bear it if anything happened to you and the twins, Evan. I love you all so much.'

'Nothing's going to happen to us, Gideon darling. The three of us are perfect. Truly. And I love you, too. So will the boys, once they . . . pop out.'

Watching them, Charles Addney felt a flush of

pleasure. How wonderful it was to see two people as much in love as they were. It did his heart good to know that they had each other, had managed to find each other in this dangerous and uncertain world in which they all lived these days. He closed the door quietly behind him as he slipped out and left them alone with their happiness in each other.

'How on earth did you manage to fall?' Gideon asked. He was sitting on the side of the bed, holding Evan's hand, gazing into that face he had come to know so intimately in the past year and now loved so much.

She shook her head, gave a small laugh. 'I don't know, darling. Just clumsy, I suppose.'

'Clumsy? You? *Never*. You're the most graceful person I know, have *ever* known, actually. Your mother said it was a fluke accident, so come on, tell me what *exactly* happened.'

Evan pursed her lips together, her eyes narrowing slightly as she wondered how best to explain. She wasn't quite sure herself how she had managed to fall in the way she had. Clearing her throat, she explained, 'I was standing in front of my desk, talking to Angharad ... Oh, have you met her? She came to the hospital with Mom and Linnet.' Her dark brows lifted questioningly.

'Yes, I've met her,' he murmured, staring hard at her. 'Are you saying she was in the room with you?'

'Oh yes, she'd come over to the store to see me. It was very unexpected, I didn't even know she was in England.'

Gideon felt his hackles rising, and he sat up a little straighter on the bed, looking intently at Evan. 'So, she was in the room. You were talking to her from behind the desk. And then *what*?'

'I reached behind me, pulled the chair towards me, the typing chair I use at my desk. I was quite sure it was right behind me, and I sat down. But it had rolled away, off to one side, and naturally I fell on the floor. With a very hard bump, too.'

Gideon nodded but said nothing. He couldn't help wondering if Angharad had caused the accident. But how could she have? She was at the other side of the desk . . . Evan had just told him that. Nonetheless, he couldn't help thinking she was responsible in some way for Evan's nasty spill.

'When you fell did she come to help you?' he wondered out loud.

'Yes, she came over to me, but she was really terrified, you know, that I might have badly injured myself, and so she just stood there, asking me if I was okay. I'd felt a stab of pain in my stomach and so I'd brought my legs up, as if trying to protect the boys. Then suddenly Ruth appeared with the water I'd asked her to bring me earlier, and Mom and Linnet were with her. Mom ran to me, got down onto the floor next to me, and I told her to call the doctor.'

Evan now lay back against the pillows, her expression one of bafflement as she murmured, 'I just don't know how I could have been so careless, falling like that.'

'You weren't careless, sweetheart, it's as you said

it was, a freak accident. Thank God you didn't injure yourself. Now, let's get you dressed. Dr Addney says I can take you home, but you have to rest all day. And tonight. Tomorrow evening we're going to Pennistone Royal instead of on Saturday.'

'But I—'

'No buts, Evan, and no arguments. That's it. I've made the decision. The doctor told me you should start maternity leave now. So I'm afraid it's no more Harte's, not until well after the twins are born.'

'Oh, don't say that! I hope there'll be lots more Hartes. Well, one Harte in particular,' Evan said, smiling at him.

'I certainly hope you're referring to me.'

'Of course I am, silly. Who else do I love but you?'

Little things kept coming back to her, things she had forgotten long ago. And yet they had been significant when they happened. Pushed resolutely to the back of her mind, they were now coming to the fore, clear and vivid as they took shape once more. And each memory was shaped and defined by one thing . . . Angharad's jealousy and envy of her.

Evan lay under the duvet in the bedroom of Gideon's flat. *Their* bedroom now, since she had moved in with him months ago. They had wanted to live together once she had become pregnant; this apart, Gideon's sister Natalie had returned from her sojourn in Sydney, and because it was her flat Evan was occupying, moving out had become mandatory.

'And why not live with me, your future husband?' Gideon had asked, adding, 'Come live with me, and be my love, and we will all the pleasures prove.'

'What lovely words.'

'Yes. But they're not mine, Evan. They're Christopher Marlowe's. However, they truly *do* reflect my sentiments entirely.'

And mine as well, she thought now, pulling the duvet up around her shoulders, making herself comfortable. Both Dr Addney and Gideon had impressed upon her that she should rest all day and evening, and she knew they were correct. She was all right, no harm had been done, but she'd had a bit of a shock. Rest was the best medicine, just as they had said to her.

Angharad.

The name hung there, floating in mid-air before her eyes.

Evan had not failed to miss the distaste in Gideon's voice when he had mentioned her sister earlier. And she completely understood why he had sounded that way. With the innovation of the platinum blonde hair and all that awful red clothing she had looked flashy, and just a little bit cheap. And especially when contrasted with their mother, perfectly groomed and turned out in a mélange of soft beiges, and Linnet in her smart black Chanel suit with its pristine white-satin collar and cuffs.

Evan cringed inside at the memory of all that dreadful red. Pretty though Angharad was, she had never looked worse than she did today. It was the hair as well; it did not suit her, was totally inappropriate. Unexpectedly, a thought struck her. Angharad had looked like Mrs Santa Claus in the red outfit and with her platinum blonde hair. Under other circumstances it might have been amusing and she would have laughed, but not today; her coming to the store dressed like that was embarrassing. And how mean-spirited she had been.

Then it came, a sudden flash of memory – and remembrances of a Christmas long ago. In Connecticut. She had been seven, or thereabouts, and Angharad around three and a half, and very jealous of her, competitive even then ... It was the Christmas that Evan's grandmother had given her a puppy, a beautiful chocolate-brown Lab with unusual green eyes. They had named him Hudson, after the river.

'Gran, Gran, I can't find Hudson! He's disappeared,' Evan wailed, worry ringing her face as she ran into the big family kitchen where her grandmother stood at the long oak table cooking for the Christmas holidays.

Glynnis was making stuffing for the turkey, giblet gravy, apple sauce and all sorts of other good things to eat.

Glancing over her shoulder at Evan, she said, 'I saw him trotting after Angharad a few minutes ago. Try the solarium, lovey. Perhaps you'll find them there, playing with his tennis ball.'

Rushing back out into the front hall, Evan now raced down the corridor in the direction of the solarium. When she came to the door which led into the room she was stunned to see Angharad pushing the puppy outside into the snow and then locking the door.

'Angharad! What are you doing?' Evan shrieked in alarm, her shoes clattering against the terracotta flagstones as she flew into the solarium. 'It's freezing outside, Hudson will die out there. It's too cold for a little puppy. He's only nine weeks old! You're a bad girl, very bad.'

Evan pulled Angharad away from the door, pushed her out of the way roughly, glaring at her and exclaiming, 'You're very bad. Bad.' Frantically unlocking the door, wrenching it open, she ran outside, glanced around, her eyes seeking the puppy. He was nowhere to be seen and her eyes filled up with tears.

'Hudson, Hudson, where are you?' she shouted, her voice quavering. He couldn't be far away, surely not, she thought desperately.

Angharad had come outside and was standing on the steps of the solarium. 'I'm not a bad girl,' she yelled at Evan. 'I hate that puppy. I hate you. It's the dog that's bad. It wee-weed in my room. So there, Miss Big Shot!' She went back inside, banged the solarium door and locked it.

Evan paid no attention to her. She was far too worried about Hudson, intent on finding her puppy. Then she suddenly spotted the little paw prints in the snow, and began to follow them, pulling her cardigan around her shoulders, shivering in the icy wind, regretting she had not stopped to get her coat.

It didn't take Evan long to find Hudson. The dog

had sunk down into a snowdrift against the terrace wall, and was whimpering.

Bending over the snowdrift she almost fell into it herself as she reached down to retrieve Hudson. He was wet and cold, trembling with fright, and still whimpering as she took hold of him firmly and lifted him out.

'Little Hudsy, here I am. You're safe,' Evan soothed. 'I'll soon have you warm,' she whispered against his wet hair, bundling him inside her cardigan, wrapping it around him, cradling him in her arms. Holding him close to her body for extra warmth, she hurried back to the solarium.

Evan turned the knob only to discover that the door had been locked by Angharad. The child stood on the other side of the French doors, making faces at her; she stuck out her tongue, then laughed.

'Open this door!' Evan demanded, banging on one of the glass panes, filled with irritation. It was cold in the garden.

'No, I won't.' Angharad put her tongue out again, swung around and ran away from the French doors.

Racing along the path, Evan went to the back door of the house which led straight into the kitchen. Stumbling inside, she brought a blast of cold air with her, which made Glynnis swing around. She looked startled when she saw Evan.

'You're going to catch your death of cold, my girl, going out without a coat in this weather,' Glynnis chastised, then stopped when she saw that Evan had the puppy dog in her arms. She also noticed that the two of them were shivering.

'Goodness me, whatever happened to Hudson? He looks very wet,' Glynnis exclaimed, frowning in concern. 'Here, give him to me, Evan, I'll wrap him in this warm kitchen towel. As for you, lovey, take off that damp cardigan at once and stand in front of the fire. You'll be warm and dry in a jiffy.'

'Yes, Gran,' Evan said dutifully, handing over the puppy, then struggling out of her damp cardigan which she then laid on the hearth.

Once the puppy was dry and nestling in a cosy bed of thick towels in his basket, Glynnis said, 'Do you want to tell me what happened, Evan?'

Evan let out a long sigh. 'I'm not a snitch.'

'I know that. But how did the puppy get outside in the first place?'

'I found him in a snowdrift,' Evan muttered, avoiding answering the question.

'Certainly Hudson can't open doors, so somebody must've put him outside, Evan. That's the obvious answer. Perhaps a little girl called Angharad, eh?'

Evan was silent.

'It *was* Angharad,' Elayne announced clearly, walking into the kitchen. 'I saw her shoving Hudson out into the snow, Grandma.' Elayne made a face. 'She's always jealous of Evan, and me, too.'

Glynnis nodded. 'I understand. Well, please go and find her, Elayne, and bring her to me. *At once.*'

Elayne rushed off.

Glynnis looked pointedly at Evan. 'I know you never want to confront her, but this time Angharad has gone too far.'

When Evan was silent, Glynnis said, 'You know that, don't you?'

'Yes, Gran.'

Within minutes Elayne came back into the kitchen, pulling Angharad along by the hand. At five she was taller and stronger, and so she was able to control the younger child, who was struggling and looked sullen.

When they came to a stop in front of Glynnis, she said in a quiet voice, 'Angharad, what you did was a cruel thing, putting that defenceless little puppy out in the freezing cold. Hudson would have soon died in that snowdrift, there's no doubt about that. You've been a wicked girl. I don't often use such a strong word with you, even though you are frequently extremely naughty. However, this time you deserve it.' Leaning closer, bending slightly, looking into the child's face, Glynnis asked, 'Now, explain why you did such a cruel thing.'

'The dog wee-weed in my room,' Angharad mumbled.

'*Oh really*. That's surprising, since you usually keep the door closed. Let's go upstairs, shall we? *All of us*.'

Glynnis, her face still grim, shepherded her three granddaughters up the front stairs and into the bedroom shared by Angharad and Elayne.

'Now, show me where the puppy had an accident,' she said.

Angharad hung back for a split second, then ran to a small, damp spot visible on the light-coloured carpet. She pointed to it. 'There! It's there.'

'It doesn't look like urine to me,' Glynnis muttered, and kneeling down, she sniffed the spot, then looked up at Angharad, her face grim again. She said, 'This spot doesn't have a smell at all. I think it's water.'

'Yes, it is, Grandma,' Elayne told her. 'She spilled it last night.'

'I thought it was something like that,' Glynnis replied, getting up from the floor. 'And now you've resorted to fibbing, Angharad. Well there's only one thing to do with a girl who lies. She's got to be left alone to think about what telling the truth means, how important it is. Girls who lie are not fit for decent company.'

'I didn't lie!' Angharad cried, glaring at Elayne.

'I believe you did,' Glynnis exclaimed. 'And it's not the first time. You're to stay here in your room until your father and mother get back from New York with Grandpa. Then we'll see what happens.'

She walked across the bedroom floor, beckoning to the other two girls. After ushering them out, Glynnis turned and looked at Angharad. 'I'm not going to lock this door, but don't you dare come out.'

Once they were back in the kitchen, Glynnis served Evan and Elayne large bowls of chicken vegetable soup and small chicken sandwiches. They ate their lunch dutifully and in total silence, afraid to speak. And Glynnis didn't say a word either.

It was much later that afternoon, when she was playing with the puppy at one end of the kitchen, that Evan heard her grandmother talking to her mother.

'There's something wicked in her, Marietta,' Glynnis said at one moment. 'Angharad tells lies, and she has a cruel streak.' As Marietta began to protest, Glynnis went on firmly, 'She was an abandoned child . . . we know nothing about her genes, now admit that's true, Marietta.'

'I'm not denying it,' Marietta finally answered in a low voice. 'But she is pretty, and she can be very sweet, you know. Very loving.'

'Yes, most certainly she can, when you're giving into her, spoiling her,' Glynnis pointed out.

Marietta did not answer.

Evan, who had listened to this exchange, kept herself hidden at the back of the kitchen, not wanting the two women to become aware of her presence.

As the memory slowly faded, Evan once again accepted that Angharad had not changed very much. She was just as envious and spiteful as she had always been. It struck Evan that Angharad had come to the store today spoiling for a fight, had wanted to upset her intentionally. And if they hadn't quarrelled she wouldn't have fallen, would she?

Evan shivered slightly and huddled deeper into the bedclothes. And then she was filled with relief that she hadn't mentioned their quarrel to Gideon. She was certain he had already spotted something in Angharad which he didn't like. His tone of voice had given him away. Angharad would never find favour with him, of that she was aware.

CHAPTER FIVE

'It's exquisite,' India Standish said, looking at the diamond tiara resting on a square of black velvet laid on the dining room table at Niddersley House. 'And I would love to wear it on my wedding day . . .' Her voice trailed off and there was a moment's hesitation before she asked, 'As long as you don't think it's too much, Grandma?'

'Do you mean too *grand*, India?' Edwina asked. Edwina, Dowager Countess of Dunvale, gazed across the table at her only granddaughter and favourite grandchild.

'Well, yes, sort of,' India admitted. 'Is it a bit over the top?' She raised a blonde brow questioningly, her eyes focused on her grandmother. 'I mean, for these days?'

Edwina did not answer for a moment. Instead she stared at the tiara, her head on one side, her eyes thoughtful. After a moment she murmured, 'No, it's not too grand for today, nor was it ever, for any day, my dear, and it's certainly not very elaborate . . . just two bands of diamonds linked by interlocking circles of diamonds, with the large circle at the front holding a diamond star in a smaller circle.'

Nodding to herself, Edwina informed India, 'It's Victorian, you know. It belonged to Adele Fairley, my grandmother and your great-great-grandmother. That's why it occurred to me you might like to wear it on such an important day in your life. It's part of your family history.'

India responded, 'Yes, I understand, and it *is* beautiful, Gran. Perhaps I should try it on to see how it looks.'

'Yes, why don't you do that.' Edwina motioned to the end wall. 'There's a looking glass over there, and plenty of light from the windows on either side.'

India rose, leaned over the table, and lifted the tiara with both hands. Moving across to the mirror, she placed the diamond circle on her head and stared at herself. She saw at once that Edwina was correct. Once the tiara was on her head, it didn't look quite so grand after all, perhaps because of the cloud of hair around her face and the simple design. And it did suit her, no two ways about that; much to her surprise, it was also comfortable to wear. For a moment India attempted to visualize herself in her wedding veil and the tiara, and unexpectedly she liked the image floating in her head. She turned around and exclaimed, 'What do you think, Gran?'

Edwina's answer was to beam at her. 'It suits you, India, and it doesn't look . . . *over the top*, as you call it. Your veil will be held in place perfectly. Now, tell me, what is your wedding gown going to be like? You told me Evan was designing it.'

'Yes, she is, and I've only seen the first sketches of it, but I love her design. We've chosen the fabric already, a pale-ivory taffeta, light in weight, because when the dress is finished it's going to be worn over an underskirt of layered net, for a very bouffant effect like an old-fashioned ballgown. The bodice is tightly fitted and there are big, puffy sleeves, slightly off the shoulder. Actually, it's Victorian in style, Gran, now that I think about it. I've asked Evan to keep it plain and understated, no embroidery on it.'

'It sounds as if it will be lovely, my dear, and I feel sure the tiara will be the perfect adornment since it is Victorian like the gown. So, are you going to wear it on your wedding day to please an old lady?'

India smiled at her grandmother, then turned again to the mirror, gazing at herself for a split second. As she swung around to face Edwina, she exclaimed, 'Yes, Grandma, I'd love to wear your tiara and thank you for thinking of it.'

Edwina returned India's smile with one equally as loving. '*Adele*'s tiara, that's how I regard it. Would you like to take it with you today? Or do you prefer to leave it here for safe-keeping?'

'I think I'd better do that, actually. You have that enormous safe and I don't even have a small one in my flat. Besides, it's only January, Gran, I'm not getting married until June. So yes, it would be much safer here for the next six months, I think.'

'I understand . . .' Edwina sat back in the chair

and watched India as she walked over to the dining table, took off the tiara and placed it on the black velvet, thinking what a lovely young woman she had become. She had the finely-drawn aristocratic looks and pale-blonde colouring of Adele Fairley, as did her cousin Tessa Fairley; in fact, the two could easily be mistaken for sisters, and often were by strangers.

'Shall I put the tiara in its box, Grandma? Or do you want Frome to do it?'

Edwina laughed. 'You'd better do it, he's far too slow these days. It'll take him half an hour to get the tiara in its box, never mind into the safe. Old age creeping up, I'm afraid.'

India's mouth twitched with laughter. 'You are funny, Gran, the way you go on about Frome getting old. He can't be more than fifty if he's a day.'

'Fifty's about right,' Edwina confirmed, still chuckling to herself. 'But he's dreadfully slow lately. You know very well I'm much faster at everything, even though I am ninety-five.'

'And quite remarkable!' India exclaimed.

'Imagine, Emma was only sixteen when I was born. She took me off to her cousin Freda's in Ripon to be brought up, at least when I was a baby . . .' Edwina stopped somewhat abruptly and sat there staring out of the window, as if remembering something from long, long ago, her eyes full of a curious yearning.

After a moment of watching her, India asked softly, 'Are you all right, Grandmother?'

'Oh, yes, I am, India, I am. And I hope I remain

so. At least until I see you well and truly married to Dusty.' Pushing herself to her feet, she continued, 'And shouldn't we be on our way to have lunch with him at Willows Hall?'

'Yes, we had better go,' India agreed, and put the tiara back in the worn, black-leather box where it belonged, then laid the black velvet cover over it. Closing the lid and fastening the small catch, India looked across at her grandmother and said, 'Shall I put it in the safe?'

'*Absolutely*. It'll be quicker, as I just said, if you do it. Come along, my dear, I'll take you to the safe. And then we'll be off. It was nice of you to come and fetch me, India. I could've been driven over to Dusty's by Rupert, you know. He doesn't have much driving to do, as it is.'

'Oh that's all right, Grandma. I wanted to come. To see you and to spend a little extra time with you.'

They crossed the hall together and went down a corridor towards the room where an enormous safe was housed. As she followed Edwina, India went on, 'I think you'd better wear a warm coat, Grandma, it's bitterly cold today, and it could snow again.'

'I will, my dear. I have a lovely quilted coat Paula got for me. From Harte's, of course.'

'Mr Rhodes, I'm sorry to bother you, but there's a Mrs Roebotham here. With Atlanta,' Paddy Whitaker said from the doorway of the studio.

Dusty's head came up with a jerk, surprise flickering in his eyes. '*Atlanta?*'

'Yes, Mr Rhodes,' the house manager confirmed. 'They're in the kitchen at the moment. Atlanta likes Angelina, as you well know.'

Alarmed though he was by this altogether unexpected news, Russell Rhodes, one of the world's greatest artists, managed to keep his face neutral. Dusty, as he was commonly known, put the paintbrush down carefully, even though his stomach was churning all of a sudden; he managed somehow to keep his movements deliberate and totally controlled. His mind was racing, trying to fathom what had happened to the child's grandmother. Obviously something had. That was why Atlanta was here.

Turning away from the easel, Dusty asked, 'What's the problem? Did this Mrs Roebotham say?'

'No, but she has a suitcase. It's Atlanta's. And the woman appears to be nervous and obviously quite worried. However, she wouldn't say a word to me, Mr Rhodes. She just repeated several times that she had to speak to you and only you.'

'I understand. I'll come up to the house with you right away, Paddy.' Moving across the floor of the studio swiftly, Dusty glanced at his watch and asked, 'Is everything under control for lunch?'

Paddy, still framed in the doorway of the studio, nodded his head. 'Angelina has finished setting the table in the dining room, and Valetta's in the middle of cooking lunch. Everything smells delicious, as usual. I have the white wine cooling. Pouilly Fumé. No problems, at least not with lunch, sir.'

'I'm sure not. Thanks, Paddy. By the way, you'd

better make sure the dining room is warm. The countess feels the cold these days, so Lady India tells me.'

'The fire's blazing and I turned the central heating on a while ago. Kept it low, though.'

'That's fine.' Dusty paused at the door and, doubting that he would be returning to his studio today, he switched off all the lights. After grabbing his sheepskin coat from the wall peg, he locked the door and walked with Paddy to the beautiful Palladian house set at the top of the hill just a few yards away.

Once inside the house, Dusty murmured, 'I'd better see Mrs Roebotham first before I greet Atlanta, find out what this is all about. Give me a couple of minutes to freshen up, then bring her to the library.'

'I'll do that, sir. And in the meantime, I'll try to get her to have a cup of tea. She wouldn't have anything before. But perhaps she will now that she knows you'll be talking to her in a short while.'

'That's a good idea,' Dusty answered, and then he hurried across the marble entrance hall and into the spacious library. The first thing he did was go into the adjoining bathroom where he washed the paint off his hands, splashed cold water on his face, and then ran a comb through his thick black hair.

He stared at himself in the mirror, thinking that he looked tired, drained. And also worried. Taking a deep breath, trying to steady himself and stay calm, he returned to the library, straightening his sweater as he went to his desk. Lifting the tweed jacket from the back of the desk chair he slipped it on, then sat down at the desk, his mind in a turmoil.

Something must have happened to Molly Caldwell, Melinda's mother, he decided, or why would a stranger be here with his child? Unless it was Melinda who was in trouble, and her mother had gone to the clinic to see her. But if that were the case why hadn't Mrs Caldwell phoned him? She usually did, wanting always to keep him informed of everything that affected his child. She was a good woman.

Propping his elbows on the desk, Dusty dropped his head into his hands. Why today? he muttered under his breath. Why did it have to be *today* of all days? India was on her way to have lunch, bringing her grandmother, the Dowager Countess of Dunvale, and he wanted everything to go right.

Trouble he didn't want or need.

But there was no doubt in his mind that trouble was about to come and hit him smack in the face.

He braced himself. Everything was about to go wrong; his gut instinct told him that, and he trusted his instinct. Always had.

'Tell me about Emma, tell me about Grandy,' India said as she drove down the driveway of Niddersley House and turned left onto the Knaresborough Road. 'You promised you would ages ago and you never have.'

'There's so much to tell, I wouldn't know where to begin,' Edwina murmured, settling herself in the car seat. 'Do you like this car, India?' she then asked, changing the subject. 'I gave it to your father, you know.'

'Yes, he told me. And I love my Aston Martin.' Giving her a quick look through the corner of her eye, she then asked, 'Are you comfortable, Gran?'

'Very. Thank you for asking,' Edwina answered, glancing out of the window.

'So, getting back to Emma Harte. Here's an idea, why don't I just ask you questions?'

'That's a very good idea, India. But surely you know a lot from your father. He was devoted to her.'

'Oh yes, I do, and from Mummy as well. Daddy always says he was one of the Praetorian Guards.'

Edwina burst out laughing, and chuckled for a second or two. 'He spoke the truth. He and Paula, Emily and her late brother Sandy, and Winston felt it was their duty to surround and protect her in every way. I must admit, I did sometimes tease your father, asking him if he and the others were ever tempted to do away with her, as the original Roman Praetorian Guards had often had an urge to slay their leader.' Edwina chuckled again.

India laughed with her grandmother, and asked, 'And what did my father say?'

'He was horrified that I could even countenance such an idea. I'm afraid that my teasing fell flat. He and his cousins were utterly devoted to her.'

'And you weren't, were you, Gran?' When Edwina did not answer, India pressed, 'You were estranged from her for quite some time. I know that because Daddy told me.'

A low sigh escaped Edwina, and she remained silent for a moment longer before finally saying, 'Yes, it's true, I was. I became estranged from her just before I went off to finishing school in Switzerland, and we weren't very close for a number of years after that.'

'Why? What happened?'

'It's such a long story, India dear, and I always get upset when I discuss it these days. I will tell you the details some other time, I promise. Let's just say, for now, that I was totally wrong. I was the one at fault, not my mother, and when I finally realized that I tried to make amends. And we became devoted to each other at long last.'

'You sound very regretful, Grandma,' India said softly, sympathy echoing in her voice.

'I am, even to this day. I think what I regret most are the years I missed knowing her, being with her, when I was a young woman. I was married to your grandfather, Jeremy, and living with him at Clonloughlin. I was so happy with him and we were devoted to your father, our only child, and I didn't give a thought to my mother. Not for a very long time.'

'My father told me he went and sought her out, that he didn't even tell you.'

'That's correct. And it was my uncle, Emma's brother Winston Harte, who told me that the moment they met was memorable. He said it was instantaneous and absolute infatuation between Emma and Anthony. And they always remained devoted to each other.' Turning to India, Edwina finished in a low voice, 'I'm glad your father had the guts to defy me and went to meet his grandmother on his own. They became close and remained close for the rest of her life, and they both benefited from the relationship.'

'You said earlier that Emma sent you off to live in Ripon with her cousin, Freda. Was that one of the things that upset you?'

Again Edwina was silent as if mulling over her answer, and when at last she spoke she found herself telling the truth. 'No, not really. I was a baby and I was given a lot of love, care and attention, and it was a pretty, pastoral place to live. Freda was a loving young woman. I knew deep down, when I was older, that Emma had done the best thing for me. We were poor and she had to work hard to support us, and she just couldn't look after me. Nor was there anyone in Armley who could. Yes, it was the right decision, even though later there were moments when I resented her for doing it. But I was far too young to understand all the ramifications. Later, I did.'

'You know, Grandma, I really admire you. The way you admit your mistakes, take responsibility for things you did which you now regret. Most people can't do that . . . admit they've been wrong.'

'Only too true, India,' Edwina murmured, 'and for you to understand that now, at your age, makes you a very smart young woman indeed. I'm proud of *you*, my dear. Now, enough of the past and Emma. Tell me about your plans.'

'Just one more question, Gran, and then I'll stop,'

India pleaded. 'I'll talk about my plans, and anything else you want to talk about.'

'All right. One more question then. What is it?'

'Everyone says Linnet is Emma's clone? Is that true? You'd know better than any other member of the family.'

'Oh yes, she's the spitting image of her, as Emma looked at that age when I was growing up and living with her. But it's not only the looks, you know. Linnet is like her in other ways. It's in the genes, I suppose. She has inherited many of my mother's mannerisms, and she even sounds like her at times. And quite aside from those things, her personality is similar to Emma's. Linnet can be brusque and blunt, just as my mother was, and she speaks her mind. Very plainly. I've always said to Paula that with Linnet what you see is what you get, and Emma Harte was exactly the same way.'

Edwina sat up straighter in the car seat, and looked at her granddaughter. 'You might find this hard to believe, but do you know, India, sometimes when I'm with Linnet I feel as if I'm a little girl again and actually with my mother. I fall back into my memories, and I'm transported back in time. It's rather strange, I must admit.'

'I suppose it is, but every time I pass that portrait of Emma in the store, I think I'm looking at Linnet – well, the woman Linnet will be when she's much older.'

A fleeting smile touched Edwina's face, and after a moment she said, 'Now come along, you promised to tell me your plans, yours and Dusty's. And what about his little girl? Will she come and live with you when you're married?'

'I don't think so, Grandma . . . Dusty feels she should remain with Mrs Caldwell, that's the child's grandmother. He doesn't want to uproot her, bring her to live at Willows Hall with us. Anyway, he always promised Melinda, that's the little girl's mother, that he wouldn't take Atlanta away from her.'

'I understand his reasoning. And that's just as well, wouldn't you say? Surely she's better with her mother?'

As Edwina said this, she felt a sudden surge of apprehension. She saw trouble on the horizon.

PART TWO

Trio

'The three clans stand together as one family.
Harte, O'Neill and Kallinski against all foes.'
Emma Harte, *A Woman of Substance*

CHAPTER SIX

Linnet wished she could go up to the moors, but she knew that it was impossible this morning. Snow had fallen during the night and the hills soaring above her along the rim of the horizon were topped with glistening white.

She had to admit that it would be unbearably cold on the 'tops', as the locals called the highest parts of the moorland and the high fells that dropped down into the Dales. The snow would make them impossible to traverse, and then there was the wind. It was always blowing up there, even in the best of weather, and today it was bound to be a bitterly cold wind.

For as long as she could remember Linnet had loved the moors above Pennistone Royal, the lovely, ancient house in Yorkshire where she had been born, and which had belonged to her great-grandmother, Emma Harte.

One day it would be hers. Her mother had told her that in great confidence. It was a big secret; no one else could know.

When she was still only a toddler, her mother had taken her up there to play amongst the heather and bracken, under a perfect sky as blue as the tiny speedwells growing in the lower fields below in the warm weather.

The moors were Linnet's special place, her haven whenever something ailed her. Her mother had told her a long time ago that she had inherited Emma's love of them.

'You're just like Grandy,' Paula would often tell her, smiling indulgently. 'Whenever you get a chance, you go rushing up there, especially when you're troubled or worried about something. That's exactly what your great-grandmother did for her entire life.'

Linnet was beset by problems on this chilly Saturday morning, all manner of troubling thoughts jostling around in her head. Sighing, she walked down the gravel path towards the Rhododendron Walk, and tried to sort out her worries in the order of their importance.

Uppermost in her mind at this moment was Jonathan Ainsley. A short while ago, Jack Figg had phoned to tell her that Ainsley was no longer in London but now staying at his house in Thirsk, and his very presence in the vicinity made her feel uneasy. Jack always called him a loose cannon and the idea that he might well be just that frightened her. It put her on her guard.

Then there was the situation with Evan's family. Uncle Robin had invited them all to stay with him for the wedding, and this was now suddenly alarming Jack, alerting him to trouble. He had voiced the thought that each and every one of them would be 'sitting ducks', should Jonathan Ainsley decide to pay an unexpected visit to his father at Lackland Priory.

'But he can't shoot them dead,' she had countered, 'all he *can* do actually, Jack, is to be very rude to them, and nasty to his father. Uncle Robin's used to that by now, I should think.'

'Couldn't they be accommodated elsewhere for the duration of the wedding festivities?' Jack had asked, and she had then suggested he speak to her mother about this. 'I suppose they could stay with us at Pennistone Royal,' she had gone on swiftly, 'or with Aunt Emily and Uncle Winston in Middleham. Allington Hall is big enough. But Mummy'll know best. Mind you, Uncle Robin won't like it if she interferes with his plans, that I *can* tell you.'

Jack had answered that Paula was head of the family and he was going to call her the moment he rang off. And then he did just that, muttering, 'And what *she* says *goes*.'

Linnet had nodded to herself as she had replaced the receiver, thinking Jack was right.

Apart from Jonathan Ainsley, Paula's cousin and the family's bitterest enemy, Linnet was somewhat concerned about Evan. Thankfully she was all right, and there were no problems with the babies, but that curious fall still puzzled her.

Evan was the most nimble person she knew, and moved around with a unique kind of elegance and grace, and Linnet couldn't for the life of her understand how Evan had missed the seat of the chair, hit the floor the way she had. It both baffled and bothered her.

Evan and Gideon had arrived at Pennistone Royal on Thursday, earlier than originally planned, and last night she had spoken to Evan about her fall when she and Julian had arrived and had supper with them.

Evan had laughed it off when Linnet had started to gently probe, and so she had let the subject slide away without making any further comment. What truly disturbed Linnet was the remembrance, so clearly etched in her mind, of Angharad standing over Evan in her office, looking down at her, doing nothing to help.

There had been such an odd expression in Angharad's eyes Linnet had done a double-take, had given her a longer, harder stare, and had been discomfited when she recognized that Evan's adopted sister was actually looking gleeful. Linnet had not failed to miss the inherent spite in her at that moment, and was enormously troubled by the strangeness of this young woman and her sudden appearance on the scene.

Angharad Hughes had not been due to come to London until next week. *She* bears watching, Linnet now decided, shrugging further into her cape, increasing her pace down the hill. I wouldn't put anything past *her* . . . she spells trouble.

When Linnet had arrived at Pennistone Royal last night her mother had asked her to stay for the whole of the coming week, so that she could help with Evan's wedding. 'Evan can't possibly do much, darling,' Paula had pointed out. 'She's so very pregnant, and after that awful fall in her office, Emily and I don't think she should be exerting herself, or doing anything physically stressful.'

Immediately, Linnet had agreed to stay on at Pennistone Royal to help her mother. They were close and always had been, and whenever she could ease Paula's burdens Linnet tried to do so.

Earlier in the week, Linnet had considered talking to her mother about making certain changes at the store in Knightsbridge, but now she realized this was hardly the right time for such an important and delicate discussion. That must wait until after Evan's marriage to Gideon next Saturday, only a week away.

The wedding was distracting her mother as much as it was Aunt Emily, mother of the groom. So how could *she* start bringing up old-fashioned windows that needed a fresh approach to suit the changing times? Or explain the importance of having a spa or suggest the innovative idea of devoting an entire floor to brides and weddings?

Surely her words would fall on deaf ears? Or if they didn't, they would certainly *irritate* her mother no end. Paula seemed set in her ways these days, much to Linnet's chagrin, and change appalled her.

Put it on hold, she muttered to herself, and continued on her way, heading closer to the walk. This had been created by her mother over thirty-five years ago or more, and she had designed it for Emma Harte. The Rhododendron Walk at Temple

Newsam, a stately home near Leeds, had been the inspiration, and Paula had copied it down to the last detail, inveterate gardener that she was.

In the summer months it was quite extraordinary to behold, the glossy leaves of the rhododendron bushes alive with colour from the giant flowers . . . white, lilac and pale pink giving way to tints of dark-rose and purple. The flowery bower was breath-taking at that particular time of the year; now, in winter, the glossy green leaves were speckled with frozen snowflakes and tiny icicles.

At one moment, Linnet stopped and glanced up at the sky. It was forbidding, curdled and cold. The wind was beginning to blow the steel-grey clouds away and quite suddenly a pale sun was visible, a pale-silver orb against the expanse of blue floating above. She was used to the sudden changes in the weather in Yorkshire, especially in the Dales where she had grown up. Rain was prevalent throughout the year; but apparently, it wasn't going to be a wet gloomy day after all, and this pleased Linnet.

Striding out, humming to herself, she began to enjoy her walk. But at the same time her busy mind was focusing once again on the Hughes family.

She was well aware that Uncle Robin would be upset and disappointed if Owen and his family didn't stay with him. Robin Ainsley had discovered a new lease on life through the advent of Evan Hughes and her father Owen, his long lost son by Glynnis Hughes. Certainly he looked better than he had for several years.

On the other hand, the Hughes family presented

problems all of a sudden, primarily because Jonathan Ainsley was in Yorkshire. There was no doubt in anyone's mind that he resented the very idea of a half-brother in the shape of Owen Hughes. As Jack Figg had said, there was no telling what a loose cannon might do.

Jack Figg believed that Ainsley was dangerous, and she had to believe Jack, pay attention to him because he had rarely if ever been wrong, especially when it came to their security, the security of their homes and the stores.

Perhaps her mother would talk to Uncle Robin, instil some sense into him, make him understand his new-found family might possibly be at risk with Jonathan floating around. Yet Robin Ainsley was a stubborn man, and full of confidence about his own judgement. He had been a Member of Parliament for years, and he was a lawyer as well, although never practising. Still, he was an intelligent man, in fact a brilliant man, as his career in government attested. Would he listen to his great-niece, daughter of his half-sister Daisy, to whom he was close these days?

No, wait a minute, Linnet instructed herself. Unexpectedly, it had just struck her that the best person to tackle Robin was his other half-sister, Edwina. They had been *especially* close throughout their long lives, shared many secrets and problems. 'Hand in glove,' was the way her mother had described them recently, pointing out to Linnet that it was obviously Edwina who had helped to facilitate Robin's long, ongoing affair with Glynnis.

That's it, Linnet told herself, and immediately came to a snap decision. She would telephone Great-Aunt Edwina the minute she got home, and explain the situation in detail. Paula might be head of the family, but Edwina was the eldest of them all at ninety-five. Furthermore, she still had all her marbles, as Linnet was well aware. Even more importantly, she had immense clout with Robin. To her he *would* listen, and he would accept her advice, Linnet was convinced.

Glancing at her watch, she realized that Great-Aunt Edwina wouldn't be at Niddersley House now. When she had spoken to India at the Leeds store yesterday, her cousin had told her she was taking Edwina for lunch at Dusty's house.

At this moment, India would be driving her grandmother to Willows Hall near Harrogate.

Drat, Linnet muttered to herself, and pressed on along the Rhododendron Walk, formulating a plan as she strode out. She would phone Willows Hall after lunch and talk to Edwina then. And she had no doubt that Great-Aunt Edwina would be delighted to jump into the fray. She had always had the demeanour of a British general commanding his troops, and loved to boss everyone around, especially her siblings.

Julian Kallinski stood at the window of the bedroom at Pennistone Royal which he shared with Linnet, looking out across the lawns.

They were covered in hoar frost on this icy Saturday, and the dark, skeletal branches of the trees were dripping long icicles which looked like miniature stalactites. The whole scene resembled a painting in grisaille, the black and white tints strikingly beautiful against the backdrop of the pale sky.

In the distance he could see Linnet coming down the Rhododendron Walk, returning home, bundled up in her favourite cape. It was bright red and she was hard to miss even from this distance.

A smile struck his mouth and his eyes brightened at the sight of his wife. *Wife*, he thought, *she's my wife*.

He suddenly wondered what he would have done if Linnet hadn't come to her senses, if she hadn't ended their silly estrangement.

No, not *their* estrangement. *Hers*, actually, from *him*.

He had never felt estranged from her, only puzzled by her strange behaviour, and achingly vulnerable to her.

After several months of their being apart he had forced the issue, forced her to see him by taking charge of the situation, and not taking no for an answer.

Fortunately, he had chosen the right moment, and she had come back to him willingly, lovingly. And during her emotional and physical capitulation to him, in the searing heat of their mutual passion, she had told him she loved him and only him, and she had finally agreed to become his wife at last.

But what if he hadn't become assertive because of his frustration, annoyance and anger? None of that might have happened. What if none of those words had ever been said? By him and by her. What would he have done ultimately? How could he have continued his life without her by his side?

It would have been difficult, most certainly, even trying, because their families were so intertwined. He and she might break up, but they would be constantly thrown together.

The three clans of Hartes, O'Neills and Kallinskis had been part of each other's daily lives for well over a century, since the day Emma Harte, Blackie O'Neill and David Kallinski had met and become best friends in the early years of the twentieth century in Leeds. And they had remained friends until their deaths.

Exile, Julian thought. I would have had to exile myself. I would have had to leave England, go to New York, and run the American end of Kallinski Industries. That would have been the only solution. It would have been dreadful, heartbreaking, a miserable existence. And my life would have been empty and banal without *her*, without my lovely, red-haired Linnet by my side.

But he wasn't without her. They were married now, and had been for over five weeks . . . Married just as they had planned to be married since their childhood . . . Their dream of marital bliss together had come true in the end.

Smiling to himself, filled with happiness, Julian turned away from the window and went over to the desk in the corner. As he passed the old Queen Anne chest he caught sight of their main wedding picture in its silver frame.

He paused, staring at it for a moment. It was the big family portrait with himself and Linnet in the centre, and surrounding them were the rest of the family. His parents, her parents, her grandmother, Daisy and Great-Aunt Edwina, and the two grandfathers, O'Neill and Kallinski, respectively. And there were their siblings and cousins and the aunts and uncles. The three clans in full force.

Julian focused his attention on his grandfather, Sir Ronald Kallinski, who had managed to stave off death in order to attend their marriage. But sadly he had died in his sleep three days after their wedding, just when he and Linnet had arrived in Barbados for their honeymoon.

His father and her parents, and Grandfather O'Neill in particular, had insisted they did not come back to England for the funeral.

'He wouldn't have wanted that, Jules,' his father had said to him, speaking in his firmest voice. 'He was thrilled to see you and Linnet married, overjoyed to know the three clans were united in marriage. "All mixed into a lovely stew," he said to me at the reception. And he was finally able to let go. He died peacefully in his sleep, and he was a happy man. We'll bury him quietly, and I'll start planning his memorial service. You'll both be here for that.'

Julian had told his father he wanted to help with the plans for the memorial, and Michael Kallinski had agreed that they would do it together. 'Remember, he was in his nineties.' His father had then added, 'And he had a great life, a *big* life. He was ready to go, he was ill. And tired, really. But as I said, a happy man because of you two. So, enjoy your honeymoon, and goodbye.' His father had then hung up, and Julian knew that all his father had said was correct. To go back would be silly, under the circumstances.

Linnet had been loving and consoling, full of sympathy, proffering wise words, and she had helped him to get through a few truly sorrowful days. And finally, after much discussion, they had wisely taken the advice of their families and remained in Barbados.

Moving away from the chest, sitting down at the desk, Julian thought of the coming week. He was going to be at the Leeds office of Kallinski Industries, and he would greatly miss his grandfather's presence there. For the past six months or so, Sir Ronnie, as he was called by everyone, had made the Leeds offices his headquarters, no longer fit enough to travel to London.

Naturally his considerable influence was everywhere, from the wonderful Post-Impressionist art and the Barbara Hepworth sculptures in the lobby to the coolness of the upper floors. Sir Ronnie had always insisted that the air-conditioning was turned on, no matter the time of year. He liked his working environment to be cool, which was why many of the women employees tended to refer to Kallinski House as 'the frozen North', and 'Iceland'.

Julian looked across at the door as it suddenly flew open, and his reflective expression was obscured by the bright smile which readily settled on his face.

There she was, his beautiful Linnet.

She hurried forward, smiling back at him, and wrapped her arms around him, held him close.

'Are you all right? You looked so sad when I came in,' she whispered against his cheek.

'I'm fine, really. I was just remembering Grandfather.'

'I know.' Linnet drew away and stared up into his dark blue eyes, almost violet in colour like her mother's. 'Don't forget what the Hartes have always said about a loved one who has died . . . *in my heart forever.*'

'Yes,' he murmured. 'I remember that.'

'And it's true, you know.'

'Yes, Linnet, I think it is. I feel that Grandfather is in my heart forever . . . that motto of your family is absolutely correct.'

She smiled at him, touched his face with a fingertip. 'You know something strange, even though I never knew Emma, I feel *her* in my heart. Sometimes I think she's all around me, loving me, guiding me, watching over me.' She put her head on one side. 'Do you think that's silly? Rather fanciful of me, Jules?'

'Of course not. And I certainly wouldn't be so arrogant as to dismiss such feelings. There's so much we don't know about this world, or the other . . . and I'm happy that you feel *she's* watching over *you.*'

Linnet stood on tiptoe and kissed him on the lips, then asked, 'Have you seen Gideon and Evan yet this morning?'

'Yes,' Julian answered and led her over to the

sofa near the window. 'Let's sit for a minute. I've several things to tell you. First, Emily came over and Gideon and I had coffee with her, then she took your mother off to Beck House in West Tanfield. Gideon is driving over there later with Evan, and he asked us to go to tea at the house, and have a look around. How do you feel about that?'

'It's great! I'd love to see how far they've come in the decoration of it. So, does that mean we can have lunch alone? Just the two of us?'

'Not exactly,' he answered, his eyes suddenly mischievous.

'Oh, who's here that I don't know about?'

'Your beloved brother, Lorne.'

'Oh goody! That's wonderful. Oh, sorry, Jules, about our tête-à-tête. You don't mind do you?'

'Not at all, darling, I've always had a soft spot for Lorne. But, actually, that's not all of it. He's here with his twin and her French friend.'

'Tessa and Jean-Claude are *here*?' Linnet sounded surprised.

'That's right, and Tessa says she's going to cook dinner for everyone, so we're in for a treat.' He grinned at Linnet. 'She's making her speciality.'

'Oh God, not *coq au vin*.'

'Oh no, she doesn't make that anymore, at least so she told me. We're going to have lamb stew.'

Linnet began to chuckle. 'Come on, let's go down to the kitchen and see what's going on. In the meantime, let me tell you about the call I had from Jack Figg just as I was leaving for my walk.'

'Something important?'

'Just that the dreaded Jonathan Ainsley is staying at his house in Thirsk. Jack's a bit worried about that.'

'I don't blame him,' Julian muttered, following Linnet out of their bedroom. 'That man's a menace.'

CHAPTER SEVEN

Dusty jumped up from the desk where he was sitting and went to stand in front of the blazing fire. His face was taut as he stuck his hands in his pockets and warmed his back against the flames.

His mind had been racing ever since Paddy had announced the arrival of his little daughter with Mrs Roebotham. The fact that the woman had brought along a suitcase belonging to Atlanta meant only one thing: the child was coming to stay with him. Which, in turn, meant that it was Molly Caldwell who was out of action, not Melinda who was in some kind of trouble. If that had been the case, Mrs Caldwell would have phoned him to explain.

'This is Mrs Roebotham,' Paddy said, now hurrying through the doorway, ushering the woman across the library floor at last.

Immediately, Dusty moved forward exclaiming, 'Hello, Mrs Roebotham. *Hello*!' He stretched out his hand and smiled, added, 'I'm Russell Rhodes.'

She took his hand and shook it, rather timidly

he thought, and murmured in a subdued voice, 'I'm pleased to meet you, Mr Rhodes.'

Paddy excused himself and disappeared, while Dusty led the woman towards the fireplace. He knew everything about her the instant she entered the room, although he had never met her before. She looked about forty, was scrubbed to shining cleanliness, not a vestige of make-up on her face, neat and tidy in her appearance, her dark clothes plain, simple, but not cheap-looking in any way at all. Her luxuriant auburn hair was brushed back and formed into a sleek twist at the back of her head to reveal a slender, high-cheekboned face that was rather attractive, and she had light eyes, greyish blue, he thought. She was slim and wiry, and of medium height, and there was something about her that was arresting, a determination in her, per-haps, an honesty and straightforwardness. He knew immediately that she was a decent woman.

Leeds, he thought. Working-class Leeds. Same background as mine. No doubt growing up in a Victorian terrace house, just as I did. They had a lot in common, although he was quite sure she was not aware of that.

'Let's sit here, shall we, Mrs Roebotham,' he said briskly.

'It's Gladys, everybody calls me Gladys, Mr Rhodes,' she said in her quiet voice, sitting down where he had indicated, crossing her ankles, placing her hands in her lap on top of her bag.

'Very well, it's Gladys then. Now, would you like some refreshments? Tea? Coffee? Or something else? Something to eat, perhaps?'

'Nothing, but thanks ever so much. Cook made me a cup of tea when I got here, Mr Rhodes.'

He nodded his understanding, and repressed the urge to tell her to call him Dusty. He knew she wouldn't, and that the mere suggestion would only embarrass her. She was probably overly impressed by this house, undoubtedly intimidated by his fame . . . the poor Leeds lad who'd made it big. The Yorkshire newspapers were his greatest boosters, always full of his fame, calling him a genius, giving him lavish accolades for his paintings.

As he took the seat opposite her, he asked, 'What's happened to Molly Caldwell?'

'She's had a heart attack,' Gladys answered calmly, but her hands were twisting together in her lap, and betrayed her continuing nervousness.

Dismay clutched at him. 'How bad is she?' he asked urgently, leaning forward, pinning his eyes on hers.

'It's serious, but her doctor is very hopeful,' she murmured and tried to give him a reassuring smile without much success.

'When did it happen? This morning?'

'No. Yesterday afternoon. It was lucky I was there. I go three times a week to help her, and I was in the kitchen doing the ironing when she collapsed. I called Dr Bloom immediately. It was him that sent the ambulance. She's in Leeds Infirmary, that's where they took her.'

'And before that, before she went to the hospital, she told you to bring Atlanta to me?' Dusty said.

'Oh, no, she was . . . well, she was sort of out of it,' Gladys explained. 'I knew what I had to do, mind you, Mr Rhodes . . . bring Atlanta to you. Molly had drilled that into me. She said if ever she got sick or anything I had to bring the little girl to you. Nobody else. Only to you. She kept an envelope in the kitchen drawer with your address and money for taxis in it.'

'I'm glad she'd told you what to do in case of an emergency, Gladys. Very glad. And you did well. Thank you.'

'I would have brought Atlanta to you last night. But it had turned seven by the time they took Molly to the hospital. Way past Atlanta's bed time. I thought it best to stay the night at Molly's house, I didn't want to alarm the child. And so I brought her here today. I spoke to the Infirmary, this morning before coming here, and Molly's doing well.'

Dusty nodded. 'What's the prognosis? Do you know? What did the doctor tell you?'

'That her heart attack was serious. But not life-threatening. Dr Bloom seems to think she'll be able to come home in about a week.'

'That's certainly good news, good to know,' Dusty exclaimed, smiling at her, filling with sudden relief.

'By the way, she's in the I.C.U., Mr Rhodes. I shall go and visit her on my way back home, even if I can only wave to her,' Gladys announced.

'That's very kind of you, and I'll go myself later this week. By the way, this Dr Bloom, is he in Meanwood?'

'Oh yes, he's our local doctor. He's been there

years. And he's only three streets away from Molly, and not too far from me either. I've written his number down for you, Mr Rhodes. I thought you might want to be in touch with him.' As she spoke she fumbled in her bag and finally brought out a piece of paper, handed it to him.

'Thanks, Gladys, thanks again for bringing Atlanta to me. Incidentally, how did you explain her grandmother's absence to her?' he asked, staring at the piece of paper, then putting it in his pocket.

'It was Atlanta who came to me in the kitchen. She said her grandmother had fallen down, had hurt her leg because she wasn't getting up. So when the ambulance arrived, I said they were taking Grandma to get her leg made better. She accepted that, and then when I told her I was bringing her to you today she was so excited that was all she could think about,' Gladys informed him, then sat back in the chair.

Dusty stood up. 'Thank you for all you've done. I'd better go and see Atlanta without any further delay. I thought it better to get the whole story from you before seeing my daughter. Now, come with me to the kitchen, Gladys, and have some lunch. Then we'll arrange for a car to take you back to Leeds, to see Molly and later to your home.'

'Oh, please, it's not necessary, honestly it isn't. I'll get off, after I've said goodbye to Atlanta. She's a good little girl, you know, very grown up in so many ways, Mr Rhodes.'

'Yes, I know. She's a treasure,' he said, escorting her out of the room. 'I'm very grateful to you,

Gladys, and I won't let you leave here without some food in you, and a car to take you wherever you want to go. And by the way, you'd better give me your phone number so that I have it handy.'

She nodded. 'Yes, I will. I don't live far away from Mrs Caldwell, just a couple of streets down.' There was a moment's hesitation, before she said softly, 'Thanks for being so nice.'

He smiled at her, but said nothing, and led her through the entrance foyer in the direction of the kitchen. He saw her looking around, staring at his paintings. But she didn't make any comment and neither did he.

'Daddy! Daddy! Daddy!' Atlanta cried the moment she saw Dusty, coming forward to meet him as he entered the kitchen, dancing towards him on tiptoes, her laughter echoing all around them. She was tall for three, graceful and slender, 'his little beanshoot', he called her.

As she came into his arms there was no mistaking whose child she was with her jet-black hair and light blue eyes. It always seemed to him that there was nothing of Melinda in her. After hugging her, kissing her cheek, he put her down on the floor and gave her a huge smile. 'We're going to have a fun weekend together while Grandma gets her leg mended.'

'Does it hurt her, Daddy?' Atlanta asked, staring up at him. Without waiting for his answer she shook her head and said, 'She didn't cry.'

'No, I don't think it hurts, darling,' he answered

and then turning to Gladys he said, 'Please stay for something to eat, it's already twelve-thirty. You must be hungry.'

Before Gladys could respond, Atlanta looked across at her and announced, 'Valetta's made spaghetti, Gladys. It's got tomatoes in it.'

'I don't think I can have lunch here, Atlanta, and—'

'Oh please, please,' Atlanta cut in, and looking at Dusty she went on, 'Make Gladys stay, Daddy, please.'

Dusty grinned, gazing down at Atlanta, and said, 'I'm having lunch with your friend India, and then this afternoon she's going to take you out. So, why don't you eat here in the kitchen, and Valetta will make some more of your favourite things, and then we'll all go for a drive.'

Atlanta nodded. 'Can I go and see Indi? I like her.'

'She hasn't arrived yet, but of course you can say hello to her . . . she's bringing *her* grandmother to see me.'

'Oh. Is she like my grandma?' the child asked, staring up at her father.

Dusty bit back the laugh that rose in his throat, and said, 'No. I think she's quite different altogether. In fact, there's a big difference. But her grandma's as nice as yours.'

'Oh goody.' Atlanta ran to Gladys and took hold of her hand. 'You'll like Indi. She's nice. She tells stories and reads to me.'

'I know how much you like that. But I really

think I have to go, lovey, I'll meet your friend India another time.'

'*Oh*. Don't go, Gladys,' the child beseeched, clinging to her hand.

'I have to visit your grandmother,' Gladys explained, and then becoming aware of the sudden tears welling in Atlanta's eyes, she said, 'Well, all right, I'll stay and have a snack with you.' She managed a small chuckle, added with a twinkle, 'I'm getting a bit peckish.'

'Like the birds!' Atlanta exclaimed, laughing. 'That's what you always say. Peckish like the birds.'

Dusty said, 'Then it's settled. Come on, Gladys, and you too, Atlanta. You can both sit here at the table, and Valetta will bring plates of her delicious spaghetti, and whatever else you want. All right, Valetta?'

'That's fine, Mr Rhodes,' the cook said, laughter in her dark eyes. Waving her wooden spoon, she turned back to her pans, stirring the contents of one of them. 'I'm almost ready to serve.'

As Dusty was leading his child and Gladys Roebotham to the table at the far end of the large, family-style kitchen he heard the sound of a car outside on the gravel driveway. Kissing the top of Atlanta's dark head, he murmured, 'Drink some of your water, darling, and I'll be back in a minute.'

'Yes, Daddy,' she answered dutifully sitting in a chair. She picked up the small glass of water and took a swallow. 'Sipping like the ducks,' she said, smiling at Gladys.

*   *   *

Dusty strode across the main entrance foyer, heading for the front door, intent on greeting India and her grandmother on the steps. As he opened the door and went out onto the terrace he saw them coming slowly towards him.

He knew better than to go and escort them inside. The Dowager Countess of Dunvale was something of a tartar, with a very sharp tongue, and was quite determined to look after herself. She resisted any help from others, and he understood absolutely. She was extremely independent and self-reliant, and he admired her for her extraordinary stamina and fortitude. After all, she was ninety-five and anything but senile. Far be it from him to undermine her confidence in herself.

India waved to him and he waved back. He wondered how she would react to the news that Atlanta was here for a week at least. He would give her all of the details as soon as they were settled in the sitting room having their aperitif. Her grandmother liked a drink before lunch, and her insistence on 'a drop of sherry', as she put it, always tickled him. He would tell India about Molly Caldwell at once, so there was no misunderstanding. Months ago she had accused him of 'lying by omission', and he had no desire to have that accusation levelled at him again.

He knew that India liked the child as much as Atlanta liked her, and her presence would not present any problems, as far as he could see. Angelina, the housekeeper, and Valetta, the cook, would keep an eye on her whilst he was painting during the morning, and he would spend time in the afternoon with her. After all, India would be at the Leeds store during the week, and she still lived at Pennistone Royal, spending only the weekends with him here at Willows Hall. No, the child would not be intrusive on them or their relationship, he decided, and then it struck him that Gladys Roebotham could be very useful. It was obvious Atlanta was attached to her, and Gladys seemed to reciprocate the child's feelings. Perhaps she would consider spending part of the coming week here looking after Atlanta.

'Excuse me, Mr Rhodes,' Paddy said from the entrance foyer.

Dusty swung around to face the house manager. 'Yes, Paddy?'

'I've put a decanter of Amontillado in the sitting room, and I was wondering if there is anything else you need?'

'I don't think so, thanks very much. Lunch in about half an hour. Oh, and Paddy, order a car for Mrs Roebotham, would you, please? It's to take her back home, with a stop-off at Leeds Infirmary to see Mrs Caldwell. And please tell her I'll be in to have a word with her in a few minutes.'

'Right you are, sir,' Paddy murmured and was gone on silent feet.

'Good morning, Countess,' Dusty said a moment later as India and her grandmother finally came to a standstill in front of him.

'Good morning, Dusty, and *countess* is far too formal. I do keep telling you that. You must call me Edwina.'

'You know I can't,' he replied, laughing. 'That's not respectful.'

She chuckled with him, and then suggested, 'Why not call me Great-Aunt Edwina? Or Grandmother. But perhaps you have a grandmother of your own?'

'No, she's dead.' Turning to India he smiled lovingly, and kissed her cheek. 'Hello, darling,' he whispered against her hair, before he ushered them both into the house.

Within several seconds he had Edwina settled comfortably in a chair near the fireplace, and India went and perched on the sofa, waiting for him as he poured Amontillado into glasses and brought the sherry to them.

'Cheers, ladies,' he said, lifting his glass, and sat down on the sofa next to India.

'Cheers,' India answered, as did her grandmother.

Staring hard at Dusty, India now said, 'You've got a peculiar expression on your face. What's the matter?'

How well she knew him, and in ways no one else ever had before.

His new tactic was to tell her everything up front, without preamble, and so he said, 'It's Mrs Caldwell. She had a heart attack late yesterday afternoon, and the woman who helps her brought Atlanta over here this morning.'

'Oh, how dreadful!' India exclaimed. 'I mean about the heart attack. How is Mrs Caldwell today?'

'Apparently it's serious but not life-threatening. She'll be in hospital for about a week, and from what Mrs Roebotham says, the prognosis is good.

I'll call the doctor later; in the meantime Atlanta's here to stay with me for a few days. Until her grandmother's better, actually.'

India smiled at him. 'Don't look so concerned, Dusty, she'll be fine with us, and I couldn't be happier. It's lovely to have her here for the weekend. We'll have some fun together. Where is she now?'

'Having lunch with Mrs Roebotham in the kitchen, but she's really looking forward to seeing you later.'

'So am I. And Grandma, you'll get to meet Dusty's little girl. She's just adorable.'

Edwina simply nodded and took a sip of sherry. No doubt Atlanta *was* adorable, and certainly India was genuine in her affection for the child, but Edwina couldn't help thinking that it was a good thing she was still only three years old. And still malleable. There was no doubt in Edwina's mind that Dusty and India would end up raising his child. His former girlfriend was recovering from a serious drug-addiction and her mother obviously had a wonky heart. She might not live long; and who could answer for the daughter . . . addictions were hard to kick . . .

CHAPTER EIGHT

Tessa Fairley stood in her room at Pennistone Royal, lost in thought. Of late, there were moments when she couldn't help wondering what the rest of her life was going to be like. What did the future hold in store for her? What was her destiny to be?

The one certainty, the one steadfast thing in her life, was her devotion and love for her three-year-old daughter Adele. Everything else was vague, up in the air, or out of her grasp, at least so it seemed to her lately.

Would she be made managing director of the Harte stores by her mother? Would she then run them herself, as she had always wanted to do? Or would her mother decide to make her joint managing director with her sister Linnet? Shared responsibilities had been bruited about in the past few months, startling her, disappointing her, putting her on guard. That was something she had *never* wanted . . . sharing the top spot with her sister.

Conversely, would she abandon her career, ambitions, and dreams of being the new Emma Harte, and instead marry Jean-Claude Deléon?

She smiled inwardly. There was just one small problem in that regard: he had not asked her to marry him. But if he did propose, and if she accepted, there would be a vast upheaval in her life and that of her child.

Since he lived and worked in Paris, she would have to move across the Channel and make a life with him there. Could she be happy in France?

Tessa almost laughed out loud. Of course she could. She was a dyed-in-the-wool Francophile, and she loved Paris, knew the City of Light as well as she knew London. Well, almost. Years before meeting Jean-Claude, she had been going to Paris on a regular basis, and Shane O'Neill, her stepfather, owned one of the most exclusive and deluxe hotels in the city, on the elegant Avenue Montaigne, off the Champs Élysées.

Then there was Jean-Claude's small country estate where he spent most weekends. Located outside Paris, near Fontainebleau, it was a picturesque country manor called Clos-Fleuri. On her first visit last summer she had taken an instant liking to it, and she felt at home there, as if she truly belonged. Apart from the beautiful grounds and gardens, the house was lovely, full of charm, and when she was there she felt enveloped in quiet luxury and comfort. There was a peacefulness about it that she cherished.

All of these points aside, Tessa was deeply in love with Jean-Claude, and she had realized from the beginning of their affair that she could be happy with him *anywhere*.

Tessa had never known anyone like him. He was loving, warm, and kind to her, and he adored little Adele. Emotional considerations apart, he was a man she respected and admired. He had a vivid intelligence, was clever, street-smart, and absolutely brilliant in his work. Yet despite his superior intellect, he never made her feel inferior. They got on well and were great companions; she had never felt that way with her former husband, Mark Longden. He had always managed to put her down and beat her up – verbally and physically.

Jean-Claude Deléon, one of the most famous men in France, if not indeed in the world, had fallen in love with her the minute he had met her. And she with him. He called it a *coup de foudre*. 'We were struck by lightning,' he sometimes said, smiling at her tenderly.

That had been last August. In the last five months they had managed to spend a great deal of time together in Paris and London, at Clos-Fleuri, and here in Yorkshire at her mother's home. And during these months they had grown closer, come to know each other most intimately on every level. It was so right, this affair of theirs, and they both knew it.

But there was a problem, and it troubled her. What would she *do* if she married him? She had always worked. Hard graft was bred in the bone of every Harte, and she was no exception. She had been brought up to be disciplined, dedicated, driven, and an achiever. Just as the whole family had. So wouldn't she be bored if she didn't have a job?

Naturally she would be bored. Bored silly. And especially since Jean-Claude worked like a Trojan himself, writing books, screenplays, plays for the theatre, and articles for newspapers and magazines. He filmed documentaries and gave lectures. He was forever occupied.

And then there was his great fame in France. He was the philosopher-king, the favourite of presidents and politicians, and a member of the Parisian elite.

Fame had its own demands. She was well aware of that; her brother Lorne, her beloved twin, was a famous actor. Fame ate up his time, just as it ate Jean-Claude's time. There were personal appearances, press and publicity, events to attend, and she knew it was all part of his work.

Tessa let out a heavy sigh and sat down in the chair at her desk. There were so many questions bouncing around in her head this morning, and no answers were forthcoming.

She glanced at the mail on her desk, which she had brought with her from London. After reading the letters and emails, she put them back in their folder and pushed it to the end of the desk, an old French *bureau plat* she treasured. Then her eyes scanned the little sitting room which adjoined her bedroom. This intimate suite of rooms had been hers for as long as she could remember, and she loved its primrose-yellow walls and yellow-and-red toile de Jouy documentary print at the windows. In this room were displayed all her favourite possessions, decorative objects, beloved books and paintings, which she had collected over the years. They helped to give the two rooms their attractive aspects and personality, bespoke her taste as well as personal preferences. It was distinctively her décor and no one else's.

Glancing at her watch Tessa suddenly realized she ought to go downstairs and find Jean-Claude and the others, offer them drinks before lunch. Her mother, who had gone to West Tanfield with Aunt Emily, had asked her to look after everyone, be the hostess in her absence.

Earlier, when she had talked to Margaret, the housekeeper had insisted on making lunch, because, as she put it, 'You'll have your hands full doing dinner tonight, Miss Tessa.' And so she had let the housekeeper take over. A short while ago, Margaret had come up to tell her about the menu. She was making hot leek-and-potato soup, a chicken pot pie, a cottage pie, and fish cakes for those who wanted lighter fare. There was green salad and cheese, as well as fresh fruit.

Margaret had then thought to add, 'And what about all this lamb stew, Miss Tessa? You've ordered far too much meat. Why, there's enough to feed an army, that there is!'

Tessa had quickly answered that there were a lot of bones in lamb shoulder and neck, and that everyone liked a stew the next day anyway, because it tasted even better.

Tutting to herself, Margaret had said no more, but she had looked annoyed as she stomped off to the kitchen. Perhaps she's cross with me because

I've invaded her territory again, Tessa thought, then shrugged. She enjoyed cooking, and if she was in the kitchen Margaret could have a night off. But the housekeeper wouldn't see it that way.

Rising, Tessa now walked through into her bedroom, and took a sage-green wool jacket out of the wardrobe. Slipping it on, she swung around and stood for a moment regarding the bed.

No one had ever shared this bed with her in all of her life. None of her siblings when they were growing up, and certainly not Mark Longden. Whenever she and Mark had stayed at Pennistone Royal after their marriage, she had asked her mother to put them in the Blue-and-White Suite. On these occasions she had been able to use her own rooms as her private place, somewhere to be alone, to rest and work. It was her quiet haven during her marriage, as it had been from childhood. Her little yellow-and-red suite was sacrosanct. No one was ever permitted to share it with her, and never had been.

Until last night. When the house was still and everyone had gone to sleep, Jean-Claude had come to her bedroom at her invitation. He had slipped into the bed with her, taken her in his arms, and held her close. They had loved each other very tenderly . . . and it had pleased her that he was with her here. He was her one true love, her soul mate, the only man she wanted, and wherever she was she wanted him with her. So her private haven was willingly opened to him, and with joy.

She never worried about the difference in their ages, but she was aware he did. He was over twenty

years older, and it bothered him. Sometimes she
chided him for that, told him not to be silly, and he
would nod, and smile, and change the subject. She
wanted to have another child, but only by him; she
wanted it even if they weren't married. But whenever she thought of bringing it up she lost her nerve.
Perhaps this weekend she would mention it . . .

The buzzing phone interrupted her thoughts.
'Hello?'

'*C'est moi, chérie,*' Jean-Claude said.

'How odd!' Tessa exclaimed. 'I was just thinking
about you.'

He chuckled. 'Nice things, I hope.'

'Oh yes, very, very, very nice things.'

'Are you coming downstairs, my Tess? I would
like to talk to you about . . . something.'

'I was just on my way out, coming down to
find you.'

'I shall await you in the library.'

'See you in a jiffy.'

She hung up the phone, glanced at herself in the
mirror, liking the sage-green wool jacket with the
cream sweater and matching cream-wool trousers.
Invariably, Tessa wore light colours, knowing how
well they suited her pale blonde colouring, and
she had discovered Jean-Claude preferred them to
darker shades.

Hurrying across the bedroom, she went out into
the corridor and down the wide curving staircase,
heading for the library, wondering what he wanted
to talk to her about.

* * *

The great Stone Hall was empty, but a fire blazed up the chimney and it was a warm and welcoming sight, as were the many large pots of gold, yellow and bronze chrysanthemums and the white orchids. Her mother always had a lovely display of plants in the Stone Hall, following the tradition started by Emma many years before. Gardening was Paula's hobby and many of the plants in the house were grown by her in the greenhouses.

Tessa's high-heeled cream boots made a staccato sound as she crossed the Stone Hall, and went into the library.

Jean-Claude swung around as she entered and he hurried over to her, kissed her cheek.

His face was cold against hers, and she exclaimed, 'Did you go out for a walk after all?'

'*Mais oui, chérie*. I needed fresh air. And to clear my head,' he explained, and taking hold of her hand he led her down the long room. 'Let's sit here, near the terrace windows,' he murmured. Once they were seated he stared into her face, his eyes searching, as if he were trying to ascertain her mood.

'What is it?' Tessa asked, frowning, staring back at him. 'You look so intense. *Worried*, even.' Anxiety suddenly flared in her, and she wondered what he had on his mind.

'No, not worried. Intense, perhaps. Tess, I am going to . . . get this out. Say it. I cannot encase it in fancy rhetoric.'

She felt herself stiffening, alerted to trouble, and she gave him a harder, more probing stare. 'I don't understand . . . what do you mean? You sound as if you're going to tell me about something . . . unpleasant. About us, maybe?'

'*Non, non, chérie*. What I have to say is not about *us*. I have been given a big assignment. For a French television network, and I wanted to explain . . . I will be out of Paris for a while, perhaps for several weeks. Possibly a month at the most. I hate to leave you, Tessa, but it is an important assignment I have been offered. I must take it.'

Relief flooded through her, and she exclaimed, 'That's fine, I understand.' She laughed somewhat weakly, and added, with a slight grimace, 'I thought you were going to announce something quite awful, like you were finished with me . . . that it was over . . . that we were over.'

Startled by her words, baffled at her lack of faith in him, he looked at her askance, and said softly, 'That will *never* ever happen . . . you must not worry about such a thing. Which reminds me, I have this for you.' As he spoke he pulled a small leather box out of his pocket and handed it to her silently.

Tessa took the box, lifted the lid, and her eyes grew wide as she stared down at a glittering diamond engagement ring. 'Jean-Claude!' she gasped, surprise echoing. 'It's perfectly beautiful.'

He beamed at her. 'Do you like it?'

She nodded. 'Of course. I love it. And I love *you*!'

He took the box away from her, took out the ring, and put it on her finger. As he did so, he said, 'Do you think I have to ask Shane for your hand in marriage? Or am I being a little old-fashioned?'

She laughed uproariously, amused at this suggestion. 'You don't have to ask him. Or Mummy. I am a divorced woman, after all . . . well, not quite divorced. Yet.'

'And will you be my wife, Tessa, once you are free?' he asked, his voice solemn, his face serious, intent.

'Oh yes, Jean-Claude, very much *yes*.'

He leaned closer, kissed her on the mouth, and told her, 'You've just made me a happy man. A *very* happy man, my darling.'

'And I'm a happy woman.' She held out her hand, gazing at the ring. 'It's just beautiful, Jean-Claude. Thank you so much.'

'It's an old ring, I had it reset. It suits you.' He smiled at her indulgently. 'I think diamonds are your stones.'

'And why not?' she asked gaily, and then sobering slightly, she added, 'But you haven't told me where you're going. Where is your assignment taking you?'

'To Afghanistan.'

She gaped at him, flabbergasted. For a split second words failed her, but after a moment she gasped, 'Oh, no, not *there*. You're going to cover the war there. You could get hurt. Why, you could even get killed!'

'*Non, non. Jamais* . . . never. I will be fine. Remember, *chérie*, I have done this many times before. I am a war correspondent, Tessa. You must not forget that. I learned long ago not to take risks.'

'But Jean-Claude, being a war correspondent is terribly *dangerous*, whatever you say,' she protested.

'That I do not deny. However, I *am* experienced, and I am not a hot head. I do not put myself in harm's way, and I have been there before when the Russians invaded Afghanistan. I know the terrain.'

'I shall be frantic with worry,' she cried, her face paler than usual, her eyes stricken. She began to tremble.

'I know that, but the time will pass quickly. It will be only a month. And thank God for cell phones. We can speak every day.'

'Please don't go—'

He held up his hand. 'My Tess, you know who I am, what I am all about. I must go. I do not have a choice in this matter. It is what I do. And you must learn to live with it.' His tone brooked no argument. He sounded suddenly tough and very determined.

'You *have* to go? You really do?' she said in a low voice.

'I do.'

'Then I *shall* have to learn to live with it,' she answered, and blinked rapidly as tears welled.

Jean-Claude noticed her tears at once, and put his arms around her, held her close. 'Nothing is going to happen to me. I promise,' he reassured her. 'I shall come back to you safely. We shall be married as soon as your divorce is final, and we will be together always.'

Tessa did not answer. She was too choked up to say anything. As he held her closer she silently prayed that he *would* be safe, that he *would* come back to her all in one piece.

CHAPTER NINE

'I need to speak with you.'

Lorne nodded, looking across at his twin sister from the window seat, where he had so often sat as a child, here in the old playroom on the top floor of Pennistone Royal underneath the attics.

Tessa stood near the ancient rocking horse, Gallant Lad, which had been ridden by their mother, aunts, uncles and cousins before them. The vibrant red, green, yellow and white paint was faded now, cracked and chipped, and the black mane had thinned with time, but oh how that beloved horse had been ridden, hugged, patted and enjoyed by so many Harte children.

Lorne waited patiently for her to speak; he was always patient with her and loving; they were the closest of friends and he knew she was not the ogre so many of the family thought she was. He noticed how pensive she looked, saw the worry flickering in her silvery-grey eyes, so like his own, and he immediately thought of that bastard of an ex-husband of hers. Well, soon to be *ex*, and he wondered if Mark Longden had been causing more trouble. Whenever he thought of him Lorne saw red, wanted to find him and thrash him within an inch of his life. He had mistreated and abused Tessa, and as far as Lorne was concerned no punishment was too harsh for him. Blackguard, he thought under his breath, using a very old-fashioned word, but one he believed most appropriate.

'Come on, tell me! Speak to me, Ancient One,' he coaxed, using the name he had invented for her when they were children, and when, at the tender age of five, she had announced to him that she was the elder twin by five minutes and therefore their mother's heir. Much to her chagrin he had never let her forget that little child's boast.

Tessa smiled her special smile, the one she reserved only for him, and giving the rocking horse a little push so that it began to move, she looked directly at Lorne and murmured, 'Jean-Claude's going to Afghanistan. To cover the war for a French network.'

'Is he really! That's great, he'll be in his element. He's such a brilliant war correspondent . . .' Lorne's voice faltered as he instantly noticed the pained look crossing her face and quickly he added, 'Oh God, Tessa, how stupid I'm being. You're worried, of course, and who wouldn't be? Reporting a war *is* dangerous, I know that. But listen . . .' Lorne leaned forward, his expression serious, intent, as he swiftly went on. 'He's been at this game for years. He knows what he's doing, he's a seasoned war correspondent and not a beginner, wet behind the ears. Please try not to worry.'

'Easy to say, brother of mine, hard to do.' She shook her head slowly. 'Very hard not to be on the verge of panic.'

He nodded, compressed his lips, understanding exactly how she felt. 'Knowing you, I suppose you told him how nervous you are about this.'

'Yes, Lorne, I did. I asked him not to go.'

'And?'

'He told me he had to, and that I would have to get used to it . . . more or less those words, anyway. He was adamant, so naturally I agreed with him.' She lifted her slender shoulders in a light shrug. 'What else could I say?'

'Nothing really,' Lorne agreed. 'In reality, you have no choice. You have to go along with him. He's a fifty-three-year-old man who's been doing what he wants all his life, especially when it comes to his work, his career. That's who he is. His own man. I doubt he could be deterred, once he'd made up his mind, not by you or me or anyone else. Look, it *is* his *forte*, after all.'

'That's right, and he's good at it. And over the last few years he's become an expert on the Middle East, fanaticism and militancy. He said to me only the other day that it's a political philosophy – waging war against the Western democracies, that is. He has the need to understand, to write about such things. That's one of the reasons he's excited about going to cover this war.'

'I realize that. Actually, he's talked a lot to me

about the Middle East, especially in the last year. But listen, Tess, the news is good, and has been since December. Things are better, most certainly, and let's not forget he *knows* the country, covered the last war there when the Russians invaded Afghanistan.'

'I know, he's told me bits about it, and anyway I read his book *Warriors*, and he covered it in that.'

Moving away from the rocking horse, Tessa walked over to the window seat, and Lorne made room for her as he had done when they were children. Leaning back against him, she murmured softly, 'I'm so afraid he might get killed.'

'He could get killed walking across the Champs Élysées,' Lorne answered. 'It'll be all right,' he went on quietly, putting his arms around her, wanting to calm and reassure her.

Tessa nodded, then sat up slightly, put her hand in her pocket and brought out the diamond engagement ring. Turning around to look up at her brother, she said, 'We're engaged,' and showed him the ring.

Lorne stared at it, then whistled, and his eyes twinkled as he exclaimed, 'I'm thrilled. *Congratulations*. I couldn't be happier for you.' He started to laugh then, looking at her with sudden amusement.

'What is it?' she asked curiously, eyeing him intently, frowning.

'When I set the two of you up, I never guessed it would actually come to this . . . *a permanent relationship*.'

'I knew it!' Tessa cried, punching his arm. 'Right from the beginning. I told Jean-Claude on our first date that I suspected you'd brought us together, and very specifically, to have an affair.'

'And aren't you glad I did?'

'You bet!' Smiling, she slid the ring on her engagement finger and showed it to him again. 'Look, Lorne.'

'It's a bobby dazzler, and so are you!' he exclaimed and then he added in a more sober tone, 'He's a good man, Tess. True blue. And he's very good for you, just as you're so good for him. And when do you plan to get married?'

'As soon as we can, and I'd really like it to be before June. I don't want to infringe on India's splashy wedding in Ireland.'

'I agree. And can I hope to be best man?'

She grinned. 'We haven't got that far. He only just gave me the ring this morning. But I'm sure he'll ask you.'

Lorne nodded. 'When does his assignment actually start?'

'In two weeks. He's going to Paris on Monday, but he'll fly directly from Paris to Yorkshire on Thursday . . . he says he's determined to attend one of our famous family weddings.'

'Learning the ropes, eh?' Lorne teased.

'I suppose. Thanks, Lorne, for getting us together in the first place. It means the world to me that you did that for me, that you cared enough.'

'Hey, come on, don't be a silly goose. Incidentally, why aren't you wearing the ring? Be careful you don't lose it, leaving it floating around in your pocket like that.'

'I'll wear it tonight, after we've told Mummy and Dad. They don't know yet, since they're both out.'

'Then we'll make it a celebration tonight.'

'That's an idea . . . Lorne?'

'Yes, what is it? You sound suddenly mournful.'

'I'm worried about not having a job after I marry Jean-Claude. I've always worked. What I mean is, I'll have to give up Harte's.'

Her twin gave her a long, thoughtful look, frowning, shaking his head. 'Is it still that important to you, working at Harte's?'

'Yes. No. I don't know.'

'You're thirty-two, darling, and you've had a lot of success at the stores. But let's not forget the rough ride you had with Mark Longden. A very bad marriage that gave you absolutely zilch.'

'It gave me Adele.'

'Yes, of course, and I know you love her, I know what she means to you. But you're a young woman, you should have happiness with a man, a fulfilled life. And how often do we find the right person? *The* one for us? I haven't yet. *But you have.* Jean-Claude is the perfect man for you, and you're going to be very busy being his wife and bringing up Adele. And what if you have a child, or indeed children, by him?'

'You're right, Lorne,' she replied very quietly, looking into the distance.

'I know you, Tessa, and you're thinking about Linnet. About Linnet being the head of Harte's, and that kills you, doesn't it?'

Tessa stared at him. She said nothing, biting her lip.

There was silence.

Neither of them spoke for a while.

It was Lorne who finally said, 'You've just got to get over this jealousy of yours. You've been rivals for years and it just makes for bad blood between you. And upsets us all.'

'I know . . . but she wants the top job desperately.'

'And she'll probably get it. Face *that* now. You'll be living in Paris with your new husband. She'll be here, right on the spot. Of course Mummy's going to give it to her.'

'I wish I could commute.'

'Don't be so ridiculous! That wouldn't work. You'd better make up your mind to forget having the power at the stores, and think of your marriage. I don't believe you can have both. And to my way of thinking, you'll be happier being Madame Jean-Claude Deléon than the new Emma Harte. That role's for Linnet. Accept it.'

Tessa stared at him. She did not reply.

'I would like to speak to the Countess of Dunvale, please, Paddy. This is Linnet O'Neill.'

'Oh hello, Miss O'Neill,' Paddy Whitaker said pleasantly. 'I'll put you through to the dining room.'

'Oh, I don't want to disturb their lunch!'

'No, no, it's all right, they've finished. Just a moment please, Miss O'Neill.'

It was India who picked up the phone in the

dining room, and said, 'Hello, Linnet, I hear you want to speak to Grandma.'

'For a minute or two, India. I hope I'm not phoning at an inopportune time.'

'No, no, it's fine. We've finished lunch, just waiting to have coffee. Let me get Grandma.'

Linnet waited several minutes before she heard that famous sonorous voice. 'Here I am, Linnet. To what do I owe this honour? An unexpected phone call from you is a rarity.'

'Oh gosh, Great-Aunt Edwina, don't say *that*. You make me feel guilty.'

'Don't be daft, and guilt's a terrible waste of time.'

'Yes, Great-Aunt Edwina,' Linnet responded and went on quickly, 'I need to talk to you about Uncle Robin and Evan's family, and it's urgent.'

'Why? Is there something wrong?'

'No. But there could be. Is it at all possible for me to see you tomorrow? I could drive over.'

'Today would be better, my dear. And if it's urgent, isn't it better we meet today? Or can you tell me about this problem on the phone?'

'I'd prefer to talk it out with you in person. I have an idea. Why don't you come to supper tonight? Tessa's cooking, she's making her famous lamb stew.'

'It sounds delicious, but I'm not sure I could eat another big meal,' Edwina protested, although she was now riddled with curiosity.

'You don't have to eat anything much, you know. You can pick, like the model girls do.'

Edwina laughed. 'Well, I am free this evening, and—'

'I could invite Robin, Great-Aunt, and we could kill two birds with one stone,' Linnet cut in swiftly. 'Please say you'll come. It's very important.'

'What actually is it about?'

'It's too complicated to explain on the phone, but let's just say this . . . I need *you* to talk some sense into *him*. About having the Hughes family stay with him. They can't.'

'Why not?'

'Because Jonathan Ainsley's unexpectedly in Yorkshire, and he might cause trouble for everyone. And especially Owen Hughes.'

'Ah yes, of course, Linnet, you are absolutely right.' There was a little pause. Edwina took a deep breath and announced in her familiar, commanding voice, 'I shall come tonight. And you must make sure Robin is there as well. You are correct, as usual. As your great-grandmother always was. Only *I* can talk some sense into my brother.'

'Thanks for agreeing,' Linnet exclaimed, her voice suddenly cheerful and breezy. 'Shall I send somebody over to fetch you?'

'No, no, that's not necessary. I have my driver. Just tell me what time I should arrive, and I shall be there promptly.'

'You'd better come before drinks. About six-thirty, if that's all right with you? Then we can have a chat before Uncle Robin arrives. Just the two of us. Oh, and it's a casual evening, Great-Aunt Edwina.'

'I am never *casual*, my dear. I shall dress for dinner as usual.'

'Could I have a word with you in private, Gladys?' Dusty said, walking across the kitchen to the small eating area where Gladys was finishing lunch with Atlanta.

'Of course you can, Mr Rhodes,' Gladys Roebotham responded, standing up, moving away from the small table. 'I'll be back in three shakes of a lamb's tail,' she said to the child, who laughed and clapped her hands with glee on hearing these words.

Dusty smiled lovingly at his daughter, and then turning to Gladys he said, 'I haven't heard that expression in donkey's years. My mother used to say that.' As he finished he laughed when he saw Atlanta's face. It was a picture.

Gladys laughed with him and said, 'It's funny the way these old-fashioned sayings always have a reference to animals in them. They certainly amuse Atlanta, she loves hearing them.'

'Indeed she does.' He guided the young woman across the kitchen and into a small hallway that led out to the back garden.

Gladys said, 'What did you want to speak to me about, Mr Rhodes?' She sounded curious.

'I was wondering if you would be able to do a bit of baby-sitting for me, Gladys? You know, come over and look after Atlanta, if it's at all necessary? She seems very attached to you, and you're so good with her.'

Immediately, a troubled look settled on Gladys's

face and she said slowly, worriedly, 'I'd love to do that, I really would, but it's a bit of a problem right now. I have a relative staying with me, who's not been well, and I can't be away for too long during the day. I'm ever so sorry, Mr Rhodes, I am that.'

'I am too,' Dusty responded, forcing a smile, filled with sudden disappointment. Over lunch he had convinced himself that Gladys would be available and that she would solve a lot of problems for him.

Observing him carefully, Gladys saw the crushed look slide onto his face, and swiftly she said, 'But perhaps I'll be able to do something to help later on. I mean, if Molly's still in the hospital and Atlanta's out here with you.'

'I'd appreciate it, if that becomes the case, Gladys, I would indeed. I want to thank you again for looking after Atlanta, for being so responsible. Now let me take you back to the kitchen to finish lunch. And whenever you're ready, Paddy will call for the car to come. It only takes the driver five minutes to get here and he'll take you anywhere you want to go.'

'Thanks ever so much, Mr Rhodes, you've been ever so nice. Any message for Mrs Caldwell if I do get to visit her for a while?'

'Yes, of course. Tell her I'm wishing her better very quickly, and that she should have the hospital call if she needs anything. You can also tell her I'll be in to see her on Monday.'

'That'll please her, it really will,' Gladys Roebotham replied, smiling up at him, thinking what a nice man he was, not at all the villain Melinda Caldwell had made him out to be. In fact he was a real gentleman.

CHAPTER TEN

Paula sat at her grandmother's old desk in the upstairs parlour making a list of things still to be done for the wedding, when a light tapping on the door brought her head up with a start.

'Come in,' she called, glancing at the door.

It flew open and Margaret sailed in, carrying a laden tray and exclaiming, 'Did you think I'd forgotten about your tea, Mrs O'Neill?'

'No, Margaret, I didn't, you never forget anything,' Paula answered, and putting down her pen she rose and went to the fireplace.

The housekeeper bustled over, put the tray on the coffee table, and then straightened. Looking across at Paula, who was now seated on the sofa, she murmured, 'I made your favourite ginger biscuits, Miss Paula.' As she spoke she dropped a piece of lemon in the china cup, and asked, 'Shall I pour the tea, or do you want to wait for Mr O'Neill?'

'Oh, that's all right, Margaret, you can pour it,' Paula answered, smiling at her. The housekeeper had grown up at Pennistone Royal and the two women had known each other all of their lives. Paula thought of Margaret as part of the family, and never paid much attention to her odd moods and moments of familiarity. She said now, 'I'm so glad Tessa wanted to cook dinner, you can have a night off.'

Margaret shook her head, said a little vehemently, 'I've been pressed into service, so to speak, Mrs O'Neill. Tessa needs a bit of help, that she does.'

Frowning, Paula exclaimed, 'What do you mean? She makes her lamb stew very quickly . . . Why does she need help?'

'I think you ought to know you're having a dinner party tonight, Miss Paula.'

'I am?' Paula sounded baffled and stared at the housekeeper in disbelief.

Margaret nodded emphatically. '*Eighteen pounds* of lamb stew! That's what Tessa ordered from the butcher. It seems a lot of meat to me but when I questioned her about it, she said there're loads of bones in neck and shoulder. Which is true, a'course.'

'I know that,' Paula answered a bit impatiently, and asked, 'But who's coming for dinner? Who are those I don't know about already?'

'Miss Linnet's invited Mr Robin and the countess, and Tessa told me that Emily and Winston are coming, and probably India and Mr Rhodes.'

'Good Lord! How many does that make altogether? About sixteen?'

'Seventeen,' Margaret announced. 'Grandfather O'Neill always has supper with you, doesn't he?'

'That's true. Perhaps Tessa didn't order too much lamb, after all.'

'I usually reckon half a pound per person, because there're a lot of vegetables in the stew.' The housekeeper gave Paula a smug smile, wanting the last word when it came to her domain. 'She's gone overboard.'

Paula nodded. 'You're right, as usual, Margaret. And I'm so sorry you've been pressed into working when we'd agreed you could have the evening off. Perhaps I'd better come down to the kitchen and help.'

'No, no, no, madame, it's not necessary!' Margaret exclaimed, reverting to formality again, her voice rising. 'I'll help Miss Tessa flour the meat and *sauté* it, and the others are preparing the vegetables at this very moment.'

'The others?' Paula raised a dark brow.

'Emsie's chopping onions, Mr Julian's scraping carrots and Lorne is peeling potatoes.' A loving smile settled on her face as she mentioned him. 'He's such a darling, Mr Lorne is, so obliging and helpful. There's nobody like Lorne. The woman that gets him is going to be fortunate indeed, a woman blessed.'

Paula bit back a smile, endeavouring to keep her face straight. The whole family knew that Margaret had adored Lorne since his babyhood and he could do no wrong in her eyes. The fact that he was now a famous actor only added to his allure. Margaret was his biggest fan and spoiled him outrageously when he came home to stay. 'Yes, Lorne *is* special,'

Paula finally murmured, and at last let the smile slip onto her face. She added, 'But you didn't mention Mr Deléon. Or Linnet. Where are they?'

'Oh, Miss Linnet's on the phone doing business as usual, I think.' Margaret beamed at Paula. 'You know she's so like Mrs Harte, open for business twenty-four hours a day, seven days a week. A right chip off the old block!'

Paula broke into laughter, then asked, 'And Mr Deléon?'

'He's sitting in the kitchen drinking coffee and talking to Miss Tessa, and looking very worshipful, I must say.'

'And I suppose Adele is with Elvira?'

'Oh yes, Miss Paula. They're having tea in the nursery.' Edging away from the fireplace, Margaret thought to add, 'I don't mind helping Miss Tessa *sauté* the meat, you know. After all, she's been an apt pupil of mine, very apt.'

'Indeed she has, Margaret, you've taught her everything she knows about cooking. Thank you for doing that. And you shouldn't mind too much when she invades your territory.'

'I don't, Mrs O'Neill. And I'll be enjoying her stew for supper and so will Joe, since there'll be so much left over. Anyway, it's my recipe.' With another smug smile and a nod, the housekeeper walked out.

A moment later Paula glanced at the bedroom door as it opened and Shane sauntered in, laughing. 'What a card she is these days, darling!' Still laughing, he joined her by the fire. 'She can sound like a tyrant at times, and then quite suddenly she's all marshmallow. There's no one like her. She moves from formality to casualness with such ease and in a way I've not seen or heard from anyone else.'

'I don't pay too much attention, Shane,' Paula replied, smiling at him. 'I never know what she's going to call me ... we all know that by now. And I don't care, she *is* part of the family, and her parents worked for Grandy all of their *lives*. She's like one of those devoted retainers of old, and she feels part of us, one of us. And let's remember, she did grow up with me, in fact she's only about four years older than I am.'

Shane nodded his understanding, reached for the pot and poured himself a cup of tea. 'But I think she's wrong about Winston and Emily coming to dinner. Winston didn't say anything to me about that when we had lunch today at the Drum and Monkey.'

'Neither did Emily when we were working at Beck House. But Emily is rather besotted with Evan at the moment, and more importantly Evan's condition ... she can't wait for those babies to be born.'

'But they're not going to be born tonight, are they?'

'Oh, Shane, don't tease, you know what I mean. She loves to be around Evan right now, and let's remember that Gideon *is* her favourite child.'

'You'd better not let Toby and Natalie hear you say that,' he warned, sipping his tea, reaching for a ginger biscuit.

'As if I would . . .' Paula paused, looked across at her husband thoughtfully, her violet eyes suddenly filled with puzzlement. Then she sat back on the sofa, shaking her head.

Shane, always tuned into her, said, 'What is it? Come on, let's have it.'

'Tessa said a funny thing the other day: she said Toby's not her best friend anymore, that she never hears from him. Well, hardly ever. She sounds a bit sad, actually.'

'Those two have been as thick as thieves since they were kids together, so I'm not surprised she's upset if he's pulled away from her. And yet that in itself is not surprising to me, Paula. They're both in the middle of divorces, and he's at a loose end, while she's suddenly involved with another man before her divorce has even come through. Personally, I think Toby's nose is out of joint. I always believed he was sweet on Tessa.' When she remained silent, Shane pressed, 'Didn't you?'

'Sometimes,' Paula admitted, and gave him a faint smile. 'Although I'm not quite sure it would have worked, no, not at all. They're so much alike in so many ways.'

Leaning forward across the coffee table, Paula continued, 'I'm quite a fan of Jean-Claude's. I think she needs an older man, one who will give her love and support, but I don't think their romance will lead to marriage.'

'Because of her career?' Shane suggested. When Paula said nothing in response, he let his eyes rest on her speculatively. 'Come on, Paula, you know that's the reason. She's very ambitious, and she always has been. Tessa wants the top job at Harte's and she aims to have it. She'll probably put it before Jean-Claude in the end.'

'Everything you say is true, but I was thinking of *him*, of Jean-Claude. *He* might not want to get married, Shane.'

'Your guess is as good as mine there, but I do know one thing . . . Tessa may look fragile, even delicate, and in need of protection, but I've always believed she has a streak of strength, even toughness in her, and she's not a Harte for nothing, you know.'

'Yes, you're right, and I've noticed that she refers to herself as being a Harte these days. It wasn't too long ago she insisted she was all Fairley. Quite a *volte face*.'

'I know. On the other—'

'Am I interrupting?' Linnet asked from the door-way, and, not waiting for her parents to answer, she hurried into the room. After kissing Paula on the cheek, she flopped down next to her father and hugged him. 'I'll only be a few minutes,' she went on. 'I know how much you both like to have this particular time to be alone together.'

'It's all right,' Shane answered, eyeing his daughter, his eyes full of love for her. Suddenly, he couldn't help thinking that today, more than ever, she looked very much like Emma Harte. She was wearing a red sweater and trousers, and the colour, which had been a favourite of Emma's, was as becoming to her as it had been to her great-grandmother.

'I bet Margaret told you I've invited Great-Aunt Edwina and Uncle Robin to dinner – she's such a chatterbox.'

'She mentioned it in passing,' Paula replied. 'I wasn't quite sure why though, unless you're simply being cordial.'

'No, there's a reason, Mummy,' Linnet admitted. 'I need to speak privately to Edwina before Robin comes. You see I've got to explain why she has to talk to him, drill some sense into him.'

'About what?' Paula asked, sounding puzzled.

'Having the Hughes family to stay at Lackland Priory during the wedding festivities. It won't work and it could be very troublesome.'

'Why is that?' Shane asked.

Paula had a flash of insight. *Jonathan*, she thought. It's to do with him. Somehow. Dismay hit her like a punch in the chest. She sat very still, as always upset when she thought of her treacherous cousin.

Linnet explained, 'Jack Figg called me this morning to tell me that Jonathan Ainsley has parked himself at his house in Thirsk. Jack believes he could easily pop over to see his father and run slap-bang into Owen Hughes. His half-brother. Jack says that kind of encounter could prove dangerous.'

'By God, that's a possibility!' Shane interjected, sounding startled.

Paula made no comment.

'Didn't you speak to Jack, Mummy? He said he was going to phone you.'

Paula shook her head. 'I've been at Beck House

all day with Aunt Emily. I guess my mobile was off. So Jack couldn't have reached me even if he'd tried. Anyway, Linnet, I could have talked to Uncle Robin quite easily . . . he does listen to me.'

'But you've enough to do with all these wedding arrangements and the reception. I thought Edwina was definitely the best *other* person to convince him they should be put up somewhere else.'

'I understand,' Paula said.

'I wish I'd come over to Beck House this afternoon after all.' Linnet shook her head. 'But Julian and I had some other things we had to do. I could have explained then, couldn't I?'

'It doesn't matter, darling.'

Shane said, 'But where *would* they stay?'

'I thought they could go to Aunt Emily and Uncle Winston . . . after all *their* son is marrying Owen's daughter. And there's lots of room at Allington Hall. The adoptees could stay there as well.'

'*Adoptees*,' Shane spluttered, 'that's a peculiar way to describe Evan's sisters, whom I assume you're referring to.'

'*Adopted* sisters, Dad,' Linnet corrected herself.

'Do be careful how you describe them to other people, Linnet,' Paula cautioned. 'You mustn't sound disrespectful.'

Shane interjected, 'You don't appear to like them by the sound of it. And I didn't know they were here *already*.'

'They're not,' Linnet said. 'Well, one of them is. Angharad. I found her strange, Daddy.'

'I see. Your mother's right, Linny, do be careful

how you speak of these girls in public. And anyone else, for that matter.'

'Yes, Dad.' Looking across at her mother, Linnet now said, 'I hope you don't mind me taking charge of this problem, Mummy. You don't, do you?'

'No, of course not.'

'You're becoming a regular Margaret Thatcher, aren't you, Linnet?' Shane teased.

'All Yorkshire women are Margaret Thatchers in the making, Dad. Bossy and controlling. Surely you know that.'

Shane laughed, shaking his head. 'You're incorrigible!'

Paula looked from her husband to her daughter and smiled in amusement. She decided she wasn't going to give any thought to Jonathan Ainsley and the trouble he might make. Nor did she want to deal with Robin. She said evenly, and with a certain sense of relief, 'I'm sure Jack is correct about lodging them somewhere else, Linnet, and thanks for taking charge. Since you've started the ball rolling, I'm going to let you continue. Go ahead and deal with Edwina and Robin, and do so with my blessing.'

'Oh thanks, Mums, I'm glad you agree. Well, I'd better go and change into something a little bit more suitable for dinner.' Jumping up, she blew her parents a kiss and hurried off.

When they were alone, Shane said, 'To me she seems more like Emma every day.' He pushed himself to his feet, went and stood in front of the fireplace. 'She's nobody's fool either.'

Paula also got up, walked over to him, put her

arms around him and nestled her head against his chest. 'I know she's smart and bright and quick, you don't have to tell *me* that. And yes, she is like Grandy. It's quite strange for me sometimes . . .' Paula paused for a moment, and then quietly added, 'I feel as if I'm listening to my grandmother speaking at times. It's as if Grandy has been reincarnated in my daughter.'

'Perhaps she has,' Shane responded, and mystic Celt that he was he didn't think there was anything odd about his reply.

Paula murmured, 'There's always the spectre of Jonathan Ainsley hanging over our heads . . .' Her voice trailed off, and she held onto him tighter.

'Let's not blow things out of proportion,' Shane answered. 'He has a house here in Yorkshire so obviously he's going to come and live in it from time to time.'

'But why *now* all of a sudden, with another family wedding pending? He wants to make trouble, as he tried to do when Linnet and Julian got married.'

'Oh, it's just a coincidence,' Shane said swiftly, wanting to soothe her. But he couldn't help wondering if he was wrong and Paula was right. These thoughts were interrupted when there was a knock on the door and before either of them could answer, Tessa walked in, followed by Jean-Claude in her wake.

Shane and Paula quickly stood apart, and Paula said, 'I hear you're making a wonderful lamb stew for dinner, darling.' As she spoke she smiled, beckoned for them to come closer. 'How are you, Jean-Claude?' she asked, moving towards him.

Shane followed, extending his hand to the Frenchman. After greetings were exchanged, Tessa said, 'I hope we're not interrupting.'

'Not at all,' Paula said. 'Let's go and sit by the fire.'

Once they were settled, Tessa looked at her mother and then at Shane, and said, 'We've become engaged.'

'This is just wonderful!' Paula exclaimed, sounding surprised. 'Congratulations, Tessa ... Jean-Claude.'

'Thank you,' Jean-Claude said and added, 'I'm glad to see you approve.'

'I'll say we do,' Shane exclaimed. 'Very much so. Congratulations.'

Tessa beamed at them, and then held out her hand, showed them her diamond engagement ring.

'It's beautiful,' Paula said, and looking from Tessa to Jean-Claude, she went on, 'And it looks as if we've now something to celebrate tonight. It's going to be a lovely dinner party with so many of the family coming. And I'd like to say welcome to you: welcome to our family, Jean-Claude.'

CHAPTER ELEVEN

The man took the key out of his pocket and inserted it in the lock of the back door. He turned it and smiled to himself as the door opened easily. Stepping into the kitchen, he shut the door and glanced around.

It was late afternoon and the light was dim in the kitchen but he resisted turning on the lights. Instead he went through into the front hall, took off his overcoat, hung it in the closet and then walked through the various rooms on the ground floor.

There were moments when he wanted to laugh out loud as he moved through the space, surveying everything, laughing again with pleasure and pride in his own deviousness.

Paula O'Neill would have a heart attack if she knew he had a key to this house. But he did, it was in his hand; now he dropped it into his pocket, still smiling to himself. He had a key to the back door at Pennistone Royal as well. She would have a triple heart attack if she knew *that*. His laughter echoed hollowly through the empty house.

How clever he had been all those years ago when he was a teenager. At that time he had had the keys copied for himself, and nobody had been any the wiser, not even his canny grandmother. And nobody had ever changed the locks at Pennistone Royal. Nor here at Heron's Nest in Scarborough.

Dumb, he said to himself. My dumb cousins are indeed dumb. Paula O'Neill most especially. She ought to have known better. Locks should always be changed from time to time. Precautions always taken. From people like him. Even Jack Figg was stupid. As if he didn't know that Figg had a tail on him. He laughed to himself. A tail was so easy to lose.

The furniture in all the rooms was covered in sheets, the curtains partially drawn, and this gave the place a ghostly, eerie feeling. Yet this did not trouble him one iota. He did not believe in the supernatural and, anyway, he had nerves of steel; nothing fazed him. Not ever.

As he went up the staircase he noted yet again how scrupulously clean the house was, thanks to the caretaker who came in once a week to check the heating system and pipes. Although the house was not used much by the family now, especially in the winter months, Paula O'Neill, nevertheless, made sure it was in top-notch condition. As some sort of ridiculous tribute to Emma Harte, no doubt, who had loved this house and favoured it more than any of her other holiday homes.

Walking into the bedroom which had been his as a boy, it never occurred to him that his cousin loved Heron's Nest as much as their grandmother had, and that it held many fond and sentimental memories for her. He knew nothing much about sentiment.

Jonathan Ainsley opened the draperies and stood looking out of the window at the gardens below and the sea beyond stretching into infinity. Heron's Nest stood on a little promontory and he had always thought his room had one of the best views in the house. He still did.

Under the pale sun the sea was gleaming brightly this afternoon. It was smooth, hardly a ripple on the surface, and it had a greyish-green patina that reminded him of the glazed-like surface of ancient jade. Automatically his hand went into his pocket, his long fingers curling round the piece of mutton-fat jade that he believed brought him Good Joss – good luck – because it had been blessed in a very special way by a beautiful and charismatic woman. Jasmine Wu-Jen. He thought of her now. He had missed her during this sojourn in Paris and London.

There had been times when he had thought of flying her in from Hong Kong, but invariably he changed his mind at the last minute. She wouldn't fit in here. She was too exotic. Too different. Too disturbing. Better that she remained where she was. In her home high on the Peak above the teeming city he had always loved, a home he had given to her when she had become *his*.

Turning away from the window for a moment he let his eyes roam around the room, taking in all of the possessions from his youth. He had never removed them from here, preferring instead to let them all stay intact on the bookshelves. Many of them were insignificant, trifling things. Odd-looking or unusual pebbles and shells from the beach, an ancient miner's lamp made of brass, a small stuffed bird in a glass case, a big jar of multi-coloured marbles, and, in another glass case, an old Roman coin he had found on the moors above Scarborough, which as a teenager he had considered his most prized possession.

He still liked to walk across the moors and along the sea cliffs, as he had as a boy. He had loved history when he was growing up and it had been easy for him to envision battles and skirmishes amongst the hills, conflicts at sea . . . those violent and bloody encounters that were part of the story of this island race he came from.

He turned back to the window and gazed out again, thinking of times past when there had been so much strife in this land, and often strife within families. Brother against brother, cousin against cousin when it came to the greatest stakes of all – such as the throne of England. The Royal Houses of York and Lancaster in mortal combat, cousins warring with each other to gain the ultimate in power . . . the crown of England. That most glittering prize.

There's nothing new under the sun, he thought suddenly. I am prepared to do battle with Paula O'Neill to get what I want. It was no longer Harte's. He knew now that this would be an impossible undertaking. But he could still have his revenge on her by destroying those things she held dear. Her husband Shane, long ago his friend . . . her children . . . and of course that little jewel, Adele Longden, her only grandchild.

He thought of Mark Longden, with a rush of bitterness. What a waste of time he had been ultimately. No guts. Jonathan was convinced that it was Mark who had betrayed him in November last year, by alerting Jack Figg that a gang of yobbos was going to rumble into Pennistone village to create havoc at the wedding of Linnet O'Neill and Julian Kallinski. The scheme had almost worked and it would have if Mark had not lost his nerve.

The woman slowed her car as she came to the end of the main road and turned onto a patch of dirt, parking under an ancient tree. As she got out of her car and locked it, she glanced at the tree, one so old its gnarled roots protruded like knotted fingers reaching out of the earth as if grasping for life. It had hardly changed, had looked like this since her childhood, when she had first come here with her mother. It had always fascinated her.

Moving away from the car, crossing the main road, she saw that the area ahead was deserted this afternoon. But then it was chilly and a sharp wind was blowing up from the sea; few people would venture out on a bitterly cold day like this, not even the dog-owners who were dedicated to their pets and made a walk along the cliffs a daily ritual.

As she finally came up onto the cliffs the woman

could see the house far away in the distance, standing on its little promontory, and she struck out towards it, striding briskly along the path high above the North Sea. Below her the waves foamed and frothed around the clusters of rocks, but farther out it was calm and flat, glittering like glass in the pale sunlight, a greenish-grey reflecting the anthracite-coloured sky.

The path led directly to the back gate of the house, and it would take her exactly nine minutes to walk there. When she had been small it had taken her double that time as she trotted along next to her mother.

She was a tall woman, slender, with a mass of black curly hair tied back in a pony tail. Her eyes were the colour of coal under perfectly arched black brows; she had a broad forehead, a sharply-defined nose and a long neck. Although she was not beautiful in the classical sense she was attractive, and very striking in appearance.

When she was a child her friends had called her Gypsy, because of her dusky complexion and jet-black hair; her colouring resembled that of the Romany women who travelled across the countryside, going from fair to fair . . . the women who lived in gypsy caravans and told fortunes by reading palms, looking into glass globes or at tea leaves.

But gypsy she was not. The woman was a mixture of Irish and Scottish. Her mother had frequently told her when she was growing up that she was a true Celt, but also a throwback to her Black Irish ancestors, who in turn were descended from the Spanish sailors shipwrecked when the Great Armada from Spain had foundered off the coast of Ireland in Elizabethan times.

Matched to her striking looks were her striking clothes – elegant, expensive and highly colourful. No shrinking violet, she usually selected vibrant colours, shades that suited her, were flattering, and made her stand out wherever she went.

This afternoon she was dressed entirely in purple, from her belted purple wool coat with sheared beaver collar and cuffs, to purple leather boots over purple trousers. Adding an extra dash of intense colour were red woollen gloves and a red cashmere scarf which was blowing about in the wind as she walked.

The woman's name was Priscilla Marney and she had grown up in nearby Scarborough, although these days she lived in Harrogate where she ran a successful business of her own creation.

She thought of that business as she strode out, worrying that she had left her small staff to cope without her on a busy Saturday. On the other hand, she had not seen Jonathan the last time he was here in Yorkshire, and later she had bitterly regretted not making an effort to get together with him.

Yesterday, when he had phoned her suddenly out of the blue, he had been most persuasive and she had given in immediately to his pleading, unable to resist him, which was usually the case.

Jonathan Ainsley.

She thought of him as she hurried along the cliffs.

How long had they known each other? She pondered this for a moment or two.

It was something like forty years . . . that seemed impossible to her, but she knew it was true. She found herself frowning in surprise as she acknowledged this. She had, in fact, known him most of her life. How remarkable that was, now that she thought about it.

They had met as children when her mother had gone to work as a summer secretary to Emma Harte during those warm-weather months when Mrs Harte lived at Heron's Nest. Once the school holidays began, Mrs Harte brought her brood of grandchildren to stay at her holiday home in Scarborough. Here she trained them to stand on their own feet and to look after themselves in every way possible.

'Emma's Boot Camp.' That was what most of them called it, and each one of them confided in her that their grandmother was either tough or demanding, or overly stern with them. Each one had a different point of view, but they all loved Grandy, as they called her.

Priscilla had had a schoolgirl crush on Jonathan in those days, and he had genuinely reciprocated her feelings, so much so she had lost her virginity to him when she was fourteen and he not much older. They had discovered sex together, and they had gone at it hammer and tongs . . . that was the way he described it, anyway. They thought they were wonderful.

In the ensuing years they saw each other off and on, and slept together off and on; he had been married to Arabella Sutton and divorced from her and had not married again; she had been married twice. Her first husband, Conner Mallone, had been killed by a bus in Manchester, where he had gone on business; she was separated from her second, Roger Duffield. At least at the moment.

Roger was currently begging her to take him back; she was resisting his overtures. It was not a good relationship and she had not been happy with him; she had recently come to believe she was better off on her own as a single woman. Her daughter by Conner, Samantha, who was now in her twenties, agreed with her, was encouraging her to 'be your own woman', as she put it.

Priscilla was well aware that there was no future, no long-term relationship with Jonathan, but old habits die hard and she enjoyed meeting him here in secret to have sex at Heron's Nest where they had first made love as teenagers.

It gave her a kick, and she was aware it turned him on. There was another thing they both appreciated – the fact that theirs was the longest sexual relationship either of them had ever had with another person.

A few steps away from the house Priscilla took out her phone and dialled Jonathan on his mobile. He answered with a curt, 'Hello?'

'It's me. I'm only a moment away from the back gate.'

'I just opened the kitchen door. I'm upstairs,' he said and clicked off.

*　　*　　*

After stepping into the kitchen, Priscilla locked the door behind her, made her way through the kitchen and out into the front hall. Here the light was dim, almost gloomy, but she did not dare put on a lamp. The caretaker lived not too far away and Jonathan was constantly worried she would notice the lights if they were on in the house, which was locked up for the winter.

Taking a small flashlight out of her pocket, she turned it on and made her way up the winding staircase. When she reached the landing she saw Jonathan hovering in the corridor and a sunny smile broke across her face.

Smiling himself, he came to meet her, regarded her intently for a brief moment and then pulled her into his arms and gave her a big bear hug. He clung to her for a moment or two, and she to him.

'It's great to see you, Pris darling, and you look wonderful.' As he spoke he held her away from him, and scrutinized her once again. It was true, she was in marvellous form, beautifully groomed and dressed. He liked chic women.

'Thank you, and so do you, Jonny. Positively blooming. I've always told you Hong Kong agrees with you.'

He made no response, took hold of her arm and led her down the corridor to his room, asking, 'You can have dinner with me later, can't you?'

'Oh, gosh, Jonny, I don't know . . .' She broke off, shaking her head. 'My staff are all alone, and we're quite busy.'

'Can't you give them a call?' He pushed open the door of his room and took her inside.

'Yes.'

'Then do it now . . . so we can be relaxed about things,' he suggested, eyeing her suggestively.

She did as he asked, using her mobile, and moments later was talking to her office. 'Everything's under control, Priscilla,' her assistant told her. 'There's no reason for you to be here. We can manage.'

When she gave Jonathan this news a pleased expression leapt onto his face; he grinned at her, exclaimed, 'And guess where I'm going to take you? The Grand Hotel in Scarborough.'

'Good Lord! What kind of an idea is that? And how's the food these days?' she asked, shaking her head.

'I don't know about the food. But who cares really? I want to take you there for old times' sake . . . Remember how we used to sneak down there for fancy teas? We weren't supposed to go to the hotel alone, and it was great breaking the rules, wasn't it?'

'Indeed it was, and especially when we came back and broke even more rules here.' She glanced at the bed longingly, her face flushing.

Jonathan followed the direction of her gaze. 'Anxious, are we?' he asked looking at her, an amused glint in his eyes.

'I'm always anxious for you, just as you are for me,' she replied in a low, throaty voice. 'And why wouldn't we be? It's been quite a while since we've seen each other.' She moved towards him, put her arms around him, brought her face close to his and kissed him on the mouth.

He responded most ardently and found himself instantly aroused as he generally was with Priscilla. He wondered if this reaction was because she was the first woman he had ever had. He wasn't sure; it didn't matter, because he had no time to ponder. None at all. He wanted her under him on that narrow bed. He wanted to do all the things he had done to her when they were teenagers, their hormones roaring, and so hot they could hardly wait to get undressed, had practically ripped each other's clothes off.

As he had undressed her then so many years ago, now he did so once more, helping her with her coat, her sweater and her boots. A few moments later he was shedding his own clothes and joining her on the bed where she was already waiting for him.

Stretching himself out alongside her, he leaned over her and kissed her cheek, held her close to him. After a while, as his hand slid down to stroke her stomach, he whispered in her ear, 'I remember how you flinched when I did this for the first time.' His hand rested between her legs, and he began to touch her gently. 'But I soon had you moaning, begging me not to stop, didn't I? As you will do so in a moment, won't you, Prissy?'

'Oh, yes, yes, you know I will,' she gasped as he continued to arouse her. Now he bent over her again and kissed her breast, sucked on it, and she found herself growing even more excited, the heat rising in her as passion flared. At one moment she thought,

I'm in my fifties. So how can I feel like this? So hot and wet and aching for him. Because I'm fourteen again, she suddenly thought, and opened her eyes and looked directly into his face as he got on top of her and brought her to him, his hands under her bottom.

'Does this feel as good as it did when I was a mere lad?' he asked, gliding inside her.

'Oh, yes, Jonathan . . . yes . . .'

They sat in the bar of the Grand Hotel in Scarborough, sipping dry martinis and reminiscing about their youth. They didn't always have a chance to share a drink and dinner when they'd been together, because they often had to rush off to keep other commitments. And so on this icy January Saturday evening, they were pleased they were able to relax, have the luxury of a drink, a meal, and no pressure to leave each other after their intense and passionate lovemaking of earlier.

They spoke for a while about themselves, their unique relationship, and their lives in general, and then quite suddenly Priscilla said, 'Your cousins were childhood sweethearts, and so were Shane and Paula.'

Momentarily startled at this reference to the family, Jonathan was caught offguard and he said in a slightly bitter tone, 'The Harte women always get what they want, no matter what that is.' His mouth narrowed into a tight line, his eyes hardened.

Priscilla glanced at him quickly, frowning. 'You sound odd, Jonny, what's the matter? Didn't you approve of Emily marrying her cousin Winston Harte?'

Catching himself in time, not wanting to betray his true feelings to Priscilla, which he almost had a moment ago, he forced a cheerful laugh, said in a steady voice, 'It didn't matter to me, Pris, and actually that seems to be a family trait, doesn't it? Several of my cousins have married each other.' He shrugged, and, making a tremendous effort, he smiled warmly, added in the nicest possible voice he could summon, 'And thankfully they all seem happy enough. Grandy would be pleased if she knew.'

'Talking of weddings, are you going to be at Gideon's next Saturday?' she asked curiously.

'Afraid not, old thing. I have to meet my French partner and his wife in Paris next weekend. Business takes up a lot of my time, you know. But I shall be returning to Yorkshire, and I was hoping there would be another chance for *us* to get together.'

Her black eyes shone with happiness as she gazed back at him. 'Oh, yes, Jonny, I'd love that. When *are* you returning?'

'On the Sunday night or Monday morning.'

'Should we have a rendezvous at the house again?' she asked eagerly, reaching out, gripping his hand. 'I always love it when we're at Heron's Nest together . . . it's so exciting in the dark, no lights, taking chances, nerve-racking chances because we never know if the caretaker will come by. But mostly it's delicious because of you and us and our youth. We recapture those days at Heron's Nest.'

'I know exactly what you mean.' He leaned into

her, whispered against her hair, 'And you're such a naughty girl, Pris, much naughtier and more experienced than you were *then* . . . oh, yes, a lovely naughty girl.'

She felt herself blushing and said softly, 'And you're *very* wicked. A wicked, wicked man, but I do love what you do to me.'

Sitting up straighter, Jonathan murmured, 'Let's not meet at the house next time. It *is* a bit dangerous, as you just pointed out. One never knows whether the caretaker might pop down to the house at the wrong time. And talking of houses, would you like to come to mine? In Thirsk. It's almost finished.'

'Oh, I'd love to! That would be wonderful.' A smile spread across her face, which seemed to shine with eager anticipation.

'Then you shall come in the afternoon. On *Wednesday*. Let's make it Wednesday to be sure I'm back from France. Come early evening, and we'll have dinner after our little romp, and perhaps you'd like to stay the night?'

Priscilla sat back in the chair, returning his gaze. She couldn't believe her luck; he was inviting her to his home, asking her to stay the night. This was something quite remarkable, a whole new twist in their relationship. Might it go even further? She stared at him greedily, her eyes taking everything in – his good looks, his handsome face, those bright, intelligent eyes. And the clothes. So expertly tailored. That cashmere sports jacket and those dark finely-made gabardine slacks. Expensive, she thought. Everything about him is expensive. Big time. He was big time. He had a big life. Might she not share it with him? Why not?

'Well, Prissy, will you stay the night? Or can't you?'

'Jonny, of *course* I can! I'd love to. Absolutely *love* to.'

'I'm sorry I can't make the wedding,' he said unexpectedly, reverting to their conversation of a moment ago. 'But sadly I won't be in Yorkshire, as I said. And anyway, I don't really like morning weddings.'

'Oh, but you've got it wrong, Jonathan. Gideon and Evan *are* getting married in the afternoon. At two o'clock.'

'Gosh, how could I have made such a mistake? Still, I will be in Paris.'

'And you'll miss the reception at Pennistone Royal,' she pointed out. 'That's a pity. And you'll miss the party after the lunch.'

'That I will,' he replied and smiled inwardly, now that he knew for a fact that the reception and luncheon were to be held at his grandmother's pile of stones and not at his father's house. She knew a lot, Pris did. He must ply her with a few more drinks and lots of sex and see what else he could glean.

CHAPTER TWELVE

'Great-Aunt Edwina!' Linnet cried, rushing across the Stone Hall at the sight of the oldest and most important member of the Harte family. 'Thank you for getting here so early.'

Linnet grasped her hand and then leaned into her, kissed her on the cheek.

'I thought it would be a good idea to really get a head start, so that *we* could have that chat you suggested. *Alone*,' Edwina said, giving Linnet a knowing look.

Smiling, putting her hand under Edwina's elbow, Linnet escorted her to the fireplace, saying as she did, 'You look wonderful in your trouser suit, Great-Aunt. I love that bordeaux colour. It really suits you.'

Edwina, looking pleased, said, 'Thank you, my dear. It happens to be the only *casual* thing I own other than a few jumpers . . . and you did say it was a casual evening.'

'Yes, I did. And you look perfect. Now, would you like something to drink?'

'A drop of champagne, if you have some handy.'

Linnet grinned at her and hurried over to the drinks table, exclaiming, 'Of course we do. Pol Roger, how does that sound?'

'Very nice, thank you.' Edwina had seated herself on a chair near the fireplace and now she turned around, her attention on Linnet, who was busy pouring the champagne. Neat and smart, Edwina thought, she always looks so well put-together. Tonight Linnet was wearing a white silk shirt with long, full sleeves, black silk trousers and a black wool cardigan draped around her shoulders. Several long strands of pearls hung around her neck. Fake, Edwina decided, but she knew the pearl earrings were the real thing since she had given them to Linnet as a present just before her wedding. Yes, she was a very smart girl. In every way.

Linnet came back to the fireside carrying two flutes of champagne, and she handed one to Edwina. They clinked glasses and Linnet sat down opposite her great-aunt.

After taking a sip of the champagne, Edwina said, 'Now then, my dear, let's get to the point. What's all this about?'

'Basically it's about Jonathan Ainsley, as I told you on the phone. Jack Figg called me this morning to tell me that he's in Yorkshire. At his house in Thirsk. His sudden arrival just before Evan's wedding is making Jack nervous. Jack thinks Jonathan is out to make trouble.'

'He may very well be,' Edwina said, her eyes narrowing slightly, and then she pursed her lips before adding, 'however, Jonathan's not going to do anything too foolish . . . he's a bully and all bullies are cowards, don't you know?' She raised a brow quizzically.

'Yes, I do. Obviously he wouldn't do anything *himself* because he *is* a coward. He'd hire somebody else to do it . . .' Linnet paused, took a deep breath and plunged in, explaining in a serious voice, 'Jack found out he was going to disrupt *my* wedding by sending in a bunch of yobbos. Who knows what they'd been instructed to do. I didn't know anything about it until later, of course. Jack hadn't wanted to frighten me.'

'And Jack thinks Jonathan might try the same thing next Saturday? Is that what you're saying?' Edwina asked, suddenly sounding troubled.

'Perhaps not *that*, but he certainly believes Jonathan will more than likely go to see his father while he's here. And he'll run into Owen Hughes and his family if they're staying at Lackland Priory. That's what I wanted to explain, Great-Aunt Edwina. They can't possibly be Uncle Robin's guests, the way he insists. They have to be housed somewhere else. In order to avoid a confrontation.'

'I think perhaps you are right, Linnet,' Edwina agreed, and giving her a very direct look, she continued, 'Although I suppose all he could really do is be rude.' She shook her head. 'He can't very well kill them in their beds. Never liked him. He was a strange boy, really, up to no good most of the time, and don't think my mother didn't know. Emma had his number all along, that's why she rearranged her will the way she did.'

Linnet pricked up her ears and leaned forward, her intelligent green eyes fixed on Edwina. 'What did Grandy actually think of him?'

'She said he was *treacherous*, and she was rarely wrong about people. So, let us continue, quickly come up with a plan of action before Robin arrives. Now, Linnet, if Lackland Priory is not a suitable place for Owen and his family to stay, what do you suggest? Where can they go?'

'Allington Hall. Emily and Winston will be happy to have them; after all, their son is marrying Owen's daughter . . . they're going to be happy to put them up, I'm certain of that. And if they can only have Owen and Marietta as their house guests, the adoptees can stay with Robin. Or, come to think of it, Great-Aunt Edwina, why not with you at Niddersley?'

'Good Lord, Linnet, I don't know about that! And by adoptees I suppose you are referring to Evan's two sisters?'

'You're right, I am, and I must tell you something confidentially . . . I didn't take to the one I met the other day. *Angharad*. She's the youngest. And a bit odd, in my opinion.'

'Angharad. That's a mouthful of a name,' Edwina muttered.

'It's a Welsh name.'

'Oh, yes, I know.' A smile suddenly illuminated Edwina's wrinkled face and her wise old eyes became brighter. 'Glynnis Hughes loved Welsh names. She was very Welsh, you know, very much into Celtic lore and all that kind of thing. I was close to her at

one point in our lives. I liked her, and I suppose—'
Edwina broke off, shook her head. 'I suppose I
was the one who helped to facilitate their love
affair . . .'

'I heard the story about Glynnis and Robin. About
them never really giving each other up. Fifty years
together. Evan told me the other day when I got
back from New York. Quite romantic, wasn't it?'

Edwina nodded. 'It was. Very. But fraught, and
they ran a lot of risks, were almost caught out
many times.'

'They should have just divorced their spouses and
married each other, that would have been the best
thing,' Linnet pronounced, sounding matter-of-fact
like Emma Harte, the great pragmatist, to Edwina.

'Glynnis didn't think like that, Linnet dear,' Edwina
confided. 'She was the one who stayed the course, in
relation to their marriages, that is. She made Robin
stay with Valerie. You see, she didn't want him to
ruin his political career.'

'Would it really have been such a scandal? Could
it have actually brought him down?' Linnet asked
curiously.

'*Absolutely*. He would have had to resign his seat,
leave Parliament.'

'Gosh, that wouldn't happen today, would it?
Politicians do all sorts of things and get away with
it! They can practically commit murder, so to speak,
without there being any repercussions.'

'That's *now*. This was *then*. The Fifties. And
things were very different, people were not so per-
missive nor so forgiving either. The slightest thing

could be interpreted as scandalous, and cause great hurt. However, let us get back to the Hughes family today. I can't see why Emily wouldn't have them to stay. The whole of the Hughes family, I mean. But if there *is* any kind of problem, you know the young women can stay with me at Niddersley House.'

'Thank you, Great-Aunt Edwina, you're a brick.' Linnet sat back, sipping her champagne, relaxing slightly, and thinking about Angharad meeting Edwina. She had to swallow her laughter. Edwina would frighten the girl to death. Or would she? There was something about Evan's sister that puzzled Linnet; she couldn't quite put her finger on it, but a word suddenly jumped into her head. *Schemer.* Yes, that was it! She felt that the girl was not only manipulative but an opportunist and a dissembler. I have to talk to Gideon about that, ask him what *he* thinks of Angharad Hughes. She had a feeling her cousin had not taken to Evan's sister.

Suddenly, hearing footsteps echoing at the other end of the Stone Hall, Linnet leaned forward and said to Edwina, 'It's Uncle Robin, and he's very early.' Putting down her glass, she got up, and again whispering, she said emphatically, to her great-aunt, '*You've got to make him understand that they cannot stay with him.*'

Edwina inclined her head, answered in a low voice, 'I know what to say, my dear. Leave it to me.'

'Uncle Robin! We're over here,' Linnet exclaimed, hurrying forward to meet him, her face full of smiles, her eyes warm, very welcoming.

They came together in the middle of the Stone

Hall, and after kissing Robin on the cheek, she asked, 'What would you like? Scotch? Champagne?'

'Ah, yes, champagne. I wouldn't mind a bit of the bubbly. Thanks, Linny. And it's so nice to see you, and looking so well. You're positively blooming.'

As Robin walked towards the fire, he called out, 'Good evening, Edwina, I see you got here before me. As usual, the early bird catching the worm.'

Linnet gave them a few minutes alone, standing in front of the drinks table, pouring champagne in a crystal flute for her great-uncle. Robin Ainsley had been Emma's favourite son, just as he had always been Edwina's favourite brother. Edwina had usually tried to be on his side, to back him to the hilt, her mother had told her long ago, when Paula had been recounting some of the family history of the Hartes. She enjoyed hearing those stories, relishing them, and she was inordinately proud to be a Harte, most especially to be Emma's clone, as the family said she was.

Putting the bottle of Pol Roger back in the silver ice bucket Linnet carried the flute of champagne over to Robin, who was sitting on the large over-stuffed sofa talking to Edwina.

'Good health,' Robin said, raising his glass first to Edwina and then to Linnet, smiling at them both.

'Good health,' Linnet repeated.

'Down the hatch!' Edwina added in her sonorous voice, and took a good swallow of the Pol Roger, thinking that she only ever drank this particular champagne here at Pennistone Royal.

Looking across at Robin, Edwina said slowly, 'I'm trying to remember why our mother had such a fondness for Pol Roger. I could swear it had to do with her brother Frank.'

'No, it had to do with Churchill,' Robin corrected. 'He was her great hero, and apparently his favourite champagne was Pol Roger. So it became hers.'

'True, but not quite the whole story . . .' Edwina threw her half-brother a somewhat smug look, and went on, 'Her brother knew Winston Churchill. Remember, he was a journalist and was constantly writing about him even before Churchill became the P.M. It was because of him that Emma stocked Pol Roger. Her brother told her it was the only one Winston enjoyed. Frank liked it, too. I remember that.'

'Got to hand it to you, Edwina, you recall everything. And you're correct about the Churchill story. Mother met him during the war, at some incredible bomb site with enormous damage, and she never let any of us forget he had shaken her hand and thanked her for her war effort.'

'It's true. I was living in Ireland, but I heard the story from Uncle Winston.'

The three of them fell silent for a second or two, and then Robin cleared his throat and said, 'When you phoned to invite me to dinner, you said you wanted me to come early, Linnet. And I see Edwina is here early, too, so I can only deduce that you have some Harte business to discuss with us both.'

'No. Hughes business, Uncle Robin. With you.

I need to explain a situation that's developed and then Edwina has something to say to you.'

He seemed somewhat taken aback, and he leaned against the pile of needlepoint cushions, frowning, looking from Linnet to Edwina, his expression nonplussed. When neither of them said anything to him, he turned to Linnet, 'Well, come on then, let's have it. Tell me what's on your mind.'

'Do you know where Jonathan is at the moment?'

Robin shook his head. 'He *was* in London. I think he went back to Paris before returning to Hong Kong.'

'He's in Yorkshire, Uncle Robin, at his new house in Thirsk.'

It was obvious that Robin did not know this and he was startled; he sat up straighter on the sofa, shaking his head. 'I haven't heard a word from him. He usually calls at some point when he's in Yorkshire, even though we're not exactly close pals at the moment. How long has he been here?'

'Several days. Jack Figg phoned me this morning to tell me his whereabouts, and Jack's worried, Uncle Robin ... He thinks that Jonathan might confront Owen or Evan if he runs into them.'

'He's not likely to do that, Linnet. *Really*.' He shook his head. 'How on earth could he run into *them*?'

'At Lackland Priory. *Your house.* You're insisting the Hughes family stay with you, and Jonathan could easily stroll in unannounced, to see you. Or perhaps he'll get wind that they're staying with you and come over, hell-bent on creating a fuss, or making trouble somehow. That's his nature, and his modus operandi.'

'Oh, my dear, I do think that perhaps you're letting your imagination run away with you. Jonathan is not a frequent visitor, I've told you that before. And especially now that he knows categorically that his inheritance is perfectly safe. He doesn't feel the need to pester me, hover around me. As for a confrontation with Owen or Evan, he's nothing to gain anymore, so why would he even bother?'

'Jealousy, envy, perversity, the desire to upset you,' Linnet suggested. 'Or get his own back at you for having the audacity to actually have another son. You name it and I bet it would fit the bill.'

'I think you're exaggerating the situation, Linnet dear,' he said again, shaking his head.

'Uncle Robin, have you forgotten that Evan was almost killed in a car crash? In a car that belonged to you? A car that was apparently tampered with. You might easily have been mourning your only grandchild at this time, a woman who's currently carrying your great-grandsons, instead of getting ready to celebrate her wedding a week today.'

Robin bit his lip, and there was a distracted air about him all of a sudden. He did not say a word, sat pondering, worry invading his face.

It was Edwina who spoke up resolutely. 'You'd better *listen* to Linnet, Robin. She's making a lot of sense. *I* suspect Jonathan is up here in Yorkshire because of Evan's marriage to Gideon. I don't trust that son of yours. Never have. And neither did our mother: she thought he was a treacherous devil.

As the eldest and head of the family, I must insist you change your plans about housing the Hughes family at Lackland Priory. They cannot be on your premises, at least they can't be your house guests. That's a dangerous game, and tempting Providence. Jonathan would be over there in a flash and the balloon would go up.'

'How would he even know they were staying with me?'

'He'd know!' Linnet exclaimed. 'I've always said he's got a spy in our camp, although no one ever really believes me.'

'Not that awful secretary at the Leeds store?' Robin asked, staring at Linnet, horror written all over his face.

'No, not Eleanor, Uncle Robin, don't look so worried. Jonathan's not going to marry her. That romance is long over. There's someone else, although I'm baffled about who it is. But as sure as God made little apples he's got someone giving him a lot of information about us. I just wish I knew who it is.'

'Can't Jack find out?' Edwina asked.

'No, because we don't know exactly where to begin. And we've gone through all the possible suspects ages ago. But one day he or she will be revealed. In the meantime, Uncle Robin, Jonathan probably knows already that Owen and Marietta and the adoptees are coming to Yorkshire on Monday, and that they are to be your honoured visitors.'

'Adoptees is not a very nice way to describe those

girls, Linnet,' Robin muttered reprovingly. 'Glynnis was very fond of them.'

Edwina guffawed and exclaimed, 'Like hell she was! She only cared about Evan, only had eyes for her biological granddaughter because she's part of you, and you know that very well. Let's not forget you don't have to keep up the pretence anymore, Robin. The whole family knows you were with Glynnis until the day she died. Well, practically. Evan was no surprise to you. You knew all about her, and Owen you'd known since he was a child. Now listen to me, my dear.' Edwina leaned closer, and continued in a tone that forbade argument, 'The Hughes family has to be lodged at Allington Hall with Emily and Winston, and if they don't have room for the two girls, Angharad and Elayne can come and stay with me at Niddersley. And that's the end of it. There will be no further debate about this matter.'

'Oh, but Edwina, I was so looking forward to being with Owen. Don't forget, I've been deprived of him all of my life . . . my son by the only woman I ever loved. I've been so looking forward to having him with me—'

'Oh, don't be such a sentimental old fool!' Edwina snapped, although not unkindly, as she cut him off. 'You can pop over to Allington Hall to see Owen whenever you want, and once the wedding is over and Jonathan has returned to Hong Kong you can visit Owen as much as you wish. Furthermore, you can go and stay with him in America after he returns there. There's nothing to stop you.'

'Oh, I don't think I'm well enough to go tripping off to New York,' Robin protested.

'You look spry enough to me,' Edwina asserted and patted his hand. 'Let us do the best we can to get Evan married to Gideon without the proverbial hitch. Once they are safely married and installed at Beck House, you can do whatever you want with Owen. My main concern is for that granddaughter of yours. She's the only one you've got to continue your family line, and don't you forget *that*.'

'All right,' Robin replied in a meek voice. 'I expect you're right, Edwina. I can't ever remember you being wrong, except for the years when you cut Mother out of your life! But everything you say tonight is true. Evan is of the utmost importance. We must, *I* must, consider her first.'

'Thank you, Robin,' Edwina murmured, falling back against the chair, looking exceedingly relieved.

Linnet smiled at him, also relaxing, for the first time that day.

Edwina sat in regal splendour, looking every inch the countess, smiling warmly and greeting everyone with her special brand of charm and graciousness.

Finally they had all arrived, and she leaned back in her chair near the fireplace, sipping from her glass of champagne and observing the scene being enacted before her in the Stone Hall.

Tonight this looked as wonderful as it had in her mother's day, filled as it was with bronze chrysanthemum plants and white orchids, the fire blazing, the candlelight flickering and the softly-shaded lamps giving off a warm glow. How welcoming it was.

There was a faint buzz of subdued conversation as everyone moved around to spend a few minutes talking to each other. It was a most cordial and convivial atmosphere, and this pleased Edwina.

My mother would be proud, she suddenly thought: most of those present tonight are her progeny, and they *are* rather special even if I do say so myself. And good-looking. She smiled to herself. Whatever anyone said about the Hartes, no one could deny how good-looking they were. She had frequently been caustic about their looks in the past, but not anymore. And after all, she was a Harte herself . . . as well as being a Fairley.

She focused momentarily on Tessa, and then Lorne. The twins were also part Fairley, and it was the Fairley looks they had inherited. They had the pale complexion, silvery eyes and blonde hair of the famous beauty, Adele Fairley, mother of Edwin, who had been her father and for whom *she* was named.

Edwina's eyes moved on to the Frenchman, and she wondered where *that* affair was going? Would he propose to Tessa? She hoped so. The best thing that could happen to Tessa would be for her to marry him.

Edwina liked the charismatic and brilliant Jean-Claude, and knew without a shadow of a doubt that he would be a stable and loving partner, and a good influence on her great-niece. How beautiful she looked tonight, the ethereal Tessa. She was wearing a pair of narrow-cut trousers, a camisole, and a narrow coat which came to her knees and was somewhat in the style of the Indian Nehru jacket. The outfit was made of silver-grey taffeta, and with it she wore silver-grey Tahitian pearls and earrings. She's just perfection, Edwina thought; she hardly looks as if she's been cooking half the day. But she had made the entire dinner, Linnet had told her earlier.

Edwina's glance moved on, this time settled on Bryan O'Neill, who stood talking with his son Shane. She was pleased Bryan was looking so well after his bout of bronchitis. Now fully recovered, he seemed as strong as ever. Tall, broad-shouldered, silver-haired, not to mention silver-tongued, he was the spitting image of his father, Blackie O'Neill.

For a second the decades slipped away, and she fell down into the past, thinking of Blackie with affection. He had been her mother's closest and dearest friend until the day he died. And he had been very good to her when she was a young girl growing up, even when she treated him badly.

Edwina sighed under her breath, thinking how unfair she had been to Blackie, who had loved her like his own. And for a while, after she had obtained her birth certificate, she had believed he was indeed her father, because his name was on the certificate. But as it turned out, Edwin Fairley had been her father. Blackie had merely lent his name.

A good man, Blackie O'Neill, Edwina mused, and his son Bryan is a good man. Good Lord, Bryan must be at least eighty-five! He certainly doesn't look it.

For a long moment her eyes rested on Shane, Black Irish like his father and grandfather, and another good man. Her mother had once said when he was young that he had an intense glamour . . . and he still possessed that glamour.

Shane was the best. He had always been there for Paula, even when she was a child. He was her rock. Edwina recalled how upset she had been when trouble had broken out between Paula and Jim Fairley and their marriage had gone awry. At the time, she had put most of the blame on Paula, but it hadn't been her fault. It had been Jim's, in reality. He was a Fairley through and through, and had inherited many of Adele's bad habits, as well as her vanity and her drinking problems. He'd had to fight alcoholism, just as Adele and his uncle Gerald Fairley had. Genes, she thought, it's all in the genes. There's simply no escaping that.

Emma had let Paula marry Jim Fairley despite her better judgement, because she was a fair woman who had no intention of blaming the sins of the grandfather on the grandson. But Emma had always said it wouldn't work, and it hadn't. Jim had been the wrong man for Paula; also, deep down she had been in love with Shane even though she had not realized that for a long time.

But then one day, long after Jim had been killed in an avalanche in Chamonix, Paula had finally married Shane, and lived the life of a contented woman at last. Her happiness with Shane was manifest in everything she did, and Edwina knew she was one woman in the world who was at peace with herself.

No sooner had this thought entered her mind than Paula hove into view, came to stand next to Shane, linking her arm through his, leaning against him. He looked down at her and smiled and drew her to him in the most intimate way.

As always, Paula was elegant, wearing an ankle-length dress of amethyst cashmere, and matching suede boots tonight. It was a colour that echoed those violet eyes, her most striking feature.

Edwina leaned forward slightly, peering at her niece. She looks worn out, exhausted, Edwina thought. And pale. She's so very pale. She doesn't look like her normal energetic self. Is she ill? Or is she worried? Perhaps about the dratted Jonathan Ainsley? Yes, maybe it was just worry, not ill health. No, she's not *ill*. She couldn't be. The Hartes are a strong and robust lot, and we all live to a great age . . .

'A penny for your thoughts, Great-Aunt Edwina,' Lorne said, drawing close to Edwina. 'And how about a refill?'

'Oh, I don't know about that, Lorne darling, I don't want to get tipsy.'

He laughed, his light eyes twinkling mischievously as he took her crystal flute and hurried over to the drinks table. Edwina watched him go, thinking it was about time *he* got married, too.

Within seconds Lorne was back at her side, handing her the glass. He touched his to hers, and murmured, 'Cheers.'

She smiled at him over the rim, and exclaimed, 'Down the hatch,' and took a long swallow.

'So, a penny for your thoughts, Great-Aunt.'

'Actually, I was thinking about your mother,' Edwina admitted. 'She doesn't look like her usual self, Lorne, does she? Or is that my imagination?'

'No, it's not. I agree with you,' he responded, placing his arm along the chair back, bending over her. In a lowered voice, Lorne went on in a confiding tone, 'I think Mum's under the weather, and I've thought that for a while now, actually. She seems somehow slightly . . . *depleted*, that's the only word I can come up with. I've asked her, and Dad as well, if there's anything wrong, and they've both denied it. In fact, they seemed truly dumbfounded that I even asked such a question.'

'Could she be worrying about Jonathan Ainsley being in Yorkshire?' Edwina suggested, looking at him keenly, her eyes not leaving his face.

'You know what, I think everyone around here tends to exaggerate about *him*, gives him too much importance. I think he's more of a spectre hovering than an actual threat. But to answer your question, yes, I think she does worry about him. And far too much, in my opinion.'

Edwina nodded, and then exclaimed, 'Oh, there's the lovely Jack. Linnet didn't tell me he was coming to supper. He's a favourite of mine, Lorne.'

'He's everybody's favourite,' Lorne answered with a laugh. 'Especially the ladies. I think I'll have to borrow a few tricks from his book.'

'I'm sure you're just as popular as he is,' Edwina chided, and went on, 'I see Emsie over there, but where's Desmond?'

'He's at boarding school, Great-Aunt Edwina.'

'Oh, yes, of course he is, and your mother is beckoning to you,' Edwina exclaimed. 'Goodness me, she looks as if she's about to make an announcement.'

When Paula made her way across the Stone Hall, heading for the staircase, everyone present knew that she had something special to say to them. All family announcements were made from these steps; it was a tradition which had begun with Emma.

Shane was behind her, and as she beckoned to Lorne, her son patted Edwina's arm and hurried to join his mother and stepfather. Linnet and Emsie were also walking over to the staircase and took up positions near their parents and brother.

'We have some wonderful news!' Paula began, reaching for Shane's hand, drawing closer to him. 'Shane and I are happy to tell you all that Tessa has become engaged to Jean-Claude!' As Paula finished speaking Tessa and Jean-Claude walked over to the stairs and stood smiling at the group as everyone called out their congratulations.

Shane exclaimed over the din, 'Let's raise our glasses to Tessa and Jean-Claude and wish them much happiness in their life together.'

Everyone did as Shane asked, and once the toasting was over, Tessa stepped forward a few steps, bringing Jean-Claude with her. 'Thank you all so much . . . If you're surprised about this sudden announcement, then I must tell you that I am too! It was just before lunch *today* that Jean-Claude asked me to marry him, and I must admit

I was taken aback. But only *momentarily* and I said *yes* to him. *Immediately*.' Turning to look at Jean-Claude, still clinging to his hand, Tessa continued, 'I think I'm the luckiest woman alive to have you.'

Jean-Claude put his arm around her, brought her closer to him and kissed her cheek, then looking around at the group of family members, he said, 'I thank you for your good wishes. And I'm the lucky one!' Turning to Paula and Shane he added, 'And I promise you both I shall treasure Tessa, take care of her always. I want you both to know she's safe with me.'

'Yes, we *do* know that,' Paula answered as Shane stepped forward to shake Jean-Claude's hand.

After that there was a lot of hugging and kissing. Linnet, Emsie and Lorne were in the forefront, enveloping Tessa in their arms, and then they went to Jean-Claude to shake his hand. And the others all crowded around, kissing Tessa, offering their congratulations and best wishes to her and Jean-Claude.

It was Tessa who finally said, 'Thanks, all of you, but I'm afraid I must now dash off to the kitchen – or we won't have any dinner tonight!'

'I shall accompany you, *chérie*,' Jean-Claude exclaimed.

'No, no, I can manage, and Margaret's there to help me. Besides, Jean-Claude, you'd better stay and get to know my family . . . those that are here tonight at least. I dread to tell you how big it *really* is!'

* * *

Bryan O'Neill walked slowly across the floor, making for his favourite grandchild. *Linnet*.

When she saw him, she gave Lorne an apologetic smile and then hurried over to her grandfather. 'I can see you're looking for me, Grandpops. Do you need anything?'

'Only a few more years on this earth so that I can bounce *your* babies on my knee,' he murmured, and took hold of her arm, led her away to a far corner of the Stone Hall. Together they sat down in a corner and Bryan, leaning forward, said, 'She may not let her ambitions go to waste just because she is marrying Jean-Claude. Knowing Tessa the way I do, I'm sure she thinks she can live in Paris *and* London, somehow commute in order to head up Harte's. She's always wanted the top job, Linnet, you know that.'

'I do, Grandfather, and you're right, Tessa may well think she can run things from Paris. But let's not forget, Mummy's still the boss and she has absolutely no intention of retiring. She's only in her early fifties for goodness' sakes.'

Bryan smiled, and took her hand in his. 'Such small capable hands,' he murmured. 'Just like Emma's. I remember her hands very well, she took care of me when I was a baby and a toddler with those hands. But then you know all that. Watch your step, Linnet, and keep your eyes peeled. As sweet and lovely as Tessa is being to you at the moment, she is still your rival. Don't ever forget that.'

'I won't, I promise, Gramps. We all know she's

the way she is because she's the first born, the eldest.'

'True. But that was never Emma's way of passing on power. The person best equipped to do the job got it. And I'm sure your mother thinks the same thing: after all, she was trained by Emma Harte.'

Linnet nodded, leaned forward. 'I've got some good ideas for bringing the store into the present. It needs a whole new approach, and I want to talk to Mummy about a few changes, once the wedding is over.'

'Yes. But please wait a while, Linnet,' Bryan replied quietly. 'She's had a lot of pressure on her since well before Christmas. Just take it easy for the moment. All right?'

'Yes. Oh, Gramps, there's Evan looking for us. Come on, let's go and see what she wants. She seems a bit concerned.'

'And she looks to me as if she's about to give birth any minute,' Bryan muttered half to himself. 'Do you think she can last another week until the wedding?'

Linnet burst out laughing. 'She'll just have to, won't she?'

Bryan simply smiled, made no further comment as they crossed the Stone Hall to the spot where Evan had suddenly paused. She was beckoning them. His eyes went across the room to Robin Ainsley, who was about to become a great-grandfather. That can't please Jonathan very much, Bryan thought, and wondered whether the black sheep of the family was planning anything diabolical for next Saturday. He prayed to God he was not.

Evan said, when they reached her, 'I got a bit out of breath and had to pause for a moment. Anyway, Great-Aunt Edwina wants a word with you, Linnet, if you could please come over to her.'

'Of course. But is she all right?'

'Oh, yes, she's perfectly fine. She says to tell you she's had a brainwave.'

Laughing, Linnet glided across to Edwina, whose face lit up when she saw Linnet moving in her direction.

'What's your brainwave, Great-Aunt?' Linnet was asking her a moment later, crouching down next to the chair.

Drawing Linnet closer, Edwina said, 'I think I've solved the problem of that wretched Jonathan Ainsley. Gideon and Evan must *elope*. And right away.'

'Not a bad idea,' Linnet laughed, although she knew it wouldn't work because of Evan's condition. The babies could be born at any moment, and she decided to say this to Edwina, who was looking like the cat that had swallowed the cream.

'Oh, yes, you're right. I'd forgotten that part. Drat. And we do have to take the babies into account. Mmmmm. Well they should have eloped a long time ago. If they had, everyone wouldn't be worried about Jonathan pulling a stunt next Saturday.'

Linnet didn't answer. She'd just had a brainwave of her own. 'I'll be back in a jiffy, Great-Aunt

Edwina,' she murmured and went in search of Jack Figg, bursting to confide her idea to him. It was brilliant; never had she been more certain of anything.

Linnet found Jack talking with Julian, and the two men welcomed her enthusiastically. Her husband put his arm around her and drew her closer to them, while Jack gave her a huge smile.

'Looking more beautiful than ever tonight, I see, Beauty,' he told her, and turning to Julian, Jack added, '*You're* one lucky chap, I can tell you!'

'Oh, I know that,' Julian answered, grinning at the older man whom he'd known most of his life.

Linnet said, 'Thanks, Jack, for your lovely compliment. But listen, I've just had a brainwave. So let's move over there, away from everyone, so I can tell you both.'

Jack nodded, and the three of them discreetly slid towards the library door where they could be alone, leaving the others grouped in the vicinity of the fireside.

'We'd better not go into the library,' Linnet cautioned, 'we'll be missed. Let's just stand here. What I have to say won't take a minute.'

'I'm all ears,' Julian murmured.

Jack said, 'Okay, Kid, shoot.'

'A few minutes ago Great-Aunt Edwina suddenly said Gideon and Evan should elope. To avoid any trouble the ghastly J.A. might bring down on them. I explained to her that they couldn't go rushing off to Gretna Green or anywhere else for that matter, because the babies could easily be premature. And of course she understood.' Linnet paused, looked from Julian to Jack, and said, 'And then I had a sudden flash of . . . *inspiration*. A great idea.'

'So tell us then,' Julian urged.

In a low voice she explained the plan that had evolved in her head in the last few minutes, her attention on Jack Figg.

When she had finished Jack nodded, his face reflective; after a moment he asked, 'Are you sure they'll do what you want?'

'I don't know, Jack, to be honest. But Gideon and I have been best friends all of our lives, and I think he'll see the sense of it.'

'Let's hope so,' Jack exclaimed, and a cheerful smile suddenly slid onto his face. 'You're a clever lass, Linnet. Very clever.'

'She is indeed,' her husband agreed. 'And knowing Gideon, he'll go along with it and he'll talk the others into it. I'm sure of that.'

'Let's go back and join the group,' Linnet murmured, edging towards the centre of the Stone Hall. 'We'll get together tomorrow, Jack, and discuss it. You *are* staying the night, aren't you?'

'Your mother and father insisted,' he said, and then explained, 'They didn't want me driving if I'd had a few drinks.'

'And you have to do that . . . you have to toast Tessa's engagement to Jean-Claude,' Linnet replied succinctly.

'Yes, indeed. And that's another story in the making,' Jack announced, looking from Linnet to Julian.

Linnet said nothing. Her face was as inscrutable as Emma Harte's had often been on certain occasions when it was wiser to conceal innermost thoughts and feelings. A still tongue and a wise head – that had been Emma's motto and it was Linnet's also.

CHAPTER THIRTEEN

There was no question in Dusty's mind that Molly Caldwell was a very sick woman, much worse than Gladys Roebotham had indicated on Saturday.

Now, on this Monday afternoon, he stood next to her bed in the I.C.U. of Leeds Infirmary, forcing a smile onto his face as she looked up at him, her dark brown eyes locked on his. She was extremely pale and strung up to drips, but the nurse had removed the one from her mouth so that she could speak.

'But you can only stay a couple of minutes,' the nurse had warned as she had slipped out of the room, leaving them alone.

'Atlanta?' Molly whispered, and looked as if she was about to say something else.

He held up his hand, and said in a gentle voice, 'Don't exert yourself, Molly, please. Let me do the talking . . . Atlanta's all right. She's with me, safe and sound at Willows Hall. Gladys brought her over to me, as you instructed.'

Molly's brown eyes lit up and she blinked, said

in a dry, parched voice, 'She's a good woman. Is Atlanta . . . asking for me?'

'Yes, she is, to be truthful. But Gladys dreamed up a story that you'd hurt your leg, so we're sticking to that. She thinks you're getting your leg mended, and that you'll soon be home. And you will be, Molly. I spoke to your doctor this morning and he's very positive about you making a full recovery.'

A faint smile touched her mouth and in a low, almost inaudible voice she said, 'Melinda must never have her, Dusty. *Never*.' There was a short pause as Molly appeared to struggle for breath, and then she whispered, *'Promise me.'*

Startled for a moment, he said swiftly, 'Of course I promise. Melinda's not really capable of looking after her, even though she is apparently getting better in the de-tox clinic.'

Ignoring this comment, Molly continued, 'Atlanta must be with you at all costs . . . *you* must bring her up.'

For a split second he searched her face and then he nodded, and trying to reassure her, he said, 'I *will* bring her up, I promise, and she'll be with me at the house until she goes to boarding school. I'll look after her until she's grown up. But listen, Molly, you'll be doing that, love, you'll be out of here in a few days, recuperating at home with Atlanta. I'll hire a nurse to look after you, and any other help you need.'

Molly made no answer, she simply gazed up at him for a long moment, her eyes suddenly filling with tears.

He noticed this at once and became alarmed. The last thing he wanted was for her to grow agitated or upset. Rest and quiet was what she needed, the doctor had told him that.

'Molly, don't fret, love, I'll take care of you and Atlanta, and Melinda as well.'

'She doesn't deserve you,' Molly muttered, 'and she mustn't have the child.'

Dusty stared down at Molly Caldwell, not only startled again by her words but also perturbed. Taking hold of Molly's hand he squeezed it and said, 'I'll come to see you tomorrow, love.'

She gave him a faint smile and her trust and belief in him shone in her dark eyes.

Outside in the corridor, Dusty paused, took a deep breath and leaned against the wall. He was worried about Molly. His gut instinct told him that she was truly ill, and that she might possibly be plagued with heart trouble for the rest of her life. Although the doctor had told him she would be able to go home in a week, he wasn't at all sure about this now. She looked drained, not at all like herself. And just before he left a moment ago, she had seemed utterly exhausted.

But then she'd had a heart attack on Friday, he reminded himself. Of course she wasn't herself. Pulling himself together he glanced around, wondering if he should ask to see the doctor again. Mr William Larchmont. The heart specialist in charge of Molly's case. It had always struck him as strange, that those *specialists* in different branches of medicine were called mister rather than doctor; odd, really, when he thought about it. Could Larchmont add anything to what he'd already said half an hour ago? Dusty doubted it. And Dr Bloom had been non-committal earlier that morning, when Dusty had telephoned him at his office in Meanwood. 'She'll pull through. She'll be all right,' he had said without really saying anything at all.

Shrugging into his sheepskin coat, Dusty strode across the foyer, nodded to the nurse at the reception desk and took the lift down to the ground floor. Crossing the lobby, he pushed through the glass doors and went out into the street; instantly, he regretted that he had sent Paddy Whitaker and the car back to Harrogate. The weather had changed in the hour he had been at the Infirmary, and for the worse.

It was a bitter, raw afternoon, bone-chilling cold, the air layered with that awful northern dampness that seemed to infiltrate the entire body, seeping into it. He lifted his head, stared at the sky, saw that it was the colour of lead, hard and unmoving, without a single cloud to give it life. It hangs there like a shroud, he thought, and shivered involuntarily, pulled up the collar of the coat, stuck his hands in his pockets as he strode out, moving as quickly as he could without actually running.

Leeds had never been his favourite place. This tough, bustling and bleak northern industrial city had always intimidated him when he was growing up, and he had been glad to leave when he won a scholarship to the Royal College of Art in London.

Funnily enough, he had immediately settled in at his digs in Belsize Park, on the fringe of Hampstead, and without a qualm; in London he had never felt any kind of intimidation. Because he was older then? Was that the reason? He wasn't sure. No, of course he knew the reason. London was a beautiful city architecturally, and beauty of any kind had always thrilled him, brought about in him a sense of enormous joy, expectation and anticipation, hope for the future. His future.

He pushed these thoughts away, wondering where to go for a hot drink; he had time to waste before he went to Harte's to collect India. They would drive back to Willows Hall together, and she would stay the night. He knew how much she liked Atlanta, and the child liked her, but he was reluctant about encouraging them to bond, wary of their relationship. He did not want to burden India with a child who was not hers; yet she constantly protested that Atlanta was not a burden.

He must strive to believe India, understand her better. It was this lack of understanding on his part that had created their problems in the first place. She was a good person, bright and intelligent, a smart young woman, and, oh, how he loved her. Loved her beauty, her sexuality, her manners. And her manner, the way she handled herself so perfectly normally with everyone, whether she was talking to the cook, the housekeeper, Atlanta, himself or her grandmother, the Dowager Countess. She treated all in exactly the same way.

A smile crossed his face, obliterating his scowls.

He had a soft spot for her grandmother, Edwina. She was quite a card, undoubtedly her own woman, and certainly a bit of a martinet. And yet she was kind, thoughtful, and it was she who had managed to ease and eventually obliterate his discomfort about India's parents being titled aristocrats.

'This is all nonsense, balderdash. In your head,' she had begun one evening and stopped when he had held up his hand in a peremptory way.

'Listen!' he had exclaimed, 'I'm not ashamed of my background, or where I come from. I'm a working-class boy from the suburbs of Leeds. I've never pretended to be anything else. And I'm proud of that, proud of what I've made of myself. And I'm not in the least impressed with titles or aristocrats, I think that kind of attitude is . . . *nonsense, balderdash*, to use your own words.'

'I understand, so what's it all about then?' Edwina had demanded, peering at him across his dinner table at Willows Hall, his Palladian mansion that he was inordinately proud of. His own stately home.

'I guess I characterize aristocrats and titles with a bygone age, a different age. With snobbery and class injustices in the past. Centuries of it, actually. This is Cool Britannia now, not Rule Britannia. Talent talks to everyone, from Tony Blair to the average man. That's how it is today in this NEW century.'

Edwina understood him perfectly; most of his words sprang from his upbringing, even though he might not admit that. Whatever he believed, his background got in the way, well at least a little bit, and she told him all of her thoughts very bluntly and he listened patiently as she endeavoured to explain.

'Perhaps you're right,' he had said when she'd finished, wanting to close the discussion, no longer concerned, or interested, in fact. 'Let's move on.'

Edwina, Countess of Dunvale, first-born child of Emma Harte, was not having any of that. Instead she said, 'Listen to me now, my young friend. My mother, Emma Harte, was born a poor girl in a mill village on the Yorkshire moors. She came to Leeds when she discovered she was pregnant, where she was helped by her old friend Blackie O'Neill, at that time a navvy on the Leeds canals and a bricklayer, and by Abraham Kallinski, a Jewish clothing manufacturer, a refugee from the pogroms in Russia. I was that child she was carrying when she was no more than sixteen herself, and I was born illegitimate. Edwin Fairley had made her pregnant, he was the son of Squire Fairley of Fairley Hall, where she had worked as a maid. When I was only six months old my mother packed me off to live with her cousin Freda in Ripon, so that she could work, make money, and so protect me. Emma said money made you safe, that it was power, and she was right. It's always been that way, hasn't it? Eventually, I was sent to boarding school, a very good one, and later I completed my education at a finishing school in Switzerland. At that time I returned to London, where I became a debutante, because by then my mother was a successful woman. *The* Emma Harte. And she had the money and standing in society to bring me out. I met Jeremy Standish, the Earl of

Dunvale, almost at once, and he fell in love with me. Head over heels, that was the way he put it. And so we were married. We had one son, Anthony, who is India's father. If there were any aristocrats around, Dusty, they were all Dunvales not Hartes, I can assure you of *that*.'

She had laughed then, and he had laughed with her, and he had sat back in the chair, scrutinizing her carefully, wondering if she had loved the earl the way he had loved her. And then, much to his surprise, he asked her, point blank, just like that, and she had answered him without a minute's hesitation.

'I adored him, Dusty. Jeremy was my ideal. You know, I worshipped him, in a sense. Wrong to do that perhaps, but nevertheless I did. He was older than I was, over twenty years older, and I think that's one of the reasons I loved him so much. There were moments, when I was a young woman, that I truly felt the need for a father figure, and Jeremy was very protective, indulgent, kind, and in a way, rather fatherly. Don't misunderstand me, Dusty, it was a love match, very much so, and we had an extremely sexual marriage. We were mad for each other. In fact, I was always surprised we never had any more children. We were always making love.'

Her bluntly-spoken words had thrown him for a moment; it seemed ludicrous to him that this old lady of ninety-five years was talking to him about sex. Then he looked at her intently, scrutinizing her yet again with those penetrating artist's eyes of his, and he saw beyond the wrinkles, the great age, saw her as he knew she must have once been. *A great beauty*. He knew without question that she had looked exactly like India did today when she had been a young woman.

As he walked on, ruminating to himself, he suddenly wondered whether he should stop off at Harte's, have a cup of tea in the restaurant, then decided against it. Instead he went into the first coffee shop he spotted.

Dusty slid into a booth, ordered a pot of tea, leaned into the corner, waiting for the waitress to return with his order.

Within seconds he became conscious of his dreary surroundings, was assailed by a mixture of old, familiar smells . . . troubling smells associated with his youth: burnt pans, cabbage on the boil, bacon frying, a whiff of gas from a leaking ring, and overall a faint odour of dampness, of wet washing. And decay. Poverty. Mean streets.

He could not bear it . . . too many unhappy memories, bad memories rushed at him and he leapt to his feet with such unexpectedness, such energy, the waitresses all turned to stare at him. Without a word he threw five pounds on the table and rushed out, not looking back. Gagging. Needing fresh air.

He struck out in the direction of City Square, walking rapidly, breathing deeply, blocking out the past, the childhood days that brought such pain, wanting to forget. Remembering was a burden.

What a relief it was to be outside, damp and icy as it was.

*   *   *

In no time at all, Dusty was crossing the road, hurrying into City Square. When he came to the statues in the centre he paused, stood looking, thinking how banal they appeared to him now. When he was a child they had seemed magnificent, larger than life, looming high above him. Now they were scaled down to size, in his eyes.

The scantily clad nymphs who stood on plinths holding up torches seemed utterly ridiculous as companions to the statue in the centre of the square. Edward, the Black Prince in his armour, seated on a black horse; beloved son of Edward III, a warrior like his father, one of England's greatest kings. Why were the nymphs there at all?

Dusty was unaware of the sudden icy wind blowing up as he stood there staring; he was momentarily mesmerized by that statue, which he had thought so magnificent when he was a little boy.

Time shattered.

The present fell away.

The past was all there was left.

Memories flooded him, memories long ago shut off, aborted from his mind. Now he lived within them . . . here in the city of his birth.

'Who's the man on the horse, Dad?' Dusty asked, staring up at his father, tugging at his hand when Will Rhodes did not immediately respond.

Looking down at his boy, his only child, his adored son, Will smiled and said in his usual gentle way, 'That's a statue of Edward, the Black Prince. A brave prince he was, too.'

'Why's he called the Black Prince then?'

'Because of his black armour. At least, I think that's the reason, Russell.'

'It's a right big horse, in't it, Dad?'

'Aye, lad, it is, and black as coal.'

Coal.

Black dust.

Black dust inhaled for years.

Silicosis.

Death.

Dusty turned away from the statue of Edward, the Black Prince on his coal-black horse, and crossed the main road to the Queen's Hotel.

He was thinking of his father as he walked. Will Rhodes had been a miner, had gone down the pits in Castleford for years. All of his life really; he had been a pit lad when he was only a very young boy.

And it was the pits that had killed him. His lungs had been ruined, destroyed by the work he did to support his little family – his lovely wife, Alice, and his beloved boy, Russell. The boy who would never go down the pits. Will would never allow that. Never. The boy who would be an artist. A great artist. The boy whose talent 'shone like the brightest moon in midsummer', that was the way his father had always put it.

His father had died young. Only forty. Amazing that he had lasted that long.

Dusty had known when his father was going to die. It was because of his strange manner, what he had said to him. 'Take care of your mam, lad.

Take care of my Alice.' Will had seemed perfectly well when he had said that, out of the blue, but he must have known death was knocking on his door. He was dead and gone within the month. And that night, when he had uttered those strange words to his son, Dusty had known something truly bad was going to happen to his dad. It was a kind of premonition.

Silicosis. That was the cause of death. Black dust had stolen the life out of Will Rhodes. A man far too young to die.

Dusty swallowed hard as he approached the hotel. He always got a lump in his throat when he thought of his father. He had loved him so much; but he had never told Will that, which was something he had regretted ever since. You must always tell those you love that you *do* love them. He never had. Never told anyone. Until he had finally said it to India Standish: his fiancée, soon to be his wife. In June. In Ireland. At Clonloughlin. Lady India Standish, the girl of his dreams.

The moment he set foot in the lobby of the hotel, which was the best in Leeds, they surrounded him, respectfully. They all wanted to help him, to please him. He was their hero, the local boy made good. Bloody good. Famous. Rich. A celebrity. Whatever that meant.

He smiled and thanked them, was scrupulously polite, and managed to get himself into the lounge, where he took off his sheepskin coat.

The waiter came immediately, took his order for

a pot of tea and departed. Dusty settled himself on the sofa, glancing around as he did. He hadn't been inside the hotel for years, and he noticed at once that it had been redecorated and refurbished, in a tasteful way. The surroundings were pleasant, comfortable, and there was a welcoming warmth in the lounge. Dusty began to thaw out, and he realized how chilled he had become standing in City Square, although he had been too lost in the past and memories to notice it then.

The past was immutable.

It was always there. You carried it around with you. Some people referred to it as baggage; he did not. The past was the sum total of himself. It made him who he was.

Dusty's thoughts went back to his father.

He had been sixteen when Will had died. It was just after he had started to attend Leeds College of Art; his father had seen that happen, at least, and he had been proud. 'No pits for you, my lad,' Will had said, full of smiles after Dusty's first day at the college. 'You're going somewhere, aye, you are that.' And his mother, Alice, always quick, had exclaimed, 'Yes, he *is*. To the Royal College of Art in London. When he's eighteen.'

Dusty remembered now, and so very clearly, the huge, proud smile on his father's face, the unexpected sparkle in those deep blue eyes. He had inherited his father's eyes and his dark hair, but there the resemblance stopped. He was much broader than his father had been, and he had a craggy, almost rough-hewn face, whilst Will Rhodes had been slightly built, thin, with refined, almost delicate features. He took after his mother's side of the family, was built like her twin brothers Ron and Ray, who had his type of muscular torso, wide shoulders, and smouldering good looks.

Leaning back against the sofa, Dusty closed his eyes for a moment, and captured behind his lids the image of his father's face.

Will was smiling, and he was happy because his only child had won a scholarship to Leeds College of Art, and in Will's considered estimation, and his mother's, there was no reason why their brilliantly talented and artistic son wouldn't win yet another scholarship to the Royal College of Art in London. In fact, they were positive he would. And he had done so. But his father was dead and buried by then.

The rattling of china brought Dusty up with a slight start, and he nodded to the waiter when asked if the tea should be poured, then thanked him as the cup was passed.

Sipping the tea, finding it warming, refreshing, Dusty suddenly wondered if people who knew they were dying tried to warn loved ones, those who would be left behind to grieve. Or *prepare* them, if not exactly warn them?

His father had instructed him to look after his mother a month before he had passed on. And Gram, his father's mother, had done the same thing only a year later.

In the same way, unexpectedly, she had told Dusty he must never forget who he was, where he came from, and what he was all about. 'And always stay close to your mam, lad. Be there for her, take care of her. She's the bravest, the kindest woman I've ever known. Don't you ever forget that, Russell. Stand by her.'

Did people get a feeling they were soon to die?

He did not know. But his mother had known, certainly she had, because she had actually told him. 'I'm dying, Dusty,' she had murmured, ten years ago, and on seeing him turn pale, falter as he walked across the sitting room towards her, she had smiled bravely, and said, 'It can't be helped, love. It's the cancer. It eats away at you, and I'm getting weaker. It's better you know, then I don't have to pretend with you or lie to you, Dusty.'

He had gone to sit with her on the sofa, taking her hand in his, staring into her face, and as he had looked into her soft, grey-blue eyes, that gentle face, he had been unable to speak. She had been his rock all of his life; she had worked and slaved so that he could go to college in London. Even though he had won that coveted scholarship, there were all those extras to pay for, and even though he had a weekend job he still needed money. And his mother provided it without a murmur or complaint. God knows how she had done it. But, thank God, he had been a success almost immediately after leaving college, and he had been able to take care of her, give her the few comforts and luxuries she deserved once he was established. Eventually he had bought her a small house in Leeds, insisted she stop working, and she had repaid him with her obvious happiness and joy at her new-found financial security. Most of all, she was proud of him, and it pleased him that he had succeeded in fulfilling her dreams for him.

'You're the best, Dusty,' she had said to him for years, her eyes full of love. 'And never forget who you are. You're the best-loved son of Alice and Will Rhodes. And remember, you have it all. Talent, intelligence, and Looks with a capital L. Let's not forget your handsome looks, Dusty. They're important in this world, and don't let anyone tell you otherwise.'

He *had* remembered all of the things they had told him: Will, Gram, and his mother. It was their love and devotion, their self-sacrifice that had put him where he stood today. That and their belief in him, their belief in his talent. That talent sometimes baffled him. He did not know where it came from, and there were times when he shook his head wonderingly, marvelling at it. It was the essence of him. That he *had* come to understand.

He was forty-two, a grown man and mature. Well, most of the time. He was about to marry; he must make *her* happy. He must be a good husband. And he must trust her, trust her judgement and her good sense. Ever since she had come back to him, after their painful quarrel and separation, he had managed to do that. And he had even told her he loved her . . . that was a first for him.

There was the child. His child and Melinda's. Molly had made him promise to bring her up. She had warned him – was that the right word? – not to let Melinda have her. Because of Melinda's drug-taking? Her terribly destructive drug-abuse? Or for some other reason? He wasn't sure.

Molly had been warning him, preparing him. *For her death.*

She knew she was going to die, just as his father, his grandmother and mother had known. They had prepared him, so it wouldn't be too much of a shock when it happened. But nevertheless, it was always a shock when someone you loved died, even if you were expecting it.

Molly Caldwell was going to die. She knew it. And now, so did he.

Dusty leaned against the sofa cushions, taking a deep breath. A wave of sadness enveloped him and he felt his throat closing with emotion. Molly Caldwell had been a good mother, and a good grandmother, and she hadn't deserved to suffer the way she had because of her daughter. Melinda had led her a merry dance over the years . . .

Dusty sat upright with a start. If Molly did die there was Melinda to contend with. She wouldn't allow him to have custody of Atlanta. No way. She would want the child for herself, to use as a weapon against him. That was the way she was made. He thought of Tessa Fairley and her battles with her ex-husband, Mark Longden. Was he going to go through the same thing?

But there was always a way to solve problems of this nature. Money talked. And Melinda did not have a savoury reputation these days. Drunk. Drugged. In and out of many beds. In and out of de-tox clinics. Unfit mother? Unquestionably.

Dusty continued to sit quietly for another half hour, turning things over in his mind, thinking of all the worst possibilities he might have to contend with. As he ruminated about the situation, one thing became crystal clear to him. He must confide in India tonight, explain his feelings about this situation, about his past with Melinda. And he must speak to her about his childhood. She had always wanted to know more about those early years and he would never tell her.

Tonight he would. He owed her that. She was going to be his wife. There should be no secrets.

CHAPTER FOURTEEN

The clock in the church tower began to strike. Inside the church the noise was thunderous, deafening. Startled from her reverie, Evan sat up with a jerk. The din continued for a few seconds longer, and then, much to her relief, all was quiet, the interior of the church suddenly without a single sound, peaceful once more.

Evan settled back against the wooden pew, waiting for Gideon and the others to return. They had left her off at the church and driven round to the vicarage, to see the vicar. She knew they would arrive at any moment; in the meantime, she was enjoying her sojourn alone here. The church had a beautiful altar, and the three stained-glass windows set high above it were quite something to behold. The jewel colours of the panes were stunning, and they sparkled brightly in the sunlight, creating rainbow reflections against the pale stone walls which were nine hundred years old, dating back to Norman times. She knew the church was considered a local treasure.

Glancing around, Evan filled with pleasure and happiness. Yesterday, the florists had worked all day and into the evening, under the supervision of Paula and Emily, creating the loveliest of flower arrangements for her wedding. The church was brimming with them. Alcoves, corners, the altar steps, and window sills were aglow with many white and pink orchids; banks of white and pink carnations filled the air with their sweet perfume, while tall white lilies and winter evergreens added a seasonal touch. The setting took her breath away. Paula, and her future mother-in-law Emily, had done her proud.

Settling back, relaxing, Evan's thoughts momentarily strayed to her great-grandmother, Emma Harte. It was she who had kept this old Norman church in good repair over the years, and had also arranged for central heating to be installed. 'You'll be warm,' Gideon told her the other evening, reassuring her, knowing how much she suffered from the icy weather lately.

This morning she was cosy in her ankle-length, pale-grey overcoat worn with matching trousers and a sweater. She was in good form, although she did feel a bit top heavy. She would be happy and relieved when the babies were born. She couldn't wait to see her twin boys, and neither could their father.

Evan smiled to herself, thinking of her genes, his genes. Twins ran in the Harte family, and seemingly she was carrying on the tradition.

Evan wondered if it would snow today. Wiggs, the

head gardener at Pennistone Royal, had announced that snow would fall this weekend. There was nothing more romantic and picturesque than a winter wedding in the snow, especially in the countryside which became a white and glistening wonderland. Her mother agreed with her about that.

Evan thought about their conversation on Wednesday. In the afternoon a troubled Marietta had come to her with an odd story. Something had happened that morning which had worried her so much she had felt compelled to confide in her daughter. As her mother had recounted the story, Evan had filled with unease herself, alerted to trouble.

Seemingly, her mother had driven down to Pennistone village with Angharad that morning, wanting to buy a few small things at the village shop.

'We were minding our own business, selecting postcards and a few other items, when a handsome man walked in,' Marietta had explained. 'He started going through magazines on the rack, then suddenly Angharad caught his eye, and I couldn't believe it! They were instantly chatting away as if they knew each other well. Angharad was flirting with him. I was angry about her vulgar behaviour with a total stranger, so I paid, and we both left the shop. I had taken only a few steps when I realized I'd left my glasses, so I went back. As I was entering the shop, I heard the woman behind the counter addressing the man as Mr Ainsley. I was shocked, Evan. I grabbed my glasses and fled.'

At this point, her mother had paused for a moment, looking at Evan through concerned eyes, and then she had finally asked, 'Could it have been *Jonathan*, do you think, Evan?'

'More than likely,' Evan had replied quietly, her unease increasing. 'There is no *other* Mr Ainsley. Except for Robin.'

Evan remembered now the genuine dismay she had experienced as she had answered her mother. How unfortunate that it was Angharad, of all people, who had met Jonathan Ainsley. She was not only a flirt but impulsive, with very little judgement about anything, and she had slept around indiscriminately since she'd been a fourteen-year-old. Evan couldn't wait for the wedding festivities to be over, when her family would go back to London, then on to New York. She loved her parents and Elayne, but long ago she had become extremely cautious, even wary of Angharad, whose behaviour left a lot to be desired. Furthermore, she knew Gideon couldn't stand her and that Linnet held Angharad at arm's length. But on Wednesday afternoon, wanting to put her mother at ease, to reassure her, Evan had gone on in a steady, level voice, 'I'm sure Angharad and Jonathan won't run into each other again, Mom. Truly. That's highly unlikely.'

Marietta had agreed, looking relieved.

Evan, however, had worried so much about this strange encounter for the rest of the day that she had finally told Gideon about it. Later that evening, when Linnet returned from a visit to the Harrogate store, they had confided in her, expressing their worries.

Linnet had listened alertly, looking troubled herself.

'I'll let Jack know immediately. There's the possibility that Ainsley knew very well who Angharad was. They might not have met by accident at all, you know. It could have been arranged to look like one, though. By Ainsley. He's sly, a sneaky chap, Jack says, and somebody's feeding him information, of that I'm certain. And listen, aren't you glad you agreed to go along with my plan?'

They had both said yes in unison. Linnet's Plan with a capital P . . . that's what she called it, and it was already in operation; Evan was delighted that it was. She felt comfortable and at ease this morning, and all because of Linnet O'Neill.

There was a sound behind her and swiftly Evan glanced over her shoulder. She saw Linnet, Julian and Gideon coming into the church along with the vicar of Pennistone Royal village, the Reverend Henry Thorpe, and she waved, her face lighting up.

It was the good-looking young vicar who led the way down the aisle to the pew where Evan was sitting at the front of the church. She stood up and smiled at him as he greeted her warmly and shook her hand. They chatted for a brief moment, until Gideon said in a low but firm voice, 'Could we get things started, please, Vicar?'

'Absolutely, Gideon. That's why we're here.'

And so in that peaceful, ancient church filled to overflowing with flowers and early morning sunlight, with only the vicar and two other people present as witnesses, Evan Hughes was married to Gideon Harte. It was exactly eight-fifteen on

Saturday morning when they pledged their troth to each other with clearly-spoken words and gold wedding rings.

This early morning marriage ceremony, conducted in absolute secrecy hours before it was due to take place, had been Linnet's brainwave a week ago. And it was Linnet who had insisted on the necessity for total secrecy.

'Nobody can know,' she had pointed out to Jack a week ago.

Nevertheless, he had been stubborn about Paula being informed. 'She *has* to know,' he had said emphatically. 'And so do Shane, Emily and Winston. The four of them control the families, the clans, and they're in charge, run everything. They'll keep their mouths shut, that I can guarantee. But they *must* be in the picture. However, I agree with you, Linnet, no one else should be told except them. For security reasons. Not even Evan's parents or Robin can know. They'll be told after the event. Everyone in the family will be told then.'

Linnet had nodded, had pointed out, 'No one can be present except me and Julian as witnesses. The marriage has to be so low-key it will go unnoticed.'

And that was the way it was.

After the simple marriage ceremony, the four of them followed the vicar into the vestry to sign the church register. Once that had been done, they all thanked the vicar for his cooperation in Linnet's plan.

When they left the church Jack Figg was waiting

outside with several of his operatives, and he came forward to congratulate the bride and groom. A moment later he was ushering Gideon and Evan towards his Land Rover, along with Linnet and Julian. Once they were settled, he went back to the vicar who was standing on the church steps.

'Thank you, Reverend. We couldn't have done it without you.'

The vicar grinned. 'Not if you wanted it to be legal, you couldn't,' he quipped. 'I was happy to be of help, and I'll see everyone later at the reception.'

With a smile and a nod Jack hurried back to his car and drove out of the sleepy, deserted village. He was relieved that nothing had gone amiss, that Gideon and Evan were now well and truly married to each other. That's all he had been concerned about: making sure there was a wedding without a hitch.

There was an air of secrecy at Pennistone Royal when they got back to the house. On the way there from the church, Gideon had telephoned Paula on his mobile, and exclaimed, 'It's done! We're married! And no one is any the wiser.' So when they arrived at the house no more than ten minutes later, Paula and Shane came rushing out to greet them on the door step.

Paula kissed Evan and Gideon, and so did Shane, and then they congratulated them. Paula led the way back into the house, heading for the breakfast room, and she explained, 'Margaret has prepared breakfast for the seven of us, but she doesn't know where you've been. No one does.' Glancing at her daughter, she said with a warm and loving smile, 'I'm glad you had that brainwave of yours, Linnet, and that you put your plan into action. You're a clever girl.'

'Thanks, Mummy, but I do feel a bit awful . . . I've deprived Evan of her beautiful wedding.' As she spoke she looked across at Evan and offered her an apologetic smile.

'I don't feel a bit deprived!' Evan exclaimed. 'I feel privileged to be a member of this family, and anyway it *was* a beautiful wedding, with you and Julian there to stand up for Gideon and me.'

Gideon said, 'She's right, you know, Linny. The main thing is that we *are* married, and because of your plan Evan's not a target. Thank God.'

They all seated themselves at the round table in the bay window of the breakfast room, and within seconds Margaret was bustling around serving ham and scrambled eggs, toast and large pots of tea and coffee, along with dishes of marmalade and butter.

Once Margaret had retreated, Jack said quietly to Paula and Shane, 'The village was half asleep and completely deserted. I spoke to the vicar, as you requested, Paula, and he's going to phone a few key villagers later, tell them the wedding was private, held earlier today because of Evan's condition. He's also arranging for the Women's Institute to give a special tea party in the church hall tomorrow, to make up for their disappointment.

You know how much they enjoy a Harte wedding.'

'That's nice of him,' Shane said. 'It might be a good idea to send down a case of bubbly for their tea party. What do you think, Paula?'

'It's a very good thought, darling. I'll have Joe run it over to the vicarage tomorrow morning.'

Gideon looked at Paula and grinned. 'I bet you had a hard time keeping my father and mother away from this little breakfast, didn't you?'

Paula began to laugh. 'In a way, yes. Emily, in particular, wanted to be here to greet you and Evan. But to be honest, in the end she understood that it would be nicer, kinder to stay at Allington Hall with Evan's parents. The only alternative was to bring them along, and I felt it would be better if we kept this really simple. Evan can rest later, and get ready for the reception without any pressure from any of us. And as soon as I phone Emily, she will tell Evan's parents about your early ceremony.'

'And besides,' Shane interjected, 'we have our work cut out for us. Once breakfast is over, Paula and I have to phone a lot of family members, Gideon, to tell them to come to the house at three rather than going to church for a two o'clock ceremony that's not going to take place.'

'Are you going to explain the early morning marriage in the same way?' Julian asked, looking from Paula to Shane.

'Indeed we are, Jules,' Shane replied. 'It's the most logical thing to do . . . Evan's looking more pregnant than ever, and why wouldn't we all be worried that the twins might be born premature? I think everyone will buy our story.'

'And if they don't, too bad,' Linnet announced. 'Anyway, to tell them the real reasons serves no purpose. It will make us all look a bit paranoid.'

'You *are* paranoid,' Lorne said from the doorway, and strolled in looking debonair in a white turtle-neck sweater and jodhpurs. Smiling hugely at them all, he added, 'I assume you were making a reference to Jonathan Ainsley when you brought up the word paranoid, Linnet. I think you all pay too much attention to him, give him too much credence. I think he's a spectre rather than a threat.'

'Perhaps you're right,' Linnet answered, smiling at her brother. 'But it just so happens that he did attempt to disrupt my marriage to Julian last month. Tell him, Jack.'

Jack Figg nodded, looking at Lorne, who had pulled up a chair and sat down next to Shane. Jack began to explain. 'My operatives and I thwarted a band of yobbos who were about to come down into Pennistone village and start trouble. Serious harm and damage to the church and everyone in it were fortunately averted.'

'How did you find out?' Lorne asked.

'We got it from the horse's mouth, so to speak,' Jack murmured. 'From someone who was involved. But I prefer not to say who.'

Gideon leaned across the table and asked Paula and Shane, 'Do you want me to make some phone calls for you? I agree that Evan should rest for a few hours, since it's going to be a long day, and into the evening. But I'm totally free.'

'Not anymore you're not,' Linnet teased. 'You're very much taken.'

'Yes, I am, and it's great,' Gideon replied, smiling from ear to ear.

CHAPTER FIFTEEN

The fruitwood casket, scrolled with silver, had stood on the Queen Anne chest for Paula's entire life. Many times in the past she had asked her grandmother where the key was, and Emma had constantly told her the key was lost. The casket had been mysterious and intriguing to everyone, because Emma would never explain what was in it, if anything.

But not anymore. Not only did it have its silver key in its silver escutcheon, but the entire family knew what the mystery box had contained: letters from Glynnis Hughes, Evan's grandmother, written in the Fifties to Emma Harte here at Pennistone Royal. And it was the letters which had solved Evan's identity. Once Paula had found the key, and opened the casket, she had discovered that Robin Ainsley, Emma's favourite son, had been the father of Glynnis's child Owen Hughes, and Evan was therefore Emma's great-granddaughter from America.

With Evan on her mind, Paula walked across the

upstairs parlour and into her bedroom, her eyes fixed on the famous casket. Lifting it down, she carried it back to her oval Georgian desk near the window and smoothed her hand across the lid. On it was a small silver plaque; it was engraved with the initials E.H. which stood for Emma Harte . . . but they could also stand for Evan Harte, and perhaps more than anyone else in the family this lovely old box should belong to Evan. After all, it had contained so many secrets that pertained to her grandmother Glynnis, and indirectly to her.

I'm going to give it to her, Paula decided, lifting the lid, looking inside at the faded, red-velvet lining. It was empty, since Paula had given Glynnis's letters to Emma, tied with blue ribbon, to Evan last year. And she must also have the diamond star, Paula suddenly thought, it will match the diamond star earrings Emily has given her for a wedding present.

Smiling to herself, almost laughing, Paula stood up and hurried into her bedroom, opened the wooden jewellery box which stood on her dressing table, and took out the Victorian star brooch. It was very old, too, and had been given to Emma Harte by Arthur Ainsley's mother, when Emma had married Arthur in the 1920s, along with a pair of matching diamond earrings. Paula was laughing to herself because she was thinking of her cousin Emily, who years ago had asked Emma if she could borrow 'those old diamond earrings of yours, Grandy'. Grandy had shaken her head and said, 'I didn't know diamonds get old, Emily, but of course you can borrow them.' Later,

Emma had given the earrings to Emily, because her mother Elizabeth had been an Ainsley.

Evan was also part Ainsley, through Robin, so she should have the brooch which belonged with the earrings, Paula thought, and everything's neat and tidy that way. She had no trouble remembering how much her grandmother liked to keep things straight in her head, in her business, and in her life. Neat and tidy, Emma had called it.

The sound of the door opening and Lorne calling, 'Mother, are you here?' brought Paula hurrying out into the parlour, the brooch still in her hand.

'Darling, what is it?' she asked, staring at her eldest son.

'Can we talk for a few minutes?' Lorne asked, joining her near the fireplace, sitting down on a sofa.

'But of course we can. You sound anxious, Lorne. Is everything all right with you?'

'It is, Mums, yes. Except that I worry a lot about *you* these days. You've seemed so tired lately.'

'I have been, actually, Lorne. Since before Christmas. But now this wedding is finally happening today, I'm sure I'm going to be much better. It's been a worry.'

'Because of that bloody cousin of yours?'

'Only partially. There's been a lot to organize with Emily, she so wanted Gideon's marriage to be perfect, and in a way she was cheated this morning. I feel sorry for her in that sense.'

'Because she didn't see Evan walking down the aisle? Standing at the altar with Gideon? Is that what you mean?'

205

'Yes, I do. But she saw the need for the secret marriage, immediately it was suggested, and the reception is going to be both beautiful and glamorous. I told her she'll see Evan and Gideon go onto the floor for the first dance, and she knows that will take the place of her being at the actual ceremony.'

Lorne shook his head, looking across at his mother, and said, in the quietest of voices, 'Do you really think Ainsley is dangerous?'

'I'm afraid I do . . . through other people acting on his behalf. He would never be caught red-handed, he's far too smart for that. Let's not forget that he is a Harte, you know, whatever else he is.'

'Too bad,' Lorne muttered, and went on, 'Jack told me a short while ago to watch myself at all times. That I could well be a target, because I'm your son, and also that I'm an easy target because I'm so damned visible as an actor.'

'You must listen to Jack,' Paula exclaimed, her voice rising. 'He's right. Maybe you should have a bodyguard: a lot of famous actors and actresses do, as you well know.'

'Not for me, Mums, thanks for the suggestion anyway. I'll keep my eyes open, and watch my step, as Jack has cautioned me to do.' His eyes went to the diamond brooch and he asked, 'What's that you're holding? The famous Ainsley pin?'

Paula smiled. 'I'm going to give it to Evan today, since she is a descendant of Arthur Ainsley, and Emily's given her the matching earrings, the ones Grandy gave *her* years ago . . . they belong with the brooch, it's a matched set. And now it's going to be complete again.'

'That's nice of you and Emily . . . passing down family heirlooms. A rather charming tradition. Anyway, I also came up to ask you what the drill is for this afternoon now that everything's going to take place here?'

'Nothing has changed, Lorne. At three o'clock, instead of arriving in the Peach Drawing Room from church, Evan and Gideon will arrive from . . . upstairs.' She laughed as she said this; her sense of humour never failed her.

Lorne laughed with Paula, and nodded. 'Then there will be the champagne reception in the Peach and Grey Drawing Rooms, and after that the late lunch at four-thirty in the Stone Hall, and once lunch is over there'll be dancing, and revels.'

'That's correct, darling, and actually, now that they're married, I feel much more relaxed. I'm going to enjoy myself. I feel as if a heavy load has been lifted off my shoulders, Lorne.'

'I'm glad, Mother. You worry too much, and all the time. Now I'm going to go off and cadge a sandwich from Margaret, and then skedaddle, have a rest and get into my dark blue suit. I'll be downstairs early in case I'm needed.'

'You'll be the handsomest man there, my darling.'

'Except for Dad,' Lorne said, pushing himself to his feet, and walking across to the door. Before leaving the upstairs parlour, he glanced back at his mother. 'Is there anything you need help with?'

'Not really, Lorne, but thanks for asking.'

'All you have to do is yell if you need me.'

'Oh, there is one thing. Will you make sure Desmond's well turned out, please? He always used to look so smart, but lately he's seemed . . . a bit dishevelled.'

'All the kids are these days, but I'll go and give him the once-over later,' Lorne promised, and closed the door softly behind him.

Paula continued to sit on the sofa for a moment, thinking of Lorne and how lucky she was. Her son had never given her a moment of worry. Ever. He was almost too good to everyone, and she frequently worried that he might be taken advantage of, especially by women. Sighing, she stood up and went to the desk, put the brooch in the fruitwood casket and closed the lid. Later she would find the little velvet box for it and take these gifts to Evan's room, with a note telling her their history in the Harte family.

'You know you can wheedle anything out of me, luvey,' Margaret said, smiling up at her favourite, who lolled against the big window in the kitchen, looking impossibly handsome. 'We're very busy in here, as you can see, but I'll make you a chicken sandwich. Mind you, my lad, you'll have to eat it somewhere else, this 'ere kitchen's teeming with the caterer's staff. Still, I'm glad your mother is having the lunch catered, it would've been too much for me.'

'Yes, it would, Margaret, my darling,' Lorne

answered, leaning forward, kissing her on the forehead. 'You've got to take care of yourself. Sometimes I think you work far too hard.'

Margaret grinned at him. 'That's the curse of this family, Lorne. Your great-grandmother set the standards around 'ere, you knows, and because she was a work addict, or whatever you call it, she expected everyone else to be just like her. She was a bit of a slave-driver, Emma was.'

Lorne burst out laughing, and then swung around when he unexpectedly heard his name. He found himself staring into the face of the caterer, whom he had known all of his life. 'Hello, Prissy!' he exclaimed, smiling at Priscilla Marney, who often did the catering for his mother's big parties and receptions. 'How're you? And how's Samantha?'

'She's great, and so am I. And you look wonderful, Lorne. I can't wait to see your next film.'

'It'll be out in a few months, and in March I start rehearsals for a play in the West End.'

'When it opens we'll come and see it. Sam and I are your biggest fans,' Priscilla said.

Lorne smiled at her, noticing in a glance that her appearance was much toned down. Usually Prissy wore flamboyant clothes in brilliant purples and red. There was a theatricality about her that he appreciated, being an actor; with her gypsy colouring and height, he thought she was a striking-looking woman. However, she was unusually low-key today . . . her wild black hair was pulled back into a neat chignon and she wore a businesslike black trouser-suit and white shirt.

Lorne said, 'If you get in touch with me later, when the play opens, I'll make sure you have house seats, Priscilla.'

'Thanks, Lorne, that's very nice of you.' She glanced at the clock on the kitchen wall. 'Isn't it getting late? Shouldn't you be changing? You're due at the church soon, you know.'

'I'd better go,' Lorne exclaimed, edging away, not wanting to be drawn into a discussion by the caterer. He was certain she knew nothing about the secret ceremony this morning. He himself hadn't been aware of it until he had joined his parents and the others for breakfast.

Margaret, bustling over, put a plate in his hands. 'Get on with you, my lad,' she said swiftly, 'and enjoy your chicken sandwich. See you later.' She almost pushed him out of the kitchen in her haste to be rid of him.

Lorne went striding down the corridor in the direction of the breakfast room. His mother thought Margaret knew nothing about the secret marriage ceremony, but he was not so sure about that. He thought his mother often underestimated the house-keeper, who was much shrewder than she and most of the family realized. The way Margaret had moved him on, when Priscilla started talking about the time, told him a lot. Not that it mattered if Priscilla Marney knew; she would know at three o'clock anyway. And she'd been working for the family for years. Everyone liked Prissy, and she was the best caterer in Yorkshire.

The breakfast room had one occupant, Lorne's

half-brother Desmond, who was sitting at the table eating a bowl of fruit salad.

'Hey, Des, where've you been all morning? I haven't seen you around,' Lorne exclaimed, walking in and sitting down next to him.

Desmond groaned. 'Doing my homework. Dad's been on my back about it.'

'Need any help?'

'No, but thanks anyway for offering. I suppose we've got to get all dressed up for the wedding. What a *bore*.'

Lorne began to laugh, and after a moment he said, 'What does it matter, Des, really? Wearing a suit and tie for a couple of hours is no great hardship. Anyway, it's only an ordinary suit today, not a morning suit, thank goodness. I hate having to get into a top hat and tails.'

'Oh, God, so do I!' the seventeen-year-old exclaimed. 'Mums wants me to wear my new navy blue suit . . . what're you wearing, Lorne?'

'A navy blue suit, that's what our mother wants us both to wear. And Dad and Grandpops, too.'

Desmond made a face. 'I wish I didn't have to go. I *hate* weddings!'

'I know what you mean . . . lots of family and all that stuff, and usually lots of quarrels and fights as well. It is a bore, in a sense, you're right. But think about this. You got home from boarding school for the weekend because of it.'

'True,' Desmond said and had the good grace to smile at his brother, whom he adored. He went on, 'Haven't you got a new girl yet, Lorne?' As he spoke a dark brow lifted quizzically, and then Desmond, Black Irish to the core, began to grin cheekily. 'I bet Mum is forever on *your* back about settling down.'

'You're right, she is. On the other hand, Desmond, I can't settle down when I don't have a woman in my life.'

His brother nodded, then leaning forward he asked, 'Can I stick with you at the wedding, Lorne? I always get eaten alive by the aunts and female cousins if I'm not careful.'

Lorne began to laugh again, and was still laughing as the two of them finished eating. That had been his fate when he'd been Desmond's age, and he understood exactly how his brother felt.

Jack Figg opened the door of the Peach Drawing Room at Pennistone Royal and stood for a moment regarding the room. It was his favourite spot in this great and ancient house and now, as he glanced around, he marvelled that it had not changed much in over forty years or more.

At this moment it was empty, since the family were all upstairs in their rooms getting dressed, and no guests had arrived for the reception. Jack glanced at his watch and saw that it was just ten minutes to two. Over an hour to go before the wedding reception began, far too soon for anyone to come yet.

Slowly, he walked across the floor to the white marble fireplace. The peach silk walls held a golden glow at this moment, as shafts of winter sunlight filtered through the many tall windows, filling the drawing room with a soft hazy light. He had always thought this was the loveliest of all the rooms, with its peach-and-cream colour scheme, elegant Regency furniture and exquisite Impressionist paintings.

Standing in front of the fireplace, he looked up at the Sisley landscape which Emma had hung there over fifty years ago, and then moved on, his eyes taking in the other two Sisleys and the two Monets which graced the walls. These five paintings would always hang there. Emma had decreed that in her will.

Jack noticed, as he glanced around, that Paula had changed nothing; she simply refurbished things as they became worn or shabby and therefore remained true to Emma's original décor.

There were flowers everywhere. Several tall crystal vases were filled with lilies, imported lilac and branches of mimosa; porcelain bowls held carnations and tulips, and Paula's signature orchids were displayed in wonderful china tubs. But no roses. That was Emma's old rule and Paula abided by it.

His thoughts centred on Paula as he moved over to one of the windows, and stood staring out at the terrace and snow-covered gardens beyond. She had looked exhausted lately, but earlier today, when he had walked around the Stone Hall with her, helping her to put the place cards on the tables, she had seemed better. For one thing, she appeared more relaxed and at ease, and lighter in spirit. Because of the secret ceremony at eight-fifteen this morning, he was absolutely positive of that.

She worried herself to death about Jonathan

Ainsley, Jack was well aware of this, and he wished there was something he could do to alleviate her worries. But he was helpless. Unless, of course, he went out and killed Ainsley. Then she would be at peace. But naturally that was impossible. Jack decided he had to find a way to stop the man in his tracks; there had to be something he could do. He must devise a plan.

Jack had been part of this family for years and he thought of it as his own, and certainly they thought of him as one of theirs. Because of his love and affection for them, he wanted to ease their burdens whenever he could, and especially Paula's, to whom he had been close for years.

A sigh escaped. He had to do something to help her immediately. More security would be a good idea; he was going to talk to Lorne about hiring a driver who was an ex-policeman. That way Lorne had proper protection. He was a famous actor, a Harte even though his name was Fairley, young and good-looking. And therefore a perfect target. Jack had said that to Lorne already. But he must make his own moves and provide protection, because Jack knew that Lorne wouldn't.

As he turned and walked back towards the double doors, Linnet suddenly appeared, and waved to him as she hurried into the room. 'I've come for my stuff,' she said as she headed towards him.

Jack nodded, put his hand in his pocket and brought out a large envelope.

Drawing to a standstill, she took the envelope from him. 'It's the mike and the earpiece?'

'Yes. Make sure the mike doesn't get muffled by the flower you plan to wear on your lapel,' he said. 'And you must hook the mike pad onto your waistband, then put the wire of the mike into it.' As he spoke he turned around, lifted up his jacket and showed her how the pad was attached to his waistband at the back of his trousers. 'Okay?'

'Yes, I understand everything. I understand about the earpiece, too.'

'What will you be wearing, Linnet?' he asked.

'A long skirt with a top, and a full-length silk coat. I chose that outfit because of all this stuff,' she explained, indicating the envelope.

'Good girl. There's nobody like you, Linnet.'

'I hope not,' she shot back. Eyeing him appraisingly, she added, 'You look very smart, Jack, very smart indeed.'

'Thanks for the compliment. Where's Julian?'

'Upstairs in our bedroom, getting changed, and I'd better go up myself, get into my clothes. I promised Evan I'd help her.' Linnet looked at the carriage clock on the mantelpiece and said, 'Goodness, it's well past two already! I'd better hurry.'

'Right, Beauty—' Jack broke off as his mobile rang. Pulling it out of his pocket, he said, 'Hello?'

'Jack, it's Pete.'

His operative sounded tense, upset. Jack exclaimed, 'What's wrong?'

'Part of the west wall of Pennistone Royal church just blew out. It's a good thing there was nobody in the church, otherwise it would have been a real bloody mess.'

'Oh, my God!'

Jack kept his voice low, but Linnet had heard his exclamation and seen his stricken face. She remained perfectly still as he stayed on the phone, listening intently.

Pete went on, 'Somebody put explosives there, or a small bomb. People would've been killed, Jack, if they'd been in the church.'

'I realize that. Have you informed the village police?'

'The vicar did.'

'Are you all right, Pete? I know you're parked across from the church.'

'I'm fine. So is Chuck who's down the street.'

'Where's Al?'

'Up on top of the hill . . . looking for yobbos. But there are none in sight.'

'Where's the vicar, do you know?'

'He's standing a few feet away from me, examining the damage to the church wall. He's with the sexton. Do you want to speak to him?'

'Yes, put him on.'

'Right away.'

A moment later the Reverend Henry Thorpe said, 'What's going on, Mr Figg? Do you know?'

'No, I don't, Vicar, but I suspect it might be the work of somebody who's disgruntled with the family. And thankfully no one was hurt.'

'*Thankfully*. And what do you want me to do?'

'I understand the police are there. Once they've done a thorough search of the church to make sure there's . . . nothing else *amiss*, the mess should be cleaned up and the hole covered with planks or boards, and tarpaulins. To keep the animals out.'

'I'll see it's done.'

'Could you put somebody else in charge, Vicar?' Jack now asked. 'I do think it will look strange if you're not up here at three o'clock to attend the wedding reception.'

'Of course I'll be there. I understand I must be present.'

'Vicar?'

'Yes, Mr Figg?'

'I think it might be more discreet, and certainly wiser, if this incident wasn't mentioned at the wedding reception. It would be very disturbing to Mrs O'Neill. Not to mention upsetting to the bride and groom if they thought they'd been targets.'

'I understand and I won't say a thing. However, the explosion was quite loud and there are now a few villagers hanging around, as we speak. What shall I tell them?'

'Nothing. Say you don't know what happened. Be very vague. Act baffled. Certainly the less said the better.'

'I'd better deal with Sergeant Lyons. He's in charge. I don't think I'll mention anything about *disgruntlement*, if you know what I mean.'

'I certainly do, Vicar. And I think that's smart. I'll see you shortly. In the meantime, there are a number of my security men in the village. If you put Pete back on I'll have a word with him, tell him to help you in any way he can. And remember, not a word about this when you get here.'

'You don't have to worry about me, Mr Figg,' the vicar said firmly. 'I'm giving the phone to Pete.'

A moment later Pete said, 'I'm on, Jack. I think it might have been a bomb. One which was probably planted during the night and triggered about ten past two.'

'Sounds right to me, Pete. The church would have been full of Hartes at that time if we hadn't made the other plan. Stick close to the police, let them know you're there to help if they need you. I'm sure they won't. Just stay in touch.'

'I will.'

Jack closed down his mobile and looked at Linnet, who had remained glued to his side. He said softly, 'Part of the west wall of Pennistone Royal church was blown out. Nobody's been hurt, but you will have gathered *that*, I'm sure. Pete, one of my men who's down there, thinks the bomb was planted during the night and triggered when the wedding was supposed to be starting. Around ten minutes past two.'

Linnet had turned very pale, and she whispered vehemently, 'It had to be Ainsley. There's no other explanation.'

'But we can never prove it. And the police are not going to find any real evidence, only the remnants of the bomb. Trust me on that.'

'What can we do?'

'Nothing, Linnet,' Jack answered quietly, shaking his head. 'The police will examine everything, check out the church to make sure it's safe, write up a report. Anyway, nothing else will happen at the church or in the village, rest assured of that.'

'But Ainsley might still attempt to hurt Evan and Gideon.'

'Not right now, he won't. He'll lay low. It's more than likely he'll leave Yorkshire, go back to Paris or Hong Kong. He's smart enough to realize that we've got our ears to the ground. He's no fool, you know. He'll be very aware that we suspect him.'

'That's what Mummy always says. We can't tell her about the bomb in the church, Jack.' She stared at him, worry in her eyes.

'You're damned right we can't! We can't tell *anyone*. Not until the wedding festivities are over. Let's keep this as quiet as we can until tomorrow. Okay?'

Linnet nodded, biting her lip.

'You still look extremely pale, Beauty. You're going to have to put on that Emma Harte face of inscrutability before you come to the reception. And by the way, for God's sake don't say anything to Evan and Gideon either.'

'I wouldn't dream of it! I'm not stupid, Jack. But if it's all right, I will mention it to Julian.'

'That's fine, but tell him not a word to anyone. We don't want to spoil their wedding reception, do we?'

'Never. I ruined their wedding by insisting on the secret ceremony.'

'You saved their lives, Linnet,' Jack murmured in a low voice, his expression serious. 'Never forget that.'

CHAPTER SIXTEEN

Gideon Harte was furious. Angry words flew to his tongue, but before he could utter one word he caught sight of his mother's face, saw the warning look on it, one he knew of old. He paid attention to her, tried to swallow his anger, stepped closer to Evan; her fingers reached for his and he held her hand tightly, loving her so much.

As he sought the appropriate words to address Owen Hughes, his wife saved him the trouble.

Evan said, 'Dad, *please*. Don't go on like this. We're all as disappointed as you. But Gid and I are *married* now, and that's that.'

'But we could have been there! *Should* have been there! We're your parents. Why didn't you invite us to come this morning?'

Ignoring the question, she said in a slightly weary voice, 'After my fall, I've been a bit nervous, and the doctor cautioned me to take everything at a slower pace, so—'

'I didn't know you fell! Why wasn't I told?'

Again she avoided answering Owen. 'Listen to

me, Dad. Gideon and I decided at the last minute to play it safe. A small wedding, no guests, just two witnesses. *No excitement. No fuss.* We knew we would celebrate this afternoon at the reception here at Pennistone Royal, when I can go to bed if I'm feeling queasy or tired.'

Gideon glanced at his father-in-law, saw the disgruntled look settling on his face, and thought: *the whining bugger.* He's thinking of himself, not of Evan. Gideon had long been aware that Owen Hughes didn't think much of the Hartes, and that he wasn't particularly impressed when he'd discovered he himself was one. He probably didn't like any of them. He was a self-involved man who was selfish to the extreme, and Gideon's sympathies lay very much with Marietta. He looked across at her now and she gave him a faint, apologetic smile and shrugged lightly. He saw the discomfort in her eyes; she was sensitive, like Evan.

Owen said, 'Well, I must admit I *am* disappointed—'

'I know that, Dad,' Evan exclaimed, showing her irritation. 'So is Mom. And also Emily and Winston. But *they* understand.'

Marietta stepped forward, went across the sitting room, took hold of Owen's arm. 'You're being a bit silly, Owen. The important thing is that Evan and Gideon are now married. You can have the enjoyment of taking your daughter into the reception a bit later . . . *and* to the strains of the wedding march. Just let it go now. *Please.*'

Owen gave her a strange look but made no

response, simply tried to shake her hand off his arm. The odd couple, Gideon thought.

Winston Harte now took charge, growing as impatient as Evan and his son. After glancing at Gideon, he turned to Owen. 'I think it's a good idea if we leave the ladies to their own devices, give Evan a chance to get dressed.'

Owen nodded, and said to Evan, 'I'll send Elayne and Angharad up to help you, honey.'

'No, no! I don't want them!' Evan exclaimed irately and without thinking, and then softening her voice, explained, 'I have Mom and Emily, and that's fine. Truly, Dad, I don't need anybody else.'

'But it's traditional for the sisters of the bride to help.'

'I don't want them, Dad, and I'm not a normal bride. After all, I am about to give birth. And right now I can't stand people hovering over me, fussing.'

'As you wish,' he said in a clipped tone and headed for the door, looking more put out than ever.

Winston smiled lovingly at Evan, squeezed her shoulder as he walked past her. 'See you downstairs, sweetheart. And whenever *you're* ready. Do take your time. People have been invited to stay through the evening, you know, there's no rush for you to make an appearance.'

'Thank you, Winston,' she replied, smiling at her father-in-law, a man she had grown to love, respect and admire. He was so kind to her, the most considerate person she had ever known.

Gideon said, 'I'll join you in a minute, Dad,' and, turning, he looked at Evan, murmured, 'Come on, darling, let's go into the bedroom for a moment, I want to talk to you.'

Once they were alone in the adjoining bedroom of the Green Suite, which they were occupying this weekend of the wedding, Gideon put his arms around Evan and held her close. 'Don't let your father upset you,' he whispered against her hair. 'He'll get over it.'

'I know he will, and I'm not *upset* . . . just annoyed with him.'

'Let it go, Evan, don't be annoyed with anybody . . . it's our wedding day. I'm so lucky . . .' He held her away, stared into her face. Never had he seen her look as delicate as she did today; there was a fragility about her that suddenly worried him. He noticed how pale she was, and her skin was almost translucent . . . he saw a small blue vein throbbing on her temple and her mouth trembled slightly, made her seem child-like, very vulnerable. His heart clenched. He couldn't bear it when she was upset, and cursed her father under his breath.

He bent, kissed her forehead. 'I'm so lucky, the luckiest man alive. I love you very much, Evan, and I promise once again to love and protect you all the days of your life.'

'Oh, Gideon, Gid darling . . . and I promise the same.' Gently, lovingly, she touched his cheek with her hand. 'I'm all right, honestly I am, and I'm so glad we took Linnet's advice and got married without a fuss. I know it was because of our anxiety about Jonathan, but it *was* a wise move in reality because I do keep feeling queasy . . . I have all morning. I was glad to have a rest after breakfast.'

'But you just said you were all right! Are you sure you don't need the doctor?' Worry clouded his face.

'No, of course I don't. The queasy feeling comes and goes, and I promise you I'm not about to drop the twins in your lap.' She smiled at him. 'But too much fuss and excitement does get to me, I guess.'

'Then take it easy, as Dad said you should. Don't hurry, get dressed leisurely. Do you need me to get anything for you?'

She shook her head. 'I'm going to do my make-up, and then Mom and Emily can help me into my clothes.'

'Come on then.' He led her across the room to the kidney-shaped dressing table in the bay window. Once she was seated on the stool he kissed the top of her head. 'I'll tell our mothers to come in, shall I?'

Turning to face him, Evan said softly, 'Not for fifteen minutes. I need to collect myself, do my hair as well as the make-up.' She grinned up at him. 'Just a little peace and quiet for a while, Gid.'

He nodded, passed his hand over her hair. 'Your wish is my command, madame.' With a smile he crossed the room, paused at the door and blew her a kiss, then went out.

* * *

The moment he stepped back into the sitting room of the suite, Marietta said, 'Is Evan feeling ill?'

'No, not really. A little queasy, she said, but she's fine actually. Please don't worry.'

'I could've killed her father. He just doesn't know when to shut up.' Marietta shook her head, her expression one of exasperation.

'He did go on a bit,' Gideon agreed, smiling warmly at Marietta, a woman he genuinely liked and considered a much nicer person than her husband. 'But Evan didn't pay too much heed to him. She's rather preoccupied with getting herself ready for the reception, amongst other things . . . like preparing for twins as well . . . etcetera, etcetera.'

His mother smiled. 'Yes, we're all a little preoccupied with the soon-to-arrive additions to the family, Gid. And so we must just excuse Owen for flogging a dead horse. And after all, he *is* disappointed.'

'Not more than you, Dad and Marietta,' Gideon couldn't help pointing out. 'But you're right, Mother, let's not hold a grudge. Evan needs a while to do her hair and make-up, and she wants to be alone for the next twenty minutes. As soon as she's ready for you both, she'll invite you in. Okay?'

'Very okay,' Emily answered. 'And later we'll all meet up in the library. The flowers for the men's buttonholes are on a card table in the library. White carnations. And there are sprays of orchids for the bride's attendants. But I'm sure Linnet's got that in hand.'

'I'll see to it that the men have a flower in their

buttonholes. Linnet can look after the ladies. And by the way, you both look smashing, Mum ... Marietta. Very elegant indeed.'

'Thanks, Gideon,' Marietta responded, very much appreciating her son-in-law, a man of great quality in her opinion. Evan was lucky, luckier than anyone she knew, because her daughter had married the man of her dreams. And who cared when and how they got married, as long as they were happy together and committed to each other? What a fool Owen was, at times; she suspected he felt overshadowed by the Harte family. Inadequate perhaps? She wasn't sure of that, but she did know he was ready to go home as soon as possible after this weekend. She was planning on staying: after all, it wasn't every day that a woman became a grandmother to twins.

Emily glided over to her son and took hold of his arm, led him to the window. 'She's not upset, is she?'

'No, Ma, she's not. *Annoyed*, though. I told her not to be. After all, it's our wedding day and I don't want anything to mar it.'

'It won't, my darling.' Wanting to get off the subject of Owen, once she knew Evan was fine, Emily remarked, 'I'm glad you think I look elegant. Evan created my outfit. Isn't she a clever girl?'

Gideon agreed, then, noticing the design, he commented, 'It's beautiful. It looks like an antique tapestry ... is it?'

'Indeed it is! Evan discovered it in the attics here. Grandy must have bought it years ago, intending to have something made and never did.'

Emily now stepped away from her son, slowly turned around so that he could get the full benefit of the design on the back of the coat. The tapestry was a greyish-blue in overall colour, the actual design woven in red and violet, soft yellows, pale orange and sage green. The evening coat was trimmed around the edge with a narrow border of brown fox and the cuffs were also made of fox.

'It's the lady and the unicorn,' Gideon exclaimed. 'And the cut is superb, Ma. Did Evan make your dress as well?'

'Yes. I asked for something very simple in pale grey and she came up with this long silk sheath.' Emily laughed, her eyes dancing. 'It's like a lovely long comfy sweater, and so easy to wear.'

'I'm afraid I wasn't so lucky,' Marietta murmured. 'Evan didn't design my outfit, and I only wish she had.'

'But you do look lovely!' Emily exclaimed. 'Only a blonde like you can wear those soft golds and browns. And I'm glad for your sake you chose palazzo trousers and a long jacket, Marietta. Even with central heating and blazing fires, Pennistone Royal tends to be draughty in winter.'

'Well, ladies, I'd better be on my way,' Gideon announced. 'Dad'll be wondering where I am. Also, I want to have a word with Jack Figg. I'll see you both later.'

As soon as the door closed behind Gideon, Marietta said quietly, 'I'm sorry Owen's been difficult, Emily—'

'Marietta, please don't apologize!' Emily exclaimed,

cutting in. 'He's disappointed because he didn't get to walk his daughter down the aisle. You know what fathers are like.'

Marietta inclined her head, went and stood near the fireplace, staring into the flames. She remained quiet, a reflective look settling on her face, seemed to be in another place. Emily suddenly realized she was still feeling embarrassed by her husband's rather silly behaviour, and decided that silence was the best way to handle the situation. Any comments she would make would only upset Marietta even more.

Emily walked across the green-and-white sitting room, and stood looking in the elaborate, gilt-framed mirror over the Georgian chest, staring at herself. She liked the way she looked today, was pleased with her new haircut and the honey-blonde shade of her hair concocted by her hairdresser.

Emily was a typical Harte – blonde, green-eyed and fair of complexion, but the bright blonde hair of her youth had deepened in the last few years, and there were now strands of silver in her tresses. The solution had been this warm, honey tone, which, she now decided, was rather flattering.

'I think Evan's been so lucky, having met and married Gideon,' Marietta suddenly announced, startling Emily out of her reverie.

She swung around to stare at the other woman, and nodded. 'Gideon's lucky, too,' Emily replied. 'Evan's a lovely young woman and we all took to her right from the start.'

A thoughtful look slid onto Marietta's face and

she seemed about to say something, then suddenly hesitated.

Emily watched her, waiting for a moment before saying, 'Is there something you want to tell me, Marietta? You look a bit troubled.'

'No, I'm not, but Owen . . . well, he's been going on at me about Gideon and Evan being related, being cousins. It doesn't matter to me, but I need to shut him up. So . . . well, I was wondering . . . could you explain . . .' Her voice trailed off helplessly.

'It's perfectly legal in this country to marry your cousin, you know. Even first cousins can marry,' Emily told her. 'But as a matter of fact, Evan and Gideon are *not* first cousins. They're cousins a couple of times removed. Here's how the lines of descent evolved, Marietta. Emma Harte, my grandmother, had a brother, Winston. We call him Winston the First in the family.' She laughed, and went on, 'Winston the First had a son whom he named Randolph, and Randolph had a son whom he named Winston, after his father. *That* Winston, Winston Harte II, is my husband, the one who just left the room . . . Gideon's father.' Emily stared hard at Marietta and asked, 'You do understand that line, right?'

'Yes, of course.'

'Now, to Evan. Her great-grandmother is Emma Harte, because of Emma's son Robin Ainsley. It was Robin who loved Glynnis, your mother-in-law, during the war years. Glynnis gave birth to Owen Hughes, who is Evan's father. So you see Evan is a direct descendant of Emma Harte in a straight line down.'

'I understand that, too, but Evan said something about Emma being Gideon's great-grandmother. Surely she would be his great-great aunt, wouldn't she?'

'She's both,' Emily answered, and went on to further explain, 'Through his great-grandfather, Winston the First, Emma *is* Gideon's great-great aunt. But she is also Gideon's great-grandmother, because my mother is a daughter of Emma, and Emma was my grandmother, hence Gideon's great-grandmother.'

'Heavens to Betsy! However do you keep it straight?' Marietta asked, laughing. 'I'm sure I couldn't.'

'Yes, you could, if you'd grown up with it as we all have. But there's nothing to worry about, you know, as far as the twins are concerned. They'll be perfectly all right, there won't be any genetic deficiencies because Evan and Gideon are related.'

'Oh, I know that, and anyway, Evan had all the tests and everything's normal. It's just that . . .' She stopped, shook her head. 'Owen is a worry wart.' There was a small pause and then she confided, 'He drives me crazy at times.'

'I can well imagine,' Emily blurted out sympathetically, and could've bitten her tongue off. A small flush crept onto her neck, and she felt embarrassed at her blunder.

Marietta burst out laughing, then confided, 'That's why I'm glad he's going to go back to the States after the weekend! But I'm staying on, I want to be here for the birth of my grandchildren.'

Emily smiled at Marietta warmly, and walked across the floor, took hold of her arm in an affectionate way. She murmured in a loving voice, 'I'm so happy you're going to be here for the arrival of the twins, and I just want you to know you are welcome to stay with us at Allington Hall whenever you wish.'

For a split second Marietta was taken aback, and then she said, 'That's so kind of you, thank you very much. Evan told me yesterday that she and Gideon are not moving to Beck House until after the twins are born. She explained there were a lot of things still unfinished.'

'That's right,' Emily replied, nodding. 'Anyway, in my opinion Evan's better off in London until the weather's better. I don't know why the two of them thought they could trot up here to Beck House every weekend. Evan seems to suffer from the cold, just like my grandmother did. Emma was always complaining that she was freezing to death. And it's a lot colder up here than it is in the south. Mind you, I expect they'll come up some weekends and stay at Pennistone Royal while things are being finished at Beck House. Winston's volunteered to help them.'

'Yes, he would, he's such a nice man.'

Emily merely smiled.

Marietta said, 'You grew up with him, didn't you?'

'I did indeed, and I was madly in love with him

by the time I was sixteen. But he hardly noticed me. He was off with Shane, chasing the girls. My heart was always breaking because of that.'

'So how did you two finally get together?'

'It was at the christening of Tessa and Lorne at Fairley Church, over thirty years ago now. Gosh, so *long* . . . how time flies. A bit of a problem arose that day about Shane, and my grandmother gave me the third degree about it, and Winston, too. Afterwards, we went for a walk, commiserating with each other . . . and I can't tell you how it came about, but he suddenly kissed me. And *wow*! That was that!' Emily shook her head. 'I couldn't believe it, couldn't believe we were suddenly in each other's arms . . . and we have been ever since.'

'That's such a lovely story,' Marietta murmured, and swiftly turned away, a sudden sorrow washing over her face.

Emily said, 'Are you all right?'

'Oh, yes, I was just remembering . . . something similar that happened to me long ago . . . but it didn't have your happy ending.'

'I'm sorry. Do you want to talk about it?'

'I don't know – *perhaps*. Well, yes, why not?' Marietta sat down on the sofa as she spoke, and Emily joined her, listened attentively while Marietta confided one of the saddest stories she had ever heard.

She wanted them to leave – her father and her sisters.

Her mother was staying on for the birth of the

twins, and this was fine with Evan. Her mother was comforting, soothing, and always loving. Her father and her sisters were irritants.

Well, no, not Elayne, who was as quiet as a mouse, sweet and simple and as adoring as she had always been. But Angharad was a dangerous presence, and Evan couldn't wait for her to leave.

As for her father, he was difficult and grudging these days, prone to temperamental outbursts if he didn't like something. His first complaint was about Allington Hall. He was put out because it was a racing stable, one of the finest in England, and forever busy, teeming with horses, stable boys and girls, other helpers, and jockeys. She loved the bustle at Allington Hall, especially during the week when everything was flying at full speed, and she also shared Gideon's pride and excitement when one of their horses had a big win.

Her father just found the whole atmosphere distasteful, the stable staff a nuisance, and he had told her so the first time he had gone over there with her to meet her future in-laws, Emily and Winston, last September. And so she had not been surprised at his annoyance and petulance when he discovered he and Marietta were staying there for the period of the wedding, instead of at Lackland Priory with Robin.

Evan had endeavoured to placate him, explaining, 'Listen, Dad, Jonathan's back in Yorkshire, and everyone feels it's wiser for you and Mom to make Allington Hall your base. You see, if Jonathan should come over to visit his father and bumped into you, there could be a lot of unpleasantness.'

'So what! I can handle that, handle him,' her father had blustered, and she had simply turned away, adding that the decision had already been made, and that was that. She pointed out she could do nothing about it, and neither could he, unless he preferred to stay at a hotel in Harrogate. 'It's up to you,' she had added.

At one point, trying to engage his interest, she had told him some of the history of the stables, how they had been founded by Gideon's grandfather, Randolph Harte, who had become one of the most famous trainers and breeders in England. It was Randolph who had been in charge of Blackie O'Neill's string of race horses, which were stabled there, including the renowned mare, Emerald Bow. This was the horse which Emma Harte had given to Blackie as a gift, and Randolph had specially trained her to run in the Grand National at Aintree. This was the greatest steeplechase in the world; it was a difficult course, with some hazardous obstacles, including the famed Becher's Brook, which had to be jumped twice during the race.

When Emerald Bow won the Grand National, the three clans had been exultant, thrilled and proud of the courageous young mare who had sailed over the difficult Becher's Brook twice with the greatest of ease, winning the steeplechase and proving herself to be the best.

Now that Randolph Harte was dead, the stables were in the hands of the Colonel, as he was known. Colonel Humphrey Swale, formerly of the British army, was an extraordinary trainer who had worked with Randolph in the last years of his life and been handpicked by him to take over one day when it became necessary.

Winston, Toby and Gideon loved the stables as much as Randolph had, but since they were occupied with the day-to-day running of the family-owned newspapers and television network, they were happy and relieved to leave the stables in the capable hands of the Colonel, who had maintained the success and profitability which had been the benchmark of Randolph's years.

Evan remembered now how she had led her father into the study at Allington Hall one afternoon last week. It was her favourite room, a charming spot with dark-green walls, green tartan carpet, comfy, worn-leather sofas and armchairs and a collection of fine country antiques. Taking pride of place in the study were the many gleaming cups and ribbons which proclaimed the stables to be one of the finest in Yorkshire, indeed in England. But he had shown no interest at all in the room, its décor, the Stubbs paintings, the antiques or the trophies; had merely muttered that horses and horse racing bored him.

Evan let out a deep sigh, thinking how much her father had changed lately. Or perhaps he hadn't . . . perhaps she simply saw him through different eyes these days . . . perhaps clearer eyes. How he did annoy her at times.

Sitting up straighter on the stool, she pushed this thought away, remembering Gideon's words earlier. He was right. It was their wedding day and she should not be annoyed with anyone. It should be a day of happiness and joy – after all, it was the most important day of her life – she wasn't going to spoil it for herself. Nor was she going to let her father or Angharad spoil it either.

Leaning forward, Evan stared at her image in the mirror. She was pale, wan, washed out, needed to make herself look pretty for her husband. And so, armed with foundations, powders, blushers, and eye make-up she set to work bringing colour and life to her face. Then she brushed the dark cloud of hair away from her face and forehead, took it back and around her ears, coaxed it into a soft sleek pageboy.

A few moments later she stood up, went to open the door into the sitting room, announced to her mother and mother-in-law, 'Mom, Emily, I'm ready. So can you help me into my dress, please?'

The two women jumped up and hurried to join her, and both exclaimed, almost in unison, 'You look beautiful!'

Within seconds Evan was stepping into her gown and being zipped up, and then she slowly turned around to show Marietta and Emily the overall effect of her special creation. They gasped in surprise.

The gown was cut in the French Empire style, which had been favoured by the Empress Josephine. It had a square neck, a very high bust line, and long, narrow sleeves. The dress was created from several layers of chiffon, which fell away from underneath her breasts, the fullness cleverly camouflaging her pregnancy.

The design was lovely but it was the colour that stunned. It was not one colour really, but many shades of blue, each one ombred into the next . . . deep pavonian-blue shading into pale sky-blue, the sky-blue changing to turquoise, the turquoise ombred into the palest of greens. The effect was sensational.

As Evan turned again, very slowly, the chiffon drifted around her in an eye-catching mélange of sea colours, and Emily said softly, 'It's like that wonderful beaded cocktail dress of Grandy's, Evan, the one Linnet and you used in the fashion retrospective last year . . . I have a feeling it inspired you, didn't it?'

'Yes, it did, Emily,' she acknowledged and smiled. 'I just loved the colours of that gown, and I was lucky when I stumbled onto this ombred blue chiffon at the Renaud Brantes fabric showroom. *Very lucky*, I thought.'

'It's exceptional, Evan,' Marietta said, 'all the colours of the sea.' Her voice was low, practically inaudible, and she continued to stare at her daughter almost in awe, thinking how beautiful Evan truly looked. And then Marietta suddenly exclaimed, 'But it's also the colours found in a peacock's tail, isn't it?'

'Why, yes it is,' Emily said, and Evan nodded in agreement.

'Don't you have a coat?' Marietta then asked, suddenly worried.

'Yes, I do.' Evan walked across to the armoire, opened it and took it off the hanger. 'It's made of the same chiffon, three layers,' Evan explained, and handed it to her mother. 'If you can hold it for me, Mom, please.'

Marietta did as she asked, and Evan slipped into the floor-length coat then turned towards the cheval mirror and settled it on her shoulders properly. It was a simple design, with a full swing back and straight panels at the front; the collar, cuffs and edges of the coat were trimmed with a rolled band of bugle beads which reiterated all the different shades of blue and green in the gown.

'Honey, it's just lovely,' Marietta murmured, 'but I do hope you'll be warm enough. Emily says the house is draughty.'

'I'll be fine,' Evan reassured her mother. 'Actually, it's silk chiffon, which is quite warm when it's layered. Now, all I need are Emily's diamond earrings and Paula's diamond star pin and I'm ready.'

'*Your* earrings, *your* pin,' Emily corrected. She moved across the room, leaned closer to Evan and kissed her on the cheek. 'You are indeed the most beautiful bride, Evan, and I'm happy and proud to have you as my new daughter.'

CHAPTER SEVENTEEN

Nettled by what he perceived as his daughter's extreme indifference to him, and still feeling slighted because he had not been invited to the early morning wedding ceremony, Owen Hughes meandered into the Stone Hall looking unhappy and somewhat morose.

As he glanced around he forgot about his displeasure for a moment, impressed by the beauty of the hall this afternoon. It had been transformed in the last few hours. Albeit grudgingly, he had to give Paula and Emily their due. Between them they had created something quite spectacular; no two ways about it, the Stone Hall was looking fantastic, had a fairytale feeling about it.

Paula's pride and joy were her glass houses where she grew her orchids, many of which were exotic and rare. She had given him a tour the other day, and he had been amazed by the extent of her collection and the variety of the hundreds of orchid plants.

Now some sixty or so of these orchids in glazed

cream ceramic pots graced the Stone Hall. There were snow-white orchids, white orchids tinged with pink or with deep pink centres, all kinds of pink orchids, solid in colour, or speckled or veined with white; mixtures of these were grouped on the mantelpiece, and on chests and tables placed around the hall; or stood in corners on special wooden stands of different heights. Others were used as centrepieces on the round tables, which had been set out for the wedding luncheon.

The latter were covered with floor-length pink silk cloths; there were pink silk cushions on the small gold chairs, which were trimmed with large pink satin bows. These tables and chairs were grouped around a small dance floor which had been put down in the middle of the Stone Hall, near the fireplace. Already lamps had been turned on, a huge fire blazed in the tall stone hearth, and overall the scene was lovely, had a welcoming warmth to it.

It pleased Owen that Paula and Emily had created this setting for Evan, and he felt a lifting of his bellicose mood. As he moved amongst the tables, heading for the library, he noticed that his place card was on one of the large tables. He saw at once that he was seated between Emily and Paula, and this cheered him even more. It was a place of honour befitting the father of the bride.

Marietta had been seated between Robin and Shane. That would please her; she liked both men and particularly Shane O'Neill, with whom she flirted outrageously he had noticed, much to his chagrin.

Owen frowned to himself as he moved on, thinking of the way Marietta had brushed aside his complaints earlier this morning. She hadn't seemed to care that Evan had gone off and married Gideon without asking them to be present. But then that was just like Marietta these days . . . she was something else. How she had changed, how independent she had become. It was the inheritance; her aunt's will had made her a rich woman, given her a new lease of life, and certainly a wholly different attitude. It was an attitude he didn't particularly like.

It irritated him that she was staying on in London, that he hadn't been able to persuade her to leave with him next week. She fully intended to remain in England for the birth of the twins, who were not due until February. So be it, he thought, and then paused as he heard his name being called.

Owen swung around, found himself almost, but not quite, face-to-face with Priscilla Marney, the caterer, whom he had met earlier in the week.

He smiled at her. 'Hello, Miss Marney.'

'Good afternoon, Mr Hughes. And you must call me Priscilla or better, Prissy, as everyone does. Can I get you anything? Would you like a drink, perhaps? The waiters will be coming out in fifteen to twenty minutes, but I can go to the kitchen, bring you a glass of wine.'

'No, no, Priscilla, but thanks anyway. I was just strolling through, admiring the Stone Hall.'

'It's charming, isn't it? Paula and Emily have done a great job.'

'Yes indeed,' he said, eyeing her, wondering why she called them by their first names.

As if reading his thoughts, Prissy exclaimed, 'That must sound rude to you, my use of their Christian names, but—'

'Oh, no, it doesn't,' he cut in swiftly, smiling at her. He liked her.

'You see, we all grew up together. My mother was Mrs Harte's summer secretary, when she was at Heron's Nest, her seaside house in Scarborough. She always had her grandchildren to stay, Paula and Philip, Emily and her brother Sandy, who's dead now, Sarah and Jonathan, and her great-nephew, Winston. And Shane always came too, and sometimes Michael Kallinski. Anyway, we all played together, shared our summers when we were youngsters.'

'It must have been a lot of fun.'

'It was. We were great chums.' A faint smile played across her mouth, as she added, 'Paula and Emily have been good to me, using my catering service.'

'You're good at what you do, Priscilla. The dinner was terrific the other night. Very good indeed.'

'Thank you, that's kind of you to say so.'

'So you know my half-brother, Jonathan . . .' He let the sentence slide away, not wanting to probe too much.

'Oh, yes, we're great friends.' Immediately Priscilla knew she'd said too much, and quickly corrected herself. 'What I mean is, we *were* good friends a long time ago. I haven't seen him in years.' She always felt the need to protect Jonny and their special relationship; he had warned her not to let anyone in the family know about them. Or anyone else, for that matter. And she would never betray him, let Jonny down. She thought of their date for next Wednesday, and a little thrill ran through her. 'Well, I must be off, Mr Hughes!' she exclaimed. 'I've got my hands full today.'

'I understand. And call me Owen,' he said to her retreating figure.

Elayne Hughes stood in the grand, very formal dining room at Pennistone Royal, where all of the wedding presents were on show, laid out on the long mahogany dining table, and on other tables specially set up in the room for this purpose. She was staring at the picture she had painted herself, as a wedding present for Evan and Gideon, studying it really.

It was displayed in a prominent place, propped up on an easel which stood on top of a Georgian chest. She nodded to herself, liking it even more than she had when she had first finished it. She had chosen to paint a spot Evan knew, a field near the family farm in Kent, Connecticut . . . golden corn blowing in the breeze, set against the dark green Litchfield Hills, a bright blue sky filled with puff-ball white clouds floating high above, and, in one corner, three red barns and two grey silos, so very typical of the area where they had grown up. She was glad now that she had had the painting framed; somehow, the ornate, gilded frame made all the difference, gave the painting a sense of substance, even of importance, and this pleased her.

Elayne knew that Evan and Gideon loved it, especially Evan, since it was a reminder of home for her. *Home.* No, Connecticut wasn't home anymore, not for Evan. Yorkshire was her home now. And London, of course, where her beloved Harte's store stood in Knightsbridge. Elayne had the feeling that Evan had come into her own skin *here*, in this beautiful county, in this extraordinary and quite magnificent house. She was happy for Evan, who had always been special, and so loving and protective of her when she was growing up. Unlike Angharad. Their younger sister had been mean-spirited, constantly playing pranks on them both, telling lies about them to their grandmother, Glynnis, and getting them into trouble with their mother. Deep down, Elayne disliked Angharad intensely, although she tried not to show it . . . Angharad was not the kind of person she had any desire to upset or make angry.

Stepping away from the painting, Elayne moved slowly around the table, looking at the other gifts, admiring them. Their parents had given Evan and Gideon a beautiful silver tea service, Georgian naturally, since their father was an expert on the Georgian period. Leaning closer, peering at the card propped up against the silver teapot, Elayne saw that Angharad's name was on it as well. So their sister hadn't wanted to give Evan a separate gift after all. How typical of her. Elayne knew she was jealous of Evan, and of her; Angharad thought they had been forever favoured, put before her, and usually referred to herself as 'the low girl on the totem pole'. How ridiculous she was at times. And how ridiculous she looked with her dyed, platinum blonde hair, all that heavy make-up, and such gaudy clothes.

At least today Angharad looked halfway decent, was dressed elegantly, since she was wearing her bridesmaid's outfit. Evan had designed it – a simple, floor-length A-line gown with a tight bodice and long sleeves. It had a high-standing collar at the sides and back, somewhat like a half-ruff, and the style and cut of the gown was Elizabethan. Made of an expensive moiré taffeta, pearl-grey in colour, it was worn over a stiffened petticoat which made the skirt stand out properly. Angharad looked good in the gown, but then all the bridesmaids did. She and Natalie, Gideon's sister, and Emsie were the other grown-up bridesmaids, whilst Adele, Tessa's little daughter, was the flower girl. She, too, had the same gown in miniature; Elayne thought she looked adorable and the soft grey suited them all.

The wedding present from Robin, Evan's grandfather and Gideon's great-uncle, was spectacular, a huge, red leather box lined in black velvet, holding twenty chased silver wine goblets. Instantly, Elayne thought of Jonathan. Angharad was convinced he would be at the wedding, was itching to meet him again, after running into him in the newspaper shop in the village. But he wouldn't be there. He wasn't invited because he was the black sheep of the family and Paula's bitter enemy. Evan had confided this the other day. But she hadn't repeated it to Angharad. Why would she break a confidence? Anyway, let

Angharad look for him and be disappointed; he was old enough to be her father. Her sister had apparently flirted with him in the shop. She was more than ridiculous, she was crazy. Not to mention promiscuous.

'There you are,' Owen exclaimed from the doorway. 'I've been looking all over for you, honey.'

Elayne swung around and broke into a smile. 'Dad, you look wonderful. So handsome in your blue suit with your white carnation. Come see my painting, so well displayed. Doesn't it look great?'

'It sure does, Ellie,' he smiled back, thinking she cut quite a swathe in the grey silk gown with her dark hair and large blue eyes. People who didn't know she was adopted often said how much she resembled him, and actually she did. Marietta once remarked that they'd grown to look alike, but he thought that was a stupid thing to say ... how could you grow to look like someone?

He gazed at the painting for a long moment, and then nodded. 'It's one of your best,' he said at last, beaming at her.

'Dad! Dad, have you seen Mom?' Angharad cried, rushing into the dining room. 'Your father's looking for her.' She hurried towards Owen and Elayne, almost stumbling over herself, looking flushed, a little flustered.

'Calm down, Angharad!' Owen was startled by her headlong swoop towards them, went on, 'She can't have gone very far ... maybe she's still upstairs with Evan.'

'Oh, by the way, why weren't we allowed to help

our sister dress?' Angharad demanded, her search for Marietta suddenly forgotten. 'It's traditional that the bride's sisters help her get ready for her marriage.'

'I know. But circumstances are not quite normal, are they?' Owen replied. 'Evan is very heavily pregnant, and she doesn't feel too well. To tell you the truth, I'm surprised she hasn't given birth already, she's awfully big.'

Angharad nodded, smiled, and said spitefully, 'Like she's about to drop four baby whales and not twin babies.'

Owen ignored this comment, but Elayne couldn't stop herself from exclaiming, 'Why are you always so bitchy about Evan? You're mean and ungrateful. She's never been anything but nice to you all of your life, and all you want to do is make nasty comments.'

'Tut-tut, Elayne, don't lose your temper on her wedding day. She'd be so put out, would think you're vulgar, now that she's become such a snob.'

'No, she hasn't,' Elayne shot back. 'She hasn't changed at all, and you know it.'

'Girls, no quarrelling, please. Not today. And especially not here. And why does my father want to see your mother?' he asked Angharad, staring at her.

'How the hell do I know?' she snapped. 'He said something about wanting to be seated near to you at the luncheon, wanted her to check.'

'Oh. I see. I don't believe he can be, actually. He's seated next to Marietta, I noticed his place card when I walked through the Stone Hall. Please go and tell him that, honey, and we'll be with you in a second. I just want to take a look at the other gifts, I hadn't realized they were on display until Gideon told me.'

'Okay, but hurry up. I don't want to get stuck with Robin.'

Owen watched her retreating figure, asking himself why it was he was suddenly beginning to distrust her. Elayne's right, she's bitchy, he thought. And that's not all. She's devious, just as my mother used to say. Glynnis was right, as usual.

The moment she walked into the library, Linnet knew that Jack had told Shane about the explosion at the church. She was close to her father, and she knew his every expression; they were all engraved on her heart. He was disturbed, she could tell that, and deeply worried. He stood with Jack and Winston at the fireplace.

Hurrying to join them, she lost no time. 'Jack told you about the church, didn't he, Daddy?'

Shane looked at her and inclined his head. 'He did, Linnet, and I can only say thank God for your foresight. Because of your brainwave, your idea to change the time of the ceremony, no one was killed.'

'It was all Jonathan's doing. But we'll never prove it,' Linnet answered. 'More's the pity.'

'That's absolutely true,' Shane agreed. 'However, I don't think we have to worry about Jonathan at the moment. He achieved what he set out to do – which was to upset us all, make us worried.'

Linnet stared at her father. 'But he meant to kill us, didn't he?'

'That's the general idea, I think. On the other hand, he has the satisfaction of knowing he's truly thrown us, and I'm certain that this gives him pleasure. Upsetting the Hartes has become his favourite hobby.'

'He won't be back for a while,' Jack volunteered, staring at Linnet.

'You mean he's not in Yorkshire?' Linnet asked, frowning, her green eyes suddenly filled with puzzlement.

'He's back in London. I think he'll stay put, or at least he won't come back up to Yorkshire. He might go to Paris, of course.' Jack shook his head, and went on, 'I have a bit of surprising news for you, Linnet. He had a visitor yesterday morning before he left.'

'Who?' she asked, her eyes narrowing as she searched Jack's face.

He threw her a knowing look.

'Not *Angharad*? Don't tell me she actually had the nerve to go over to Thirsk to see him?'

'She did indeed.'

'When did you find that out?'

'A short while ago. Yesterday, my men tailing Jonathan saw a woman in a head scarf and dark glasses visit him at his home, and he made a note of the number plate on her car. He decided to check it out later in the day and did so. Then when he heard about the explosion at the church he thought he'd better tell me about her. The car is registered to Winston.' As he spoke he glanced at Winston, who nodded.

'So she borrowed your car, is that it?' Linnet said.

'One of the stable cars, actually, Linnet,' Winston answered. 'Apparently she phoned Emily from Edwina's, asked if she could come over, borrow a car to go sightseeing. Emily said of course she could. It was Edwina's driver who dropped her off.'

'Well, well, well, she doesn't waste any time, does she?' Linnet muttered. 'The odds are she'll see him in London . . . if *he's* interested, that is. What do you think? The three of you know him.' Her eyes roamed over Jack, her father and Winston, speculative and appraising as she held their collective gaze.

'He'll see her, if only to pump her, get information,' Jack announced, sounding positive.

'Or he could be interested in her as a woman,' Winston suggested.

'That's true,' Shane muttered. 'He harbours a weakness for women, always has, and the younger the better.'

'You'd better have her watched, Jack,' Linnet exclaimed.

'I'd already thought of *that*, Beauty. It's done.'

Shane took a step forward, put his arm around his daughter and pulled her closer. 'Don't worry, darling, at least not this weekend. Jonathan Ainsley's out of the way, and I'm positive nothing else is going to happen.'

'Sometimes things happen when he's *not around* . . . usually most of the time, wouldn't you say, Dad?'

'True,' Shane murmured, hugging her tighter. 'However, as I pointed out a moment ago, he's thrown a spanner in the works, and that's enough for him.'

'Oh, Daddy, I hope so.'

She sounded so forlorn, she who was always cheerful, upbeat and stoical, that Shane looked down at her, put his hand under her chin. Staring into her upturned face, he said, 'Come on, get it together, Linnet. You're a Harte and an O'Neill, and you're married to a Kallinski. *You* are the embodiment of the three clans. You've got to play that role today. Nothing less will do, my darling. You must be the very best of all of us.'

She nodded, took a deep breath.

Leaning down, Shane kissed her forehead. 'That's my girl . . . *our* girl.'

'This is it, chaps,' Winston said, straightening, standing his full height. 'Here come the troops . . . the bridesmaids, the ushers, and the bridegroom as well.'

'I'd better go and help the girls with their sprays.' Linnet gave her father a huge smile and glided across the library.

'Hello, Adele darling,' she said, when she spotted the three-year-old. 'You look so pretty.'

'Thank you, Auntie Linnet,' the child responded, 'Mumma says I'm going to carry a nosegay.'

'That's right, sweetheart, and here it is.' Linnet put the miniature bouquet in her niece's hands and kissed the top of her silver-blonde head.

Angharad sidled over to Linnet, holding the spray of small green orchids and asked, 'Where exactly am I supposed to pin this?' Adele drew closer to Linnet, looking startled, perhaps even a little afraid. Linnet took hold of her hand.

'Just below your shoulder, on the left side.' Linnet indicated her own spray which was already pinned to the lapel of her jacket. 'A bit higher than mine, though.'

Angharad nodded, glanced around and exclaimed, 'Oh, there's a mirror on the wall there. Come on, Elayne.' They rushed across the room.

Emsie came over to her sister, and whispered in Linnet's ear, 'That adoptee is definitely gross.'

'Sssh. Someone might hear you, and you'll catch it.'

'You started it,' Emsie shot back, and then grinned at Linnet and asked, 'How do I look?'

Linnet couldn't help laughing. 'You've become awfully conscious of your appearance these days, Emsie, my lass. You who never cared at all, was always in the tack room grooming the horses! What's going on?'

'I made a decision,' Emsie announced and looked over her shoulder at Natalie, Gideon's sister. 'I'm going to work on one of our newspapers like Natty does.'

'Are you now?' Linnet said teasingly. 'I always understood you were going to be a jockey.'

'I never said *that*!' the seventeen-year-old protested, flushing. 'And you know it.'

Linnet merely smiled and said to Natalie, 'Pick your spray, dear one, and I'll pin it on for you. Yours, too, Emsie, if you bring it.'

Natalie hurried to Linnet and hugged her. These

two were great friends; they had bonded as children, and they actually looked more like sisters than cousins. Natalie Harte had inherited Emma's red hair, just as Linnet had, along with her green eyes and pretty complexion.

Stepping away from Linnet, breaking the loving embrace, Natalie said, 'I suppose Mummy is with Evan and Marietta, isn't she?'

'Yes, they're upstairs. They'll come down about two forty-five. I thought we could get one or two photographs of the bride and groom, with the bridesmaids and ushers before we all go into the reception. What do you think?'

'The three photographers are all set up, Linnet, just the way you wanted. I have one in the Cream-and-Gold Drawing Room, and another in the Grey Sitting Room. I kept the Peach Drawing Room free, for the reception, as you said. The third photographer has a set-up ready in the Garden Room. This way, everyone can move from one room to the next, and with the set-up more or less in place the photographs will be done quickly.'

'Thanks for organizing this for me, Natalie, I really appreciate it.'

Natalie was staring hard at Linnet, and didn't say a word for a moment, and then in a low voice she hissed, 'Are you wearing an earpiece?'

'Keep your voice down. Yes, I am, so I can stay in touch with Jack.'

'I see. But *why*?' Natalie probed, riddled with curiosity.

'To make sure everything's running smoothly,

that's all,' Linnet fibbed, and turned to Emsie. 'Just look at you, Emsie, you are a silly goose, you've got the orchid practically upside down. Come here, let me fix it.'

'Oh, there's Great-Aunt Edwina and Uncle Robin!' Natalie said suddenly, sounding excited, and, handing her orchid to Linnet, she asked, 'Can you do me first, please, so I can go to Edwina? I just adore her, and she does need looking after.'

'Like the Earl of Warwick in his armour astride his destrier needed looking after,' Linnet scoffed. 'She could be Warwick's second-in-command, in fact. She looks as if she's about to lead a charge into the Lancastrian hordes.'

Emsie giggled, and it took Natalie a lot of self-control to keep her face straight. Linnet could be very amusing at times.

'Gosh, she's coming this way,' Emsie muttered. 'Quick, Linnet, get my orchid on.' Emsie looked down when she felt a tug of her dress, and frowned. 'What's wrong, Adele?'

'Where's Mumma?'

'I think she went with Grandma to the Stone Hall.' Taking hold of the child's hand firmly, she added, 'We'll go and find her in a second.'

Adele smiled up at her, clinging to her hand. 'All right, Emsie.'

Edwina said, 'Ah, Adele, my darling girl, you look a picture today, you do indeed. A very pretty picture.'

'Thank you, Great-Aunt Edwina. So do you.'

Edwina chuckled at this unexpected comment.

'Out of the mouths of babes and sucklings,' she murmured, and turning added, 'Good afternoon, ladies. You are both so fair and charming in your lovely frocks, and you, Linnet, should always wear pale blue.'

'As you must always wear purple, Great-Aunt,' Linnet answered.

He felt like part of them, and they thought of him as family, yet he was the outsider.

Jack Figg was well aware of this, but it did not trouble him one iota. He cared about them all in different ways, loved some more than others; in a sense, they were his only family now, with all of his blood relatives dead and buried.

It was just before three o'clock, and he stood in the Grey Sitting Room watching in amusement as his two favourite redheads, Linnet and Natalie, bustled around like sergeant majors, lining up the family for the big wedding portrait the photographer was impatiently waiting to take.

His eyes followed the two young women alertly, and as he noticed how skilfully they moved people around, he realized that what they were doing had a lot to do with the colour coordination of the different clothes. They both held clipboards and kept conferring with each other, stepping back and viewing the group as a whole.

How clever. Somebody had created a colour plan for the wedding, especially the photographs; more than likely Evan with her eye for clothes and her colour sense. As he continued to watch with great interest, he saw this plan take shape. Brilliant, he thought. Just brilliant.

All of the male members of the family, without exception, were wearing dark-navy business suits, white shirts and pale blue ties. Each man had a white carnation in his buttonhole, just as he did, and of course he was dressed in a navy blue suit, too. He had been told to wear that colour, and obviously so had all the other men.

The four adult bridesmaids, Natalie, Emsie, Elayne and Angharad, were beautiful in their long pearl-grey taffeta gowns; little Adele wore the same dress in miniature and was enchanting. The grown-up girls had green orchids pinned on their left shoulders; Adele carried a bouquet of the same green orchids.

Linnet was dressed in a pale blue silk suit with a long, well-tailored coat and long skirt, while her sister Tessa was in a pale bluish-grey caftan which had blue beading around the neck. Their cousin, India, had chosen a long Nehru-style tunic and narrow pants made of heavy silk and this was the same pale bluish-grey as Tessa's caftan.

Snap, he thought. Navy for the men; grey for the bridesmaids; pale blue or bluish-grey for these three. Colour coordination indeed.

Jack's eyes scanned the other women. Paula, his great favourite, wore a long, violet-coloured velvet coat and a violet chiffon gown underneath; Emily had chosen a tapestry coat predominantly greyish-blue, with small touches of soft colour, while the mother of the bride, Marietta, was in gold brocade over dark brown silk.

Glancing along the rows, he found another touch of gold brocade, this time worn by Elizabeth, Emma Harte's second daughter, while Daisy, her daughter by Paul McGill, was dressed in a splashy magenta shade.

Great-Aunt Edwina, the eldest of Emma's daughters, wore her favourite deep purple. Jack smiled broadly. God bless her, he thought, she just keeps on ploughing the seas like a great old battleship. He adored Edwina, whom he considered to be the greatest character he had ever known.

Finally, he found another pool of rich purple and gold. Sally, Countess of Dunvale, India's mother, wore a long, gold brocade coat over wide trousers of gold-coloured silk, and her sister, Vivienne, had chosen a purple cut-velvet coat and dress that echoed Edwina's deep purple.

What it boils down to is a mixture of dark navy, pearl grey, and greyish-blue predominantly, Jack decided, with strong colour from the violet, purple and magenta, these shades balanced by the gold brocade.

And at the centre of this rather simple colour plan stood the bride in her shimmering blue-on-blue ombred chiffon that reflected all the shades in the sea. How beautiful she was.

Jack smiled wryly to himself. He, the most conventional of red-blooded heterosexuals, had certainly learned a lot from Emma Harte. More than he had realized until today!

The family portrait is going to be spectacular, he thought, silently congratulating Evan for her foresight. She must have guided the women in their choices of colour, even been insistent.

Seemingly all was completed. Linnet and Natalie took their own places, and the relieved photographer got ready to start when Shane stepped forward.

'No, no! Stop! Wait a minute,' he cried, looking at the photographer. Then he shifted his gaze, looked at Jack. 'What are you doing down there, Jack? You're supposed to be up here with us. We need you for this shot in particular.'

'But I—'

'No buts, Jack. *You're family*. Come up here and stand with me and Paula.'

Jack did as he was told, unable to utter a word. He was overcome with emotion.

PART THREE

Duo

Fortune is not satisfied with inflicting one calamity.

Publilius Syrus: *Maxim 274*

CHAPTER EIGHTEEN

Linnet was so excited, filled with such elation, she picked up the phone and dialled Evan's home number without a second thought, wanting to convey her pleasure immediately.

After numerous rings, just when she was about to hang up, Evan was saying hello.

'It's Linnet!' she cried, 'and I can't get over your sketches for Harte's wedding gowns. They're fantastic! Whenever did you design *fifty* dresses? When did you find the time?'

Evan chuckled. 'I'm thrilled you like them, Linnet. I designed at least twelve of them for *you*, when I was creating your wedding gown last year. But we finally decided to go with the Tudor Princess look in the end, so I just put the rest away. The others I've created over the past few years, in my spare time. I liked most of them so I kept them. I did throw a few away, the ones I thought weren't very good.'

'You didn't! That's a crime. Please keep everything you design in the future, and let *me* be the judge. You're far too critical of yourself.'

'I promise I won't ditch a thing, not even a rough sketch. How's that?'

'Just great, and thanks for sending your portfolio over to the store. I do appreciate it, and I hope we can start putting a few of the designs in work very soon. For all those June weddings that will be coming up.'

'Of course we can. I'll send you an email about some of the seamstresses I've used, and which designs I think they'll handle best. How's that?'

'So you can't come to the store? Is that what you're saying?' Linnet asked quietly. 'Not even to discuss the gowns with me?'

'Oh, Linnet, I wish I could. But Dr Addney has simply forbidden it,' Evan murmured, at once understanding Linnet's disappointment, and need for her to be at Harte's. 'He says I have to take it easy, stay at home and rest, not exert myself in any way, or get myself agitated. But listen, you can come over to the apartment, can't you? We could look at the sketches here, make our plans, choose the seamstresses.'

'It's a great idea, but unfortunately I'm really jammed today.'

'That's all right. We'll do it later in the week. Whenever . . . Actually, Mom's here, she's going to go with me to meet Emily at that apartment in Belgrave Square. The one which belongs to her friend, Lavinia Constable, who's off to Los Angeles. I think Gid might have mentioned it to you?'

'Yes, he did. The other day. And isn't it a funny coincidence that it's near Emma's house in the square?'

'That's the best part, being so close to Paula and Shane. As far as the flat is concerned, it's only a rental for a year, Linnet. But the great thing is that it has been renovated. It's brand new, and *unfurnished*. So we could use our own things. Gid's really excited, he's seen it already. If I like it, then it's a done deal, because he thinks it would be perfect for us, if only on a temporary basis.'

'Since Gid likes it, I'm sure *you* will, and if it's halfway decent rent it for the year. You can't continue to live in Gideon's bachelor flat once the twins come. You'll be cramped to death.'

'I know. I thought we'd be able to furnish the apartment quickly, maybe find a lot of the things we need at Harte's.'

'You will, and I'll help you. So will Emily. We'll make it liveable for you, at least, hopefully before the babies are born.'

'We'll have to hurry then,' Evan said, laughing.

'You do feel okay, don't you?' Linnet asked, concerned.

'I'm great, honestly, and I'm sure I'll deliver in February, which is when I'm supposed to.' There was a moment's hesitation before Evan continued, 'I'm so sorry you only have India to help you at the moment. I know how tough it can be at the store. When is Tessa coming back from Paris?'

'In a few days, once Jean-Claude goes off to Afghanistan. He wanted her to spend some time with him at his home. Did she tell you she's going to meet his son?'

'No, she didn't. But that's nice, and it's a good

idea, don't you think? Now that they're engaged.'

'Yes,' Linnet agreed, and added softly, 'My mother told me last night that Tessa's divorce should be through at the end of this week. So they can get married fairly soon.'

There was a silence.

Linnet said, 'Have I lost you, Evan?'

'No, I'm here,' she answered. 'I was just startled to hear that bit of news. Will Tessa be leaving Harte's, moving to Paris?' Her voice was low, almost conspiratorial.

'I don't know anything . . .' Linnet left her sentence unfinished, and then cleared her throat. 'I don't think she's said a word to Paula.' The other line began to shrill, and Linnet exclaimed, 'Let's talk later today, Evan. I've got to take this.'

'I'll call you after I've seen the flat,' Evan responded, and hung up.

Linnet pressed the other button. 'Hello? Linnet O'Neill.'

'It's India,' her cousin said. 'Have you got a moment?'

'Yes, of course. Is something wrong, India? You sound strange.'

'I think I've got a problem – well, a sort of *developing* problem.'

'Here or at the Leeds store? Or is it personal?'

'*Personal*,' India announced and then sighed. 'Mrs Caldwell, that's the grandmother of Dusty's child, if you remember, has taken a turn for the worse. I just got off the phone to Dusty, and he posed a very difficult question. I didn't know how to answer him. I need your advice, Linnet. Can I come along to your office?'

'*Absolutely*. I'm free right now.'

Several seconds later India walked into Linnet's office, came over to her desk, sat down and blew her cousin a kiss. 'Sorry to do this at ten o'clock in the morning, but I simply don't have the answer for Dusty. I'm a bit baffled.'

Leaning over the desk, Linnet suggested, 'Tell me what it is, let's go from there.'

'Dusty thinks Molly Caldwell's going to die. He's had a premonition about it for over a week now, he says, and his dilemma is what to do about taking the child to see her grandmother before she does die. Should he? Or would it be better if he didn't?'

'Wow, that's a tough one.'

'Don't tell me. I've wrestled with it for the last hour.'

Linnet sat back in her chair, a reflective look settling on her face. She closed her eyes, concentrated for a few moments; then she snapped her eyes open, sat up, and said to India, 'Let's just analyse it . . . let's bring it down to our own personal level . . . For example, if Paula were dying, would we tell Tessa to take Adele to see her grandmother?'

India bit her lip, shook her head. 'I don't know.'

'Okay, look at it this way. If Great-Aunt Edwina, your grandmother, were dying, and if you had a child of your own, and your child had been close to Edwina, what would you do?'

'I think I'd take her to see Edwina. For Edwina's sake as well as the child's.'

'I feel the same way. And after all, India, Atlanta doesn't have to be *told* her grandmother is dying, now does she?'

'No, she doesn't,' India agreed. 'I have a feeling Dusty's concerned about Molly's condition, how she looks physically, whether or not she's hooked up to drips. He doesn't want Atlanta to be frightened, and I also have a feeling he thinks Atlanta should perhaps remember her grandmother the way she was the last time they saw each other.'

'Do you want to go back to Yorkshire? Help Dusty with this?'

'Yes, I think it would please him, make it easier for everyone, in a sense. On the other hand, it's Thursday and I've only been back here for three days and a bit. My desk is piled high.'

'I know, so was mine. Do you have anything truly pressing, India?'

'Not really. But I should follow up on some of the clothes and accessories we ordered for spring. Then again, I suppose a day won't make too much difference. I could leave tomorrow morning, early, and meet Dusty in Leeds.'

'Is it pressing? Is Mrs Caldwell actually at death's door?'

'Not exactly, as far as I know. However, the woman who helps her told Dusty that Molly was getting weaker, and also fretting about Atlanta.'

'Then go today. Go now, India,' Linnet said. 'You can be in Leeds in several hours. Why waste time?

Tempt providence? I think it's awfully important that the child sees her grandmother again, and is given a proper explanation about why she's in hospital. Also, I think it's important for Molly Caldwell to see her granddaughter . . . so she can die in peace. And you should be with Dusty, as his fiancée.'

'I'd planned to go with him, if he did decide to take Atlanta to see Molly.'

'I believe that to be very fitting, compassionate,' Linnet said, in a low, soft voice.

'Yes. And thanks, Linnet, for helping me to help Dusty make a decision,' India answered, the faint Irish lilt echoing behind her melodious voice. She gave her cousin a little smile. 'I know he'll go along with whatever I suggest.'

After India had left, Linnet began to collect Evan's sketches from her work table where they were laid out. She put them carefully into the portfolio, thinking about India's upcoming marriage to Dusty. Evan had designed a beautiful crinoline gown of ivory taffeta for India. Edwardian in style. How talented she was.

A long, heavy sigh escaped as Linnet tied the string on the portfolio, put it at the back of her work table and returned to her desk.

She sat staring into space for a few minutes, thinking about Dusty Rhodes and the problem he would face when Molly Caldwell did die. She now knew quite a lot about Melinda Caldwell; Gideon had made it his business to find out as much as he could in order to protect India.

The woman was dangerous, no question about that. She was a drug addict, could be violent, and apparently she was difficult to deal with. There was no way she would give up custody of her child, Linnet was quite certain of that. And so was Great-Aunt Edwina, who had worried aloud about India to Linnet, during the wedding festivities at Pennistone Royal this past weekend.

'It will be a replay of the Mark Longden situation which Tessa had to cope with,' Edwina had pronounced dourly. 'Just you wait and see. Dusty's in for a lot of trouble, mark my words.'

'What can we do?' Linnet had probed as she guided Edwina away from her sisters with whom she had been standing – Elizabeth, Emily's mother, and Daisy, Paula's mother and Linnet's grandmother. They both were consistently curious about the entire family and loved family intrigue and gossip. In fact, it often struck her that they thrived on it.

Edwina, not one to miss a trick, had given Linnet an amused glance and said, 'Yes, better to find a quiet corner to chat. My siblings are very nosey.'

Linnet had laughed, taken Edwina to the other end of the Stone Hall, and Edwina had gone on, 'I shall advise Dusty to get a top-notch solicitor to handle the situation. Maybe we can avoid a court case if he has the right firm. Better use the one Emma and Paula have always used. Mmm, that's a good idea. And then there's *money*. That might well be the answer.' All this had been said in a decisive tone and Edwina's dour mood had lightened as she spoke.

'Money isn't always the best currency, though,' Linnet had answered succinctly.

Edwina had given her an admiring look. 'Spoken like a true Harte, dear Linnet. And I must tell you this, while I think of it. I rely on you to stand by India, in your very clever and daring way, just in case I'm not around, that is.'

'Are you going somewhere, Edwina?' Linnet had asked swiftly, addressing her by her first name as she often did.

Edwina had laughed hilariously. 'No, I'm not planning any trips. But you never know, I might just pop my clogs, even though that would be such a nuisance. I've so much to do at the moment, so many engagements.'

Linnet had thrown her arms around her great-aunt, hugging her tightly, laughing with her, once again thinking how extraordinary she was. An absolute original.

And Edwina's right, Linnet now thought. Dusty must have the proper kind of representation and the best law firm behind him. That was the imperative. She made up her mind to talk to Paula later today about this, get her mother to introduce him to the solicitors she used, Crawford, Creighton, Phipps and whatever. They were big-time. And that's the kind of lawyers Dusty would need to deal with Melinda, if the occasion arose.

No sooner had this thought entered her head than the phone rang. When she picked it up and said, 'Hello? Linnet O'Neill here,' it was her mother who spoke.

'Good morning, Linnet dear,' Paula said. 'Are you very busy at the moment?'

'No, Mummy, I've just been going over some really gorgeous sketches for wedding gowns, Evan's designs. I'd love to show them to you, if you've got a minute.' It had suddenly struck her that this was possibly a wonderful opportunity to broach the idea of an entire floor devoted to brides, one of the projects on her back burner.

'I'd love to see them but not now. We have a problem. A very serious problem. Could you come to my office?'

'You mean *now*?'

'At once, Linnet.'

'What's wrong?' she asked, her voice rising.

'Just come to my office, Linnet, *please*.'

'Right away, Mummy.' Linnet dropped the phone in the cradle, jumped up and went out. As she left the outer office she told her secretary where she was going, and headed for the chief executive's suite, almost running down the corridor, suddenly worried and growing nervous.

Her mind was racing as she pushed open the door of her mother's domain, and said to Jonelle, one of her secretaries, 'The boss lady sent for me.'

Jonelle smiled at her. 'Go right in, Linnet.'

Stepping into the spacious and beautiful room, which had been Emma's office from the day the store opened until her death, Linnet went cold when she saw Jack Figg sitting on a chair next to her mother. Paula was perched on the edge of the sofa, looking the epitome of elegance in her well-tailored black suit, but also very tense, taut.

Apprehension flooded Linnet, but she swallowed it back, controlled herself as she walked towards them, saying, 'Mummy . . . Jack . . . what's going on? What's the matter?'

'Hello, Linnet,' Jack said, sounding a bit weary. His voice was gruff, and Linnet thought he looked extremely tired. He had dark rings under his eyes.

She stared at her mother.

Paula stared back, smiled at her somewhat falteringly, and patted the sofa. 'Come and sit with me, darling. Jack has some news. News I regard as rather bad, if not, indeed, disastrous.'

Without responding, Linnet did as she was bidden, went and sat next to her mother on the sofa. She was eaten up with curiosity.

'Would you fill Linnet in, please, Jack?' Paula said, sighing.

He nodded, but for a moment he didn't say anything. He sat gazing at the two women, mother and daughter, heirs of Emma Harte, who had always worn her uniform both literally and figuratively. Today mother and daughter were both dressed in the same kind of smart black suit Emma had favoured, obviously couture, expensive, and worn with white shirts. Both in high heels. But no jewellery except for pearls on their ears, watches on their wrists, and plain gold wedding bands on the appropriate fingers. Just like Emma. Her style. And right down to the last detail. Intelligent, brilliant women. Kind and loving women. He couldn't bear it if anything ever happened to either of them. He cursed silently to himself, frustrated, and boiling inside.

Taking a deep breath, Jack looked at Linnet and said calmly, 'I have excellent reasons to believe Angharad Hughes has hooked up with Jonathan Ainsley.'

Linnet nodded. 'I'm not going to say I'm surprised, Jack, because I'm not. We had a discussion about this very thing the other day. The day of the wedding.'

'We did indeed, and Shane even speculated that this might well happen, pointing out that Jonathan had a terrible weakness for women, especially young ones.'

'What have you found out?' Linnet asked, feeling a sudden tension in her chest.

'As you know, Angharad went to see him on Friday morning at his house in Thirsk. What happened at that meeting we've no way of knowing, but she was there for about thirty minutes, no longer. Ainsley then went to London. Angharad was at the wedding, as we all know, but she left Yorkshire first thing on Monday morning. She took the early train to King's Cross, and checked in at the hotel owned by George Thomas, her father's old friend.'

'And her father and mother returned to London on Tuesday, along with their daughter Elayne,' Linnet pointed out. 'I believe Owen Hughes and Elayne left for New York yesterday. Isn't that so?'

'It is,' Jack replied, nodding. 'Marietta is still at the hotel. She's staying until Evan gives birth, she told me that at the wedding reception. And I'm sure everyone knows this.'

'We do. And she's with Evan at this moment.' Linnet glanced at her watch. 'I believe they are presently on their way to view an apartment in Belgrave Square, which was arranged by Emily.'

'That's right,' Paula volunteered. 'Emily's old friend, Lavinia Constable, just did up the place only to get a marvellous job offer to do the sets for an important movie in Los Angeles. She's gone away for a year.'

'So we know the whereabouts of *all* the Hugheses,' Jack said acidly, 'including Angharad.'

'Is she in London with *him*?' Linnet probed.

'She's actually in Paris. But then, so is he,' Jack answered, throwing her a pointed look. 'One of my London chaps was tracking her from the moment she stepped off the train at King's Cross. We know everything she did on Monday. She checked into Thomas's Hotel off Cadogan Square, then went to the hairdresser's around the corner, later spent an hour or so shopping at Harvey Nichols. That evening, she went over to Jonathan Ainsley's apartment in Grosvenor Square, around seven, and stayed until ten-thirty. Obviously having dinner, or whatever. She went back to see him at his apartment on Tuesday afternoon for an hour only. That night she had dinner with her parents, and George and Arlette Thomas at the hotel. Elayne was present as well. Angharad went shopping again on Wednesday afternoon, ate alone with her mother on Wednesday evening, and flew to Paris this morning. Very early.

When she arrived in Paris she checked into the George V Hotel. My Paris operatives have her under permanent surveillance now.'

'So J.A. was already in Paris, eh?'

'He was, Linnet. He flew in early on a private jet on Wednesday morning. He's been ensconced in his flat on Avenue Foch ever since.'

'Something's going on between them, that's patently obvious,' Linnet now ventured. 'I think they must have planned to meet in London when she saw him at Thirsk on Friday. They made a date, probably because he couldn't spend any time with her then.'

'*Correct!*' Jack agreed. 'He had just put his luggage in the car and was ready to leave the house when she drove up. He went back inside with her. But not for that long, as I said: half an hour maybe.'

Paula interjected, 'What transpired between them, whatever it was, made them want to see each other again. They clicked in some way, that's what I think. He was rushing up to London, and she knew she was going back there, so they made a date. And during their encounters in London he decided to invite her to Paris, and she probably was thrilled to go.' Pausing, Paula stared hard at Jack. 'That's the way I see it, anyway. Don't you?'

'I think you've pretty much got it right, Paula.' Jack glanced at Linnet and then back at Paula. 'I must pose a question to you both. Is it personal? Is it a sexual liaison? Or is he using her to get information about Evan and Gideon? Or about

Owen and Marietta? Or the entire Harte family? What's *he* up to, in other words.'

'Maybe it's both – business and pleasure,' Linnet muttered. 'Certainly she could be very useful to him. It's like having a spy right in the bosom of our family. And Owen's. Don't forget, he hates *all* of us.' Linnet leaned back against the chair, disliking Angharad more than ever. She was such a gross, gushing, vulgar woman: Linnet couldn't bear her. Nor could Tessa and India. Angharad had tried, during the short time she was in Yorkshire, to make friends with them, ingratiate herself, to infiltrate their group, but without success. Each one of them found her unbearable; even Evan had distanced herself from Angharad, who seemed to brush up everyone the wrong way. Linnet was well aware that Natalie and Emsie had also been totally turned off, fled for their lives whenever they saw Angharad on the horizon.

Paula said, 'She's *useful* to him. *Dangerous* to us, Jack. Let's face it, she knows everything that's going on in her own family, and also ours probably. Evan and Marietta are in constant contact. And no doubt there's a lot of chit-chat passing back and forth, there usually is in families.'

'Mummy, Evan doesn't like Angharad! She confided in me, and she's not close to her, never was, in fact, not even when they were children. If you want my opinion, Evan actually *hates* her. I know it's a strong word to use, but I think she does. As for Gideon, he can't abide her either. I know he blames her for Evan's fall. He told me.'

'Does Gideon think she pushed Evan? Something like that?' Paula asked, her eyes narrowing.

'No, because Evan says Angharad never touched her. However, Gid believes she managed to get Evan so worked up, so agitated and nervous she missed the chair, fell onto the floor. He is *convinced* that if Evan had been alone in her office the accident wouldn't have occurred. He has this idea – that somehow Angharad goaded Evan, yes, that's what he believes, even if we don't.'

'So, as far as we know, those two dangerous people have become cohorts . . . but for what reason?' Jack wondered out loud. 'We must find that out. *How? Who can help us?*' Jack sat back in the chair, rubbing his chin with one hand, looking thoughtful.

'I would say there is only one person. *Marietta,*' Paula pointed out. 'Neither of her sisters likes Angharad, apparently, so there's only the mother left. That's the one person Angharad would confide in, anyway.'

'Don't you think, under these circumstances, she might be wary of talking to her mother? Anyway, she'd never admit to plotting something diabolical with Jonathan Ainsley. Would she?' Linnet asked.

'Damn right she wouldn't!' Jack exclaimed. 'But you have a point, Paula, about Marietta. Angharad would more than likely make a point of seeing her, especially if she were having an affair with Ainsley. She would want to show off. She's a young woman, full of life and energy, and he's a good-looking, very rich, sophisticated older man, also from the Harte family. She just might want to boast she's snagged him, because she undoubtedly sees him as a catch.'

Jack jumped up, walked over to the window, stood looking down at the busy traffic in Knightsbridge. But he was oblivious to everything; his mind was working in the strange ways it often did, as he tried to envision what Angharad would do, what would motivate her to boast to her mother? Spite? Envy? Jealousy of Evan? Right on, he thought.

After a few seconds, he turned to face Paula and Linnet. 'Listen to me. She *won't* confide in Marietta if Ainsley's plotting something bad. She probably *will* confide in her mother if she's having an affair with him. She won't be able to resist doing so. She'll feel more competitive with Evan than ever.'

'So what do *we* do?' Linnet asked. 'In the meantime?'

'Get Marietta on our side,' Paula suggested.

Jack smiled for the first time that morning. 'I don't think that will be very hard, do you, Paula? All we have to do is explain the situation to Marietta, tell her that Evan and the twins might be in serious danger. I don't think she'd want anything to happen to her daughter and her first grandchildren, do you?'

Paula shook her head. 'No woman would take that risk.'

Linnet said, 'Marietta has to be told how *dangerous* Angharad actually is, if she's involved with J.A., and then she'll help us, I'm sure. Perhaps she knows Angharad has gone to Paris, and maybe she'll go over, too. To visit her.'

'Only Marietta can get to the bottom of the situation,' Jack murmured. 'We *must* find out what's going on.'

'Evan and Gideon have to be told about Angharad and Jonathan, they can't be left in the dark,' Paula interjected. 'Maybe we can invite them for drinks this evening, and Marietta as well.'

Linnet nodded. She did not trust herself to speak. She suddenly had such a dreadful sense of foreboding, of trouble ahead, that she felt incapable of saying anything at all.

CHAPTER NINETEEN

Linnet and Jack Figg left the executive suite, and Paula turned to her work, taking a manila folder off the top of a pile at one end of her desk.

She attempted to study the first page of the current balance sheet, but found it hard to concentrate. Images of Jonathan Ainsley intruded. A sudden thought occurred to her, and she sat up straighter in her chair; her mind had unexpectedly focused on her cousin, Sarah. She used to be close to Ainsley, but was now more inclined to take the family's side. But wasn't she a better judge of his current situation than Marietta Hughes? The latter would have to rely on the veracity of her daughter, and would the girl *really* tell her mother the truth?

Maybe she would. On the other hand, what if she didn't actually know the truth? There were a variety of elements involved here, and in her opinion Angharad Hughes was no match for the deadly Jonathan Ainsley. Evil though he might be, he was a brilliant man with a keen intelligence, and he was a past master of deception and dissimulation.

To her way of thinking, Sarah Lowther Pascal, whom Paula truly believed was now on the side of the family, was the one person who would see everything as it really was, through very clear eyes. Sarah had convinced her last year that she was opposed to their cousin, because she had come to understand how dangerous Jonathan was, and that he fully intended to do the Hartes harm if he could.

Reaching for the small red book that contained all of the family phone numbers, she found Sarah's direct line at her Paris office and punched in the numbers.

Sarah answered within seconds, and Paula said, 'Hello, Sarah, it's Paula.'

'Paula, hello!' Sarah exclaimed. 'How are you?' Her lovely rather mellifluous voice was friendly and very warm.

'I'm fine. We were all sorry you couldn't make it to the wedding, especially Emily, but we understood your problems. Is Chloe feeling better?'

'Yes, she is, thanks for asking. Bed rest and the right antibiotics seem to be doing the trick. Her viral bronchitis is clearing up. She really wasn't well enough to come to Yorkshire, and frankly I just didn't want to leave her. Also, Yves was snowed under. He's preparing a new exhibition of his work, and he always gets so involved himself with the mounting of it. Anyway, I'm sure it was a lovely wedding, and that everything went well.'

'It did, thanks to Linnet.' Paula took a deep breath

and plunged in, told Sarah about the early morning secret ceremony, the reasons for it, and then gave her details of the explosion at the church. 'Thank God nobody was hurt, because there was nobody in the church,' Paula finished.

Sarah was aghast at the other end of the phone and she cried, 'But he's gone mad! Why on earth is he so destructive? So determined to hurt the family? It just doesn't make sense.'

'It's because of the past, Sarah. He feels cheated of what he thinks is rightfully his . . . that will never change. He's *obsessed*.'

'Our grandmother did what she thought was right, what she believed to be the best. It had nothing to do with you or me or anyone else. None of her children or grandchildren were involved in the making of her will. Why can't he get that through his head?'

'I don't know, and quite frankly I think he's delusional,' Paula responded. 'He's sick in the head, as far as I'm concerned. And he's being grossly unfair . . . he still gets his dividends from Harte Enterprises, as we all do, Emily sees to that. He has the trust fund Grandy made for him, and he's a rich man in his own right, a talented businessman who's made millions for himself because of Emma's legacy to him. So why this vendetta?'

'You said it yourself, Paula . . . he's sick.'

'And a loose cannon. Jack Figg has absolute proof he's involved with Evan's sister, Angharad Hughes. Apparently she ran into him in the newsagent's shop in Pennistone Royal village, and according to Evan's mother, who was there, they kind of . . . flirted with each other. Since then Angharad has visited him at his house in Thirsk, has met him twice in London. And now they're both in Paris. They flew separately, and she's staying at the George V, but she's obviously there because of him, no two ways about that in my mind, and Jack Figg's also.'

There was a total silence at the other end of the phone, and then, after this short pause, Sarah said, 'So *that's* who it is.'

'What do you mean?'

'He phoned me early this morning, suggested dinner on Saturday. He said he wanted me to meet a protégée of his. I wasn't sure what he meant by protégée, but anyway, I put him off because Yves is so busy with the exhibition.'

'Could you go? Would you go? For me? For the family, Sarah? We simply need to know if he's using her, pumping her for information in order to monitor us and get to us. Or is it simply a middle-aged man's lust for a much younger woman? A twenty-three-year-old platinum blonde with a pretty face and sexy body.'

'Twenty-three. Good God, he's cradle-snatching!'

'That he is . . . if it's a sexual involvement. But it might be all business. Linnet believes Angharad is one of those *hungry* women who is hungry for everything. Men, money, the good life. It's possible he has a business arrangement with her. She's envious of Evan. I don't think there's any love lost there, from what Linnet has told me. There's nothing like envy, is there?'

'Only jealousy perhaps,' Sarah murmured, thinking unexpectedly of Shane and how much she had loved him once, and how jealous she had been of Paula long, long ago.

Paula said, 'So, Sarah, what do you say? Will you consider going to dinner with him on Saturday? Just to assess their relationship?'

'I'll not only consider it, I'll do it!' Sarah exclaimed with sudden vehemence. 'I need to know for myself what he's up to.'

Tessa was happy that they had come to Clos-Fleuri after spending three days in Paris. She had grown to love Jean-Claude's lovely old country house, and it was the perfect place for Adele to roam around in, with so many odd nooks and crannies that could charm a child. Elvira liked it here, too, and enjoyed tramping around the grounds with Adele in tow.

Now, as she sat at the dressing table in her bedroom, putting on make-up, Tessa thought about the next few days. Jean-Claude's only child was coming to spend the weekend with them, before Jean-Claude flew off to fulfil his assignment in Afghanistan and she returned to London.

Tessa was looking forward to meeting Philippe Deléon. He was thirty-one and an artist who lived in the South of France, not married, and something of a loner. He was a talented painter, according to his father, and was finally beginning to get the recognition he deserved. She had spoken to him several times on the phone and he sounded nice, and she found herself wanting him to like her.

Jean-Claude had chuckled when she had said this to him yesterday, and he had answered, '*Mon Dieu, chérie*, how could he not like you? Please, do not worry so much.' After that there had been no further discussion about Jean-Claude's son. She knew he had been brought up by his mother in the South of France, in a little town called Beaulieu-sur-Mer, between Nice and Monte-Carlo, visiting his father in Paris during the school holidays.

Picking up a comb, Tessa ran it through her silver-blonde hair, and then walked over to the armoire. Within seconds she was dressed in a white silk blouse, white wool trousers and a white cashmere jacket with hand-embroidered front panels. Stepping into high-heeled beige suede shoes, she walked over to the window, parted the draperies and looked out.

It was a very clear night, with a huge full moon floating low in the ink-black sky. It cast a silver sheen across the frost-covered lawns and the bare trees, dark and skeletal in the moonlight. Bereft, she thought, the garden looks bereft and sad and very eerie in this silvery light. An involuntary shiver ran through her as she lingered, staring at the ghostly landscape. Then she stepped away quickly, letting the curtain fall from her hands, and returned to the dressing table. After spraying herself with the perfume, she put on pearl earrings and slipped her engagement ring onto her finger. Looking at it for a moment, she thought of Jean-Claude and his impending trip to Afghanistan next week.

How it worried her, this assignment covering

the war. All she could think about were guns and destruction and death. She dare not let him know how concerned she was because it would upset him, and that was the last thing she wished to do. She wanted him to go off with a clear head; she did not want him worrying about her whilst he was away. He needed to be totally concentrated on what he had to do, but she did have her moments when panic overwhelmed her. She had had so many losses in her life at different times, and she could not bear another one.

Jim Fairley, her father, taken from her when she was just a toddler. Killed in an avalanche in Chamonix; David Amory, her grandfather, who was also killed in the avalanche. And then there was her half-brother, Patrick, such a dear sweet boy, who had died of a rare blood disease when only in his teens. And even the failure of her marriage to Mark Longden was a loss, in a sense, because to her any kind of failure was in itself a loss.

A sigh escaped, and she bit her lower lip nervously. She must control herself, be strong and courageous. Nothing was going to happen to Jean-Claude. He would be away for only a month, at the most, and he was an experienced war correspondent, used to dodging bullets and staying safe. He had told her that he never took risks, that he wore a flak jacket, as did most journalists and war photographers, and that he had every intention of staying alive . . . so that he could come back and marry her.

Marriage. The word bounced around in her head

all of a sudden. She wasn't even divorced yet from Mark Longden, and she was engaged to another man and prepared to start a new marriage, a new life with him. But she was sure of Jean-Claude, knew full well how much he loved her, just as she loved him with all her heart. And she knew that this time the marriage would work, because of who Jean-Claude was, what he was as a man. Brilliant, with a high intellect, a writer and philosopher of no mean repute, he was also kind, loving, generous, compassionate and strong of heart. He had a loving soul, a gentle soul.

Mark Longden had been *killing* her soul, destroying her spirit, just as he had hurt her physically. And she was relieved and happy that he was gone from her life. He was now in Australia, thanks to the extraordinary deal her mother had made with his lawyers, and he could not come back to England for a very long time. Not if he wanted to keep the money Paula had given him in the divorce settlement.

And within the next couple of weeks her divorce would be final, and she could marry Jean-Claude whenever she wished. He was anxious for them to marry as soon as possible, and she felt the same. The thought of being with him on a permanent basis now filled her with a rush of happiness, and she swung away from the dressing table, hurried across her bedroom, which served as a dressing room. Gliding through the open door into Jean-Claude's bedroom, which she shared with him, she glanced around.

At this moment he came hurrying out of his own

dressing room, struggling into a tweed sports jacket. His face lit up at the sight of her, and he exclaimed, 'Tessa, you look beautiful, *chérie.*'

'*Merci beaucoup, monsieur.*' As he came to stop in front of her she leaned forward, kissed his cheek, added, 'I'm going to see what Adele is doing.'

Jean-Claude laughed, his warm brown eyes sparkling. 'A moment ago she was sitting in the kitchen with Elvira.'

Smiling, Tessa began to edge out of the room. 'I'll just pop downstairs and see her,' she said, and went on, 'She must be feeling tired, she's had such a busy day for a small child.'

'I'll join you in a few minutes,' Jean-Claude murmured, walking over to the small desk in a corner of the room. 'I have a business phone call to make, but it won't take long.'

Adele was almost four, and she had suddenly sprung up in the last few weeks, looked rather tall for her age. With her exquisite little face, grey eyes and pale blonde hair she was the spitting image of her mother, a beautiful child who was sweet natured and docile.

Everyone fell in love with her, and Lourdes, Jean-Claude's cook, was no exception. For this long weekend in the country, and with several house guests, she had travelled from the house in Paris to do the cooking, and Hakim had accompanied her. Although Gérard was the houseman at Clos-Fleuri, Jean-Claude had decided extra help was necessary and Hakim had been a willing volunteer.

When Tessa walked into the wonderful, old-fashioned kitchen, Adele was eating a light supper and talking to Elvira in the most animated way. Tessa noticed at once that Lourdes and Hakim were looking on, their affection for her child written across their smiling faces. It pleased her so much that Jean-Claude's staff had fallen in love with Adele the first time they had met her. All of them, both in Paris and here, had made the child feel comfortable, welcomed her warmly, with smiles and a few kind words. And Adele had responded in kind. Not all of them spoke English, but a few gentle words in French had been significant, and somehow Adele had known they were saying nice things to her by their tone of voice and expressions.

'Mumma!' Adele cried when she saw Tessa coming across the kitchen, and she made to jump down from the table. But Elvira put a restraining hand on her arm. 'You have to finish your supper, Adele,' the nanny said softly.

Tessa nodded to Hakim and Lourdes and then sat down next to Adele. 'Hello, darling. What did you have for supper tonight?'

'Fish, Mumma, a little itty bitty fish with mashed potatoes and *petits pois* . . . that means peas.'

Tessa smiled. 'I know, and so you are learning French, are you?'

Adele nodded. 'Lourdes is teaching me the name of . . . food. It's a beginning, she said, and *pomme de terre*, that's potatoes. *Viande*, that's meat, and I told you about peas, and then there's *crème caramel*, that's a custard, and *lait*—'

'Is milk,' Elvira cut in, adding, 'Come along, Adele, please finish your supper like a good girl.'

'Oh, I've finished, thank you.' Turning to her mother she said, '*You're* not having fish tonight, you're having *viande*. Lamb. Jean-Claude likes lamb, Lourdes told me that. Where is Jean-Claude, Mumma?'

'Right here, *ma petite*,' Jean-Claude announced from the doorway and came into the kitchen. He rested a loving hand on Adele's head, bent down and kissed her, then took a seat next to Tessa. Looking across at Hakim, who was filling an ice bucket, he asked, 'Has my son arrived yet?'

'Fifteen minutes ago, *monsieur*. Gérard took his suitcase upstairs.'

'*Bien*,' Jean-Claude said, and then, putting an arm around Adele, he asked, 'Now, *ma petite choux à la crème*, how was dinner?'

'Very nice. *Merci*.' She smiled up at him.

He smiled back, and gazing at Tessa lovingly he said, 'So she's learning French. I think that is charming.'

'When can I meet Philippe?' Adele now asked, peering into Jean-Claude's face.

'Soon, I think. I'm sure he will come down in fifteen minutes or so. To join us for an aperitif before dinner.'

'Oh, goodie! He's going to be my big brother, Mumma said so.'

'Of course he is . . . your mother spoke the truth.'

Adele slipped off the chair, planted her feet on the floor. Elvira said firmly, in a quiet tone, 'But you've not had any dessert.'

'Thank you, but I don't want any, Elvira.' Reaching for Jean-Claude's hand, the child went on, 'Can we go to the little room? So I can watch my Cinderella tape? Please, Jean-Claude.'

'And why not,' he replied, rising, winking at Tessa and taking Adele's hand firmly in his.

The child swung her head and exclaimed in her high little girl's voice, 'Thank you, Lourdes ... *merci beaucoup*.' And then she and Jean-Claude left the kitchen.

CHAPTER TWENTY

Whatever they said about him, no one could ever accuse him of not being thorough. He had been trained by Emma Harte to be just that, and she had instilled in him the absolute need to pay attention to detail, and, most importantly, to leave nothing to chance.

His thoroughness had now brought him to this desk at six-thirty in the evening, where he sat down and opened the black leather binder that held all of the information he had garnered about the Hughes family.

From the moment Evan Hughes had been pronounced one of the great-granddaughters of Emma Harte, Jonathan Ainsley had employed a team of American and British investigators to provide him with everything he needed to know about each and every one of the Hughes family. Cover all your bases, that was *his* motto.

His eyes settled on the name ANGHARAD HUGHES, and he scanned the page which told him a few things about her. Twenty-three years old. An abandoned baby who had been adopted by Marietta and Owen Hughes when she was only a few months old. Reasonably well educated. An expert in Georgian antiques, trained by her father. Considered wild in her teenage years. Sexually attractive to men of all ages. *Well, he knew that, didn't he?* Beautiful. *He was very well aware of this, also.* Not very close to her sisters Evan and Elayne; something of a loner, in fact. Closer to her mother than to Owen Hughes. Never really a favourite of her grandmother, Glynnis Hughes. Etcetera, etcetera.

Jonathan sighed and closed the leather binder. He had had all this information for months; obviously nothing new had come up on her, or any of the other family members. And certainly the things he truly needed to know would never appear in a dossier.

Why was she pursuing him?

What did she want from him?

Had she been planted by the Hartes to spy on him for them?

He had voiced one of those questions in London . . . 'What do you want from me?' he had asked the night she had come for drinks with him at his flat in Grosvenor Square.

'Nothing,' she had replied. 'Just to see you. I sure thought you were the most handsome guy I'd ever seen when we bumped into each other in the village shop. But I told you that when I came to your home in Thirsk.' She had shrugged and added, 'I guess I thought you were flirting with me . . . I kind of . . . well, you know . . . fancied you.' She had shrugged again and eyed him, and he had thought: bedroom eyes, she has bedroom eyes, and wondered where that very old-fashioned expression had been dredged up from. And later that evening she had made quite sure he understood that she was available, ready, willing and able . . . and planning to stay on in Europe for a while. As long as he wanted, in fact.

He had known, been absolutely certain, that he could have taken her to bed there and then; in fact, he was very well aware that was what she wanted. But as attracted as he had been to her, he nonetheless paid attention to the small voice in his head that warned him to be cautious. The last thing he needed was a woman in his bed who was running back to the Hartes, to report to them about his sex life, his business life, his associates, and anything else she might manage to glean if she were around him for any length of time.

And so he had sent her packing that night, seen her the next afternoon for tea at the flat. And against his better judgement he had asked her to join him in Paris.

She had jumped at the invitation, and from the look on her face he had understood that she would jump through hoops for him . . . in bed. He wondered what else she would do for him if he asked her nicely?

Leaning back against the chair, Jonathan's eyes drifted around the library, his favourite room in the apartment on the Avenue Foch. It was elegant without being pretentious, and it was sumptuously comfortable. Designed by one of

Paris's leading interior designers, the library was panelled in bleached oak, furnished with priceless antiques, such as two handsome Louis XV chests and a beautiful standing clock by Le Roy, which were balanced by comfortable sofas and deep armchairs upholstered in dark red velvet. The carpet was Savonnerie and the paintings on the walls were from the Impressionist period: two were Degas ballet dancers, while an extraordinary Sisley hung over the carved antique fireplace. Whenever he looked at the latter he thought of his grandmother's Sisley, which hung at Pennistone Royal, and smiled smugly. His was so much better, one of Sisley's finest works, a true prize, something to be proud of and to cherish.

Rising, he walked over to the fireplace, and stood with his back to the logs burning brightly in the grate, his thoughts again on Angharad Hughes. He had invited her for drinks, and then dinner this evening, but he had no intention of taking her out to one of his favourite haunts. He couldn't possibly let himself be seen with her in public.

She was a beautiful young woman, underneath all that muck she put on her face. But the hair was positively ghastly. Nonetheless, he had wanted – no – needed, to see her again, to explore the *possibilities* . . . of her, to take her to bed, if only this once. Tonight. He knew there would be no argument from her; but he had to be sure she was on the level, was merely interested in a relationship with him, was not on some kind of mission to gather information.

He would assess her again when she arrived for

drinks, and make up his mind about her. Then he would have dinner with her at the apartment, whatever his final decision, and send her back to the George V if necessary, but only after he had enjoyed her company in his bedroom.

There was a knock on the door, and his houseman, Gaston, came in and stood discreetly in the doorway. 'Marie-Claire wishes to know if you would like caviare with the aperitifs, Monsieur Ainsley?'

Jonathan shook his head. 'Not this evening, Gaston, *merci*.'

The houseman nodded and withdrew, closing the door behind him as he returned to the servants' quarters of the spacious apartment.

Jonathan was not particularly crazy about caviare, disliking the strong fishy taste, and he certainly didn't want Angharad Hughes tasting and smelling of it. The last time he had eaten it was with Priscilla, on one of their hot dates in Scarborough, and the taste had lingered for too long.

Priscilla Marney. Of course. She could perhaps help him, help him to make the right assessment of the Hughes girl. Prissy had catered the wedding reception last week. And she was observant. Maybe she could enlighten him, but without knowing she was doing so. Prissy was jealous of other women, and also put out with him at the moment for cancelling their rendezvous in Thirsk. Yesterday. It was meant to have been yesterday. But if he phoned her now, and sweet-talked her, made her think he was unhappy not to have seen her, he may be able to glean a few useful titbits.

Returning to the French *bureau plat*, he sat down, picked up the receiver and dialled her number in Harrogate. She answered within seconds, and he said softly, 'Hello, Prissy darling. It's Jonathan.'

'Yes, I know,' she replied, her tone not revealing her mood to him.

'I'm calling to tell you how much I'm missing you at this very moment, sweetie. I'd really been looking forward to seeing you yesterday, having you all to myself at the house in Thirsk.'

'So had I,' she replied, still not softening.

'I know you're upset with me, Prissy, but you mustn't be. I'm going to make it up to you, I promise. I will definitely be back in Yorkshire next week, and that's why I'm calling now. I want you to come to the house in Thirsk, spend the day with me and the night, as we'd planned to do yesterday.'

When she did not respond, Jonathan said in a soft, throaty voice, 'You know I can't resist you, darling girl, and I must see you before I go to Hong Kong. Please say yes, you'd make me so happy.' He hoped he sounded appealing and sincere.

'All right,' she answered slowly, almost reluctantly. 'But you haven't said *when* next week, Jonny. I hope I can make it.'

'I was thinking of next Thursday. A week today. I'll fly in early to Yeadon, so we can meet for lunch, and then we'll have the afternoon and the evening together. How about it, sweetie? Come on, say yes, Priscilla. You know how I feel about you.'

It seemed to him that he suddenly felt the lifting of her cool, somewhat begrudging mood flowing down the telephone line. 'Oh, that's wonderful, Jonny! Yes, that's a really good day for me. And I'm missing *you*, aching to see you. I was so looking forward to our little rendezvous, I really was, and I felt really deflated yesterday, bloody let down, if you want the truth.'

'Don't be. Look what's in store for you . . . for us. Together at Thirsk. No staff. Just the two of us, having a long sexy day and night together . . . think of *that*, Prissy.'

'Oh, Jonny, yes, it'll be great!'

'My God, Prissy, you sound so loving and sexy, I wish you were here with me now . . . what I would do with you . . .'

'Oh, Jonny, *I* wish I were there, too.'

'I think we'd better change the subject,' he replied, suddenly laughing, pleased he had won her round. He could get her to eat out of his hand. 'Tell me what happened at the wedding. You weren't very forthcoming the other day.'

'Oh, I know, forgive me. But I was very upset when you cancelled our date.'

'So how did it go? What did I miss?'

'Well, you certainly missed the fireworks, if I can call it that. Linnet changed the time of the wedding. The two of them – Gideon and Evan – were married in a secret ceremony at eight-fifteen in the morning.'

'Oh, really! Why was that?' He made himself sound surprised.

'Evan hasn't been feeling well. The twins are due in March, but she looks awfully ready to give birth. Anyway, she hadn't been up to snuff, and the early ceremony was just a precaution actually. According to Margaret, everyone was worried that the excitement of the ceremony with all the family in attendance might cause Evan to go into labour.'

'I see,' he said. 'But what about the reception?'

'Oh, it went very well, and I must say everyone was all turned out in their Sunday best. You'd have enjoyed it, Jonny, being with your cousins and your father.'

'Yes, I'm sure I would,' he answered in a composed, neutral tone. 'And you saw my father, did you?' he probed, wanting to bring in the Hughes family.

'Yes, looking very handsome. Marietta Hughes was looking after him; she was wonderful with him.'

'And what about her adopted daughters, Pris? What are they like? Evan's sisters? Are they as beautiful as she is?'

'Not really. Elayne is rather nice, a brunette, she's the middle one, but the youngest, Angharad, is just awful.'

'Oh dear, is she the ugly sister then?'

'Not ugly ugly,' Priscilla answered, sounding as if she disliked Angharad. 'But cheap looking. She has this horrendous hair, sort of spikey and dyed platinum. A cute face, I suppose, but she wears tons of make-up. She's got a wonderful figure, mind you, Jonny. And she acts sort of sexy. For a moment I thought Lorne might go for her, but I was mistaken. He couldn't stand her. Do you know, nobody can.'

'And why is that?' he asked, his interest fired.

'I don't know. I didn't really get to chat with her. I was very busy, you know. But later, when I was having a cup of tea with Margaret in the kitchen, she told me that none of the Harte girls like her at all. She's tried to make friends with them, but they shun her, *really shun her*. Margaret says Evan can't stand her. Neither can Gideon.' Priscilla took a deep breath, and lowering her voice she confided, 'I heard on the grapevine that Gideon blames her for Evan's accident.'

'Really! Is that so? But actually, I didn't know Evan had had an accident.' This was true; Jonathan's hand gripped the phone. 'Do tell me.'

'Apparently Evan fell in her office, before coming to Yorkshire for the wedding. She missed her chair and fell onto the floor. She had to go to hospital because everyone was certain there was going to be a miscarriage. Or problems at any rate.'

'But why would Gideon Harte think it was the sister's fault?'

'Because she visited Evan at the store unexpectedly, and they had a row. I *heard* they all believe she went there to pick a quarrel. To upset Evan. Margaret heard Marietta saying to Emily that Angharad has always been envious of Evan, and never more than now. Because of Gideon, the Hartes, and all of that stuff.'

'Oh dear, don't tell me there's trouble at t'mill,' he murmured.

'That's not just possible, it's a *probability*!' Priscilla announced. 'Evan's father and sister have gone back to New York, but then I'm sure your father told you they'd left sooner than expected.'

'Of course,' Jonathan said. He knew this, but it was not his father who had kept him so well informed. However, he had no intention of letting Priscilla know this. He asked, 'And what about the awful sister? Where is she?'

'She's in London with her mother, but I don't think she's all that welcome, as far as Evan and Gideon are concerned. Wiggs, the gardener, told me that Gideon wants her to return to the States as well. Oh, and by the way, Jonny, here's a bit of news. Tessa became engaged to the French writer.'

'Oh, yes, so I'd heard,' he exclaimed, chuckling to himself, now recognizing that what Angharad had said about some members of the family was absolutely true. 'I'm really sorry I missed the wedding,' Jonathan hurried on. 'Just think, *we* might have sneaked a few hours together over the weekend.'

'Oh, Jonny, don't tease me so . . . you're getting me going, getting me all hot and bothered.'

'Now, now, Priscilla, be a good girl until next week.'

Her answer was a long sigh.

'I'll call you on Monday, darling,' he murmured, and they hung up.

Jonathan rose, walked over to the fireplace and stood looking at his Sisley. That smug smile of his played around his mouth . . . he was not really seeing the painting, though, only Angharad Hughes. In his mind's eye. So they didn't like her, eh? None of them, or so it seemed. Perhaps she was the genuine

300

thing after all. Just a hot little girl on the make, looking for a rich older man to be her sugar daddy, to take care of her. Well, why not? He wouldn't object to that.

He experienced a little rush of excitement . . . for her. He couldn't wait for her to arrive now. He wanted to study her once again, question her, get her view of the Hughes family and the Hartes. It might be very telling, and certainly interesting. His best champagne would loosen her tongue, no doubt. But then again, she sounded like a girl after his own heart; she might even be very useful to him, especially if he asked the right questions. That was always the key, wasn't it? Asking the right questions. That way you usually got the right answers.

When, an hour later, Angharad Hughes walked into the library, Jonathan was pleasantly surprised. On the few occasions he had seen her she had been badly dressed. But tonight she looked quite stylish in a black wool dress, very high-heeled black shoes worn with lacey black stockings. The stockings were all wrong, and the dress was cut far too low, but what an improvement. She had made an effort for him, or so it appeared.

He rose from the chair, moved across the floor to greet her as Gaston showed her in and then swiftly departed.

'Hi!' she said as they met in the middle of the room.

'It's nice to see you again,' he replied in a neutral voice, stretching out his hand.

She took it in hers, shook it, and then moved closer, stood on tiptoe and kissed him on the cheek. 'That's what *I* feel like doing!' she exclaimed, eyeing him flirtatiously. 'I expect you think I'm forward, don't you?'

'Not really,' he said, allowing a smile to surface. 'A little bold perhaps, but certainly a girl who knows what she wants.' Drawing her towards the fireplace, he said, 'I hope you like champagne, or do you want something else?'

'I want a lot of things, but sure, the champagne is fine for now.' As she spoke Angharad took a seat on the large sofa, and patted the cushion next to her. 'Why don't you sit here?'

Preferring to keep his distance for the moment, Jonathan shook his head. 'I'm going to sit opposite you . . . so I can look at you, my dear.'

'And do you like what you see, then?'

'I like the way you're dressed this evening, Angharad. You look quite elegant.'

'I know that's what you like – elegance, stylishness. I'm not too sure of myself with clothes . . . You'll have to help me. You will, won't you? Teach me, I mean?'

'About clothes?'

She gave him a long appraising look, and said, 'Yes, what did you think I meant?'

He was wondering how to reply, whether to lead her on or not, when the door opened to admit Gaston, which saved him the trouble of answering her.

Gaston placed the tray he was carrying on a table

set up for that purpose, and after popping the cork he poured the Dom Perignon into crystal champagne flutes, brought them over to the fireplace on a silver tray.

'*Merci*, Gaston,' Jonathan said. 'I'll ring when I need you.'

'*Oui, monsieur.*'

Once they were alone, Jonathan stood up, went over to the sofa and touched his glass to Angharad's. 'Happy days!' he said, immediately stepping back, sitting down in the chair again.

'And happy nights!' she said.

It took all of his self-control to keep his face straight, and he remembered how he had thought her a little tease the day she had appeared unannounced at his house in Thirsk. She had displayed the same suggestive characteristics then, said similarly cheeky things. Well, she *was* only twenty-three. Was this the way the young behaved these days? He thought of Jasmine Wu-Jen and her superb elegance and sophistication, and shoved the thought to one side. He did not want to be burdened with *those* memories tonight.

Angharad said, 'I told you in London, I was real disappointed you didn't come to the wedding. I was looking all over for you. Why didn't you come?'

'Unfortunately, I had an emergency in London.' He frowned. 'I thought I told you that on Monday, when you came for drinks.'

'You didn't say *emergency*, you said you had a pressing appointment. Was it with a woman?'

'That's none of your business.'

'I know. But was it?'

He shook his head in exasperation, slightly annoyed, and then found himself saying, much to his surprise, 'No, it wasn't, it was business.'

'That's great,' she answered, crossing her legs, smiling at him, then taking a sip of the champagne. She eyed him over the glass, slightly parting her lips as they lingered on the rim. 'If you'd been at the wedding I was going to get you into a quiet place, just so I could . . . you know, get close to you . . . maybe even smooch with you. Would you have . . . kissed me back?'

Startled by the question, he lifted his glass, took a sip from it, settled in the chair, regarding her thoughtfully. She had the most extraordinary legs, long and shapely, and the tight-fitting dress revealed voluptuous breasts and a beautiful figure. She moved suddenly, pushed herself deeper into the cushions on the sofa and immediately her skirt rode up; he caught his breath as he realized she was not wearing underwear – at least not much.

Jonathan stood, walked over to the table and poured himself another glass of champagne, returned to his chair, asking as he did, 'Was it a nice wedding? Did you enjoy it?'

'No, I didn't!' She said this sharply, sat up a bit straighter, smoothed her skirt.

Her expression had instantly changed, he noticed. Her face was tight, suddenly tense, and there was an unexpected hardness in her dark brown eyes. 'Because I wasn't there, is that the reason?' he probed, wanting to lead her on, discover her true feelings.

'No, not really. I was *disappointed* you weren't there, but I knew I'd see you in London. You said you'd have me over for drinks. I didn't enjoy the wedding because . . . my parents were caught up in Evan, Elayne was being mean to me, and everyone else was cold and . . . uppity. Snobs, the lot of them.'

'So that's what you think about my family, is it?' he asked, his eyes narrowing.

'*You* think it, too, don't you?' she shot back swiftly.

He was silent, staring at her with growing interest.

She said, 'I've heard whispers about you. I've heard that you're the black sheep. Are you?'

A slow smile spread across his lean, handsome face, and his bluish-grey eyes twinkled. 'I've heard that rumour, too, Angharad, but it doesn't do to listen to rumours, you know.'

She laughed, leaned back against the cushions once more, and he caught a glimpse of a red garter belt as her skirt rose, and quickly glanced away. 'I hope you *are* the black sheep. I love black sheep,' she said.

'Do you now?' He put his glass down and leaned forward, closer to her, his eyes on hers. 'And why is that?'

Laughing quietly, Angharad pushed herself up, staring back at him. Provocatively, she licked her lower lip, said very softly, 'Because I'm the black sheep in my family. Well, they don't call me *that*, but they've always said I'm . . . a bad girl.'

'And are you, my dear?'

'What do you think? Sure I am, and I love it, love being a bad girl up to her wicked games.'

'And what are those?' he demanded in a low, amused tone.

She patted the cushion, 'Come on over, I'll whisper in your ear. Better still, I'll show you.'

Since he had decided to take her to bed tonight, Jonathan saw no reason why he shouldn't start the proceedings a little earlier than planned, and went to join her on the sofa.

Immediately, she took hold of his hand and brought his palm to her mouth, licking it then letting it go. Gazing up at him, she leaned closer to him, and whispered, 'On Monday night you asked me what I want from you. I never said. Shall I tell you now?'

He nodded, intrigued. It seemed to him that sex emanated from her, was like a haze around her, and when she said nothing, he pressed, 'So tell me, what *do* you want from me?'

There was a little silence; finally she said, '*Everything*. That's what I want. *You*. All of you. And you can have all of me. I'll even give up the other men for you.'

His bright, intelligent eyes, now brimming with shrewdness and calculation, roamed over her and he said softly, 'Would you give up *everybody* for me?'

She gaped at him, not understanding, exclaimed, 'I have nobody else to give up, only my boyfriends. Who do you mean?' Unexpectedly, the answer came to her at once, and she cried, '*Them*. Do you mean them? My father and mother, my sisters?'

He nodded, his eyes not leaving her face.

She began to laugh hilariously before shaking her head and explaining, 'They don't mean anything to me. Anyway, they gave *me* up a long time ago. They've only ever been interested in Evan. She's the biological child. I'm the adoptee.'

'*Adoptee*. That's a strange way to describe yourself, Angharad.'

'That's Linnet's name for me, for *us*. She calls me and Elayne the adoptees . . . I heard her say it.'

'That's not nice, but rather typical of the Hartes, I must admit. And how do you feel, Angharad?'

'I couldn't care less.'

'What I meant was, do you feel like an adoptee?'

'I've always felt like an adopted girl. It doesn't matter, though, I'm my own woman. I have been for as long as I can remember. I said to hell with them a long time ago.'

'I understand . . .' His voice trailed off. She was gazing at him with such intensity and there was such a look of yearning on her face that he was quite startled. For a moment she was utterly vulnerable.

Angharad said in a low voice, 'In the village shop . . . I wanted to grab hold of you and kiss you. Did you feel like that?'

'I was certainly attracted to you . . . didn't you notice that I flirted with you a little bit?' He smiled faintly, remembering.

'I did.' Leaning against him, she kissed him on the mouth.

He was taken by surprise, but found himself kissing her back, not resisting as her tongue slipped into his mouth and her hand slid onto his crotch. Although she was exciting him, he took hold of her hand, lifted it off and then drew away from her. 'Let's not rush this,' he murmured.

Without saying a word, Angharad swung her legs across his lap, took hold of his hand and lifted her skirt. 'Feel how much I want you,' she whispered.

CHAPTER TWENTY-ONE

The child carried the small bouquet of flowers in one hand, and held onto her father's hand with the other. Together they walked down the corridor which led to Molly Caldwell's room at Leeds Infirmary.

'Is Grandma going to come home with us, Daddy?' Atlanta asked anxiously, looking up at Dusty. 'Is her leg better?'

'I think it is, yes,' he responded in a low voice, smiling, wanting to be reassuring. 'Still, she might need a bit more rest, sweetheart.'

The little girl nodded her head, made no comment, and a moment later they were standing outside Molly's room. Bending down, Dusty explained, 'We can't stay long you know, we mustn't tire Grandma. But guess what, I've got a surprise for you.'

'A surprise? What is it?' she asked excitedly.

'If I tell you now it won't be a surprise,' he teased.

'Please, Daddy,' Atlanta beseeched, her blue eyes

looking soulful in her heart-shaped face.

'I'll tell you half of it now, okay?'

She smiled at him beguilingly and nodded.

'India's coming to lunch with us, after we've visited Grandma.'

A huge smile illuminated her face and she squeezed his hand. 'I'm glad Indi's coming with us! What's the rest of the surprise?'

'Oh, no, Miss Nosey Parker, you'll have to wait for that.' With that, he knocked on the door lightly, turned the knob and walked in, saying quietly, 'Here we are, Molly.'

Molly Caldwell's face lit up at the sight of Dusty and her granddaughter in the doorway. 'Come in, come in,' she exclaimed, her weary face a picture of sudden happiness, her eyes shining.

Letting go of her father's hand, Atlanta half ran, half skipped across the hospital room, and when she got to the bed she thrust the flowers at Molly. 'These are for you, Grandma.'

'Aren't you a little love,' Molly said, her eyes settling on Atlanta's face as she searched for signs of change. Atlanta looked perfectly beautiful, her cheeks pink and healthy, her blue eyes as bright as bluebells and her hair a shining mop of dark curls.

'You're such a pretty girl, darling. *My* pretty girl.' Leaning forward, she kissed Atlanta's cheek and brought the child closer so that she could embrace her, then said, 'We'd best put the flowers in water, don't you think?'

'Good idea,' Dusty agreed, closing the door and

walking over to the bed. 'Perhaps I should give them to one of the nurses?'

'Yes, you should.'

Dusty bent and kissed Molly on the cheek, his eyes quickly scanning her face as he tried to ascertain how she was, how much progress she had made. 'How do you feel?'

'Much, much better indeed ... They've been wonderful to me here, I'll be on my feet in no time.' Leaning back against the pillows, she continued, 'Would you take the flowers now, please, Dusty, so that they can be put in water? And thank you for bringing them, they're beautiful.'

He simply smiled at her, saying nothing, took the flowers from her and moved away. He strode over to the door and went in search of a nurse and a vase.

Atlanta moved nearer to her grandmother and took hold of her hand which rested on top of the sheet. 'I'm glad your leg's better ... Did it hurt, Grandma?' she asked, her head on one side, a questioning look on her face.

Molly shook her head. 'Not really, darling, just a little bit.'

Atlanta continued to gaze at Molly, her eyes solemn, her voice serious when she said, 'You didn't cry when you fell down ... you were brave.'

'Mmmm,' was all that Molly could say. She was suddenly unable to speak. She was filled with emotion. She loved her three-year-old granddaughter more than anything in this world, wished she could live long enough to see her grow to womanhood. But she knew that was not to be. Swallowing, blinking back the tears, Molly said, 'And have you enjoyed staying at Willows Hall with Daddy?'

'Oh, yes, Valetta's nice and so is Paddy, and Angelina. But I miss you, Grandma. Come home.' As she spoke her voice quavered slightly and her eyes grew large in her delicate face.

'I will, as soon as I can, but in the meantime I think it's nice for you to stay with your father.' Molly tightened her grip on the child's hand, and gently pulled her forward so that they were closer together, their faces almost cheek to cheek.

Against Atlanta's hair, she said softly, 'I want to tell you something about your father, Atlanta. He's such a *good* man, kind and gentle, but also very strong and dependable and trustworthy.' Molly paused, leaned away, and studied her granddaughter. 'Oh, I do hope you understand what I'm saying, lovey,' she murmured. 'But you're so young.' Bringing a smile to her face, Molly added in a stronger voice, 'Your father loves you very much, wants only the best for you. Remember that. Always listen to him and do what he says.'

Atlanta blinked, drew even closer to her grandmother, kissed her cheek. Her voice was a whisper when she said, 'I love my daddy.' Looking suddenly sad, the child touched Molly's cheek. Molly caught her hand in hers, kissed it, wondering what would happen when she was gone. But Dusty wouldn't let her down; she had confidence in him. He would withstand all pressure from Melinda, she was certain of that.

Atlanta asked, 'Can you come and live at Willows Hall, Grandma? And Gladys? Can she come, too?'

'Perhaps. It would be lovely, all of us together, wouldn't it?'

Atlanta nodded, her face lighting up. 'And Indi, too. She's nice, Grandma! We're having lunch, do you want to come?'

'I'd love to, but I just told you, I have to stay in the hospital for a while. When I come home we'll have that lunch, *a special lunch*, just the three of us. You and India and me.'

'I wish you could come home now,' Atlanta persisted, her face as solemn as her voice was plaintive.

The door suddenly opened, interrupting them. Dusty was standing there, a big smile on his face. 'I found the other half of your surprise, Beanshoot,' he exclaimed, and he stepped aside to reveal Gladys, who was hovering immediately behind him. 'Look who's here!'

'Gladys!' Atlanta cried and ran to hug her friend. Gladys hugged her back. Then releasing Atlanta after planting a big kiss on her cheek, she went over to Molly.

'Hello, Gladys dear, thanks for coming.'

'It's good to see you looking so much better,' Gladys answered, meaning every word. Molly had improved in the last few days. 'And I'm sorry I couldn't come yesterday, but I was seeing my sister off. To Canada.'

'Oh, she's gone, has she?'

'Yes. And she's much better, fully recovered, and we've mended all of our fences.'

Molly murmured, 'Doesn't do for sisters to quarrel. I'm glad all is right again.'

'Right as rain.'

'It was India's idea actually,' Dusty said, pulling a chair up to the bed and sitting down in it. 'She thought that you and I would have a few minutes alone to chat, if I sent Gladys with Atlanta to pick her up at the store.'

'That was clever, and I *am* glad to have you to myself for a few minutes,' Molly replied, leaning back against the pillows. 'I'm so happy you brought Atlanta, Dusty. I've missed her, and I've been longing to see her.' She gave him a warm smile, and added, 'And she's doing so well with you, but then she always has. She's happy to be with you, and she loves India, from what she says.'

'*You* haven't said if you're coming to the wedding, Molly. It would please us both so much if you would. I'll arrange everything for you, make it as easy as possible . . . the travel, all that.'

There was a small silence.

Molly Caldwell stared at him, at a loss; her face was unreadable.

Dusty swallowed, held his breath, waiting for her response. He wouldn't have even brought this matter up a few days ago, since he had believed her to be at death's door. But she looked so much better today that he had been taken by surprise; since arriving here this morning he had reversed his opinion. Maybe she wasn't in danger of dying after all, at least not yet, perhaps not for a long while.

Clearing her throat, Molly finally said, 'You know I'll come if I can. It pleases me that you've found the right woman, someone you can share your life with. It also comforts me that Atlanta will have a mother when I'm no longer here to look after her. Remember, Melinda can never have her, Dusty. I told you that when I first came into the Infirmary, after my heart attack.'

'Yes, you did, but don't you think Melinda would fight me? I don't believe she would let me have custody of Atlanta without a struggle.'

'What you say is true. On the other hand, if you have a good solicitor representing you I think you would win, and perhaps without even having to go into a court of law.' A sudden sadness swept across Molly's face, and she sighed heavily as she thought of her only child, a young woman lost to her, lost to everyone for so long now. A ruined life, a wasted life, she thought, then, taking a grip on herself, she said in a voice laden with sorrow, 'You wouldn't find it difficult to prove she's an unfit mother, and that is exactly what you must do if . . . I die . . . when I die, I mean.'

'Because of the drugs, the drinking?' Dusty began and then stopped, shaking his head. 'You don't think the de-tox clinic is working, do you?'

'Perhaps it is, for the moment. But I know her only too well, and I know she'll soon be up to her old ways . . . She has the wrong friends, Dusty, as you well know, and she goes right back to them every time she's clean. It's only a matter of days before she's hooked on drugs yet again.' Molly fell silent for a moment, before she finished, 'She's my daughter, and I love her, but I can't help her, I don't think anyone can. And so I must think of her child instead, my granddaughter, *your* child, Dusty. *What's best for Atlanta*, that's all I can think about these days. You have to promise me again that you will fight to gain *sole* custody of Atlanta.'

'I promised you before, and I promise you again,' Dusty reassured her. 'I'm fully aware that Melinda is a lost cause . . . If only I could help her – I've tried, Molly.'

'Nobody could have tried harder, and you've been wonderful to her, and to your child. And to me as well, and for that I am ever so grateful.' Leaning forward, Molly now took hold of his hand and held onto it tightly. 'I want to impress something on you, Dusty . . . something you must never forget. Atlanta would be in mortal danger if she lived with her mother. Melinda is careless, irresponsible, selfish, and undisciplined. And uncontrollable when she's drunk or doped up. Please don't ever let that innocent child be alone with her mother *ever*—' Molly's voice broke and tears came into her eyes. She began to weep.

Dusty put his arms around her, held her close, trying to comfort her, wanting to give her a measure of peace, to make her understand that he *understood* all that Melinda was. Molly's words had been unremitting, stark in their unvarnished honesty and truth. He would never forget them.

'Please don't upset yourself so, Molly, you know

you can rely on me,' he said, stroking her back, continuing to hold her in his arms.

After a few minutes, Molly's weeping became quieter, and eventually it abated. With an effort, she pulled away from him and looked up into his face. 'I'm sorry,' she whispered, 'I didn't mean to break down like that, Dusty. It's just that I worry about Atlanta all the time; she's so small and vulnerable, so defenceless.'

'But she has me, and I will never let anything happen to her.'

Molly nodded, reached for a tissue on the bed-side table and dried her eyes. 'I trust you. Forgive my tears.'

'There's nothing to forgive.' Wanting to change the subject, to cheer her up, Dusty now exclaimed, 'When I spoke to Gladys last night, asked her to join us here today, she told me that she would be available to help me out, do a bit of baby-sitting for me. That was good news.'

'The best,' Molly agreed. 'Now that her sister Gertrude has gone back to Canada, and as long as I'm in the Infirmary, she's available. She loves Atlanta, and the child is happy with her, she's used to being with Gladys. They get on well.'

'That's the impression I got.' Dusty said, 'You haven't told me what the doctors say, Molly. How are you, really?'

'Dr Bloom's a bit noncommittal, he doesn't say much,' she answered, 'but then he's my general practitioner, and he put me in the hands of a heart specialist. As far as the specialist here at the Infirmary is concerned, I'm on the mend. He's a good man, Mr Laver. That's my news.'

Dusty felt a lightening of his worry, a lessening of the tension in him. 'What great news it is! I'm thankful you're going to get better, Molly. To tell you the honest truth, I've been worried to death about you.'

'I know. But it'll be all right. I'll be all right. You'll see.'

It did Molly Caldwell's heart good to see her grand-daughter getting on so well with India Standish. The young woman who was going to marry Dusty Rhodes was beautiful in a delicate, cool blonde way. But her looks were not all that important to the older woman. What pleased Molly, and gave her such reassurance, was the gentleness and kindness she detected in India. That she loved Atlanta was patently obvious, and the feeling was undoubtedly mutual.

Her mood was one of optimism and relief. Gladys and Atlanta had returned with India, and suddenly her little hospital room at Leeds Infirmary seemed crowded, especially since Dusty's presence was so potent. He seemed to take up all the space. For a moment or two she studied him surreptitiously, trying to see him objectively.

That he was handsome there was no question; his dark good looks were strong and somewhat rough-hewn, as if he had been carved from some great and ancient boulder dragged down from the moors. Heathcliff, she suddenly thought. Grandly masculine, carved from granite in great strokes, a thing of nature, mythic, powerful, gypsy dark. It was the eyes of course that bespoke his lightness, his spirituality, his sensitive nature. A deeper blue than the speedwells that grew in the fields below the moors, bluer than the sky that soared above, they were a supernatural blue.

And then there was his talent. A gift from God. Talent such as his was rare, sublime, transporting in its beauty. Molly Caldwell had always admired artistic talent, whatever field the artist had chosen. Yet she especially loved the visual arts, and Dusty's paintings had stunned and beguiled her long before she met him, before he had known Melinda and fathered her granddaughter.

There was no hope for her own child, not anymore. Melinda was on a journey of self-destruction, a journey she had embarked upon long before Dusty Rhodes had strolled casually by and fallen, momentarily, into her sexual trap. He had been wise to move out and on, Molly understood that. He was a man with a purpose in life, a talent he needed to use, great ambition to fulfil. He had wasted little time with the demented woman Melinda had become.

It was only later, when he had discovered there was to be a baby, his baby, that he had done the correct thing, done an about turn and come back to Melinda. But he had not remained long in that maddening circus of dysfunction, a circus populated with her crazy and crazed friends. Instead he had moved on again, knowing he must save himself, accepting with the best will in the world that he could not save her.

Dusty had been a good father – diligent, responsible, caring and loving. He must have Atlanta, she said to herself silently, as she watched him now, holding Atlanta on his knee, turning to talk to India . . . there was so much love in his eyes for them both. It brought a flush of genuine happiness to Molly's face, and she looked intently at Gladys, who nodded, understanding exactly what she was feeling, also recognizing that this room, at this moment, was full of unconditional love.

CHAPTER TWENTY-TWO

Linnet knew the moment she walked into Paula's office that her mother was annoyed with her. So sure was she of this, she hurried forward, exclaiming, 'Hello, Mummy,' and sat down in the chair opposite her, determined to jump-start the conversation, before Paula had a chance to say anything.

'Good morning, Linnet,' Paula replied, looking up from the papers spread out on her desk. 'I under-stand—'

'Oh, Mummy, I'm sorry to interrupt, but before we get into a discussion about the Easter Fashion Week, I just want to explain something.' As she spoke, Linnet took a sheet of paper out of a folder, continuing, 'I've written you a memo about a plan I have. I just finished it early this morning, and I want you to have it now.' Linnet leaned across the desk and handed the memo to Paula.

'Thank you.' Paula scanned it swiftly, and said, 'Well, I'm relieved to have something on paper. Your father mentioned to me that he had spoken earlier to Bonnadell Enloe, and that she told him in passing that you'd been making inquiries about her spas. Do you have an idea about opening one of her spas here at the store? Is that why you called her?'

Leaning forward, her expression eager, Linnet exclaimed, 'Yes. I do! That's what my memo is about.'

'But where would we put a spa?' Paula asked, her voice rising.

'Where the hairdressing salon is now. It's really quite large and—'

'And where will the hair salon go? There's no other available space,' Paula cut in, sounding suddenly exasperated and annoyed. Her irritation showed on her face.

'I explain that in the memo, but frankly, I don't think we need a hair salon anymore. Business has been awfully slack lately. In my opinion, that space would be better utilized as a spa.'

Paula was flabbergasted, and she sat back in her chair, staring at her daughter in disbelief. 'What makes you think a spa will do any better than the hairdressing salon?' she demanded in a cold tone.

'Women love spas. Especially young women who work hard. They enjoy relaxing at a day spa, having a massage, a facial, pedicures, manicures, and other special treatments. I think we'd have a big success if we opened one.'

'Do you really?' Paula shot back, still sounding sharp and put out. 'And have you considered the cost of remodelling the space? It will be enormous.'

'But it won't,' Linnet countered. 'Once the hair

salon equipment is removed, like the banquettes, hairdriers, and sinks, we'll be left with a large empty space. All we have to do is build wooden cubicles, little individual areas of enclosed space for the massages and treatments. I've got it all worked out, and I believe that an Enloe spa would work in the store just as well as they work in Dad's hotels around the world.'

'I don't know about this, Linnet, I think it will be a lot more costly to remodel and rebuild that space than you think. Furthermore, I'm not sure you're right about getting rid of the hair salon. And who's going to run the spa, if we should build one? The store? Or the Enloe Company?'

'I'm not sure, I hadn't quite figured that out. But it might be simpler for us if we did use the Enloe Company. That's why I put a call into Bonnadell on Friday.' Linnet gave a little laugh. 'She didn't waste much time in telling Dad, did she?'

'No, she didn't. She spoke with him early this morning about something else, but your call came up. Anyway, for what it's worth, I think she's very interested in the idea of a spa at Harte's of Knightsbridge, but—'

'Oh, Mummy, that's great!'

'But that doesn't mean that *I am*, Linnet,' Paula pressed on. 'I will have to give this considerable thought. I'm not sure you're correct, you know. And if the Enloe Company are running the spa, how are we going to make money, tell me that? What's in it for Harte's? I really think you have to do a great deal of research on this—'

The shrilling of the phone brought Paula up short, and she picked up her private line. 'Paula O'Neill here.'

'Hello, Paula, it's Sarah. Sorry I couldn't phone you earlier. I had some meetings with two of my suppliers, and they went on longer than I expected. Anyway, here I am, reporting in as promised.'

'I'm assuming you and Yves had dinner with our cousin on Saturday.'

'No, Paula, we didn't. But only because Jonathan asked to change the date to Sunday evening. Of course I agreed, because I'd promised you I'd do it, and as it turned out Sunday was far better for Yves. So . . . we met him at the Relais Plaza in the Plaza Athénée last night.' There was a pause at the other end of the line and Sarah sneezed, then said, 'Sorry about that,' and went on, 'We met for drinks and dinner and—'

'Was the girl in question with him? Or was it his protégée, so called?' Paula interrupted, anxious and now growing impatient to know.

'It was Angharad Hughes, she's his protégée, and do I have a story for you!'

'I'm all ears, I can't wait to hear everything. But would you mind if I put you on the speaker phone, Sarah? I have Linnet here with me . . . Linnet, say hello to Sarah.'

Taking the phone from her mother, Linnet said, 'Hello, Auntie Sarah. Thanks for helping with this. Mummy's been so anxious and worried about J.A. And upset, especially about the church being damaged.'

'I can well imagine, Linnet. Jonathan's become troublesome. Well, I hope we get to see you when you next come to Paris. Now, may I speak with your mother, please?'

'Here she is.' Linnet handed the phone back to Paula.

'So, Sarah, tell me the story. And may I put you on the speaker?'

'*Absolutely*. No problem. So here goes. It was certainly Angharad Hughes who accompanied him, but a very different Angharad Hughes than *you* could ever *imagine*, I'm quite certain of that.'

'What on earth do you mean?' Paula asked, mystified.

'I think I'd better begin this story at the beginning,' Sarah announced, her lovely voice echoing around Paula's private office. 'Early on Friday morning, I had a call from Jonathan, asking if he could possibly change the dinner date to Sunday. After I'd agreed, he said he needed a favour. When I asked him what that was, he explained he wanted my advice about women's hairdressers, also where to buy elegant women's clothes. When I suggested couture houses such as Pierre Balmain, Valentino and Givenchy, he said he didn't have time to wait for pieces of haute couture to be made to measure. He needed the clothes at once.'

Sarah paused for a split second, and Linnet exclaimed, 'Don't tell me he got her all dressed up in couture! *Not Angharad*. What a laugh that is! She's such a strange-looking girl, a bit cheap-looking actually.'

'I know what you mean,' Sarah continued. 'Anyway, I agreed to make a hair appointment with a good hairdresser, either Carita or Alexandre, and told him I would take him to Madame Valencia, the woman who makes some of my clothes. She has a small *atelier* on Avenue Montaigne and usually has a small selection of elegant, handmade pieces in stock. He told me the young woman was of medium height and a size eight. Like you, I was very anxious to find out what their relationship was. I got there early and picked out a few things. When he arrived with Angharad I was appalled by her appearance. She was lathered in heavy make-up, and oh, dear, that frightful platinum-blonde hair. I couldn't believe my eyes.'

'So he bought her some chic clothes and did a make-over on her, is that what you're saying, Sarah?' Paula asked, instantly understanding that if Jonathan Ainsley was going to all that trouble he was embarking on a special relationship with Angharad. If he were not, if he were treating her merely as a one-night stand, he wouldn't be buying her stylish clothes. She said this to Sarah, who agreed with Paula. 'He's spent *real* money already on her.'

'I'm very curious,' Linnet interjected. 'What did he select for her?'

'A tailored grey-flannel skirt suit, which I'd liked and had pulled out for him to look at. The jacket had a feeling of Givenchy to it, and there was a silk camisole, which also fit her. He spotted a grey-wool overcoat, trimmed down the front with chinchilla. That was another choice, along with a plain black day dress and a cashmere overcoat, as well as a black velvet cocktail suit,' Sarah finished, then added, 'That was about it, except for accessories.'

'And how did she look in the clothes?' Linnet asked, riddled with curiosity. 'I mean, the clothes didn't change her *looks*, did they?'

'No, of course they didn't,' Sarah replied. 'But they fitted her well, and suited her. After buying grey and black shoes, bags to match and gloves at Madame Valencia's accessory boutique, Jonathan took her off to Carita to have her hair done.'

'Just finish about her appearance,' Paula requested. 'What did she wear on Sunday night and how did she look?'

'She looked absolutely stunning. I hardly recognized her, to be honest,' Sarah confided, and then she rushed on, 'She was wearing the grey flannel suit, grey overcoat, and the grey accessories. But that wasn't the point. What stunned me was her hair. It had been dyed a lovely rich russet brown and had a few blonde highlights. All that heavy make-up had disappeared, too. She looked very fresh-faced, with a lot of emphasis on her eyes, well applied make-up. But just a light dusting of powder on her face and pale pink lipstick.'

'How very interesting,' Paula murmured thoughtfully. 'So it appears that he is extremely taken with her, wouldn't you say, Sarah?'

'Yes, indeed. Frankly, he's transformed her, well, at least her appearance. Yves thought she had the look of a young Audrey Hepburn, and, to be honest, so did I. By the way, she was wearing pearl-and-diamond earrings which looked real, but obviously they could have been fake.'

'To my way of thinking,' Paula remarked, 'this kind of attention means he's sleeping with her and plans on keeping her around. At least for a while. But is it merely a personal relationship or do you think he is using her as a conduit to us through her mother? *That* is the crucial question, one which concerns me.'

'Look, it's hard to say whether or not she's supplying him with information about the Hartes, how could I possibly know *that*?' Sarah answered swiftly and in all honesty. 'But I will hazard a guess . . . I believe it to be more of a sexual liaison than anything else.'

'What brings you to that belief?' Paula asked, even though she trusted Sarah's judgement.

'Angharad's obviously hugely besotted with him, hangs on his every word, clings to him. At least she did on Sunday evening over drinks and dinner,' Sarah explained. 'As for Jonathan, he can't take his eyes off her, nor can he keep his hands off her either. The lust, the passion were obvious not only to me but to Yves as well. My husband, by the way, thought she oozed sex appeal,' Sarah finished with a small dry laugh of amusement.

'I'm hoping it *is* a sexual affair, and nothing else,' Paula informed Sarah, her voice suddenly brisk. 'She's too close for comfort, as far as Evan and Gideon are concerned.'

'Yes, I know,' Sarah answered quietly, understanding Paula's worries and all the ramifications. 'But if this is any consolation, I think he might actually be falling for her. *Hard*. In a serious way . . . I've never seen him act quite like this since the days of Arabella Sutton.'

'What makes you say that?' Paula asked, her tone still crisp, businesslike and commanding.

'The look in his eyes, the expression on his face, the way he's somewhat . . . *solicitous* of Angharad. He was very much in love with Arabella Sutton, and when it all blew up he was devastated. Truly he was, Paula. I know because I got him through that awful period years ago. He's never loved a woman since . . . oh, he's had plenty, that I know only too well since I've usually had to entertain them. But this one, well, it could be the real thing just as it was with Arabella. To quote Yves, and if you'll excuse the expression, Angharad's got him by the short hairs, she's sexually entrapped him, that's what Yves said when we got home on Sunday evening. And Yves has a lot of insight into our cousin.'

'I see.' There was a moment's silence on Paula's part, and then she asked, 'Are you planning to see them again?'

'Oh, yes, since I promised to help you with the situation. I invited them to dinner later this week. Jonathan's going to let me know, but he did murmur something about taking off for Hong Kong. I must tell you, Paula, Angharad looked crushed when he said this, and Jonathan quickly added that he wanted to show her the sights. So he's obviously hooked.'

'For the moment,' Linnet remarked pithily. 'But we can't leave things to chance, Mummy.' All of her attention was on Paula when she added, 'Evan and Gideon have to be informed of this development at once, and so does Marietta. In fact, the entire Hughes family has to know. They have to be warned not to give Angharad any information about Evan's movements, or any of our movements, for that matter.'

'You're absolutely right,' Paula responded, nodding. 'And what's your opinion, Sarah?'

'The same as Linnet's. They should be warned off her, warned to keep her at arm's length.'

'I think she ought to be ostracized by the family, cut off completely,' Linnet announced in a tough voice. 'As a matter of fact, I'm going to see that this happens. And immediately. We can't afford any slip-ups here.'

'That might not be necessary, Linnet,' Paula pointed out. 'It could be that her family will do that without any encouragement from you.'

'True,' Linnet conceded, although she didn't entirely agree with her mother's assessment of the Hughes family.

After thanking Sarah and asking her to continue to socialize with Jonathan, Paula hung up, switched off the speaker phone and stared across the desk at Linnet. 'I know you'll talk to Evan and Gid, but what about Marietta? Are you sure you want to break this news to her, or should I do it perhaps?'

'Oh, Mummy, don't bother, you've so much on your plate all of the time. I'll talk to her later today. I think I have to do it in person actually, don't you?'

'That would be nicer.'

'I like Marietta, she's a lovely woman, and I think she's going to be horrified when she hears about Angharad's behaviour.'

'Very disloyal.' Paula shook her head. 'But then I've gained the impression that Angharad's not on such good terms with anyone.'

'No, she's not. Leave it to me. By the way, what do you think of Sarah's opinion about the situation?'

'She's always been very intelligent, smart, and sharp-eyed. So I tend to trust her judgement. And I am absolutely certain she *is* on our side. She thinks he's dangerous. Sarah's been turned off Jonathan for a long time now, and only stays in touch with him to help me.'

'You do really believe that, don't you, Mummy?'

'Yes, I do, Linnet. I trust Sarah all the way . . . you see she wants very much to be part of the family. She'll do anything she can to get back into my good books again.'

Linnet nodded. 'Okay. Anyway, about the spa idea, will you consider it?'

'I'll *think* about it. But I'm not sure you're right about closing down the hair salon . . .' Paula's voice trailed off. Her head was buzzing and she suddenly felt tired out, yet the clock on her desk told her it was only eleven o'clock. Taking a deep breath, she went on slowly, 'Do the research I need, Linnet, and then we'll talk again.'

'I'll have it for you in a few days, Mummy. In the meantime, did you call me in to talk about the Fashion Week at Easter? Or the spa idea?'

'The spa, actually. I was curious after your father mentioned you'd been talking to Bonnadell Enloe.'

'I see.'

Leaning across her desk, Paula said in a warmer tone, 'There's another thing, Linny, don't you think you have your hands full at the moment? Evan's on maternity leave for three months and Tessa's now engaged to Jean-Claude. Eventually she will leave Harte's, you know.'

'I wouldn't count on that!' Linnet cried, sitting up straighter in her chair. 'She'll want to have the top job and commute from Paris to London, you'll see.'

Paula sat back, staring at her daughter, but she made no comment. She had a strange feeling that Linnet was correct; Tessa had not yet given up on the idea of taking over as head of Harte's one day. After all, she had considered herself to be the Dauphine since childhood and perhaps she would find it hard to relinquish this idea. But what of Jean-Claude? Wouldn't he find that hard? Object? On the other hand, maybe he wouldn't. Perhaps he liked the idea of a young wife with modern ideas and a career.

'Is something wrong, you have a funny look on your face, Mums,' Linnet said with a frown.

'No, I'm fine,' Paula reassured her. 'I was just thinking about Tessa, and perhaps you're right, maybe she will want to . . . cling on. However, I'm not retiring. Nor do I plan to for a very long time. You should all remember that.'

'I'm sorry I'm late,' Marietta apologized as Evan greeted her in the entrance hall of Gideon's flat.

'It doesn't matter, Mom, I was just making lists of the everyday things we're going to need for the new apartment. Kitchen stuff and all that.'

Mother and daughter hugged, and then Marietta took off her top coat, hung it in the hall closet, and followed Evan into the sitting room, explaining, 'The estate agent delayed me.'

'Real estate agent?' Evan repeated, looking at her mother, her lovely, bluish-grey eyes full of questions.

Marietta took a seat opposite her in the sitting room and explained, 'That's one of the reasons I wanted to see you today, to tell you something. I'm going to take an apartment here, Evan. Not only because of you and my grandchildren, but because I love London, and I realized I want to spend part of the year here.'

'Oh, Mom, I think that's just great! And it'll be wonderful to have you and Dad here, getting to know the twins. I bet he's real excited, isn't he? And Robin must be thrilled as well.'

At first Marietta didn't respond. She simply sat in

the chair, staring at Evan blankly, wondering how to break the news to her, hoping she wouldn't be upset when she understood how things really were.

'*Mom*. What is it? You're looking peculiar.'

'No, I'm not, I'm just wondering how to explain to you that your father won't be spending much time in London, Evan.'

'Oh, you mean because of his antique business, the shops?'

Taking a deep breath, Marietta said, 'I'm leaving your father. We're separating.'

Evan leaned back against the cushions on the sofa, gaping at her mother, completely taken by surprise. For a split second she was rendered totally speechless, and then at last she said, 'Oh, my God, why didn't you tell me before? Tell me you were planning this?'

'Because I didn't want to upset you when you were about to get married, and also because of your pregnancy. It was bad enough that you had the fall in the office, all Angharad's fault, I'm positive of that. She's worse than she ever was . . .' Marietta paused, shook her head. 'Your grandmother used to say we didn't know anything about her, what kind of people she came from, and Glynnis was right. She used to say it's all in the genes, and she was correct. Angharad was a foundling . . . left on the doorstep of the church.'

'Mom, please don't digress. Tell me about you and Dad. Why *are* you splitting up?'

'Goodness, Evan, how can you ask that? You and I talked about my marriage last year . . . you know very well it hasn't worked in years. And less now than ever.'

'Since your aunt left you everything? That's part of it, isn't it?' Evan suggested, gazing at her mother intently. '*Isn't it?*' she pressed.

'Not as far as your father's concerned, no. It doesn't matter to him that my aunt left me her entire estate, and made me quite wealthy. He's not interested in the money, he's doing very well himself these days.'

'But surely he's sort of put out? Kind of . . . ticked off? Because you're now independent and can do what you want. In a way, her money has set you free.'

Marietta nodded and looked off into the distance for a moment, a faraway look settling in her eyes. And as she thought of the past, all that had happened between her and Owen, a shadow fell across her face. For a moment she was unable to speak, to explain further. All she could think about was the past . . . and the past was immutable. *That* she *had* come to understand in the last few years. You could never escape the past. No, not ever, no matter how hard you tried.

Watching Marietta acutely, Evan recognized that her mother was wrestling with something in her own mind, and she decided not to probe, or pester her. Better to wait for her mother to tell her what she wanted to tell her in her own time. And so Evan kept still on the sofa, her hands resting lightly on her stomach, as if protecting her boys. She couldn't wait for them to be born now; she longed to hold them in her arms, and longed for her body to be back to normal. There were times, like right now, when Evan felt like a beached whale.

Marietta suddenly sat up, and spoke, saying, 'Our marriage went wrong a long time ago, Evan ... when you were small. I left your father at that time. But eventually I came back for many reasons, mostly because of you. But it was only to discover that he—'

'Had taken me for himself,' Evan said, cutting her mother off mid-sentence. 'And that's why you adopted Elayne and then Angharad, isn't it? Because you wanted girls of your own, for yourself. And you wanted a family.'

'Yes, that's true. We discussed this, you and I, last summer. Adopting the girls was Glynnis's idea. She loved me and she loved her son and she loved you ... we were all so important to her. And so she begged Owen to take me back, and eventually he did but—'

The telephone jangled, and interrupted Marietta. 'I'll get it, don't move,' she instructed, jumping up and going to the phone. 'Harte residence,' she said, smiling across at her daughter as she spoke.

'Is that you, Marietta?'

'Yes, it is, Linnet.'

'Hello! I'm so glad you're there. I need to see you and Evan about something. Can I come over? Take you both to lunch? Or better still, perhaps I can bring a picnic lunch over from Harte's?'

'Let me just ask Evan what her plans are, Linnet. Hold on a moment, please.' Covering the receiver,

Marietta looked over at her daughter. 'Obviously, you know it's Linnet. She wants to take us out to lunch, or bring a picnic lunch over, she says she needs to speak to us both. So which do you prefer? Or do you have a doctor's appointment or anything?'

'No, Mom, I'm free all day, and I think I'd prefer a picnic lunch, wouldn't you?'

'Why not, it'll be lovely.' Marietta now spoke to Linnet at the other end of the phone, saying, 'It's fine for you to come over, and Evan says she'd love a picnic lunch and so would I. What time should we expect you, Linnet?'

'In about thirty minutes, if that's all right?'

'Yes, I'm sure it is. See you later.' Replacing the receiver, Marietta returned to the chair, and sat down. 'What can I do, Evan? She's coming in thirty minutes. Shall I set the table?'

'Yes, let's do that, Mom, but did Linnet say why she's coming over?'

'No. She just said she needed to talk to us both, that was all.'

'I see.' Evan sat very quietly, her heart sinking, pondering for a moment. Then she looked at her mother, her eyes narrowing and asked softly, 'Where is Angharad? Do you know?'

'No, I don't, not really. She said she was going to go to the South of France, perhaps via Paris,' Marietta replied.

'I see.'

Marietta gave Evan a sharp, probing glance. 'Why do you look like that?'

'Like what, Mom?'

'Come on, Evan, don't play dumb. You know very well how you're looking . . . like someone who knows what this is all about but isn't going to say. *Conspiratorial*, that's how you look.'

'Don't be silly!' Evan cried, shaking her head. 'How could I know why Linnet's coming to talk to us? But I do have an imagination, and I suspect it could be about the dreaded Jonathan.'

'Oh, God, no, not that.' Marietta turned pale.

'Well, maybe not,' Evan said quickly, not wanting to alarm her mother. 'Listen, let's not speculate. Let's get back to Dad, and your marriage. How did he take it, I mean when you told him?'

'With his usual indifference,' Marietta murmured, slowly standing up. 'I'm going to set the table for lunch, Evan. I'd prefer to drop the matter of my separation for the moment. We can discuss it later after lunch, when we're alone again.'

'All right,' Evan agreed, pushing herself to her feet. 'I'll hold you to that, you know.'

'I don't doubt it,' Marietta muttered.

CHAPTER TWENTY-THREE

Marietta opened the door, and Linnet came breezing into the apartment as if she didn't have a care in the world, carrying several large Harte shopping bags, exclaiming, 'Hello! Here I am with lunch. Hot vegetable soup, mixed sandwiches and fruit. I hope it tempts you.'

'It sounds yummy,' Marietta answered, taking some of the shopping bags from her. 'Let's put all of this in the kitchen. Do you think I should reheat the soup?'

'The containers keep it fairly hot, but why not?' Linnet followed Marietta, helped to take the food out of the bags, and then returned to the hall and hung up her top coat.

A moment later Evan came out of the bedroom, hurried into the sitting room and greeted Linnet warmly. 'What a nice surprise, Linny, you coming over today.' Dropping her voice, she then asked, 'Is this about Jonathan Ainsley? Or Angharad?'

'Both. But let's have lunch first. This news can wait.'

'All right,' Evan answered, knowing better than to argue. 'Can I get you anything?'

'Not right now, thanks. I'll just have water with lunch. Where do you want us to eat? In the kitchen or in here?'

'I think it's easier in the kitchen, don't you?' Evan said. Linnet nodded, and together they walked over to join Marietta in the next room.

Within minutes, Marietta was serving the soup, as Linnet told Evan about the meeting with her mother that morning regarding the day spa. 'And I think with a little luck she'll go along with it,' Linnet finished, sounding upbeat, very positive.

'Oh, I do hope so. It'll be great to have a spa, won't it? I'd certainly make use of it, and so would you.'

Linnet began to laugh. 'Let's not forget it's for the customers, not us.'

Evan laughed with her, and went on, 'When are you going to break the news about the floor devoted to brides? Soon, I hope.'

'Yes, very soon. Later this week, in fact. I'm just finishing the various memos. Then I'm going to jump in the deep end and give them all to her, along with my plan for the next couple of years. I hope Mummy sees what I see, and that she will share my vision.'

'Do you mean you're going to mention the six small cafés in the food halls as well as everything else?' Evan asked, experiencing a flicker of apprehension. 'Like the deli and the cheese bar?'

'Well, yes, I am. I'm doing memos on *everything*.

I think it's easier to comprehend a plan when it's down on paper. Anyway, my mother's always liked memos, you know.'

Marietta was listening to them talking with great interest, and when there was a break in their conversation, she said, 'I certainly like the sound of a floor devoted to brides, that's a great idea, and so is the spa. I've become addicted to *them* in the last year, they're so pampering, relaxing.'

Evan glanced at her mother, then turning to Linnet, she said, 'By the way, my mother's going to take an apartment here. She's planning to spend part of the year in London.'

'That'll be lovely. After all, you're going to have grandchildren growing up here. And where's the flat? Or haven't you found one yet?' Linnet asked. She liked Marietta, was interested in her plans.

'I have. It's just off Sloane Street, and I think it would work well for me. I'd love you both to see it.' Marietta stood, picked up two of the empty bowls and carried them to the sink; Linnet followed with hers, and a moment later the two women were putting the rest of the food on the kitchen table.

'How about a cup of tea?' Marietta asked, filling the kettle and plugging it in.

Evan shook her head.

Linnet said, 'I think I'd like a cup after all. Thank you, Marietta.' She sat down, took a cucumber sandwich and bit into it. Evan followed suit and they ate in silence. In fact, silence reigned even after Marietta had joined them at the table; all three of them concentrated on lunch, not wanting to embark on what might prove to be a difficult and disturbing conversation.

Once lunch was over, and the dishes cleared away, it was Evan who broke the silence. 'All right, Linnet, give us the bad news,' she prompted. 'Because I'm sure it's bad, isn't it?' She held her breath as she waited for Linnet to answer, knowing she wouldn't like what she was about to hear.

'*Peculiar*,' Linnet replied, and then carefully told them the gist of the conversation Paula had had with Sarah in Paris earlier that morning, not missing out one detail.

The two women were both startled and shaken to hear that Angharad was with Jonathan in Paris, but it was Marietta who was the most disturbed. She had blanched when Linnet had embarked on the story, and now she looked as if she was about to burst into tears.

Evan appeared calmer, and she discovered she was not all that surprised to learn that Angharad had hooked up with Jonathan; it had always seemed a probability to her, ever since her mother had relayed the story of their odd encounter in the village store.

'I had a horrible sinking feeling that something like this would happen,' Evan remarked, looking from one woman to the other. She gave her mother a long glance. 'Glynnis once said something to me about bad seed in reference to Angharad, and she was quite prophetic, don't you think, Mom?'

Marietta could only nod at that moment, so upset was she.

'She's not only promiscuous and greedy, she's selfish and careless, and far too casual about her life. Not to mention utterly disloyal,' Evan said in a cold voice. 'My God, she'd sell us all out for a hot night in bed with Ainsley, and a few glittering toys.'

'Lots of nights in bed with him, and lots of glittering toys,' Linnet corrected. 'But that's her business. I'd like to discuss *my* business with *you*.'

Evan nodded but made no comment.

It was Marietta who exclaimed, 'How could she do this? Get involved with the man who is the family's deadly enemy. It's unbelievable!'

'Did she know that?' Linnet wondered out loud. 'Did she realize he was the enemy?'

'Sure she did!' Evan cried, her anger coming to the surface. 'She's heard us discuss Jonathan, heard us complain how troublesome and dangerous he is. But she doesn't care, because she doesn't care about us. She never has. There's something oddly detached about her, and that condition dates back to our childhood. She was a nasty kid and she hasn't changed. Talk about self-involved, she takes the prize.'

Marietta suddenly exclaimed, 'She has now become *our enemy*.'

'Indeed she has,' Linnet agreed, 'and that's what I want to talk to you about, Marietta . . . Evan.' Leaning forward, Linnet continued, 'We know what Angharad's up to, in the sense we know she's after *him*, and that she's also after his *money*. You've

343

made that clear. She wants bed, board and bling. But what is *he* after? My mother is worried that J.A. sees her as a conduit to the Hartes, and especially to you, Evan, and also Gideon. She's part of your family, your sister, and it would be so easy for her to find out everything about your life, your movements, your plans.'

'Oh, no, not from me she won't!' Evan shook her head vehemently. 'She's been off my list for quite a while now. I don't want anything to do with her, not ever again.'

'And neither do I,' Marietta announced, pulling herself up in her chair, trying to bring her swimming senses together. 'Angharad has gone over to the other side, and therefore I shall cut her out of my life.'

'I'm glad to hear that.' Linnet offered Marietta a warm smile, reached out and touched her hand resting on the kitchen table. 'I'm sorry she's betrayed *you*, all of you, but now that she has, has shown her true colours, you can't have anything to do with her. None of you—'

'But I just said that,' Marietta snapped, cutting in.

'I know. However, what about Owen and Elayne? Where would they stand if they knew? Where will they stand when they do know?'

'Next to us,' Evan answered. 'We'll be standing side by side. Elayne, for sure, knows she's a . . . *bitch*.'

'That's true,' Marietta concurred. 'And Owen understands what she is. He's very aware that

Angharad's not a very nice person. I don't believe we have to worry about him or Elayne.'

'But they must be told,' Linnet pointed out. 'They must know she's with Jonathan Ainsley, must know everything I've told you today. Will you call Owen, Marietta? Do you want me to do it?'

Marietta did not respond at once, and hesitated.

Evan said, 'I'll call Dad.'

'No,' Marietta shook her head. 'I'll do it.'

'*Mom*, please. I think that's a bad idea.'

'You know what . . . I should call him,' Linnet now interjected. 'If I call there will be more of an *impact*.'

'Probably,' Marietta murmured.

Evan nodded.

'Then it's settled. I'll phone him later today at the shop in Connecticut, and I'll explain that Angharad has to be totally ostracized. She cannot know anything about any of the Hartes or the Hugheses.' Linnet paused, took a drink of water, and added, 'Of course there is just the possibility that she's not a conduit to us, and that J.A. has truly fallen for her, is only interested in her, just as Sarah believes.'

'Let's not take any chances,' Marietta remarked. 'Angharad has always been jealous of Evan, seen herself as the neglected child. She got it into her head years ago that we favoured Evan and Elayne, and she would often accuse me of holding Evan up as the shining example of excellence, showing Evan off as the star, as she put it. And nothing could be further from the truth.'

'She's bitter,' Evan said in a subdued voice, feeling cold and uneasy.

'You know, Marietta, Angharad is not likely to be in touch with Evan, but she may well phone *you* from Paris. After all, you're her mother.'

Marietta shook her head. 'No, she won't, Linnet.'

'Doesn't she stay in touch?'

'Not really.'

'She might call you to boast though,' Evan suggested.

'Oh, definitely,' Marietta said. 'If she's got something worthwhile to boast about.'

'About Angharad,' Marietta began, when they were finally alone. 'What I wanted to say, Evan, is that—'

'Please, Mom, I don't want to talk about Angharad. Or Jonathan Ainsley,' Evan interrupted her in a peremptory manner. 'Not right now. I'm much more interested in talking about your separation from Dad.'

Marietta walked across the sitting room and sat down in the large armchair near the fireplace. After a moment, she said, 'There's not much more to tell. Your father and I have separated, and that's that. As I told you, he seemed indifferent, as if he couldn't care less.'

'I don't mean now, Mom, I mean years ago. *Earlier*. Before Linnet arrived, you told me you had left my father when I was little. Why?'

Marietta looked across at Evan and did not answer immediately. She leaned back in the chair, crossed her legs, stared into the distance, as if staring back, looking at times past. In a sense, that was exactly what she *was* doing. 'I want to be honest with you,' she answered finally. 'As honest as I can possibly be, Evan. I owe you that. Things were not all that great between us when you were small, but that wasn't the real reason I left your father then.'

'So why did you?' Evan probed, anxious to know, to understand at last about her parents' marriage. Lately it had baffled her.

'Because I . . . I fell in love with another man.'

Evan gaped at Marietta, momentarily startled, and then recovering herself swiftly, she asked, 'Who was he? Tell me about him.'

'His name was Val Timball, and we'd known him in London, your father and I. He was an artist and set-designer, very talented, mostly working in the theatre in the West End. He came to New York to do the sets for a Broadway show, and we saw a lot of him. During the months he was living in Manhattan something happened between us – we fell in love with each other. He'd always had a yen for me, and I was very unhappy with your father by then. Val and I became involved, very heavily. When he went back to London he begged me to go with him. He wanted me to get a divorce and marry him. I couldn't do it, Evan. I realized I couldn't leave you.'

'But you just said you left Dad.'

'I did go to London, yes. But only because Val became very ill. His sister Solange told me he was begging to see me, so I went, intending to spend only a few days. But I loved him so much I had to stay with him. And he needed me. I told your father I had left him because I wanted to be with Val, and he went crazy. He flew over immediately, came raging into London, made a helluva stink and stormed out again without really listening to me, or trying to understand. He vowed to divorce me for adultery. His behaviour antagonized me more than ever.'

'And you stayed with Val for how long, Mom?'

'Only a few weeks. You see, as it turned out, Val was dying. He had a rare form of leukaemia,' Marietta's voice quavered, and she stopped, took a deep breath. After a moment she began again, speaking softly. 'It was impossible for me to leave him to die alone. Not when we loved each other the way we did. But he didn't last long, not even a month. I felt my whole world had fallen apart that summer. Val was dead. Your father was determined to divorce me. And he'd vowed I would never see you ever again. That he wouldn't allow it.'

Stunned for a moment by this story, Evan said nothing, sat waiting for Marietta to continue, as she knew her mother eventually would.

'It was your grandmother who intervened between us. She was furious with your father, told him he was being immature, that he was lacking in compassion,' Marietta explained. 'She talked us both into getting back with each other. He didn't really want to, and in a way, neither did I. Because by then I understood we couldn't really be happy.' Marietta sighed heavily, and shook her head. 'I did go back to him, but only because of you. I wanted to bring you up, love you, be a good mother.'

'He took me away from you, though, didn't he? Isn't that the best way to describe what happened?'

'Yes. It was kind of a retaliation, I think.'

'Is that when your depression started?'

Marietta nodded, and her face changed, became taut with tension as she continued to talk. 'It just came over me one day. I couldn't get out of bed. I had very dark feelings all of a sudden. I was baffled, I didn't understand what was happening to me. At first, I thought I was sad because of Val's death.' She shook her head vehemently. 'It was awful, frightening. I lived in a dark world. Then suddenly the depression lifted, and I was fine, better. Six months would go by, and then something would trigger the depression again, and I'd stay in bed afraid of everything, of everyone. Terrified, actually. Eventually, of course, I saw a doctor, got help, medicine.'

'I remember how you gradually seemed to get better, Mom, when I was growing up. But I also remember how you'd suddenly be ill again, and seemingly for no reason.'

'I might still be like that if it weren't for my Aunt Dottie, God bless her. She's the one who sent me to a new doctor last year, told me to get a life. And—'

'That's what you're doing,' Evan interrupted. 'Good for you, Mom! You have a *right* to be happy. And so does Dad. Maybe he'll be better off alone, too.'

'I think he will, Evan. And I bear him no ill will, you know.'

'I realize that. It's not your nature. Do you want to talk some more about your depression?' Evan now asked, looking at her mother intently. 'I'm happy to listen, if it helps.'

'Perhaps another day, honey. I'm worried about Jonathan Ainsley at the moment. Do you think he'll try to hurt you and Gideon, Evan?'

'Not at the moment . . . I think he's too busy with Angharad. And by the way, Mom, I tend to go along with Sarah Pascal. I think J.A. has fallen hard for Angharad and that he's not trying to get information out of her about us.' Evan suddenly began to laugh. 'He might even be suspicious of *her*! He might believe she's been sent to spy on him by us. Wouldn't that be a laugh?'

'I suppose so,' Marietta concurred, although this was said without much enthusiasm. 'I can't help worrying about you, worrying about your safety.'

'Everything's going to be all right. We've lots of security, in every possible way, even though you might not be aware of it.'

'Do you mean bodyguards, that kind of thing?'

'Yes, I do. I'm fully protected at all times, as are all the Hartes. Try to relax, Mom. Jonathan's not going to win, he's not going to get the better of us.'

'Isn't there anything the family can do about him interfering in your lives? Causing trouble?' Marietta asked.

'I'm afraid not, Mom. You see, he himself never does anything. He employs others to do his dirty work, and even then that is impossible to prove,' Evan pointed out.

'Perhaps he'll get his comeuppance,' Marietta muttered, thinking out loud. 'Perhaps Angharad will be his downfall. With a little luck.'

Much later, after Marietta had left, Evan lay on the sofa in front of the fire, half dozing, and thinking about her mother's life. It hadn't been very happy for the most part; in fact, it had been quite hard at times. But then life was never easy, it never had been, not for anyone. And for some it could even be catastrophic.

Evan was glad her mother had found her way out of that awful maze of depression and loneliness, and she understood perfectly well why Marietta wanted to live in London now.

A new beginning, a fresh start, Evan thought suddenly. This is a wonderful chance of renewal for her . . . a new apartment, in a town she knows and loves, the great expectations of being a grandmother, of watching the boys grow, of being with me, having me to herself without Dad's interference.

As she dozed off a smile settled on Evan's face. She was truly glad her mother was going to be here in England part of the year, and she would do her best to help her be happy, make Marietta part of their lives, give her the daughter's love she had been cheated of so long ago.

And she would try not to be angry with her father for too long, even though she was at this moment.

CHAPTER TWENTY-FOUR

Linnet sat staring at the latest sales sheets spread out on her desk, for a moment thinking she had misread them. But as she scanned them a second time she saw that the figures were as bad as she thought. Every department on the three fashion floors which were under her aegis had done badly.

It's not possible, she muttered under her breath, still staring at the columns of numbers. She realized with a sinking feeling that sales for last week had been very poor, if not disastrous.

Leaning back in her chair she frowned, wondering why her mother had not mentioned these figures to her. Paula got the sales sheets several days ahead of her; but then perhaps her mother hadn't had a chance to study them either. She herself had been busy preparing a number of detailed memos for Paula, and Paula appeared to have been overly preoccupied with Jonathan Ainsley.

It seemed to Linnet that her mother was constantly speaking to Sarah in Paris, almost every day, in fact, and to what purpose? she wondered.

All Paula heard from Sarah was that Jonathan was obviously besotted with Angharad, and vice versa.

It pleased Linnet that these two schemers were caught up with each other, entwined figuratively and physically. Thus enraptured, they would leave the rest of them alone, she believed. And hoped. At least for the moment.

Gideon tended to agree with her. They had met for a drink the day after she'd had lunch with Evan and Marietta, and Gideon had confided his feelings to her. Because they had grown up together and were best friends, there were no holds barred, and he had poured out his genuine fears. 'She's evil,' he had said at one moment. 'I saw the wickedness in Angharad the afternoon I met her at the hospital, after Evan had that fall. I still blame that woman for Evan's accident, I think she got Evan very upset. We have to wait and see what happens next.' He had smiled and added, 'I do believe Ainsley has met his match. I think Angharad Hughes is a real piece of work. She'll lead him a merry dance.'

Linnet sighed, then looked down at the figures once more. They loomed up, hit her between the eyes. Damnation, she muttered under her breath. Things were much worse than she had realized.

Her memos to Paula, which she'd worked on for days, were about updating the London store, bringing it into the twenty-first century, and those figures now told her how important this was. Actually, it was vital.

Every aspect of the store needed overhauling. All the windows required a new look, the displays on the various floors had to be glamorized and in general merchandise had to measure up to the new age they were living in. She had understood this for a long time, if the truth be known, but visiting Harte's in New York, and other department stores in that city, had brought it home with a vengeance.

She believed Harte's in London was beginning to lose a bit of its cachet. Oh, it was still elegant, a landmark, and world famous, but to her way of thinking it had become a trifle staid, especially for the new generation shopping today.

Linnet was smart enough to know that the latest sales figures for her fashion floors didn't spell disaster for Harte's, but at the same time she understood that they were indicative of a trend. If something really drastic wasn't done the retailing company might, within the coming year, be on a downward slide. She knew Harte's wasn't losing money. At least not yet, she muttered to herself. But she also was aware that this could happen if innovative ideas were not put into work, innovations that would appeal to the new generation, pull customers into the store, savvy young women with specific tastes and needs.

Jumping up, she went over to her work table, picked up the *Financial Times*, which she had dropped there when she had come in that morning. Rustling through its pink pages, she finally came to the stock prices, scanned the pages until she found Harte's. Nodding, she let out a small sigh of relief. The shares were stable; in this morning's paper, they were even up a little in price.

Although she was reassured, Linnet knew she had to pursue her plan, no matter what. She suddenly felt stronger, more determined and resolute than ever to force through her ideas, *most* if not all of them. Somehow she had to find the means to convince her mother that they had to move ahead, that they could not remain sitting here in what Linnet called 'the doldrums'. Her mother lived in the past, caught up with the regime of Emma Harte, and Grandy's memory.

Seating herself at the desk, she picked up the phone and dialled India, who was working at the Leeds store this week.

India answered her private line immediately. 'India Standish here.'

'It's Linnet, India. How are you? How's Dusty? Oh, and little Atlanta?'

'They're both great, thanks. But how're you? You sound tense, Linny,' India replied in her lovely soft way, the hint of a brogue behind the lilting voice.

'I am a bit anxious. Listen, belatedly, I just got around to looking at this past week's sales figures for the fashion floors, and they're awful. Actually, India, they're *appalling*. I don't mind telling you, I'm alarmed.'

'But January's always a bad month, don't forget that. And anyway, this is the first year we haven't had the January Sale. I don't know why Aunt Paula decided against it, but I think it was a mistake,' India confided.

'So do I, but I can't tell her that, she's already

irritated with me about my plans for the future,' Linnet replied.

'Oh, drat! I so hoped she would go along with you, and with us, Evan and me as well as you, and *our* ideas. What's she objecting to?'

'Actually, she hasn't seen them all yet, the plans, I mean. I'm just finishing my memos. But she wasn't too thrilled when I spoke to her about the spa.'

'Gosh, and that's one of the best ideas you've had,' India exclaimed, sounding very surprised. 'I wonder how she'll react when you mention the quick-food snack bars.' India chuckled. 'I don't think she'll be too happy, Linny.'

'I know. But we have to bring this store into the new century. Listen, the reason I called you was to ask you how the Leeds and Harrogate stores did last week, especially in the fashion departments?'

'Very well, actually,' India responded. 'I was a bit surprised, to be honest. But as you know, the Leeds fashion floors do very well, at least in the twenty-to-thirty age group. Those clothes have a lot of appeal, and don't forget we have hundreds of young women studying here, at Leeds University and the technical colleges. We do record business.'

Linnet had listened carefully, and now she said swiftly, 'You know, we might develop clothes for this category here at the London store. I think we've neglected that age group a bit.'

'That's true,' India agreed, and then said in a rush, 'There's another thing. Ever since Atlanta's been living with us I've become interested in children's clothes and toys. Last week I devised a way to bring the toys and clothes departments together in adjoining areas. That's going to help boost sales, I think. I'm trying some new children's clothing manufacturers, as well.'

'Sounds to me as if the Leeds store is a few jumps ahead of us, cousin of mine,' Linnet laughed.

India laughed with her. 'I'm merely trying to do the best I can.'

'You go well beyond that, India. What about the Harrogate store?'

'It's doing okay. Do you want me to send you the sales sheets?'

'No. Just keep up the good work.'

'I will. Any more news about the dreaded Angharad and her beau, if we can call *him* that?'

'It's the same old stuff coming across the Channel from Sarah, you know the drill . . . He's besotted with Angharad, etcetera. However, Gideon believes our Mr Ainsley has met his match.'

'In what sense?' India asked, obviously puzzled.

'Gid doesn't like Angharad Hughes, he was unusually wary of her the first time he met her. He says she might well get the better of Ainsley.'

'I'll be there to cheer her along,' India answered dryly.

'So will I. Listen, where will I find you this weekend? At Willows Hall, I presume.'

'Yes, in fact I'll be staying there from tonight on. I like being with Atlanta, who's just adorable and I've become very attached to her since she's been living with Dusty. I know it's only Thursday, but I decided to go over there later today. It's been a little

357

lonely at Pennistone Royal with only Emsie to keep me company – and she's always doing homework. It's not the same when the rest of you are in London. Anyway, are you coming up this weekend, Linnet? If so, maybe we'll get together . . . the four of us.'

'That would've been nice, but we're staying in London. Julian is going to finish the final bit of work on the memorial for his grandfather. He'll be with his father on Saturday morning, and I intend to be at the store here. But Mummy's coming to Yorkshire with Dad. And possibly Lorne.'

'Tessa hasn't been to the Harrogate store for over a week, so I decided I'd better go in there on Saturday morning, so that's where you'll find me if you need me. Or I'll be with Dusty.'

After hanging up, Linnet continued to work on the memos for her mother, and when she finally had them exactly right, as right as she could get them, she wrote an additional memo based on India's innovations at the Leeds store, pointing out how successful they were.

Finally, she printed out everything on her computer, put the pages in a folder, then locked the folder in a drawer in her desk. She would give them to her mother tomorrow, before Paula went to Pennistone Royal for the weekend.

Glancing at the clock on her desk, Linnet saw that it was four o'clock. Rising, she went out of her office, heading for the fashion floors, wanting to see what was happening in the store. It was a ritual with her, as she knew it had been with Emma Harte, the founder, and her great hero. They all called her Emma's clone in the family. And that was what she aimed to be. The new Emma Harte. That was her ambition.

Several hundred miles north of London, India Standish was doing the same thing at the Harte store in Leeds. After completing her paperwork, she went out of her office, heading for the fashion floors.

India had been trained by Linnet, and so her modus operandi was almost identical to her cousin's daily regime when it came to going out onto the floors: do a walk-through in the morning, around noon, if possible; and another walk-through in the afternoon, at about four o'clock. Just like their great-grandmother had done. Linnet was always reminding her of that, and also reminding her of Emma's discipline and hard work.

Thursday was usually a good day for the store, with plenty of young women and girls moving around, looking at everything, and especially in Fashion. India noticed that today was no exception. The clothing areas were busy, and naturally this pleased her no end.

India was intelligent, and had been exceptionally well trained, and one of the secrets of her success was that she *listened*, and very scrupulously so, to everyone. However, she paid the most particular attention to Linnet, and endeavoured to ascertain her moods. She had detected her cousin's tenseness, and anxiety about the sales figures. Linnet's concern had given her pause for thought and she tended to agree with Linnet that their great emporium in Knightsbridge needed an overhaul.

But like Evan, India trembled at the thought of Paula's wrath. There was no doubt in India's mind that their lady boss would see red when she looked at Linnet's memos this weekend.

Paula's become a little set in her ways, India thought, as she headed down the floor. She doesn't want change because she reveres Emma Harte. That is where the problem lies. Paula resisted Linnet's pleas to move on, and into the future because she was *rooted* in the past. With Emma. Abiding by her wishes voiced long ago.

India, somewhat lost in her thoughts about Paula and Emma, did not notice the woman who had started to follow her and was edging closer. It was only when the woman accosted her by grabbing hold of her arm, that India was stopped in her tracks. Half turning, she exclaimed, 'What are you *doing*? Let go of me! Who are you?'

And then, as she stared at the woman, she shrivelled inside when she recognized the face. It was Melinda Caldwell. How could that be? She was in a de-tox clinic. No. Not anymore.

Struggling to get free of the woman, but caught in her tenacious grip, India, nevertheless, managed to move out of the aisle by pushing at the woman, manoeuvring her behind a rack of clothes, pinning her against a wall. Despite her appearance of pale blonde fragility, India Standish was strong physically, and tough mentally. Still struggling to get free, but not wanting to make a rowdy scene, India leaned against Melinda and hissed, 'Let go of me. *Now*. If you don't you'll find yourself in *very serious trouble.*'

'You're in trouble. You and that bastard Dusty Rhodes. You've kidnapped my child,' Melinda shrilled, her tone high-pitched.

'Be quiet. And let me go!' India insisted in a tough voice. 'Now, do you hear? Let me go at once.'

'I know she's at Willows Hall with him. And you. *Whore.* My mother told me where my child is. Did you think my mother wouldn't tell me?' Melinda was shouting and pushing against India, trying to move them both away from the wall.

Suddenly, unexpectedly, India took a step back, and as Melinda moved forward, without letting go, India smashed her hand down on the other woman's arm, coming down hard. The small signet ring on India's little finger cut into Melinda's wrist and immediately she let go, releasing India.

At this moment, one of the sales women was frantically hurrying towards them, having just noticed the altercation, and India called to her, 'Get Security at once!' Then she turned back to Melinda Caldwell, who was now backing away. It was India's turn to grab, but Melinda was extremely swift. Darting away from India, she fled down the floor, heading towards the escalator, jumped on and rode down.

When the security officers arrived only a split second later, Melinda Caldwell had left the fashion floors and disappeared from sight. Once India had quickly explained that she had been accosted by a crazy woman, the men took off, heading for the ground floor.

'We'll find her, don't you worry, Lady India,' one of the security men promised before heading for the escalator.

India nodded, said nothing, but she thought: No, you won't. She's gone. She's already out in the street.

After thanking the young woman who had called Security, India went back to her office, feeling slightly shaken. Mostly she was worried about Melinda Caldwell being out of the clinic, and now on the loose in Yorkshire. She was dangerous and unpredictable.

Sitting down at her desk, she picked up the phone and dialled Dusty's private line at Willows Hall. When he answered, she told him, 'Dusty, Melinda's not in the clinic. She's in Leeds.'

'My God! How's that possible? How do—'

'How she got out I don't know, but she was here at Harte's,' India cut in swiftly, interrupting him, and then continued in the calmest of voices, 'She accosted me, was verbally abusive, and said she knew you had her child, that her mother had told her Atlanta was at Willows Hall.'

'Good God, no!' Dusty exclaimed heatedly. 'Don't tell me she visited Molly at the Infirmary! This is just awful. But what happened with you, darling? She didn't hurt you, did she?' he now asked worriedly. 'Are you all right, India?'

'I feel slightly shaken, but I'm all right. Unfortunately, Melinda escaped just before Security arrived. She fled down the escalator, and probably out of the store immediately. I'm sure they haven't found her, even though they were fast on her heels. I just wanted to warn you, Dusty, that she could very well be on her way to Willows Hall at this moment.'

'I understand, but that won't do her any good. She can't get into the grounds, not the way Jack Figg has this place fixed up. It's very secure, tight as a drum. When are you leaving the store?'

'Very soon. I'm just waiting for the security men to come and report to me. In the meantime—'

'Just a minute, here's Paddy. Give me a second.'

'I will.' India clutched the receiver and held her breath, waiting for Dusty to come back to her. She could barely hear Paddy's voice as he spoke to Dusty, but she pricked up her ears when Dusty said, 'This is just dreadful. Tell her to hold on a minute, please.'

Suddenly Dusty was back, and he told India, 'Gladys is on the other line. Melinda was seen by one of Molly's neighbours, who phoned Gladys. Apparently, Melinda was trying to get into Molly's house in Meanwood, but Molly had the locks changed recently. Smart move. I think I'd better speak to Gladys. Stay in touch, and let me know when you leave work.'

'I will, Dusty. It won't be very long, and try not to worry.'

'Please, India, do get a move on . . .' His voice trailed off.

'I'm safe in the store.'

'Are you now?' he asked, sounding doubtful.

'*Yes*. I'll be on my way after I've seen the security officers.'

Once she had hung up the receiver, India cleared her desk, and turned off her computer. A few moments later the two security men came into her office through the open door. 'Not a sight of her, Lady India,' Mack Slater said.

He was the senior of the two and had worked at Harte's for years. He continued, 'She went out of the store by the front entrance, and was gone by the time we hit the street. The doorman saw her running down towards City Square. He *thinks*. It might not have been her at all. Who was she, Lady India? Do you have any idea?'

India, deeming it far wiser to say nothing, shook her head. 'Sorry, Mack, I don't know who she was. Obviously someone a bit demented, though.' India gave him a faint smile and shrugged. 'The world is full of crazies, these days, isn't it?'

'You're right, things aren't what they used to be, not by a long shot. Sorry we weren't able to nab her,' Mack finished.

'You did your best, and thanks, Mack, and you too, Jerry.'

The security officers took their leave of her, and it took India several minutes to get her things together. As soon as she had packed her carry-all, she stepped over to the cupboard and took out her sheepskin coat and a woollen scarf. She had just shrugged into her coat when the phone began to ring.

Leaning over her desk, she lifted the receiver. 'Hello?'

'It's me,' Dusty said. 'I have bad news. Molly Caldwell had a heart attack a short while ago. She's back in intensive care. Melinda's doing, I have no doubt. She went there to see her and caused this to happen.'

'Oh, that poor woman, how terrible,' India murmured. 'Do you want me to go over to the Infirmary, Dusty? Is there anything I can do?'

'No, nothing. And she wouldn't even know you at the moment, she's out of it, from what I understand. The Infirmary phoned me five minutes ago to give me the news. They'll stay in touch with me.'

'What about Gladys, what did she have to say?'

'What you know . . . that a neighbour had spotted Melinda trying to get into Molly's house. Gladys had been out shopping, and another neighbour said Melinda had been banging on Gladys's door as well. To no avail, obviously, since she wasn't there. Gladys is going over to Molly's now. Apparently there's a small suitcase full of papers, which Molly told her to bring to me as soon as possible when she visited her the other day.'

'And is she bringing the case to you now? Is that the idea?'

'I thought it was best. Gladys is somewhat alarmed by Melinda's sudden appearance, and I don't blame her. Apart from bringing me the suitcase, I thought it was wiser to have Gladys tucked away at Willows Hall. Don't you agree, India?'

'So that Melinda can't get at her, is that what you mean?' she asked.

'Indeed it is. Who knows what trouble Melinda might cause for Gladys.'

CHAPTER TWENTY-FIVE

Recently Jack Figg had insisted that Tessa, Linnet, India and Evan all use discreet black town cars with ex-military men as drivers. In other words, vehicles not easy to spot and drivers who were actually bodyguards. At least during the week, when their schedules rarely varied and they were easy to track and to target. His aim: to protect the women from Jonathan Ainsley's possible menace.

Of the four of them, it was India who insisted on using her Aston Martin when she was in Yorkshire at the weekends, and Jack had been unable to dissuade her. He was still trying.

And now, as she sat in the black sedan which had picked her up at the store, she leaned forward and said from the back seat, 'I'm sorry, Larry, I forgot to tell you that I'm not going to Pennistone Royal this afternoon. Would you take me to Willows Hall instead, please?'

'No problem, Lady India,' Larry Cox answered in his polite but cheerful voice.

Settling comfortably in the seat, India's thoughts suddenly turned to Jack Figg. It occurred to her that she and Dusty urgently needed his advice, if not indeed his help. Melinda Caldwell spelled trouble. Not only for Molly Caldwell, but for them as well.

Taking out her mobile phone, India dialled Jack's number, and when he answered immediately, she said, 'Jack, it's India. Hello.'

'It's nice to hear your voice, India. Is everything okay?' he asked, his voice sharp.

'I think Dusty and I need your help.'

'What's wrong? Tell me about it, take your time.'

Speaking in a low voice, India explained, 'Melinda Caldwell came to the store today, made a bit of a fuss. With me.'

'Where are you now?'

'In the car with Larry, going to Willows Hall.'

'I understand. Let me ask the questions, it's easier for you, and much more discreet.' He trusted Larry, but he deemed it wise to be careful.

'I agree,' India replied.

'Was this an unannounced visit, India?' Jack now asked.

'Very much so. She's supposed to be undergoing treatment. I was taken by surprise actually, Jack.'

'Understood. So, now she's out of the clinic and floating around Leeds . . . that's what you're telling me, isn't it?'

'It is. This afternoon the encounter was unpleasant, to say the least. And she more than likely went to see her mother as well.'

'At Leeds Infirmary? Or is Mrs Caldwell now back at home?'

'She's still in hospital. Dusty told me a short while ago that Mrs Caldwell has had a bit of a setback, another heart attack this afternoon. I think from what Melinda said to me, she did visit her mother today.'

'Oh, God, no! And too bad about Mrs Caldwell. I hope she's going to come through this all right.' Jack cleared his throat. 'When was Melinda released from the de-tox clinic?'

'That's just it. Dusty thinks she wasn't released, that she just left of her own accord.'

'I see.' Jack paused but only for a split second, then asked, 'How was she? Demented? Sane? What? Tell me what you thought when you saw her.'

'She was angry. Looking back, she seemed quite sane but *very* angry, as I just said. I believe it was anger driving her.'

'She's a problem, India, and a dangerous one. I think we must find her as soon as possible.'

'Can we get together this evening, Jack? To go over everything. Are you in the vicinity? Or in London?'

'I'm in Yorkshire, but not too close. As a matter of fact, I'm in Scarborough at the moment.'

'Good heavens, don't tell me you've gone off to have a winter break at Heron's Nest,' India exclaimed in astonishment.

Startled by this comment, Jack answered swiftly, 'Funny you should say that, but I actually went to Heron's Nest today. To see the caretaker. She

369

thinks somebody's been using the house from time to time, over the last month or so. When Paula told me the other day, I decided to look into it myself.'

'And?'

'No *and*, India. As of this moment anyway. A few interesting thoughts on my part, but I can't actually target a person, at least not yet. And to be honest, nothing's been disturbed as far as I can tell, nor have any locks been forced.'

'Then how does the caretaker know somebody's been going there?'

'Good question. Apparently lights have been seen there several times, and little things seem out of place, so the caretaker says.'

'Who'd want to go to Heron's Nest in February? It's icy cold in Scarborough. None of *us* would go there right now. But perhaps somebody wanted to have an illicit rendezvous, something like that,' India commented and laughed. 'Heron's Nest is such a private place . . . in certain ways.'

A moment ago Jack had pricked up his ears, and now he asked, 'Why did you mention *rendezvous*, India? Are you suggesting that members of the family are accustomed to using Heron's Nest for assignations?'

'Do you mean my generation or my mother's? Who are you referring to when you say *family*? There are a lot of us . . .' After a pause she added, 'From several generations.'

Jack chuckled. 'That I know, and I'm certainly not thinking of your grandmother Edwina, or Robin, that's for sure. In fact, I *was* thinking about your generation.'

'I doubt it. I mean, who of us would go *there*? Toby? He's about the only one who's fancy free at the moment, and in the middle of a divorce. But his wife is in Los Angeles, so he can play around in London if he wants. He doesn't have to hide.' When Jack didn't respond, India asked, 'Well, don't you agree?'

'Yes, I do. It's a good point.'

'Why is Aunt Paula so upset that someone might have been there?' India probed, sounding baffled.

'I think she was worried that the house had been broken into, that there might have been a robbery.'

'I see. You know, Jack, none of my generation have ever been as involved with Heron's Nest as my mother's generation. Heron's Nest was very important to them all when they were growing up. They went every summer to stay with Emma. They called it Emma's Boot Camp.'

'I remember only too well, I often popped over to chat with your great-grandmother about business. Tell me something, do they still talk about those years at Heron's Nest?'

'Oh, yes. Mummy told me quite recently how much she loved the house and that Paula had often hidden her there, when she was having the secret love affair with Daddy. And Linnet once explained that her parents used to meet there on the sly, when Paula was trying to get a divorce from Jim Fairley.'

'Now I understand why you link it to romantic doings,' Jack murmured. 'This is interesting information, thanks. But getting back to Melinda Caldwell, I'll put a couple of my operatives on it immediately, and I'll talk to my pals with the Leeds police, chaps in the C.I.D. I must alert them as soon as we hang up, explain that she's a drug-addict and probably dangerous. I'm assuming she didn't hurt you?'

'No, of course not. But she tried,' India answered, and went on, 'She attempted to break into her mother's house in Meanwood today. I don't know the address but I'll check with Dusty and call you back.'

'Good. And I need a description of Melinda.'

'She's about my height, blondeish-brown hair, striking face with high cheekbones. Actually, I was surprised that she looked as good as she does. She was wearing black jeans and a black coat.'

'Okay. I've got that. Will you ask Dusty to phone the de-tox clinic and talk to her doctor, please? It's important we understand her condition.'

'I will. And Jack, I was wondering, *is* there any chance of seeing you this evening?'

'Why not? I'll be finished here in about an hour, so I could be at Willows Hall around seven-thirty. How's that?'

'Oh, Jack, it's great, and thank you so much. I'll be back to you shortly with the address in Meanwood.'

'Thanks, India, and try not to worry. We'll soon have this in hand.'

It was not long before India Standish called Jack again, this time with the information he required.

She also told him that Dusty had already spoken to Dr Jeffers at the de-tox clinic, only to discover that Melinda Caldwell had not been discharged. The doctor had informed Dusty that he was anxious for her to return to complete her treatment.

After thanking her, Jack clicked off and dialled two of his operatives who covered Yorkshire for him, as well as talking to his friends in the Leeds police force. Then he sat back and sipped his cup of tea, relaxing for a moment now that the problem of Melinda Caldwell was in competent hands. Another loose cannon was all he needed.

Jack had meandered into the Grand Hotel in Scarborough just before India had first called him about her problem, and had settled himself in the lounge where afternoon tea was served. He had ordered a pot of tea and a toasted teacake, but now, as he glanced around, he thought of the times he had come here with Emma for afternoon tea. And a rather grand tea it had been in those days, with a selection of finger sandwiches, scones with strawberry jam and clotted cream, and rich pastries. All too much for him now and far too fattening.

As he relaxed and caught his breath after a busy day, his thoughts wandered to India's comments about Heron's Nest. He chastised himself for being so stupid; why had he focused on the younger members of the family instead of the older generation, his generation? Of course none of the kids, as he called them, would go to Heron's Nest, especially in the depth of winter. It had no special meaning for *them*; but it did have great significance for Emma's grandchildren who had summered there with her for years. Naturally they would have a special attachment to that lovely old house by the sea.

Their salad days, he thought now, how we all remember our youth with such affection. We think of them as golden days because life seemed eternal then, and we thought we were immortal.

Rummaging around in his pocket, Jack found the small notebook he used for jotting down reminders to himself, took a pen out of his inside top pocket and listed all of Emma's grandchildren who had come to Heron's Nest when they were children. He then added the names of Shane O'Neill and Michael Kallinski, because they, too, had been constant visitors. After scrutinizing the list he put the small notebook away and finished his tea.

Paying his bill in cash, he nodded to the waitress and walked outside to his car. Within minutes he was on his way to Harrogate, driving across the moors. Mentally, he was thanking India for pointing him in the right direction. Because of her he now had a few clues, and a possible candidate for the role of intruder, the person who had invaded the winter solitude of Heron's Nest.

'What's in the suitcase Mrs Caldwell sent?' India asked, hovering in the doorway of the library at Willows Hall.

Dusty was sitting at the desk sorting through the items, and he glanced up on hearing India's voice. 'Her will, other papers, various things,' he replied, his face lighting up at the sight of her. 'You look wonderful,' he added, 'come in, don't stand there, darling.'

Smiling, India moved across the room, as always fluid and graceful in her movements. She was wearing a long crimson cashmere caftan, trimmed around her neck and down the front with gilt braiding, and her silvery gold hair was tied back in a pony tail. Her only jewellery were large gold hoop earrings, a watch, and her sapphire engagement ring.

Dusty jumped up and took her in his arms. He hugged her tightly to him, saying against her hair, 'I'm so sorry for what happened today, India. You don't deserve any of this. Melinda Caldwell is my problem, not yours.'

'Don't be daft,' India exclaimed, using one of her grandmother's favourite words. 'You're not responsible for her behaviour. And perhaps she isn't either, poor thing. I think she could be on drugs again, don't you?'

Staring hard at her, his blue eyes narrowing, Dusty asked, 'Did she seem doped up to you at the store this afternoon?'

'No, to be honest, she didn't. As I told Jack, she was angry, really furious.'

He sighed heavily. 'Unfortunately, I think Melinda's a lost cause. No one can help her, in my opinion. I hope Jack's people are able to find her but God knows where they'd look.'

'He's got the police on it as well. Apparently he knows some detectives in C.I.D. and he told me they have lots of contacts,' India explained.

Dusty nodded. 'They're all good lads. I know

some of the C.I.D. blokes, and they'd be aware of all the places where drugs are sold . . .' His voice trailed off. 'I just hope to God she doesn't start using again.' He stared into India's face, his eyes clouding. He knew Melinda would do just that. Her days were numbered.

Shaking off his dour mood, Dusty said, 'Molly's such a wonderful woman. She wrote me a lovely letter and put Atlanta's birth certificate and the key for the suitcase in the envelope.' He gestured to the items spread out on his large Georgian desk. 'There's a copy of her Last Will and Testament, and a letter to her solicitors attached. An envelope with a thousand pounds in cash in it, a little bag of jewellery, all rather nice stuff, and the deeds to her house. She owned it outright, you know. Oh, and there are two bank books for her savings accounts. Needless to say, she's left everything to Atlanta.'

'Obviously she would,' India remarked. 'I suppose she wanted you to have all this for safekeeping, since she's in the hospital.'

'That's the only reason it could be.' Dusty bit his lip and looked at India. 'I wonder if Molly suspected that Melinda might get out of the clinic and come bothering her?'

'Who knows, Dusty. The main thing is the suitcase is safe now that you have it.'

Paddy knocked on the door and came into the library. 'Excuse me, Mr Rhodes, I just wanted you to know that Mr Figg's arrived.'

'Thanks, Paddy, please show him in, and I think we'll have drinks in here, it's very cosy.'

'Right, sir. Mr Figg's just freshening up. In the meantime, shall I open a bottle of white wine?'

'That sounds good,' Dusty responded, and looked over at India who had gone to stand in front of the log fire blazing up the chimney. 'Or do you prefer something else?' he asked her.

'White wine's lovely, thanks.'

Paddy nodded and left.

Dusty walked over to the fireplace, put his arm around India and stood next to her, enjoying the warmth of the flames. 'Did you tell Jack he should plan on staying the night?' Dusty asked, looking down at her.

India shook her head. 'No, I guess it didn't occur to me, but it *is* a good idea, now that you mention it. He would have such a long drive to Robin Hood's Bay, if he were planning to go home tonight.'

'I know he sometimes stays at one of the hotels in Harrogate, but I am going to offer him a bed here. It's much more comfortable.'

Bending down he kissed her on the forehead and said, 'I have a surprise for you.'

'Oh. What is it?' Her eyes were on his, a questioning look in them.

'My painting of you is almost finished. At long last. I hope to show it to you on Saturday.'

'Oh, Dusty, how wonderful!'

'I hope you're going to like it,' he murmured.

'How could I not? You're the greatest painter there is today.'

'Ah, my bride-to-be is truly prejudiced,' he laughed, his blue eyes twinkling.

At this moment Jack walked in, a smile spread across his face. Hard on his heels came Paddy, carrying a tray of glasses and a bottle of white wine in a silver ice bucket.

'Jack, welcome!' Dusty exclaimed, moving forward, taking Jack's outstretched hand, manoeuvring him into the library and over to the fireside.

'Thanks for inviting me, Dusty,' Jack said, and then turning to India hugged her to him. 'It's good to see you, India.'

'Hello, Jack. I do hope it wasn't too bad a drive over those moors.'

He chuckled. 'It was a bit, and I must say they can be hellishly treacherous in the winter. But I made it safe and sound.'

'We want you to be safe and sound tonight, Jack,' Dusty interjected. 'And that's why we insist you stay here. You can't be driving all that way to Robin Hood's Bay.'

'But I can go to a hotel,' Jack began, and was immediately cut off by Dusty, who exclaimed, 'I won't hear of it. My home is your home, and listen, mate, it's a lot more comfortable here than at any hotel.'

'Well, thank you very much,' Jack responded, accepting the invitation gracefully.

'Come and sit with me here,' India said, taking a seat on the sofa and patting the one next to her. 'It's lovely and cosy near the fire.'

Dusty said, 'What would you like to drink, Jack?'

'I think I'll join you in a glass of white wine, please.'

'Make it three glasses, thanks, Paddy.' Dusty looked over at his house manager as he spoke, and added, 'Dinner in about forty-five minutes? Is that all right?'

'It's fine, sir,' Paddy replied and brought the tray of drinks over to the fireplace. The three of them took a glass, and thanked Paddy, who smiled in return and disappeared.

After clinking glasses, Dusty moved over to the fireplace, stood with his back to it again. There was a moment of silence and then Dusty said, 'I know it's far too early to ask if you have any news . . . but I just wanted to say this. I'm really grateful for your help, and I'll do whatever I can to assist you. Just say the word, Jack.'

'I'm not sure how you can help, unless you know any of Melinda's haunts in Leeds, where she might go. Or who her friends are here.'

'I'm afraid I don't,' Dusty answered, frowning slightly. 'You see, she hasn't actually lived here for some years . . . she moved to London and never came back much, except to see Atlanta, who has lived with Molly since she was a baby.'

'I see.' Jack blew out a puff of air, obviously in frustration, looked off in the distance for a split second. Then he said, 'India told me you'd been in touch with the de-tox clinic . . . Were they forthcoming about Melinda's condition?'

'They're very open, Jack, they don't try to hide anything. Although she still needs treatment, I got the impression she was clean again, but that they hadn't finished their therapy sessions. She's always called it their brainwashing, but I do think it helps.'

'I understand. I have one of my operatives watching Molly's house, since Melinda might try to break in again. And he's keeping an eye on Gladys Roebotham's house as well. Just in case she shows up there. What I am hoping is that we find her in Meanwood and not—'

'On a cold slab,' Dusty cut in, and lifted a dark brow quizzically.

Jack shook his head. 'I wasn't going to say that, Dusty. However, let's hope she doesn't end up in the morgue. I was going to say I hope she's not found with a drug-dealer or druggies, because that would mean she's back on heroin. It is that, isn't it?'

'Yep. And any other drug she might be able to get her hands on. Melinda is one of those people who is addictive by nature. It's a sickness really, to be perfectly honest.'

'I know that. Anyway, if anything comes up, they'll call me.' Jack patted his tweed jacket. 'I've got my mobile on at all times. Now, how's Mrs Caldwell doing?'

'She's the same. No change,' Dusty said quietly.

India now said, 'Unless you two have anything else to discuss regarding Melinda, I'd like to change the subject, if you don't mind.'

'Change away, darling,' Dusty murmured, pushing a smile onto his face. 'It does get dreary talking about drug-addicts, not to mention rather painful when I consider the ramifications here.'

Jack nodded in agreement. 'All I want to say is

that we are at a disadvantage, Dusty, when it comes to finding Melinda Caldwell.'

'Oh, I know that, I know only too well.'

'Jack, can we talk about Heron's Nest for a moment?' India asked, turning slightly on the sofa, looking at him. 'I was wondering why Mrs Hodges thought someone had been in the house recently?'

'Dust,' he responded laconically and then grinned when he saw the baffled look on India's face.

'What on earth do you mean?'

'The disturbance of dust. She told me the house gets very dusty because it's so old, and several times lately she's noticed marks in the dust that accumulates in a week.'

'How extraordinary!' Dusty exclaimed, looking over at Jack nonplussed. 'Dust, eh?' he laughed suddenly.

'Let me explain,' Jack said. 'If someone walks across a dusty floor there might not be actual footprints, but the dust will be – disturbed. I suppose that's what she means. Anyway, Mrs Hodges also says that upstairs one of the bathrooms has been used. Apparently this particular bathroom has a tap that constantly drips unless it's turned off very, very hard. She found it dripping recently. She also found some black hairs on a cushion in one of the bedrooms. Quite a few little things like that have caught her attention. Then one of her neighbours reported seeing lights in the house. Well, to be completely accurate, someone saw a light bobbing around not so long ago. I think it might have been someone using a flashlight.'

'Mrs Hodges is quite the detective, isn't she, Jack?' India exclaimed. 'She'll be bringing you D.N.A. samples next.'

Jack couldn't help laughing, and then he said, through his laughter, 'Yes, she's a regular Miss Marple. And anyway, she *did* bring me a D.N.A. sample, or rather she drew my attention to the black hairs. I have them in a glassine envelope, although I must admit I have no one to match them to, India. Nor has a crime been committed.'

'As far as we know,' India responded somewhat pithily.

'Our own Miss Marple says nothing's been stolen from Heron's Nest,' Jack pointed out.

'And there hasn't been a murder,' India shot back.

'What *are* you two talking about?' Dusty asked, totally baffled, his attention going from one to the other.

Jack explained about Heron's Nest, and then glancing at India, he asked, 'Don't tell me you've never taken Dusty over to Scarborough to see Emma's lovely old house by the sea?'

'Not yet,' India admitted, then a sheepish grin spread itself across her face, and turning to Dusty she went on, 'Don't you remember? Last year, after the stabbing, I said I'd love to take you to Emma's seaside house to have a few days' rest and recuperation.'

'Oh, yes, now I do. And after I agreed to go, *you* changed your mind for some reason.'

'Yes, because Linnet discouraged me. She said the house had been locked up all winter, and that there was only Mrs Hodges to do a bit of dusting.' She burst into laughter. 'Sorry about all this play on your name . . . *Dusty*.'

He grinned at her and swallowed down the last drop of his wine, walked across the room, poured himself another glass, then said to Jack, 'Would you like some wine?'

Rising, Jack followed him to the drinks table at the other end of the library. 'Why not? Since I'm not driving tonight I can indulge a little. Thanks, Dusty.'

India said, 'I know it's not either my mother or my father who's having an illicit relationship with someone else and using Heron's Nest as . . . a love nest.' She laughed.

He came back to the sofa, a smile on his face, and sat down next to her. 'And it can't be either Paula or Shane. Nor is it Emily or Winston. So who can it be?'

'Not Sarah Pascal, who lives in Paris and hardly ever sets foot in Yorkshire, and certainly not Amanda, who's constantly travelling, or her twin, Francesca, who's married with lots of kids.'

'And Alexander is dead,' Jack pointed out. 'I know Michael Kallinski was one of the gang who was always there, attending Emma's Boot Camp. But he's divorced and can do as he wants.' Jack pulled his notebook out of his jacket pocket and looked at the list of Emma's grandchildren. Glancing up, he stared at India. 'That leaves only one person . . . *Jonathan Ainsley*.'

'I know! I just thought of him myself. But listen, Jack, Jonathan's single, so he can see anyone he wishes. Furthermore, he has a house of his own at Thirsk, a flat in Grosvenor Square, a farm in Provence and a mansion on The Peak in Hong Kong. Why would he need Heron's Nest for a secret rendezvous?'

Jack shook his head, his expression one of puzzlement.

Dusty said, 'Perhaps the lady lives in Yorkshire, and for some reason can't travel very far. A husband? Kids? A career?'

'All possibilities, yes,' India murmured.

'Jonathan's a very sophisticated man, so who would be a candidate up here in Yorkshire?' Jack wondered aloud.

'Obviously somebody we don't know,' India volunteered.

Jack added, 'And now he's tied up with Angharad Hughes . . .' His sentence trailed off.

Listening to them, Dusty had a brainwave, and he exclaimed, 'Here's a thought, you two. If a man or a woman comes back to a place they knew in their youth, it's because they loved that spot, have happy memories of it. *Sentimental reasons*. That's why somebody went back to Heron's Nest, maybe to meet an old love. Someone from the past. Someone who feels the same way.'

'Brilliant!' India exclaimed.

'Yes, very clever thinking indeed, Dusty,' Jack agreed. 'I must put *my* thinking cap on, go back to those days in my mind. I was frequently at the house, visiting Emma.'

'Think about the things everyone *did*, Jack, that

might help you to recall a forgotten face, maybe an outside person who came to stay, or just visit for the day.'

'Good idea . . . they played tennis . . . swam . . . did the usual things young people do. Of course, Emma often invited me to tea at the Grand in Scarborough; in fact, she took everyone to tea there often, and to dinner as well.'

'You've jogged my memory, Jack,' India cried, sitting up straight on the sofa. 'Mummy told me that she and her brother Winston, with Emily in tow, used to steal out at night to go to the Grand Hotel for drinks. In the Cocktail Lounge, she said. They felt very grown up. But they got caught once. Emma's summer secretary spotted them there, and threatened to tell Emma, unless they promised never to go there again. What about that summer secretary, she—'

'Priscilla Marney,' Jack said, interrupting her, the name coming to him from out of the blue. '*Of course*. Priscilla's mother was Emma's summer secretary. They lived in Scarborough.'

India was staring at him. Her face had gone pale, her eyes were wide. 'Jack, Priscilla works for Paula. She does all the catering. She catered Evan's and Gid's wedding. She's right in our midst.'

'I know,' he said, his voice sombre. 'I even saw her bustling around at the reception, but she's so much a part of the furniture I didn't think anything about it, her being there, I mean.'

'Maybe there's nothing to think,' India suggested, hoping this were true.

'That's possible. Just because she knew Jonathan years ago doesn't mean she knows him now.' Jack leaned back against the velvet cushions, his mind whirling, sudden memories flooding back.

'I wasn't much older than any of them, you know, just eighteen and learning the ropes,' Jack told them. 'My uncle had worked for Emma for years, and I was sort of his protégé, and she made me her protégé. She took me by the hand and led me, treated me like one of the family, my uncle as well.'

India said, in a worried voice, 'If Priscilla Marney is seeing Jonathan Ainsley then she's the spy Linnet's always going on about. For a long time Linny has insisted that there was someone in our midst who was involved with Jonathan. And telling him things.'

'It might *not* be her,' Jack murmured. 'But I can assure you, I *will* find out. And very swiftly.'

'Seems like he might have moved on, though,' Dusty suggested. 'Isn't he now caught on Angharad Hughes's hook, flailing around in gay Paree?'

'That's right,' India said.

CHAPTER TWENTY-SIX

India could see his silhouette in the moonlight.
Dusty was standing at the window, looking
down into the gardens below, and he was utterly
still, as rigid as stone.

After a second or two of watching him from the
bed, India slid her feet to the floor and went to
him, moving across the bedroom swiftly. She put
her hand on his shoulder, her touch light.

He turned at once, looked down at her. In the
light from the wintry full moon outside the window,
she saw the residue of tears on his face.

Moving closer to him, she touched each cheek
with her fingertips, gently wiping the dampness
away. He put an arm around her, drawing her to
him, holding her tightly without speaking.

In the silence of the room she could almost hear
his heart beating in unison with hers. She thought:
I love him so much, I can't bear it when he's in
pain.

As if reading her mind, Dusty murmured, 'What a
mess I've made of all this, not handling the situation

with Melinda differently. And now you have to suffer because of it.'

'That's not so, and don't beat yourself over the head,' India replied softly. 'You did what you thought was right, did the best you could. No one can ask more than that.'

'I did try with Melinda . . .' he sighed. 'I do wish I'd looked after Molly better. I ought to have built her a small house on the property: she and Atlanta would have been safe here with me, with us. And I would have been around for Atlanta whenever she needed me.'

'It's not too late to do that, Dusty!' India responded, moving her head away from his chest, looking up into his eyes, as dark as lapis in the dim light. 'I think that's a grand idea, building a home for Molly and Atlanta here. Let's do it.'

He did not reply for a moment; there was sadness in his voice when he said, at last, 'It's too late now. I've left it too late.'

'What do you mean?' she asked, immediately struck by the sorrow echoing.

'I don't think Molly will survive the heart attack she had today. I didn't tell you how massive it was.'

'Oh, no, don't say that. She was doing so well. And she seems to be a strong woman. Hopefully we can go and see her tomorrow at the Infirmary. We should try at least. Perhaps we can talk to her doctors. And I'll go with you, if you wish.'

He inclined his head. 'Yes, let's do that . . . it will cheer her up.' His voice was suddenly lighter, more positive.

'And we can tell her about building a house for her. It will give her a boost. It's something for her to look forward to, Dusty.'

'Yes, we'll do that. I hope they'll let us see her.'

'They will, darling, I'm certain. Come on, come back to bed, it's the middle of the night.'

'I'm sorry. Did I wake you? I just couldn't sleep.'

'No, you didn't wake me . . . I just know when you're not there . . . even when I'm sleeping.'

Once they were back in bed he pulled her to him, wrapping his arms around her, whispering, 'Whatever would I do without you? You're always there for me, no matter what. I love you.' There was a pause before he added, 'You see, I can say it now.'

'And I love you,' she murmured against his bare chest, nestling closer. 'And you'll never have to do without me. I'll be with you for the rest of my life.'

'God, I hope so!' Pushing himself up onto one elbow he looked down into her eyes, a faint smile flickering around his mouth. Then lowering his face to hers, he kissed her deeply, and within only a few seconds his passion flared, and so did hers for him.

'Oh, my darling, my darling India.' He brought his lips to her breasts, his hands moving over her body, touching her everywhere, his desire for her rampant.

India responded ardently, with a passion that matched his, her hands fluttering over his stomach and down onto his thighs; he sighed languorously as she began to stroke him. A moment later he was above her, staring down at her. Wanting to become part of her, he took her to him almost roughly. She cried out as he entered her, and she cleaved to him. They began to move together rhythmically, rapturous in each other's arms and spiralling into ecstasy.

And suddenly Dusty felt all of his pain and anguish begin to dissolve and it was as if it had never existed. What a blessed relief it was, this absence of pain. It was because of her . . . His love. His life.

Jack Figg had never seen anything quite like it before. The most beautiful portrait of a woman he had ever set eyes on. Yet to say it was beautiful would not be enough, would not do it justice, he realized that.

The painting was so mesmerizing he could not tear his eyes away from it, held as he was by the glory of the woman's face and the breathtaking background spread out behind her.

Dusty had painted a landscape that was magnificent and could only be English: a canopy of dark green trees set against a pale blue sky scattered with puffy clouds, half golden in colour as if they were filled with sunlight. The lawns below that shimmering summer sky were lighter green, gave way to a patch of dark earth in the foreground, where the garden seat was placed. It was upon this sofa-like structure that the woman reclined.

The woman's face was heart-shaped, with a narrow nose, high cheekbones and finely-arched brows above large, silvery eyes. The face was pale, set on a slender neck and framed by a mass of silver-gilt hair, long and silky and gleaming brightly in the painting. The face and the hair seemed to jump out at him, looked so very real he wanted to lean forward and touch them.

The portrait was of India, of course, but an India Standish *he* did not know, had never seen before. There was a sensuality about her, a half-dreamy, half-knowing look in those brilliant eyes, and the red mouth, plump and half open, was positively voluptuous.

India had the look of a woman in love who had just been well loved, and naturally he did not know *this* India. She was the India known only to her lover, Russell Rhodes, who had painted this portrait of her from his very soul. The painting was a testament to that love, his adoration of her.

Her long body was stretched out on the garden sofa which was covered with a burgundy-velvet throw. She wore a filmy outfit of black chiffon, loose and casual, composed of harem trousers and a draped top. This fell away from her shoulders to reveal white arms, marble-like in their perfection. Her longish feet were bare, the nails painted to match the dark-red throw.

Jack knew it was a portrait that would cause a sensation – if ever it were shown. But naturally it would be shown. Dusty wouldn't be able to resist doing so. In Jack's opinion it was one of the most extraordinary paintings he had ever produced, staggering in its beauty.

'Come on, mate, say *something*,' Dusty exclaimed, moving closer to Jack, who was still entranced in front of the easel. 'Even if you don't like it, say something, Jack.'

'Actually, I'm absolutely speechless,' Jack said at long last, finally turning away from the portrait to regard Dusty. 'It's so captivating, so breath-takingly beautiful I don't know how to express myself adequately.' Jack shook his head. 'Well, I suppose I can say, in all truthfulness, that it's sensational, heart-stopping and truly staggering. You're a bloody marvel, Dusty. A genius. It's Classical Realism taken to utter perfection. No wonder they've always said you're the new Pietro Annigoni.'

Flattered at Jack's reaction though he was, Dusty couldn't resist teasing him. Giving him a long, hard stare, he said, 'Is that all you can say, Jack? Bloody hell, that's not much of a reaction after almost a year of slog on my part.'

For a moment Jack was taken aback. He blinked, and then, when he suddenly realized Dusty was pulling his leg, he began to chuckle. 'I meant every word, you scoundrel. It's going to cause quite a stir when you show it.'

'Yes, I know.' Moving away from the easel, standing back, Dusty studied his portrait of India, and, glancing at Jack, he added, 'It will look even better when it's framed. And *she's* the bloody marvel, if anybody is,' he finished.

'Thanks for letting me see it.' Jack stood watching Dusty throwing the sheet over the painting, continued, 'When are you going to show it to India?'

'I told her she could see it on Saturday. Tomorrow, in fact. I hope she likes it.'

'How can she not?'

'People have a funny knack of seeing themselves quite differently from the way others see them . . . they have a unique way of looking at themselves . . . as if with one eye only. They get a half-blind picture,' he finished with a laugh.

'I guess they do: that's very well said.'

'Let's go and have another cup of coffee before you get on your way,' Dusty said, leading Jack away from the painting. After locking the studio door behind them and pocketing the key, Dusty led the way to the grand Palladian house on the hill. Neither man spoke. Both were lost in their own thoughts.

After taking his leave of Dusty, Jack left Willows Hall, drove through Harrogate and took the Ripon road in the direction of Pennistone Royal. It was a lovely day, cold and crisp with a brilliant sun high flung in a pale blue sky.

Before going down to breakfast that morning, Jack had checked in with his two operatives as well as his pals at Leeds C.I.D. None of them had had any luck; there was nothing to report about Melinda Caldwell and her whereabouts. Nor had Dusty heard from the hospital. After finally making a call to the nurses' station at the Infirmary, Dusty had explained to Jack that Molly's condition was unchanged; she was still in the I.C.U. The day nurse had promised to give Dusty a ring if there were any new developments.

As he drove, Jack's thoughts swung to Jonathan Ainsley and Priscilla Marney. Were those two really old lovers? Had they recently been meeting in secret at Heron's Nest? Jack pondered this for a short while. Then it suddenly struck him that Priscilla would have been awfully young when he'd first seen her at Heron's Nest. Thirteen? Fourteen? Could she have been having sex with Jonathan then? No, too young, he decided. On the other hand, kids today had sex at that age . . . but forty years ago?

Jack sighed to himself as he drove along, wondering if he was on a wild goose chase, going to Pennistone Royal to talk to Margaret. This trip was all India's idea. Before leaving for the Leeds store earlier that morning, India had suggested he ought to go and talk to Paula's housekeeper. 'There's not much she doesn't know about this family,' India had pointed out. 'Don't forget, her parents worked all of their lives at Pennistone Royal for Emma. Margaret grew up there, along with Paula and all the cousins. That's why she's so familiar at times. Maybe she would know if Jonathan and Priscilla were once an item.' India had laughed, and added, 'She's quite gossipy, you know, at times. On the other hand, maybe those two were secretive about their relationship even then, if there was one, of course.'

Jack had instantly seen the sense in talking to Margaret, and before setting out he had phoned Paula at the London store. He had only one question for her: which bedroom had been Jonathan's when they were growing up? As she had described the room, Jack knew at once it was the one which Mrs Hodges had insisted was disturbed and where she had shown him the black hairs on the pink cushions. 'New cushions,' the caretaker had thought to point out to him yesterday. 'Mrs O'Neill bought 'em last summer, when she was titivating the house.'

So here he was, heading to Pennistone Royal on the pretext of checking the security system. He had used this ruse to explain the reason for his visit to Margaret, realizing he might change his mind about discussing Jonathan and Priscilla with her. He had decided to feel his way on that.

It was not long before Jack reached the back gate of the great stone house. After punching in the security code, he drove up the back drive slowly, cautious because of the horses that were frequently around. The back drive was deserted this morning; not even Wiggs, the head gardener, was anywhere in sight. Once he turned the bend, just before reaching the cobbled back yard, he spotted Wiggs poking at a bonfire which was blazing on a patch of dark earth.

Slowing the car, Jack rolled down the window and greeted the head gardener with a cheerful, 'Hello, Wiggs!'

''Morning, Mr Jack. It's a right fine day.'

'It is indeed.' As he drove into the yard and got out of the car, Jack felt a rush of nostalgia as he sniffed the smoke of the bonfire. His father had loved to garden, was forever burning twigs and leaves. It was an old, well-remembered smell, and for a moment it brought a lump to his throat as his childhood flashed before him.

Shaking off his past, Jack strode towards the kitchen door, knocked and walked in, exclaiming, 'Top of the morning to you, Margaret—' He broke off when he saw Priscilla Marney sitting at the kitchen table with the housekeeper. Somehow he managed to keep his face neutral as he said, 'And hello, Priscilla!'

'Good morning, Jack,' she answered with a faint smile.

It was Margaret who instantly jumped up, came over to him, a beaming smile lighting up her motherly face as she greeted him in a warm voice. 'It's a good job you're here, Jack,' she then exclaimed, taking his arm, leading him to the big deal table in the middle of the spacious kitchen. 'I had a real problem buzzing Prissy in twenty minutes ago. I couldn't make that there switch work. I think it's on the blink, do you know. Anyway, I had to go outside and find Wiggs, send him down to open the gate. Do you think there's a shortage or something?'

'It's possible, Margaret. I'd say it's rather lucky that I decided to do a check of the system here today, and only because I was in the area.'

'It's lucky for us, it is that, Jack! Now sit yourself down, luv, and how about a cup of tea?'

'I wouldn't say no.' As he lowered himself into a chair directly opposite Priscilla, Jack couldn't help thinking that it was very fortuitous that *she* was here, obviously on some kind of catering business. Sometimes when things like this had happened in the past he would tell himself: *It was meant to be*. It was as if some unseen but knowing and omnipotent hand had arranged things specially for him, to his liking. And this is what he thought now. Here was the one and only Priscilla, at his disposal, so to speak, and all he had to do was think of the best way to set her up and draw her out. With a little luck he might well be able to trap her into spilling the beans.

Pushing a big smile onto his face, he now said in a friendly, interested voice, 'And how's the catering business doing, Prissy?'

'Very well, Jack, thanks. I've been extremely busy lately . . . no, I can't complain at all.'

'I'm glad to hear it. You certainly catered Evan's wedding beautifully.' He nodded, went on, 'You grew up to be a talented lass, you really did. Why, I can remember you when you were a gawky little schoolgirl in Scarborough. I often used to come across you at Heron's Nest when I went over to see Mrs Harte.'

Priscilla stared at him, obviously taken by surprise at this mention of the past. And Heron's Nest. She simply nodded. And he wondered if he was imagining it, but hadn't her face paled slightly? He wasn't sure. Wanting to breach the little gap, break the silence, Jack went on, 'How's your daughter? Samantha, isn't it?'

A smile struck her face now, and her dark eyes lit up. 'Yes, it is, and she's terrific, Jack, thanks for asking. I'm very proud of her.'

'Oh, she's a lovely girl,' Margaret interjected, bringing the cup and saucer to the table, sitting down, pouring Jack a cup of tea. 'And she looks just like her father, Conner, the spitting image. God rest his soul.'

Vaguely Jack remembered that Margaret had told him some years ago that Priscilla's husband had been knocked down by a bus in Manchester. 'Such a young man, too,' Margaret had added at the time.

Margaret said, 'Do you want something to eat, Jack?'

'No, thanks very much though.'

Sitting back in her chair, Margaret said, 'Emily's going to have the christening here—' She stopped, noticing the disapproving expression on Jack's face, cleared her throat and corrected herself quickly, saying, 'Miss Emily wants to have it at Pennistone Royal because of tradition, and Miss Paula agreed. Anyway, it's a better place than Allington Hall. Prissy's doing the catering, of course.'

'That's why I'm here this morning.' Priscilla gave Jack a small smile, and unexpectedly confided, 'I've brought the proposals over, the plans and menus for Emily and Paula to look at this weekend. Oh, and I'm doing the wedding as well.'

For a moment Jack was baffled and he frowned, asked, '*Wedding*? What wedding?'

'Tessa's, of course,' Margaret answered before Priscilla had a chance to respond. 'Miss Paula told me last weekend that the divorce is more or less final. I believe Tessa will marry Mr Deléon any minute now. In London, at a registry office. That's the plan. But everyone will come up here for the reception, and to spend the weekend. So we certainly need Prissy.'

'But he's gone to Afghanistan. To cover the war,' Jack murmured, his brows drawing together in a jagged line. 'I don't think Tessa will be getting married just yet,' he explained. 'Not for a while.'

'Oh, but she will,' Priscilla cut in. 'The minute he's finished his assignment they'll be married. Paula told me that on the phone only the other day. That's why I had to draw up the second proposal. I've worked around the clock on it for the last few days. Paula wanted it by today because she's arriving later this afternoon.'

Jack simply nodded.

Priscilla picked up her cup of tea, took a sip and it was then that Jack noticed she was wearing a wedding band with a small sapphire engagement ring next to it. He now recalled that Margaret had mentioned something about Priscilla remarrying several years ago. He couldn't help wondering if she was still married; if she was, perhaps that was the answer, the reason why she was meeting Jonathan at Heron's Nest. If she *was* meeting him, that is. Between her busy catering business, her daughter and her marriage she would perhaps be far too busy to meet him in London. Or anywhere else, for that matter.

Unable to resist, Jack now asked, 'You *did* get married again, didn't you, Prissy?'

'Oh, yes, but I'm separated from Roger.'

'Oh, I'm sorry.'

'Don't be, he's not good enough to lick her boots!'

Margaret announced, leaning forward, giving Jack a knowing look. 'Can't hold a candle to Priscilla, that he can't.'

Priscilla shrugged. 'We all make mistakes sometimes,' she remarked. 'It hasn't worked out for me. Still, no harm done.' Quite suddenly she smiled, and it was a brilliant smile. 'You know what they say, there's more fish in the sea than ever came out of it,' she said, unexpectedly looking pleased with herself.

'Hooked a good one, have you?' Jack asked before he could stop himself.

Priscilla blushed scarlet, but did not answer him. Jack decided she didn't have to . . . words were not at all necessary. Her face told him the whole story.

Margaret laughed. 'Priscilla's got a lot of admirers, you know, Jack, and you can see why.'

'Indeed I can. And I must say I'm delighted at your enormous success in business. Mind you, Priscilla, you deserve it. The food at Evan's wedding was delicious. And talking of Evan and weddings, will you be catering Jonathan's? Or isn't he getting married in Yorkshire?' As Jack asked this loaded question, his eyes did not leave Priscilla Marney's face.

Margaret exclaimed, '*What*?' Her eyes were wide in astonishment.

Priscilla said not a word. Incredulous, she sat staring at Jack, obviously stunned. Her face suddenly turned a violent red, and just as quickly that brilliant colour drained away and she paled, was as white as bleached bone. She opened her mouth to say something, but no words came out. There was only a strangled cry of despair.

Margaret cried, 'What did you say, Jack? That Jonathan Ainsley's getting married? That takes the cake! Who is he marrying?'

'Evan's sister,' Jack answered, his eyes still on Priscilla who was now shaking like a leaf in a high wind. '*Angharad Hughes*. You know who I mean, Margaret. The platinum blonde who was one of the bridesmaids. She was—'

'Oh, God! Not *her*!' Priscilla screeched, her voice shrill and pained. 'Not that ugly, vulgar American girl!'

'Not so ugly, anymore, so I'm told. Nor so vulgar either, according to Linnet,' said Jack, gazing at her.

'What are you gabbling about?' Margaret asked swiftly, glancing worriedly at Priscilla and then back at Jack, shaking her head.

He said, 'I understand that Angharad and Jonathan are in Paris together. According to Linnet, who got it from ... Paula, Angharad is now an elegant brunette dressed in couture clothes, all of the finest quality and of the best taste. And the expensive jewellery is also of the finest quality, at least that was what Linnet was told. I also understand they're going off to Hong Kong, so he can "show her the sights", to quote Linnet quoting Paula's source. Apparently he's fallen head over heels for Miss Hughes.'

'But she's horrible,' Priscilla spluttered in an angry voice, tears coming into her eyes. Her mouth began to tremble and she could not proceed, so distressed was she.

Jack said, 'It seems her make-over, accomplished by the most talented of hairdressers, make-up artists and couturiers, has been very successful. So successful, I'm told, Angharad now looks like the young Audrey Hepburn. And let's not forget she *is* only twenty-three. Nothing like young flesh to turn on an old geezer like Jonathan Ainsley.'

Priscilla cried out, but her words were unintelligible. She began to groan, and then she burst into tears. Bringing her hands to her face, she sobbed as if her heart were breaking.

CHAPTER TWENTY-SEVEN

Priscilla lay on the big sofa in front of the fire in the library. After helping her into the room, Margaret had put a match to the paper and logs in the grate, covered her with a tartan blanket and brought her a brandy, had told her to gulp it down, explaining that it would help her.

But Priscilla had taken only a sip, then put the glass on the coffee table. She felt nauseous, realized she wouldn't be able to keep anything inside her, least of all the Calvados. She was still in a state of extreme shock.

Jack Figg's sudden and totally unexpected announcement that Jonathan, *her Jonny*, was with that awful girl in Paris had truly been the most terrible blow, the worst since she had been informed her darling Conner was lying dead in the morgue in Manchester.

When Jack had said Jonathan was going to marry Evan's sister, she was so stunned and hurt and upset she had completely lost control, become hysterical. Now they knew she had been having an affair with him . . . they couldn't help but put two and two together. For a while, as she had lain here, she had been embarrassed by this, but now that feeling had passed. She didn't have to explain herself to them, or anyone else for that matter. She was a grown woman; she'd done nothing wrong.

Closing her eyes, Priscilla tried to relax, but this was impossible. She was still tense, discomfited, and filled with unease. And then there was the jealousy – how insidiously it had crept up on her, filling her with hatred for the girl, and for him.

How untrustworthy Jonathan Ainsley was, not to mention being a dyed-in-the-wool liar. He had kept cancelling their romantic rendezvous in Thirsk, first because he had been delayed in London on business, and couldn't return to Yorkshire. So he said. And then because he was in Paris, the second time. He had murmured sweet endearments to her over the phone, promising her so much, and all the time he'd held the phone, his other hand had been on the girl. Evan's little sister. Twenty-three. Delectable. *Young flesh*, Jack had called Angharad Hughes. How right he was. What man in his fifties, especially a voluptuary like Jonathan, could resist her?

Picturing them together in bed in his Paris flat sent a terrible wave of hatred rushing through her. *Bastard*. He had promised to take her to Paris so many times and he never had. Suddenly, the mere thought of him buying the girl expensive clothes and fabulous jewellery was too much for her to bear. She began to tremble. Despair, anger, hurt and disappointment coalesced together into a tight, hard ball inside her. She began to weep uncontrollably. Pushing her face into the cushions, she sobbed and sobbed until there were no tears left; exhausted, she lay still.

Eventually, Priscilla discovered she was unexpectedly calm, and her self-control slowly returned. It was then that a cold and bitter detachment finally settled over her, and she contemplated revenge.

Margaret sat on a small chair next to the sofa, holding Priscilla's hand. 'Are you feeling better?' she asked, in a kindly tone, staring at her.

Swallowing hard, Priscilla nodded. 'Yes, thanks, Margaret. I'll soon be back to normal.' She forced a small smile. 'Sorry I got so upset. You've been very kind.'

'Jack says you went into shock . . . you did, you know, I agree with him there.'

Priscilla merely nodded, said nothing.

Margaret went on slowly, 'Whatever made you get involved with *him*, luvey? Jonathan of all people. He's a bad lot.'

Biting her lip, Priscilla shook her head. 'I'd known him all my life . . . he sought me out at different times . . . pursued me, really. He was very flattering, even loving.'

It was Margaret's turn to remain silent. She just sat holding Priscilla's hand, glad she was no longer weeping and moaning. Although she felt sorry for her in certain ways, Margaret was also silently chastising her for being such a foolish woman. But then more women fell for the bad lads than she cared to think about. She knew quite a few who'd toppled into that trap.

There was a knock, and Jack appeared in the doorway. 'Do you feel better, Prissy? Can I come in for a few minutes?'

'Oh, yes, that's fine.'

Closing the door of the library behind him, Jack crossed the floor and sat down in an armchair, facing Priscilla on the sofa.

Margaret immediately got up off the stool and moved away, made to leave, deciding it was perhaps better for Jack to talk to the caterer alone.

'It's all right, Margaret.' Jack glanced at the housekeeper. 'You don't have to leave. In fact, I think it would be a good idea for you to stay.'

'If you want me to, Jack,' she answered, and went over to the other sofa, settled herself there.

'Yes, I do want you here,' he said. Smiling at Priscilla, his eyes filled with sympathy, Jack murmured in a warm voice, 'I must apologize to you. I'm afraid I upset you greatly, blurting that out about Jonathan Ainsley, the way I did. But I'd no idea you were in any way involved with him.'

'Nobody knew,' Priscilla informed him in a low voice.

'And why was that?' Jack gave her a penetrating look.

'He wanted to keep it a secret.'

'I see.' He leaned forward, staring at her even more intently. After a moment, he asked, 'Because you're married? Was that the reason?'

'Not really,' Priscilla replied, and hesitated before

adding, 'He knew I was separated, and that I'm planning to divorce Roger Duffield.'

'But *why* the secrecy? I don't understand.'

'He didn't want the family to know about us,' she answered at last. 'The Hartes.'

'I see.' Jack now sat back, staring off into space for a moment before saying, suddenly, 'Did you never wonder why he insisted on keeping your relationship a secret?'

'Occasionally. But, well, I . . . well . . . I wanted to be with him, so I just accepted it. Accepted his terms.'

'You've been meeting him at Heron's Nest, haven't you?'

'Yes,' she responded laconically, looked down at her hands, shame-faced.

'Why there?'

'Because it meant something to him, and to me, as well. You see, we'd first made . . . been together there when we were teenagers. So Heron's Nest was special to both of us. It seemed to excite him, meeting there in secret.' She blushed, looked embarrassed, turned her head, gazed into the fire, wondering why she'd told him this.

Clearing his throat, Jack continued, 'Presumably he had a key?'

'Oh, yes, ever since our teenage years. I believe he'd made a copy then, and Paula has never changed the locks.'

Dismayed though he was about this lack of security, Jack kept his face neutral as he went on in a quiet but firm tone, 'I have to tell you something very important, Priscilla. And I need your full attention.'

Nodding, she said, 'Yes, I'm listening, Jack, I really am.'

'There's a good reason why Jonathan Ainsley wanted to conceal your affair. He didn't want Paula to know about you and him, because *he* is *her* sworn enemy, a deadly enemy of this entire family, in fact. If Paula had known how close you two were, she would not have used you as her caterer and he would have lost his informant.'

Sitting up straighter on the sofa, swinging her legs to the floor, Priscilla gaped at him askance, her face turning extremely pale. 'But I wasn't his informant!' Her eyes wide, her voice rising, she added, 'I *swear* I wasn't! And you're wrong, Jack, he wasn't and isn't an enemy of the family. I would have known.'

'Not necessarily. Didn't it ever occur to you that it was strange he never attended any of the family functions and gatherings?'

'He always planned to come!' she cried vehemently. 'He told me he was coming, but then he was suddenly called away, to Paris or Hong Kong. Or somewhere. I thought that was his life; after all, he is a big tycoon.' She shook her head. 'I never ever told him anything about Paula, or the family. I didn't know anything. No one ever confided in *me*.'

Jack got up, walked over to the fireplace, stood with his back to it, enjoying the warmth. After a moment, he began to speak once more, saying to the caterer, 'You must have told Jonathan at different times that you were about to cater a special event for Paula, didn't you?'

Priscilla could only nod.

'So in a way you *were* a conduit to the family, if unintentionally so. He certainly knew when the entire family would be here at Pennistone Royal, for example.'

'Yes,' she whispered, dismay lodging in her stomach. 'That's true. But I never knew he was their enemy. He always acted as if he were on the best of terms with them. You must believe me.'

'He's a clever chap, isn't he, Margaret?' Looking over at the housekeeper, Jack smiled sardonically. '*And dangerous*.'

'Oh, that he is,' Margaret agreed. 'He'd love to kill us all off, that he would.' She gave Priscilla a hard stare, hoping her words had penetrated.

'*Never!*' Priscilla cried, excitedly, her emotions getting the better of her. 'I don't believe you! That's not Jonny. You're exaggerating, I know you are.'

'I'm afraid not,' Jack exclaimed coldly, starting to get exasperated with her. 'Margaret is telling you the truth, as indeed am I. There's no reason for either of us to exaggerate or lie to you, Prissy. To what purpose? Jonathan wants to destroy Paula and the family and that's a fact.'

Priscilla Marney sat rigid on the sofa, gaping at Jack, hardly able to take this all in. But she accepted, as she looked into his eyes now blazing with anger, that this man spoke the truth. She was aghast and perturbed. How could she have been with Jonathan and not known any of these things? Not understood his evil intentions? Nervous, now even afraid, she suddenly wondered where her judgement had been.

And her common sense. A fool for love, she thought disdainfully.

When she continued to remain silent, Jack asked her, 'Did you know about the problem at the church on the day of the wedding?'

'No. What do you mean?' she asked, looking at him alertly, her eyes widening.

Without answering her, he said, 'But you did know the time was changed? You haven't forgotten about that, have you?'

'No. They got married in the early morning and Margaret said it was because Evan hadn't been feeling well and everyone was worried about her condition . . . the pregnancy . . . premature birth.'

'Actually, those *were* worries, but not exactly the reason the time of the marriage was changed. The family were concerned, actually they were afraid that Jonathan might attempt to do something to harm Evan and Gideon. So Linnet devised a plan, and how right she was to do so, as it turned out,' Jack said. 'At two-fifteen in the afternoon, the original time of the wedding, part of the west wall of Pennistone village church blew out. Because a bomb had been planted in the church. During the night, we believe. We're sure it was Ainsley's doing, but naturally we can never prove it.'

Priscilla stared at Jack, shaking her head. 'I went to London on Sunday. I didn't hear about the explosion.' She felt as though she had just been hit in the stomach with a cricket bat. Unnerved, shocked beyond belief, it took her a moment to get hold of herself. 'Oh, my God, no! It's not possible, Jack.

I *know* him, know him better than anybody. He wouldn't do anything so wicked.' She was almost in tears again, as she finished, 'Why would he?'

'Because of his hatred,' Margaret told her, once more speaking up. 'He's jealous and envious of Miss Paula, and of Evan, now she's in the picture.'

'How do you know it was *him*?' Priscilla demanded, her eyes nervously turning from Margaret to Jack. 'He wasn't even in Yorkshire on the day of the wedding,' she protested. 'So how could he put a bomb in the church?'

'You don't think he'd be foolish enough to do his own dirty work, do you?' Jack stared at her intently, his eyes narrowing, wondering how dumb she really was. 'Surely you're smarter than that, Prissy?' He shook his head, his face grave. 'No, no, he employs people to do his bidding, not that we would ever be able to prove that in a court of law.'

Priscilla turned away from Jack and addressed the housekeeper. 'Margaret, listen to me, you've known me most of my life, since I was a young girl. Please, talk to me straight,' she pleaded. 'Is all of this true?'

'Oh, yes, luv, it is. You've been involved with a monster for years, I'm afraid, and more's the pity.'

'But I didn't know. I really didn't, Margaret, Jack, I never knew, I swear to God I didn't.'

Margaret felt duty bound to make Priscilla understand the seriousness of all this, and she said in a stronger voice than usual, 'Miss Paula's been worried for years that he would do her harm, and harm the family as well. Worried sick, she's been. After Sandy fired Jonathan Ainsley he turned against them, all those years ago, it was. You see, earlier, just after Mrs Harte died, he'd begun to claim he'd been cheated in her will. Wasn't true, that. *I knows*. His hatred has only grown. He *is* evil. And dangerous.'

Suddenly undone by these unexpected revelations, Priscilla was now totally convinced that Jack and Margaret were telling her the absolute truth. She was unable to speak, so sick at heart was she; she sat on the sofa, her arms wrapped around herself, feeling icy cold all over and numb with shock. All this was a nightmare. What a stupid fool she had been, and for years. *He had used her*.

As if he understood exactly what was going through her mind, Jack moved across the floor, sat down next to Priscilla on the sofa. 'You were duped, Prissy, I'm sorry to say.'

Tears came into her eyes. 'I believe I was, Jack, but let me say once again, I never told him anything about the family . . . I only ever mentioned the parties I was catering and then because I thought he had been invited, that he'd be there. There was nothing else I could tell him. I didn't know anything.' When Jack was silent, she pressed, 'You do believe me, don't you?'

'Yes, I do, Priscilla.'

'I suppose Paula's not going to use my catering services anymore . . .' Her voice trailed off, and she looked at Jack questioningly.

He saw at once the fear in her eyes, the shadow crossing her face, and he understood then how dependent she was on Paula for her business. For the first time, he felt a little sorry for her. 'Perhaps not,' he responded at last. 'I'll explain everything to Paula. But you cannot be in contact with Jonathan ever again. You do understand that?'

'Whatever makes you think I would want to be?' she asked, a brow lifting, her tone scornful.

He studied her for a moment, and saw at once the vengeful look in her eyes.

Jack left the two women alone in the library, and went off to check the main control box of the security system. Originally, he had said that this was his reason for visiting Pennistone Royal this morning, so why not make it the truth and not a ruse? Also, Margaret had mentioned that the switch in the pantry was actually on the blink. Maybe there was something wrong.

Walking through the kitchen, heading towards the basement door, he stopped when his mobile phone rang.

'Jack Figg here,' he said, leaning against the deal table.

'It's India, Jack.'

'Hello! I was going to give you a ring later, tell you what a clever girl you are. I've just had a long, productive chat with Priscilla Marney, quite by chance.'

'Oh, that is good. At least I hope it is. Jack, listen to me,' she rushed on, 'I rang you about something else. I'm afraid Molly Caldwell died a short while ago.'

'Oh, *no*. I'm so sorry. Poor lady. I'd better phone Dusty, ask if there's anything I can do to help.'

'Do it later, Jack, he's rushed off to the hospital. Molly put Atlanta's name on the hospital papers as her next of kin, so he has to sort it out. Dusty wanted me to call, to let you know that Molly passed away.' There was a slight pause. 'Any news of Melinda?'

'I'm afraid not. But I keep checking in with my chaps and the police. I'll ring them again when we hang up.'

'Thanks. Let's speak later.'

'You've got it, lovey.'

They both clicked off.

Jack immediately dialled his two operatives in Leeds. There was still no news of Melinda, and when he spoke to his friends at Leeds C.I.D. they had nothing to report. 'It's like looking for a needle in a haystack,' his pal Ted Fletcher explained, and Jack had to agree with him. He knew that it would be impossible to find Melinda Caldwell. Until she ended up in a hospital. Or in the morgue.

Although he was pleased he had been able to solve the Heron's Nest mystery, he was suddenly submerged in worry as he headed down into the basement to check the electrical panels. India and Dusty would never rest with Melinda Caldwell on the loose. He wondered if there *was* a way to find her. He doubted it.

CHAPTER TWENTY-EIGHT

Paula O'Neill was crossing her bedroom at Pennistone Royal when the phone began to ring. Hurrying to the bedside table, she picked it up. 'Pennistone Royal.'

'Hello, Mrs O'Neill. It's Bolton.'

'Good afternoon, Bolton. Is everything all right over there at Lackland Priory?' she asked, wondering why Robin's butler was phoning her.

'Yes, it is. But Mr Ainsley hasn't seemed like himself for the last few days . . .' He left the sentence unfinished.

'Perhaps you should call his doctor, Bolton, have him come over to look at him. Or would you like me to give the doctor a ring?'

'I don't think he's ill, Mrs O'Neill—' Bolton stopped, hesitated, then went on cautiously, 'I think perhaps he's troubled about something, and I was wondering if you could drop in over the weekend? On the spur of the moment, so to speak. I wouldn't want him to think I'd interfered.'

'Of course I'll come to see him, Bolton, that's no

problem. And actually, I have a very good reason for coming, so you don't have to worry. Mrs Marietta Hughes is our house guest this weekend, and naturally she will want to see Mr Ainsley.'

'Thank you, Mrs O'Neill. Should I tell Mr Ainsley you'll be dropping by?'

'No, no, I don't think so,' Paula replied swiftly. 'Let's make it a surprise. We'll probably come tomorrow morning for coffee. I'll give you a ring before we set off.'

'I'll be waiting, and thank you again, Mrs O'Neill.'

'Until tomorrow morning, Bolton, and I'm glad you thought to call me,' Paula said and hung up. She stood with her hand resting on the phone for a moment, wondering what could be troubling Uncle Robin. He had seemed perfectly well the last time she had seen him. For a moment she thought of asking Great-Aunt Edwina if something was wrong with him. Instantly she changed her mind, cautioning herself not to stir anything up.

Walking over to her dressing table, Paula ran a comb through her short black hair, refreshed her lipstick, and then went to look at herself in the cheval mirror standing in the corner. She had left for Yorkshire directly from Harte's, and was still wearing her regulation black skirt suit.

Glancing at her watch, she opened one of her closets, pulled out a wine-coloured wool trouser-suit, and quickly changed. A moment later she hurried towards the door leading into the upstairs parlour. Automatically, she stopped to touch the fruitwood casket on the Queen Anne chest, but of course it was no longer there. She had given it to Evan. Shaking her head, pursing her lips, she went into the adjoining room, reminding herself that the habits of a lifetime never died.

Paula positioned herself at the window, looking out at the moors, thinking of her grandmother. Emma Harte had been the fairest of people, and she herself prided herself on her own fairness. So why was she being so hard on Linnet? And perhaps unfair?

On the way to Yorkshire Paula had glanced at her daughter's detailed memos, and for a few moments she had been enraged by them. Since Tessa and Marietta were in the car with her, she had had to put them back in her briefcase to study at the weekend.

Staring at the bleak hills, she shook her head, dismayed with herself, and then a thought struck her. Everything Linnet was suggesting they do at the store cost money. A lot of money. And she didn't want to make that kind of outlay.

Turning away, Paula went and sat down at her desk and looked at the folders containing the memos, sighing to herself. And then she remembered how she had wanted to make changes when she was a young woman. But she had made a very big mistake. Was that why she was fighting Linnet? Was she afraid her daughter would make similar errors? Hers had almost cost her the Harte stores . . .

There was a knock, and the door opened as Margaret came rushing in carrying the tea tray, followed by Jack Figg.

'Hello, Paula,' he said, hurrying towards her, a wide smile on his face.

'Jack, it's lovely to see you!' Rising, Paula went to meet him, gave him a big hug, and then took a seat on the sofa.

Putting the tray on the coffee table, Margaret said, 'Here it is, Miss Paula, and I found them there ginger biscuits you like.'

'Thanks, Margaret.'

As Jack sat down on the sofa opposite Paula, Margaret threw him a quick, knowing glance and said in a stage whisper, 'Don't miss out a thing, tell her *everything* that happened this morning.'

When Margaret retreated, Paula eyed Jack in amusement, and they both began to laugh as the door closed behind the housekeeper.

'She's a card.' Jack shook his head, still smiling. 'She takes after her mother.'

'That's true, anyway—' Paula broke off at the sound of the ringing phone, and jumped up, went to her desk in the window area.

Jack glanced around, his eyes approving. He felt a sudden surge of nostalgia for the past. How many times he had sat on this sofa, having tea with the one and only Emma, his dearest friend. He couldn't remember how many times, now that he thought about it, but the teas he had shared with her had been very special.

The upstairs parlour was full of comfort and charm; he loved its sunny yellow walls, colourful chintz fabric on the sofas, mellow Georgian antiques and glorious paintings.

The remarkable thing was that it had never changed much, and it was all Emma's work, every bit of it. She had had a great eye, and extraordinary taste, the finest. Paula simply refurbished it from time to time when this was required. Everyone congregated here, as they had always done. It had often struck him that the upstairs parlour was the centre of this great house around which everything flowed.

It was particularly cosy and welcoming this afternoon, with the huge fire blazing in the hearth, the silk-shaded lamps casting a soft glow . . . such lovely contrasts to the dark moors with their snowy caps just visible through the windows. And then there were the white orchids which Paula grew in her glass houses, pots and pots of them standing around the room.

Paula came back to the fireside, sat down and said to Jack, 'That was Shane, he's delayed at the Leeds office, so he won't make it in time for tea. But he hopes you'll stay to dinner, and so do I. You will, won't you?'

'That's a nice invitation, Paula, I hope I can. I have to check several ongoing things, but hopefully I won't have to rush off to London. Thanks for asking me.'

'You know you're at home here, Jack, part of the family. And by the way, Marietta's here, she came up with me and Tessa this afternoon. For the weekend, so she'll be lovely company for us all.'

Jack was surprised. 'Really! I thought she would be hovering around Evan at this stage of the pregnancy.'

'She's rather smart, you know, not the typical fussing mother, and when I invited her she jumped at the invitation. As Marietta put it, she doesn't want to be an albatross around Evan's neck. She thinks Evan and Gideon should have plenty of time to themselves.'

'Wise woman. Linnet told me she's looking for a flat in London.'

Paula nodded but said nothing more about this. Her violet eyes were focused on him intently, and she studied him for a long moment. She wondered, suddenly, what the family would have done without him all these years? He had been devoted, loyal, their fierce defender and protector.

As Jack became aware of her fixed, unblinking scrutiny, he laughed. 'Ah, Paula, I recognize that look of yours. I suppose you want to know about Heron's Nest.'

'Actually, I was thinking of you . . . how wonderful you've been to us over the years. Your devotion and loyalty have been remarkable, Jack.' She gave him a small smile. 'But you know *me* too well: of course I want to know about Heron's Nest. Was there a robbery?'

'No, of course not. Don't forget, there was no sign of breaking and entering, which was puzzling to me.' Finishing his tea, putting down the cup, he relaxed against the plump cushions. 'You should have changed the locks at Heron's Nest years ago,' he admonished, mildly.

'I should?' She frowned. 'Oh, God, don't tell me someone got in with a key?'

'Correct.'

'Who was it?' she asked, looking suddenly perplexed.

'Jonathan Ainsley.'

Paula stared at Jack in astonishment, and then asked, 'But why on earth would he want to go there in winter? Or at any time of the year? To what purpose?'

'It was his secret hideaway, his love nest. He was meeting someone there.'

'Who?'

'Priscilla Marney.'

'Good God, Jack, not Prissy!' Paula shook her head in bafflement, then exclaimed, 'I'm simply astounded.'

'Let me tell you the story, the one I managed to unravel this morning.'

Paula simply nodded and sat back on the sofa, giving him her entire attention. She let him speak without interrupting him.

'And so,' he finished ten minutes later, 'that's the unfortunate tale of our Prissy and the dastardly Jonathan Ainsley. She's been a fool. He duped her, pulled the wool over her eyes. But basically, Paula, I think she's a decent woman, honest, trustworthy, if rather stupid. And I doubt very much that she was ever any kind of conduit to you and the family. She says she never knew anything. Or did she?' he asked, staring hard at Paula.

'No, she didn't. Other than the dates of my various parties, dinners and other family functions. Why would she know anything about my life?'

'India says Margaret's a bit gossipy,' Jack murmured, doing a little fishing, hoping to prompt her.

'Yes, she is, but it's harmless stuff, Jack. Margaret truly doesn't know anything about our lives either, except what goes on here when we're at Pennistone Royal, so she couldn't tell Prissy a thing.'

'I understand,' Jack answered, but he thought Paula was wrong about Margaret, making a misjudgement. She knew much more than Paula realized, India had been certain of that.

Returning to the subject of Heron's Nest, Paula said in a low, saddened voice, 'Poor Prissy, how foolish she's been. She certainly didn't need to become entangled with that dreadful cousin of mine. How did it happen?'

'Oh, it's been going on for years, started when they were teenagers. By the way, she's worried you're not going to use her anymore. I think she depends on *your* business to keep her catering service going.'

Paula nodded. 'I believe she does, actually. I'll think about keeping her on, and perhaps we'd better get the locks changed at Scarborough, although maybe it doesn't matter anymore.'

'Oh, it does, it does indeed. You just never know. I'll arrange for it to be done.'

'You said you told Priscilla that Jonathan Ainsley was engaged to Angharad Hughes. But is that *really* true, Jack?' Paula gave him a sceptical look.

'I'm not sure, although I'm inclined to think so. Still, there are those who might say I'm merely making an assumption.'

'Tell me all about it, explain why you've come to this conclusion.'

'She's been wearing a large diamond ring for a couple of days, Sarah told you that, and my Paris man also informed me. I had a phone call from him a couple of hours ago, and since he's permanently assigned to Ainsley he knows his every movement. Anyway, to cut to the chase, he discovered a few things which seemed pertinent, add up to what easily could be a marriage in the making.'

'Sarah would know if he's getting married, Jack! He's always told her everything – well almost everything.'

'I know that, Paula. Just hear me out. My operative knows one of the women who works at Harry Winston on the Avenue Montaigne, where the ring was bought. He found out from her that Angharad was introduced by Ainsley as his fiancée, and the woman made the comment that the young mademoiselle is perfect for him. Because he wants to start a family.'

'Surely that's just gossip.' Paula gave him a sharp look, shook her head.

'You're right. On the other hand, leaving the ring and all that aside, I learned a couple of hours ago that Ainsley and Angharad Hughes visited a fertility clinic in Paris, a very famous one. *This afternoon.*'

'Good heavens, he's thinking of *babies*!' Paula sat up with a jerk, totally taken aback.

'Why not? He wants an heir. Obviously. And she's certainly of child-bearing age at twenty-three. Perhaps that's one of the reasons he's fallen for her.

Her child-bearing potential. How does that saying go? An heir and a spare.'

Paula sat quite still on the sofa, staring at Jack, thinking about what he had just said. She was at a complete loss for words. The whole idea of Angharad Hughes involved with Ainsley to such an extent was disturbing.

Jack was waiting patiently, expecting some pithy or acerbic comment, but none was forthcoming. And so he broke the growing silence between them. 'Announcing to Prissy that Jonathan Ainsley was getting married so threw her off balance, she lost it completely, behaved with such emotional distress and hysteria that I knew at once it was *she* who was involved with him.'

Looking at Jack intently, her eyes narrowing, Paula asked in puzzlement, 'Why were you focused on her to begin with?'

'I'd figured it out, thanks to India. I'd asked her if any member of her generation was having assignations at Heron's Nest. She ruled that out, suggested I look at her mother's generation, your generation. I did. Of course I knew none of you girls would have been involved with Jonathan when you were growing up, yet remember it was Jonathan's room that Mrs Hodges pinpointed. I suddenly wondered what outsiders had visited Heron's Nest in those days.' Jack took a deep breath, and finished, 'I remembered Emma's summer secretary, which led me to Priscilla, the secretary's daughter.'

'So it was all a matter of clues and clever deduction on your part. Well, I've always known you were exceedingly astute, and I'm glad you solved it, Jack, and—'

Abruptly, Paula stopped as the door flew open and Tessa burst into the room. For a split second she stood poised in the doorway, as if frozen in place. To Paula her eldest daughter looked like a ghostly figure standing there, dressed entirely in white and with a face as white as the clothes she was wearing.

There was no doubt in Paula's mind that something was terribly wrong, and she jumped up, went to Tessa, who came rushing towards her, exclaiming, 'Mummy! It's Jean-Claude. He's vanished. In Afghanistan. I don't know what to do!'

Paula pulled Tessa into her arms and held her tightly, trying to soothe her as sobs suddenly broke free. 'He'll be found, Tessa, he's probably been found already. Come on, darling, come and sit down with me and tell me all about it.'

Jack had risen, too, and went to the two women. Putting a hand lightly on Tessa's shoulder, he said gently, 'Your mother's right, Tessa. Come to the fireside. Do you want me to get you anything – a cup of tea, water? Or maybe a brandy?'

Tessa stepped away from her mother, shook her head. In a faltering voice, she whispered, 'I'm scared that . . . he's . . . been killed.'

'No, no, don't even say that! I'm sure he hasn't,' Paula responded in a firm tone, wanting to reassure and calm her daughter. She took hold of Tessa's hand and drew her across to the sofa. They sat down together.

Jack threw a couple of logs onto the fire, and then returned to his seat. He knew it was better, much wiser, for him to keep quiet, to leave this to Paula. A mother was always the best person to help a daughter who was in distress, as indeed Tessa was at this moment.

Paula said, 'You just found out?'

'Yes. Philippe, Jean-Claude's son, just phoned me from Paris. If you remember, I told you I'd met him at Jean-Claude's country house. Anyway, Philippe called me on my mobile, explained that ten minutes ago he'd had a call from the head of the news division at the network. The man told him that his father was missing, that he'd vanished three days ago. While he was on a special mission. After those three days had passed without any further communication from Jean-Claude, the entire network was beginning to worry. Then the cameraman showed up in Kabul and phoned Paris, told the head of the news division that he'd become separated from Jean-Claude, had no idea where he was. The cameraman had made it back to Kabul on his own.'

'This is terrible, very worrying, I admit, but we mustn't think the worst, Tessa,' Paula said, reassuring her as best she could. 'Just because he's missing doesn't mean he's been killed.'

'He could have been captured,' Tessa mumbled through her tears. 'If anything happens to him I don't know what I'll do.'

Paula put her arms around Tessa again, and held her close. 'And that's all Philippe was able to tell you?'

'Yes. He didn't know anything else. He'll stay in touch, he promised.' Tessa groped in her jacket pocket, pulled out a handkerchief, patted her streaming eyes.

'When was the last time you spoke to Jean-Claude?' Paula now thought to ask.

'On Monday. He told me he wouldn't be phoning me for the rest of the week. He explained he was leaving Kabul, that he was onto something he wanted to check out. He said not to expect a call until this weekend, but I do wish he hadn't made that rule.'

Paula, continuing to soothe her daughter, glanced across at Jack. Her expression signalled that she wanted him to say something.

After a moment's thought, Jack remarked quietly, 'That's understandable, Tessa. If he's on a special story, he obviously doesn't need to be worrying about *you* worrying about *him*, just because you haven't heard from him. Telling you not to expect a call was a wise thing to do.'

Tessa didn't say anything. Sitting up, smoothing her hair, she looked across at Jack and nodded her understanding. 'I suppose you're right, he does have to concentrate on his work, and be on the alert in such a dangerous place.'

There was a small silence, no one spoke.

Tessa shifted on the sofa to look at her mother. Swallowing, she said in a slightly quavering voice, 'I'm pregnant. I'm expecting Jean-Claude's child.'

'Oh, Tessa, darling, why didn't you tell me before?' Paula exclaimed, a wide smile lighting up her face, then it slipped slightly.

'Because I wanted to tell Jean-Claude first, and now I can't,' she mumbled and the tears started again. In a choked voice, she added, 'I hope he's safe . . . what if something's happened to him? Whatever will I do without him?'

'Listen to me, Tessa,' Paula said in a strong voice. 'He's a seasoned war correspondent, from what you've told me. He's not going to take any chances, no chances at all. He'll call this weekend, as he promised. I can almost guarantee that.'

Rising, deciding he ought to leave Tessa and Paula alone, give them privacy, Jack said, 'You must have faith, Tessa, and your mother is right, you know. Jean-Claude won't put himself in danger.' Looking at Paula, he added, 'I'll leave you two alone to talk.'

'Do try and stay for dinner, Jack. We'd love it if you could.'

He smiled at her, and left, reminding himself that she was shock-proof. As head of the family she was used to carrying so many burdens . . . What a marvel she was, so courageous.

CHAPTER TWENTY-NINE

Years ago, Emma had assigned a pleasant bedroom to Jack, and it was still his. He frequently stayed there, especially when it was too late for him to drive home to Robin Hood's Bay on the coast.

After quietly closing the parlour door behind him, Jack went upstairs to his room. He felt tired all of a sudden, needed a few moments of respite, a chance to catch his breath. He had to phone India, to ask how Dusty was doing, and put in a few calls to his various operatives in the field. But first he had the need to relax and collect his thoughts.

Once inside the room, he glanced around, struck yet again by its lovely soft colours and its comfort. He placed his mobile on the bedside table, took off his jacket and shoes and lay down on the bed, his hands behind his head.

Staring up at the ceiling, he thought about Tessa's announcement of a moment ago. Paula had taken it in her stride, as she usually did when unexpected things happened in the family. And single women having children was not such an unusual thing in this day and age. However, he was very much aware that if something had happened to Jean-Claude in Afghanistan then Tessa would be distraught. He couldn't help wondering where Lorne was this weekend. Was he expected? If he was, it would be a blessing.

The warbling of his cell phone broke the silence in the room, and Jack reached for it. 'Jack Figg here.'

'Jack, it's Ted. We've got a body. At the morgue in Leeds. A young woman. She was found in a car parked in a side street, not too far away from Roundhay Park. No I.D. on her, but she fits your description.'

'Oh, Jesus,' Jack said. 'How did she die, Ted?'

'Medical Examiner's not exactly sure yet, but more than likely it's an O.D. No bruises or wounds on her. Dead since last night, around midnight, according to the coroner.'

'You say there's no I.D. on her. Didn't she have a handbag? Anything in her pockets?' Jack asked, thinking that the lack of identification was peculiar.

'No, in answer to both your questions. Car door was unlocked, key in the ignition, but no sign of a handbag.'

'And no drug paraphernalia, no needles, nothing like that?'

'Not a bloody thing, Jack. Bit of a mystery how she died. And where she died. It could have been in the car. Maybe not. Listen, Jack, what's the chance of identifying her?'

'I would if I could, but I've never met Melinda Caldwell.'

'Family?'

'The sad thing is her mother passed away this morning. At Leeds Infirmary.'

'Mother and daughter dying within hours of each other!' Ted exclaimed. 'And I'm up a creek without a bloody paddle, that's the way it looks to me.'

'Her former boyfriend, the father of her child, will identify her, I'm sure. Let me talk to him, and I'll be back to you shortly.'

'I'm grateful, Jack. Thanks.'

Going over to the desk, Jack sat down and dialled Dusty's number on the house phone, and when Paddy answered he said, 'It's Jack Figg, Paddy. I'd like to speak to Mr Rhodes, if he's available.'

'Yes, he is, sir. I'll put you through.'

A moment later Dusty was on the line. His voice was flat and subdued, as he said, 'Thanks for calling, Jack. India said you might. I did manage to get things sorted out all right at the Infirmary.'

'I'm sorry about Molly Caldwell, Dusty. I actually thought she was going to make it.'

'So did I,' Dusty replied, but he hadn't, not really. He'd known she was going to die.

'Dusty, I just had a call from Ted Fletcher of Leeds C.I.D. They've found Melinda.'

'She's not all right, is she? I can tell by the sound of your voice. Is she . . . dead?'

'Yes, I'm afraid so.' Clearing his throat, Jack then proceeded to give Dusty all of the information he had received from Ted. He finished quietly, 'There's nobody else to identify her, Dusty, only you. Will you do it?'

'There is somebody else, there's Gladys Roebotham. But Gladys is here at Willows Hall, looking after Atlanta, and I think that's what she should be doing. Yes, I'll do it, Jack. Where do I have to go?'

'Nowhere. Stay there. I'll come and get you, take you to the morgue.'

'Come on, Jack, don't be silly. I'm a big boy. I can drive to Leeds by myself.'

'It's a lousy experience, Dusty, having to identify someone you've known who's lying on a cold slab. Listen, I'm at Pennistone Royal. Give me half an hour, I need to have a word with Paula before I leave.'

'Jack, before you hang up, did she die of an overdose?'

'They're not sure what she died of, but it could be an O.D. She died last night, around midnight.'

There was a silence, then Dusty muttered, 'I'll see you shortly, and thanks, Jack.'

On Saturday morning Paula decided to go to Lackland Priory early. And she went alone. It had occurred to her that if something were troubling Robin and he needed to talk, it would be best if they were by themselves. Marietta could visit him later, over the weekend, or perhaps he would be able to come to dinner tonight.

Before leaving, she had gone to Tessa's bedroom and spoken to her for a few minutes, hoping to reassure her. But her eldest daughter had been worried and morose, expecting to hear the worst about Jean-Claude at any moment. Nothing Paula said alleviated her anxiety, and Tessa's lack of sleep didn't help.

On the short drive to Robin's house Paula ran the events of yesterday through her mind. It had turned out to be Black Friday in a sense, or as Shane had said at dinner, 'Bad Day at Black Rock', quoting the title of one of his favourite old movies.

'Two deaths,' Margaret had muttered to her as she had served the smoked salmon. 'There's bound to be a third. Everything goes in threes, you know that, Miss Paula.'

That a mother and daughter should die so close together had sent chills running down Paula's spine when Jack had told her about Molly and Melinda. Then he had gone to take Dusty to the morgue in Leeds, promising to be back in time for dinner at eight. And he had kept his promise.

As she drove along the main road, Paula's thoughts centred on Priscilla Marney and her unfortunate involvement with Jonathan Ainsley. How flabbergasted she had been to hear about it, and now she was faced with a decision about using Prissy's catering service. Although Prissy had only herself to blame, Paula couldn't help feeling a little sorry for her. To discover she had been so flagrantly used must have been galling for Prissy. Jack had said he believed Priscilla was decent and loyal, and so she would probably keep her on. She would talk to Shane about it later.

As she turned into the driveway, Paula couldn't help wondering what was awaiting her at Lackland Priory. Before she even turned off the ignition, the front door opened and Bolton was waiting for her on the step, greeting her cheerfully as he escorted her inside the lovely old house.

After taking her coat, the butler showed her into the morning room, where Robin was having breakfast and reading the newspapers.

'What a pleasant surprise,' Robin said, getting up, kissing her on the cheek. 'When Bolton said you'd be popping in I had him set another place. Would you like breakfast?'

Sitting down opposite Robin, Paula shook her head. 'Just coffee, thanks, Uncle Robin.'

Bolton brought her the cup of coffee and quickly departed, and Paula went on, 'It's such a gorgeous day, lovely and sunny and quite mild.' She laughed. 'As if I have to tell you that, this room's full of sunshine.'

Robin smiled. 'Where are you off to so early, Paula?'

'I'm meeting Emily in West Tanfield. We have to do a few things at Beck House. And as I knew I'd be driving right past the priory, I thought I'd come in and say hello. How have you been feeling, Uncle Robin?'

'Not bad, not bad at all. Of course I worry about Evan and the twins. I can't wait for them to be born.'

'Neither can she, I'm sure of that.'

'Everything's all right, isn't it?'

'Oh, yes, please don't worry. She's going to be perfectly fine.' Paula took a sip of her coffee and went on, 'Marietta is with us for the weekend, and I was wondering if you'd like to join us for dinner tonight.'

'That sounds like a nice idea, Paula, but I'd planned to see Edwina.'

'She can join us, too, unless you want to be alone with her.'

Robin was silent, and then after a moment, he said, 'Well, we can ask her, and I think she'd like that. We love coming to Pennistone Royal.'

Leaning across the table, Robin now said, 'Shall we take a walk in the garden? As you said, it's a gorgeous day and I want to discuss my roses with you.'

Paula was taken aback, and looked at him swiftly. Noting the anxious look in his eyes, she said, 'Why not? But you're going to need a warm coat.'

A few minutes later, both of them bundled up in coats and scarves, Robin led Paula around his garden, explaining, 'I don't like to speak about private family matters when there's so much staff around.'

'I understand. But you trust Bolton, don't you, Uncle Robin?'

'Of course, he's been with me for years and he's most devoted, but it doesn't hurt to be careful. The less people know, the better.'

'I agree. Now, I know you didn't invite me out here to talk about the rose bushes,' Paula said pithily, glancing around. 'But they really do need to be in the sun, and I think those bushes over there will get too much shade in the summer.'

'I know, I plan to dig 'em up when the ground's not so hard. If I'm still here.'

'Oh, you will be, I've no doubt about that. So, what did you want to talk to me about?'

'Two things. Firstly, I want you to know that I have left Evan my mews house in Belgravia. To all intents and purposes it's Edwina's mews, but I bought it from her years ago. For Glynnis. The deeds have always remained in Edwina's name, but Anthony knows the deal, no problem there. However, I felt you should be in the picture, since you run all the family business.'

'Thanks for telling me, Uncle Robin—' Paula cut herself off, biting her lip, her expression worried.

Robin said, 'Don't even think about Jonathan. He never knew I bought it all those years ago. The arrangement is that when Edwina dies, Gideon will "buy" it as an investment. You see, Jonathan has always believed the house is Edwina's, and that she simply allowed me to stay there whenever I wanted.'

'All right, that works for me. And thank you for filling me in, Uncle Robin. You said you had two things to discuss. What else is on your mind?'

'I have created a trust for Evan's twins. I used John Crawford, your solicitor, even though he's semi-retired. I've known him donkey's years, and he is the most honourable and trustworthy of men. Again, you don't have to worry about Jonathan finding out because for years I've had a trust fund in the States. It was for Glynnis. She never touched it and it reverted to me with her death. I was thinking of making Owen the beneficiary, but I've changed my mind. It will be for Evan's twins.'

'I see.'

'You have an odd look on your face, Paula,' Robin murmured, staring at her intently. 'What is it?'

'Are you sure Jonathan couldn't trace it?'

'I am. You see, I created the trust for Glynnis in the 1950s, with money I had invested in the States. Anyway, the twins won't inherit the trust until they are twenty-one. Believe me, Paula, John has made sure everything is absolutely watertight.'

'Of course. I know how brilliant he is. But I do have a question, if that's all right?'

'Fire away, Paula dear.'

'Why did you change your mind about Owen Hughes?'

'He doesn't need the money, but that's not the real reason.' Robin shook his head, and a sudden sadness settled on his face. 'He doesn't like me, not really, Paula, and he hasn't made much of an effort towards me. I understand that. He was brought up by Richard Hughes, and Richard was his father in the best sense of that word. I think in his mind I'm just his mother's lover, and as that I perhaps don't rate too high.' Robin took her arm, smiled at her warmly. 'Besides, I prefer to look to the future . . . Those twins also carry my genes . . . and they are certainly the future.'

PART FOUR

Solo

There shall no evil befall thee, neither shall any plague come nigh thy dwelling. For he shall give his angels charge over thee, to keep thee in all thy ways.

Psalm 91

CHAPTER THIRTY

To Linnet, Harte's was the most wonderful place in the world. She had been going to this great emporium in Knightsbridge almost from the day she was born. Actually, she had even gone there before she was born, because Paula had worked at the store right up to the day before her due date.

Linnet thought of it as an enchanted place, magical even, filled with thousands of items of extraordinary beauty, literally everything the heart could desire, at least when it came to material things. She knew and loved every part of the store, founded by her great-grandmother, especially the fashion floors which she ran. And the magnificent Food Halls . . . Emma had been so proud of them, and Linnet felt the same way. Her mouth always watered when she passed through them: they were unique, there was nothing to compare to them in the entire world.

Harte's was for her an Aladdin's Cave. It had been her childhood playground . . . and now it was her true domain.

On this Monday morning there was no one else in the store but her, except for the cleaners and security, and Linnet moved from floor to floor, taking everything in, making copious notes, and endeavouring to visualize the changes she hoped would come to fruition. Some areas received much more of her attention than others, such as the fashion floors, the floor where the beauty salon was located, and the one where mattresses and beds were sold. Those definitely have to be relegated to the furniture department, she muttered under her breath, glancing at the offending mattresses before heading for the escalators.

Having arrived at the store at six o'clock, Linnet was now ready to go back to her office to review her notes and work out a strategy. She glanced at her watch as she went down on the escalator and was surprised to see it was already eight. She had spent two hours out here; how the time had flown. It occurred to her then that everything she had seen this morning was now indelibly stamped on her brain. She was lucky she had a photographic memory and could recall things easily, and in a visual way, without too much effort. It often made her work easier.

When she came to the management floor, she paused in front of the portrait of Emma Harte in its alcove in the corridor. She had been a beautiful woman, looked elegant in her pale blue dress and emeralds, but it was not the beauty that Linnet saw at this moment. Instead it was the power of Emma's face. The portrait seemed to exude that power and a special magnetism.

Stepping closer to the oil painting, Linnet whispered to it aloud, 'You've got to be with me on this, Emma. You've got to back me to the hilt.' Glancing around to make sure there was no one listening, Linnet added softly, '*You promised me.*'

Leaning forward, she touched Emma's face in the painting. 'I am with you all the way,' she heard Emma say, as if from a distance, and she smiled at the face in the portrait and moved on.

Linnet told herself she was daft in the head, the way she talked to her great-grandmother of late. The strange thing was, Emma spoke back to her . . . at least Linnet believed she did, was absolutely certain she heard Emma's voice. When she had confessed this to Julian, her husband had not laughed, had simply said, 'I believe you, Linny, but don't tell anybody else.' And she hadn't; nor did she want to. Emma was in her heart and soul, and in her head most of the time. And she did not want to share her.

Once Linnet was sitting behind her desk, she studied her notes, jotted down additional thoughts, and then sat back, contemplating her mother. Paula had agreed to see her this morning, to discuss the memos she had taken to Yorkshire over the weekend. But Linnet was nervous about doing it today, having sensed over the weekend that her mother was on edge, worried about Tessa, and Jean-Claude's disappearance in Afghanistan. Then there had been the trouble with Priscilla Marney, lover of Jonathan Ainsley.

Leaning back in her chair, Linnet thought about

that situation for a moment, a grim smile on her face. At least her mother had had the good grace to admit to Linnet that she had been right. She had always insisted that there was someone in their midst telling Jonathan about them, but no one had believed her. 'She only spoke to him about the events she catered,' Paula had pointed out. Linnet thought her mother was being a trifle dismissive, and had countered, 'That's bad enough, isn't it, Mummy? *He* always knew when we were all gathered together in one place. He could have dropped a bomb on us.'

Her mother had protested about this comment, and had immediately gone on to tell her about the deaths of Molly and Melinda Caldwell. The moment they had hung up on Saturday afternoon, Linnet had phoned India to commiserate with her in general, and then she had spoken briefly to Tessa, who was so distraught it was impossible to make her feel any better.

Linnet knew that she must telephone her sister now, to ask if there was any news about Jean-Claude.

Pulling the phone closer, Linnet dialled Pennistone Royal. It was Tessa who answered, her voice high-pitched with tension.

'It's Linnet. Have you had any news?'

'No, not a word,' Tessa answered, sounding sorrowful. Linnet knew that Tessa was disappointed it wasn't Jean-Claude himself calling.

'I'm a nervous wreck. I really feel like going to Paris, being there with Philippe, but Lorne says that's a silly idea. Anyway, I'm trying to work here in the library on my laptop, and then I'm going to go to the Harrogate store this afternoon. Lorne keeps telling me I have to keep busy.'

'Is he there with you?' Linnet asked.

'Yes, thank goodness. Mummy and Dad have gone to London this morning.'

'How's Adele?'

Tessa's voice lifted slightly when she exclaimed, '*Wonderful.* I'm trying to spend lots of time with her, she cheers me up.' There was a small pause, and Tessa dropped her voice to a whisper as she asked, 'Did Mummy tell you?'

Linnet said, 'About what?'

Tessa detected the puzzlement in her sister's voice, and replied, 'Obviously she didn't. I'm pregnant . . . Jean-Claude and I are having a baby.'

'Oh, my God! Tessa! That's great. Congratulations—' Linnet suddenly stopped. 'No wonder you're so worried,' she hurried on, 'I mean, being pregnant makes everything even more worrying than ever, doesn't it? But he'll make it . . .' Her voice trailed off lamely.

'Yes,' Tessa said, sounding suddenly very tired. 'I've got to believe that he will. That keeps me going.'

'If you don't feel up to driving over to the Harrogate store today, maybe India can pop in.'

'She has her hands full, wouldn't you say? What with the Leeds store and Dusty. And all his problems.'

'I suppose so. On the other hand, their problems

are not as troubling as yours. Let me know if I can do anything, and please phone me if you have any news. We're all anxious, Tessa.'

'I will, I promise. The minute I hear.'

A few seconds later Linnet was speaking to India, who was just about to leave Willows Hall for Harte's in Leeds. 'I'm glad you're coping all right, India,' Linnet went on. 'But Tessa sounds terrible. Depressed and sad, and no wonder. I told her not to worry about the Harrogate store today, I mean going over there. Is there really any need?'

'No, and I did mention that yesterday, Linnet. Still, Lorne's there and he's telling her she should keep busy. She's trying, God bless her. I'm praying for her, and for Jean-Claude. I can just imagine how she feels. Desperate. I'd feel the same way if Dusty were missing in a war zone.'

'So would I. How is Dusty?'

'Oh, you know him, he's like the Hartes: *tough*. And so he's coping. He's a real trouper when things go wrong. He's been really sad about Molly though, grieving, and also very troubled about the way Melinda died. But . . . well . . . he's handling things. Actually, he's planning their funerals at the moment.'

'Oh, God, what an awful task he has. By the way, India, what has he told Atlanta?'

'Nothing about her mother's death. Atlanta doesn't, I mean, didn't, know her mother well, in fact, hardly at all. It was Molly who brought her up.' India sighed. 'He told her that her grandmother had gone on a trip to see the angels, and left it at that.

Naturally she asked a lot of questions, but we've managed to appease her for the moment. And she's very fond of Gladys, who's here with us and who's turned out to be a jewel.'

'I sometimes wonder about *us*, India. I mean about the family. We do seem to have more than our fair share of troubles.'

'It's funny you should say that, I made the same remark to Dusty at breakfast.'

'Paula says that it's because we're such a big family, and there are so many of us, with the clans, there're bound to be problems and a crisis a minute. That was the way she put it.'

'I expect she's right. I've got to run, Linny, but I'll talk to you later.'

Tessa's news about being pregnant had stunned Linnet for a moment or two. She thought of her elder half-sister as being very calculating, and clever about running her life. Especially these days. There had been the awful débâcle with Mark Longden and the bitter divorce, but in the end it was Tessa who had ended up the winner and with what she wanted: her freedom, her child, and Mark Longden as far away as possible.

She also wanted to be the head of Harte's one day. Had she now discarded this ambition? If she asked Grandfather Bryan, Linnet knew he would laugh in her face. He had forever told her that Tessa Fairley would always be her rival. No matter what. And of course he was correct. On the other hand, Tessa was now involved, and deeply so, with a famous man who lived in another country, and she was carrying his child. Did she still want the top job? Did she mean to commute between Paris and London? Did she still think of herself as the Dauphine, her mother's rightful heir?

Linnet could only wonder about that at this moment. She had no answer for herself.

Opening one of the folders on her desk, Linnet looked at the emails which had passed between her and Bonnadell Enloe. She had more or less worked out the deal with the American businesswoman, who had made such a big success out of her day spas, aptly called *Tranquillity*. There was no doubt in Linnet's mind that the day spa at Harte's would be successful. She was absolutely confident about it.

Turning to a second folder, she went through the notes she had made when she had interviewed Bobbi Snyder. Bobbi was an old friend of Marietta's, from the days when Marietta had been single, an art student and living in London. Bobbi was also an American, who had stayed on in London after Marietta had left. She had married an Englishman and had a daughter, and had run the Fashion Floor at Harvey Nichols for a number of years. When Marietta had learned from Evan that Linnet needed a high-powered executive to launch the bridal floor, Marietta had recommended her old friend.

As yet Linnet had been unable to hire the admirable Bobbi, but she was hopeful that she would be able to do so in the not-too-distant future.

The third folder on her desk was about her own

fashion floors. As she opened it, Linnet grimaced, still feeling dismal about the low sales figures. This morning, as she had walked through Fashion, she had been even more convinced that they needed a whole new look.

The fourth folder was about opening a sumptuous shopping area for luxury goods, if her mother would agree. There was a big question mark in Linnet's mind about that. The other doubt she had, as did Evan, was her mother sanctioning a series of snack bars in the Food Halls. Closing that particular folder, after a quick glance, Linnet suddenly wished she had never given it to Paula to look at this weekend. More than likely it would probably rub her up the wrong way.

Closing her eyes, Linnet tried to envision the great emporium as she saw it . . . how it would look in three months . . . in six months' time . . . in a year from now. And what she saw in her mind's eye thrilled her. Somehow she had to make her mother see Harte's as *she* saw the store – not the way it was now but the way it could be. A new look . . . modernity . . . fresh ideas . . . flair as well as taste . . . delectable clothes from talented young designers . . . as well as the great personal services the store provided. Affordable real jewellery as a counterpart to high-priced jewels . . . a floor that catered to brides and only to brides . . . with services . . . a wedding-planner . . . even a link to honeymoon travel . . . and the day spa designed to pamper women of all ages.

Sitting up in the chair, Linnet exclaimed out loud,

'A shake-up. That's what Harte's needs. A shake-up and a shove into the Twenty-First Century!'

I'll say *that* to my mother, Linnet now thought, anticipating the meeting. And I'll ask her to name me Creative Director. She knew her mother would, since it had been her father's suggestion some time ago. Her mother listened to him; she always had.

Picking up the phone, Linnet dialled Evan, who answered after a few rings.

'Are you all right?' Linnet asked. 'You don't sound so great.'

'Hi, Linnet! I'm okay, I guess. I'm just so big . . . HUGE. And I have a feeling Robin and Winston are going to pop out any minute now, much sooner than expected.'

'Oh, Evan, you've chosen the names!'

'I forgot to tell you. Gideon and I decided on them last week. I like the sound of Robin Harte and Winston Harte the third, don't you?'

'I do indeed. But will your father?'

'Oh, you mean we should have used Dad's name for one of the boys?' There was a pause, and Evan let out a long sigh. 'I can't worry about that, you know. Anyway, Robin is Robin Owen, so that should pacify him. But he hasn't been overly friendly with us, Linnet. I haven't really told you I guess, but he's been quite cold to Robin, Winston and Gideon, and I wouldn't call his attitude warm towards me, either.'

'No, you didn't say a thing, but how awful. What's wrong, do you think?' Linnet asked.

'The Hartes, that's what's wrong. I am one. I

married one. I'm carrying little Hartes. I think he has quite a hatred for the family. Deep down, that is. He probably doesn't even know it. It's probably well and truly buried.'

Startled by these comments, Linnet was silent for a moment.

Evan said, 'Are you still there, Linny?'

'Yes. Listen, if he hates the Hartes the way you say, you don't think he would betray us, go over to Angharad, do you?'

'No, of course not!' Evan exclaimed. 'He doesn't have much time for her. And I know he loves me. He just has to get over this . . . jealousy he has. That's what I think it is. So does my mother. I came to London, got a job at Harte's, fell in love with a Harte, discovered I *was* a Harte. The way he sees it, according to my mother, is that he lost me to this powerful family. He forgets that he's a Harte, too.'

'But he hasn't lost you, has he, Evan?'

'No. However, he is in the process of driving me away.'

'Is he coming back for the christening?'

'Oh, yes, I'm sure he will, and listen, he's not really all that peculiar with me. Just a tiny bit remote, removed. Let's move on. Are you seeing Paula today, to discuss all the new ideas?'

'Yes, I am. So keep your fingers crossed.'

'Fingers crossed. And I know you'll be successful.'

Brilliant sunlight pouring into the library through

the tall windows slanted across the desk where Tessa was sitting, and brought her up with a start. Blinking, she turned her head, looked out of one of the windows, realizing that the first vestiges of spring were suddenly in evidence.

Standing up, she strolled over to the window fronting onto the moors, and saw, much to her surprise, that the snow which had capped the moors over the weekend had melted. And in the gardens there was a hint of fresh green buds poking out of the ground.

She had the unexpected urge to go outside, to get a breath of fresh air, to walk for a while. She had been cooped up here in the house for several days, and had done nothing much but cry and worry, and pester Philippe in Paris. He had been so kind and thoughtful, always ready to talk to her, to soothe her shattered nerves; she had grown to like Jean-Claude's son more than ever.

They had taken to each other a few weeks ago, when they had been at Clos-Fleuri together, and now the relationship had been truly cemented in the sharing of their mutual worry. Although Philippe was not at all like his father in character or personality, he looked like him, and had a similar voice. It was a comfort to speak with him, to meet such a generous reception, particularly since he sounded so much like Jean-Claude.

Jean-Claude, where are you? What has befallen you? Why don't we hear from you? These questions rumbled around in Tessa's mind, and her chest tightened at the thought that he might well be already dead. There had been total silence since last Monday. A week ago exactly. No one had heard from him.

Picking up her cell phone from the desk, Tessa walked out of the library and went to the kitchen. Pushing open the door, she said to Margaret, 'I'm off for a walk, be back in ten minutes.'

'Wrap yourself up well, Tessa my lass,' Margaret said, as always her tone motherly and concerned. 'I'm making ever such a nice lunch and you're going to eat some of it, even if I have to force it down you.'

For the first time in days, Tessa actually laughed. 'I'm not still four years old, you know, and you won't have to force me, I'll have something.'

'Yes, you'd better, now that you're eating for two.'

Tessa made no further comment, simply retreated, took one of her mother's heavy top coats from the hall cupboard, put it on, went out into the cobbled yard.

How on earth does she know I'm pregnant? Tessa asked herself, and then shook her head wonderingly. Margaret had always known everything that was going on in the family, and how she found out had always been a mystery. Tessa was not upset that the housekeeper was aware of her condition, in fact she didn't care who knew. At this moment all she cared about was Jean-Claude's safety.

She thought of the baby as she walked down towards the Rhododendron Walk. It had not been planned, and she had been startled initially when she had realized she was pregnant. Her surprise had turned to happiness; she was thrilled to be carrying Jean-Claude's child, and she knew that he would be, too, when she told him.

Now she regretted that she had held back, not confided her happy news before he had gone off to cover the war in Afghanistan. Of course he would have had to go, because he had a contract with the network; on the other hand, perhaps he might not have undertaken what was probably a dangerous mission had he known he was going to become a father.

Last night she had lain awake for hours, mostly worrying about bringing up a child by herself, if the worst happened and Jean-Claude never came back. Eventually she had fallen asleep, and on awakening this morning she had chastised herself for being so stupid. She was already bringing Adele up without a father, and knew exactly how to do it. And she wasn't really alone, she was surrounded by a loving family, and a very large one at that.

No more negative thoughts, she admonished herself as she tramped on, her hand in her pocket, curled around the cell phone. I've got to be positive, get on with my work, attend to Adele. I must be cheerful for her, put up a good front, and I must take care of myself for the baby's sake.

Grandy did it all alone, and so can I, if that becomes necessary. After all, I'm a Harte, and the Harte women are tough. We're also competent and enterprising, and we can handle anything.

With the baby coming it was obvious now to

Tessa that she would have to take time off from Harte's . . . for a short while? Or even permanently? And what would she do ultimately about her career? Could she commute from Paris to London? Perhaps it *was* viable. Maybe she could spend three days in London during the week, and have long weekends in Paris. They had discussed all this several times, and Jean-Claude had made it clear it was her decision.

Could she be head of Harte's in the top job and a commuter? She wasn't sure. And did she really want that job after all? She had always dreamed of having it, but not every dream came true. And wasn't a happy marriage with a wonderful man and children the best dream of all?

CHAPTER THIRTY-ONE

Although she was extremely pale, Linnet thought her mother had never looked more beautiful than she did this morning. The pallor enhanced her black hair and violet eyes, made them appear all the more dramatic.

As usual, Paula was elegantly dressed in a crisply tailored suit that was a strange but beautiful colour – not quite purple not mulberry, but an odd mixture of the two. With it she wore a pale pink camisole, a pink silk Chanel flower on one shoulder and large pearl studs on her ears.

As Linnet walked across the floor to her mother's desk, Paula looked up and said, with a slight smile, 'Good morning, Linnet.'

''Morning, Mummy. You look gorgeous today, and so much better than last week. I thought you seemed quite worn out.'

Paula nodded. 'I felt it, too, but despite everything that happened this weekend, I did manage to get a little rest. Pennistone Royal has always been very restorative for me, as it was for Emma.'

Sitting down, Linnet remarked, 'I spoke to Tessa a short while ago. Still no news about Jean-Claude.'

'I know,' Paula sighed. 'We must be positive, for her sake, help to keep her spirits up. My feeling is that he's alive. I hope I'm right.'

Linnet wondered whether to mention Tessa's pregnancy, decided against it, and getting down to business she asked, 'Did you get a chance to look at the memos?'

'I did, and you certainly put an enormous amount of work into them, not to mention detail. I had a lot of reading.' Paula looked intently at her daughter. 'A lot more detail than I required, by the way.'

Linnet gazed back at Paula, thinking that her mother's face had become a little stern, even disapproving, although her voice was still mild. 'I suppose you were a bit overwhelmed,' Linnet began. 'I know I—'

'Not so much overwhelmed as annoyed,' Paula interrupted in an unusually tetchy tone for her. 'From what I read, it seems to me you would like to revamp the *entire* store. Have you considered how much money it would cost to do that?'

'Not the whole store, Mummy, I certainly don't want to do that! But I honestly do think Harte's needs a big shove into the Twenty-First Century.'

Taken aback, Paula exclaimed with a hint of acerbity, 'Do you really now?'

Knowing she had just said the wrong thing, Linnet leaned forward and in a conciliatory voice she murmured, 'Please don't be angry. I've done a great deal of research into retail marketing and merchandising, and I've also trekked around the rival stores this past week. Harvey Nichols, Harrods and Selfridges were on my agenda. What I saw tells me that our competitors are thinking on similar lines. They're revamping, opting for a new image, a more modern look, focusing on a younger generation of women shoppers. They're also going for a whole new brigade of talented young designers, as well as established names like Chanel, Valentino, Armani, and so on. They're looking ahead, Mother.'

'We're so much above those stores,' Paula said in the same tetchy tone. 'To begin with, Harte's has become an institution over the years. We also happen to be a tourist attraction, and pull a lot of foreign visitors into the store. Those things aside, we give the very best personal services in London, and of any store anywhere in the world. We can't be compared . . . we are absolutely *unique*.'

'Everything you say is true, Mummy, I don't deny that. And yes, we *are* an institution, but we're starting to look just a tiny bit *staid*. We can continue to be an institution, appealing to our core, and very devoted, customer, while being more up-to-date. And yes, we *are* a tourist attraction, but that doesn't mean we sell merchandise to them. Most just come to *look*.' Linnet paused, sat staring at her mother before finishing, 'And I agree with you that we give the best personal service there is. But what we need for this new world we're living in is a bit of pizazz as well. Something a bit extra to back up everything we already are.'

Paula was carefully studying her daughter, her

expression reflective. After a long moment, she answered in a cold, rather remote voice, 'You must pull back here, Linnet, be less extreme. I will not permit you to jump into all this revamping . . . because, very simply, I don't agree with you, and I certainly *do not* approve of it.'

Linnet felt her heart plunge to her shoes, and she experienced an intense rush of disappointment.

'You mean you don't approve of anything I've suggested?' she asked in a subdued voice, thinking of all the time, energy and effort she had put in. But mostly she was distressed because she was certain she was right; if they did not bring a few more up-to-date ideas into the store, in a year from now profits could start dwindling.

'Don't sound so miserable and down in the dumps, Linny,' Paula suddenly said in a kinder tone. 'I don't think I expressed myself very well.' Smiling more warmly at Linnet, she went on, 'What I'm trying to say is that I don't approve of this huge *overhaul* you've indicated we need. Because, very truthfully, I don't think it's necessary. However, I'm going to give you the go-ahead on several of your ideas.'

Linnet sat up straighter, holding her breath, and filling with relief.

Paula was shuffling through the memos, and looking up, she announced, 'The floor devoted to brides is a great idea, and I think it will work well. God knows where you'll put Mattresses, but then, that's your problem. Anyway, to continue, you can plan the Tranquillity Day Spa as well. By the way, did you make a deal with Bonnadell yet? A tentative deal?'

Linnet nodded, feeling less dejected, regaining some of her enthusiasm and exclaimed, 'I did make a lot of progress with her, and, most importantly, she's agreed we can do the remodelling of the beauty salon ourselves. That'll save us money, because we'll be using Charlie Fromett's department, his carpenters and other workers, rather than her architects and designers. A big saving there. I said *if* you approved the spa, she could sell her products in the beauty department as well as the spa itself. That works for her and the store, gives us more profit.'

'I assume her people would run the spa for us?' Paula said.

'I talked to Dad, and he thought we'd be better off using her people, who naturally are properly trained therapists, and know the benefits of all the products. That's the way the spas are run in the O'Neill hotels.'

Paula nodded. 'He told me he'd spoken to you, and he seems to think it's a good idea for us to open a day spa.'

So that's why she agreed, Linnet thought, but said, 'Thanks, Mummy, for letting me go ahead with the spa. I know it will be an attraction, pull young women into the store, and hopefully into the fashion areas afterwards.'

'Who's going to run the bridal floor, Linnet?' Paula now asked, eyeing her quizzically. 'Evan's on maternity leave for three months, and you have enough to do.'

'I've found the right executive to run Brides.'

Swiftly, Linnet told her mother about Marietta's friend, Bobbi Snyder, then thought to add, 'And there's another thing: we don't need to spend a lot of money to revamp the mattress department. Obviously, the walls need repainting and we must put down new carpeting throughout, but the rest is a facelift, all cosmetic.'

'Yes, I realize that,' Paula replied, rising, walking across the office. She stood looking down on Knightsbridge for a moment, then turning to face Linnet she continued, 'Finally, Linnet, I want you to understand one thing. I will never, and I do mean *never*, endorse this idea of putting snack bars in the Food Halls. The mere idea of this makes me shudder, in fact it is very offensive to me. Those Food Halls are now a legend, renowned worldwide, and I won't have them tampered with.'

'But, Mummy, honestly, the snack bars could easily be fitted into a corner here and there, we could find the space.'

'Please don't argue with me, Linnet. I will not have those idiotic snack bars in the Food Halls. Harte's has plenty of restaurants . . . the Bird Cage, Far Pavilions, London Bridge, and the coffee bar. We don't need any more. *Understood?*'

'But—'

'I said *no!*'

Paula sounded so angry Linnet shrank back in the chair.

As Paula started to walk back to her desk something happened to her. And she was very conscious of it happening. Her entire office seemed suddenly to fill with white light. It became supernaturally bright and startlingly so, blinding her.

Continuing across the room, she felt her steps begin to falter and she staggered in the direction of a chair, feeling the overwhelming need to sit down.

'Mummy, what's wrong with you?' Linnet shouted, observing the change in Paula. Jumping up out of her chair, she ran to her mother, helped her to sit down.

Paula could not speak for a moment. She felt sick, very nauseous, and was hit by the most blinding headache. Her hands went to her head, holding it. Her neck hurt.

'Mummy, what's wrong?' Linnet cried.

'Don't know. Call 999. Get an ambulance. There's a terrible pain in my head. Oh, God. The pain!'

Linnet flew to the phone on her mother's desk. It was programmed to individuals, and she punched number two.

Jack said, 'Yes, Paula—'

'It's not Mummy, it's me!' Linnet cried, her voice shrill. 'My mother's ill. Get an ambulance. It's her head. I think she might be having a stroke.'

'I'm on it.' Jack slammed the phone down.

Linnet punched in the number one, the direct link to Shane's office. Her father picked up after three rings. 'Hello, Paula—'

'It's Linnet.' Her voice wobbled as she continued, 'I think Mummy's having a stroke, or something, Daddy. Jack's calling an ambulance. She's complaining of pains in her head.'

'I'll be there in five minutes!' Shane hung up.

Running to the door, Linnet wrenched it open, startling Jonelle, who glanced up, frowning.

'Go to my office, please. Get my coat and bag. And hurry. My mother's ill. There's an ambulance coming. I think she's having a stroke.'

Stunned, Jonelle gaped at her and then ran out of the executive suite, heading towards Linnet's office.

The four of them sat in the hospital waiting room: Shane, Linnet, Emily and Jack. Each one of them looked morose and worried as they waited for news of Paula's condition. They had been there for two hours, and after worrying out loud, and talking for part of that time, they had now fallen silent, each lost in their own thoughts.

But at one moment Shane suddenly sat up in the chair where he was slumped and exclaimed, 'Jack, how terribly rude I am. I forgot to thank you for suggesting to the ambulance men that they bring Paula here to King's Hospital.'

'They would have anyway,' Jack replied. 'In my experience, those ambulance men and paramedics know what they're doing. They were immediately telling me this was where they planned to bring her, explaining that King's is the best neurological centre in London. I think it's more than likely one of the best in England, if not *the* best. They have very advanced methods and techniques here, a great reputation.'

'I'll be glad when we know what happened to Mummy this morning,' Linnet murmured, her voice low, troubled, her expression anxious. 'I feel so awful, Daddy. I'd just had an argument with her about the store, and then she fell apart, had the attack or stroke, or whatever it was. It's my fault,' she whispered, sounding tearful.

'Don't be silly, darling,' Shane reassured her gently, taking hold of Linnet's hand in an attempt to comfort her. His face was anguished, his dark eyes flooded with anxiety. 'An argument isn't going to bring on something like this. It's a medical problem.'

Emily, staring across at Shane, asked quietly, 'Do you think it *was* a stroke?'

'I don't know, Emily, I don't even want to hazard a guess. I'm just praying that whatever it is, Paula comes out of it all right.'

'I think Paula's had a brain haemorrhage,' Jack ventured.

'What makes you think that?' Shane looked at the security chief intently, his expression puzzled, his eyes on Jack.

'The symptoms. Linnet told me her mother had complained of a blinding headache, of feeling nauseous. That she had terrible pains in her head. I'm not sure that those are the symptoms of a stroke. Also, I noticed when they were lifting the stretcher into the ambulance that Paula's face had dropped down at one side. That can be a symptom of brain damage. But I'm just making a guess.'

At that moment the door opened and the doctor they had seen earlier stepped into the room. 'Mr O'Neill,' he said, 'I have some news for you.'

Immediately, Shane leapt to his feet, strode over to the door, nodding. 'Please, Doctor, come inside, tell me what happened to my wife this morning.'

'Mrs O'Neill has suffered a sub-arachnoid haemorrhage,' the doctor said in a calm voice.

'What exactly does that mean, sub-arachnoid?' Shane asked, perplexed.

'This is a specific form of haemorrhage, caused by a weakness in the wall of the vessel which supplies blood to the brain,' the doctor explained.

'What caused it?' Shane asked.

'We don't know why it happens, we never do really. This weakness in the blood vessel wall is called an aneurysm, which is a word you might be more familiar with.'

'Yes, I am,' Shane answered, nodding his head

'Anyway, the best answer I can give about this type of haemorrhage is that it happens when the pressure of the blood tears an aneurysm wall,' the doctor told him.

'And the blood goes into the brain, is that what happens?'

'Yes indeed, Mr O'Neill. It goes into the tissues surrounding the brain. This is called the sub-arachnoid layer, hence the name of the haemorrhage.' The doctor put his hand on Shane's arm sympathetically. 'It's such a small amount of blood, you know, just ten cc, which in layman's terms is about a thimbleful.'

'My God, so little.' Shane stared at him in astonishment.

'Unfortunately, it can be disastrous.'

'Is my wife going to be all right?' Shane asked now, his tone low, concerned.

'Mrs O'Neill is very ill. We plan to operate tomorrow morning very early.'

'Why not today?'

'We're still in the process of giving her tests, Mr O'Neill.'

'Can I see her?'

'I'm afraid not, she's undergoing tests, as I just said. We'll be in touch.'

Shane nodded. 'Thank you, Mr Gilleon, for explaining everything, and for looking after my wife.'

The doctor took Shane's outstretched hand, shook it, nodded to the others and left the room as briskly as he had entered it.

'So you were right, Jack,' Shane said, striding over to join the others. 'I hope to God Paula is going to get through this—' He stopped, turned his head abruptly, then walked over to the window. His eyes had filled with tears and he didn't want the others to see him in this state of upset.

But Linnet was aware of what had happened to her father, that he had broken down, and she went over to him, took hold of his arm. 'It's all right, Daddy,' she murmured gently, 'Mummy's going to be fine, I just know it. She's going to make it.' Sliding her arm through his, she drew even closer and whispered, 'You know what she always says: the Hartes are made of the strongest steel.'

'Let's hope so,' Shane muttered, brushing his eyes with his hand, then putting his arms around his daughter, holding her tightly as if never to let her go. Paula was his life, and he knew that Linnet knew that. She had always been aware of how much her parents loved each other, and had for all of their lives.

And as he held his first-born daughter to him, he offered up a silent prayer: Oh God, let her live. Let my Paula live.

CHAPTER THIRTY-TWO

On Monday night Linnet went home and spent part of the evening weeping in Julian's arms. Even though her husband tried to convince her that she had not been responsible for her mother's collapse, she nonetheless kept blaming herself.

It was only when she had exhausted herself with crying and was quiet and still on the sofa that he finally spoke to her a little sternly.

'Nobody causes anyone to have a brain haemorrhage, Linnet!' he exclaimed, giving her a long look. 'It's just as your father told you, a medical problem. And think about this, Paula hasn't looked well ever since we got back from our honeymoon in January.'

'That's true,' Linnet responded, sitting up straighter, her eyes on his. 'She kept saying she was merely tired, or had done too much, and there had been two weddings to cope with, ours and Evan's. But perhaps something else was happening . . . to her health.'

'More than likely it was. And you must stop punishing yourself like this. It wasn't your fault. Remember that.'

Linnet just inclined her head, and, reaching out, she took hold of Julian's hand. 'I've come to realize, especially in the last couple of years, that Mummy's a real *worrier*. And she's done a lot of worrying lately . . . about that awful, horrible Jonathan Ainsley, and Robin's health. I know she went to see him on Saturday, because Dad told me today that something was troubling Uncle Robin. And she apparently worried all weekend about Tessa, and Jean-Claude being missing. At least that's what Daddy was explaining after we left the hospital this afternoon.'

'I don't think worrying about problems caused the brain haemorrhage either, darling. It's always a medical situation, as I just said.' Julian shook his head, let out a small sigh. 'I do feel sorry for Tessa, it must be hell, living on her nerves, waiting for news about Jean-Claude.'

'She's pregnant,' Linnet blurted out. 'She told me this morning, when I spoke to her on the phone. Before Mummy collapsed.'

Julian looked at Linnet alertly, his mind racing, his deep blue eyes now focused on her intently. 'Well, that changes the picture all around, doesn't it?'

'Yes, it does. She sounds happy about the baby, but I suppose she's worried that she might be bringing the child up without a father—'

'But she's already doing that,' Julian cut in

peremptorily. 'And Adele seems no worse for it. She's probably better without that loud-mouthed Mark Longden around. Thank God your mother dealt with him smartly, packed him off to Sydney.'

'He wouldn't have gone quite so readily if Mummy hadn't given him that huge settlement.'

'Money talks,' he said, smiling at her. 'But as you always say, there are many other currencies.'

For the first time in hours Linnet smiled, leaned into Julian and kissed him lightly on the mouth. 'I can't imagine being married to anyone else but you, Jules.'

'Don't even let that thought cross your mind,' he shot back in a stern way, but she knew he was teasing her.

Linnet said, 'Emily and Dad were going to phone the family, explain what happened to Mummy. Oh, God, I do hope she'll pull through.' Her eyes filled and she brought a hand to her trembling mouth.

Reaching for her, Julian pulled her into his arms, and held her close to him, stroking that red hair he loved so much. 'Stop it, darling. You must stay calm. Please don't think about her not recovering. Send out positive thoughts, good vibes. Promise me.'

'I will, I promise,' she murmured against his chest.

They sat like that for a while, wrapped in each other's arms on the sofa in front of the fire. They had not yet bothered to look for a larger place, and were living in Julian's bachelor flat in Chester Street. It was perfectly adequate for them at the moment; they both liked the area, and the flat's close proximity to her mother's house in Belgrave Square pleased Linnet.

Julian Kallinski's thoughts were very much centred on his mother-in-law at this moment. He was putting up a good front in order to support Linnet, reinforce her natural courage, but deep down he was troubled, and worried about Paula. By an odd coincidence his mother's sister, Ashley Preston, had died of a brain haemorrhage several years ago; now he remembered his mother telling him at the time that few people survived a brain injury of that nature. Almost everyone died within several days, if not sooner. He prayed to God that Paula would be one of the lucky ones. He didn't know how Shane would go on without her, or how any of the family would manage. Paula McGill Harte Amory Fairley O'Neill . . . my God, he thought, what a name . . . she had been christened Paula McGill, for her grandfather Paul McGill, Harte for Emma, Amory because that was her father David's surname. Fairley came from her first marriage to James Fairley, and O'Neill because she had married Shane, the love of her life . . .

He suspected that Paula was the love of his father's life. Michael Kallinski had never married after divorcing Valentine, his mother, and over the years Julian had somehow slowly come to realize, mostly through observation, that his father was utterly devoted to Linnet's mother. Oh, Michael, Michael, he thought suddenly, you should have cured yourself years ago. Moved on, Dad. Loving Paula was a lost cause. Linnet was convinced that

Jack Figg was in love with Paula also, and knowing how astute his wife was, Julian believed she was right.

But neither man had been anything but a good friend in Paula's mind, of that he was absolutely certain. She had only ever had eyes for Shane. Just as he had only ever had eyes for this bundle of contradictions in his arms. How he loved his Linnet, and all the more because of what she was, who she was. A total, dyed-in-the-wool Harte. Loyal, stubborn, loving, enterprising, strong, intelligent and brave. It would be her bravery that would bring her through this ordeal. He had loved her since they were children growing up together, and he had never ever doubted her courage and her determination to overcome all odds.

He felt her stirring, and moving away slightly, he said, 'I bet you haven't eaten all day, have you?'

Sitting up, Linnet shook her head. 'No, and I'm not really hungry, I don't think I could eat anything.'

'I have to, I'm starving.' As he spoke, Julian got up and walked across the living room, heading for the kitchen. 'Mrs Ludlow left supper ready for us, Linny.'

'What is it?' Linnet struggled to her feet and went after him, suddenly realizing she felt slightly nauseous because she, too, was hungry, had a rumbling tummy.

'Look,' Julian murmured, lifting the lid of a pan on the stove. 'Beef stew. And I know there's smoked salmon in the refrigerator, as well as salad, cheese and fruit. Surely you can take a few mouthfuls of something?'

'I think I'd better, I do feel rather empty.' Turning the gas ring on underneath the stew, Linnet continued, 'I hope Dad's all right. He went back to his office. I should have invited him over to have supper with us.'

'Knowing Emily, she took charge of him. Want to bet he's having dinner with her and Winston right at this moment?'

'I won't take the bet, because I know you're right. Of course he's with them. They're his best friends . . . all of his life.'

On Wednesday of the same week, two days after her collapse, Shane O'Neill knew at last that Paula's life had been saved by the team of doctors at King's College Hospital in South East London.

Not only had her life been saved, but the doctors had informed him that there was every chance it would be a productive life. The operation on her brain had been an outstanding success, so they believed.

Once he had hung up the phone in his office, Shane wept with relief. The strain of the last few days had taken its toll, and as strong and courageous as Shane was, the thought of losing Paula had crippled him. Somehow he had managed to keep a calm façade for everyone's sake, but he had been afraid and even panic-stricken at times.

Now, with this good news in his possession, he began to ring the family. He phoned his father first, because he was well aware that Bryan O'Neill was nervous, and fretting over Paula, and that kind of pressure was too much for a man in his eighties to take.

Then he phoned his children, who were as joyous as he was, and who promised to inform other members of the family whilst he called Emily and Winston.

On Saturday morning Shane was finally allowed to see Paula, and when he walked into her room at King's Hospital he was initially startled. There was no bandage on her head, even though he knew she had had a brain operation. He mentioned this to Mr Gilleon as he was led by him into the room, and the surgeon said quietly, 'New techniques, you know.'

Paula was filled with relief at the sight of Shane, and after a brief word with her, the doctor left them alone. 'For just a short while,' he added as he closed the door behind him.

After kissing her cheek, Shane pulled a chair up to the bed, and sat down, took hold of Paula's hand. 'Oh, darling, what a relief it is that you're all right. We've been worried sick.'

'I can imagine . . .' A wry smile touched Paula's mouth and she said, 'I didn't remember anything, Shane. Yesterday, the surgeon explained what had happened to me, that I was very ill and had had a brain injury.'

Shane nodded, 'Mr Gilleon told me you've been very lucky.'

'Yes, I know I have. But what happened? I remember talking to Linnet in my office on Monday morning . . . the rest is a blank.'

'Linnet said you were standing at the window, looking out. Then you walked back to your desk, but seemed to be faltering, staggering, and she rushed to you, got you into a chair. You asked her to call 999 for an ambulance, and you told her your head hurt. The ambulance came to the store and you were rushed here. The surgeons operated on your brain on Tuesday.'

'It's funny, I don't recall any of it . . . the doctors told me I had classic symptoms when I came in, the right side of my face was askew, and I was terribly sensitive to light.'

'And how do you feel today, Paula?' Shane scarched her face, peering at her, finding her remarkably unchanged in her appearance.

'Tired. A little weak. Very dazed, in a sense.' She offered him a faint smile and settled back more comfortably against the pillows. 'In the family we've always said the Hartes are made of steel. Well, at least one of us now has *platinum* inside as well. *Me*.'

Shane couldn't help laughing, and he touched her cheek gently. He was full of happiness that this woman, whom he loved and who had been part of his life since his childhood, was now out of danger. 'I know all about the platinum,' he said. 'Mr Gilleon has told me a few things about the operation, and he explained that they use platinum coils to seal off the bleed.'

'Yes, I know *that*, but I'm afraid I haven't taken in everything. I guess I'm still a bit out of it.'

'Not surprising, when you think about it, angel. Well, here goes, see if you can understand what they told me. I'll try and make it simple. The surgeons find the aneurysm through the use of X-ray and radiographic techniques apparently, by passing dye up a catheter in order to locate it precisely. Once they've found the aneurysm, they thread platinum wires along the tube. As I understand it, Paula, the hole in the blood vessel is actually sealed by the platinum wires, which form coils. They're in place permanently in your brain and prevent any further bleeding.'

'Isn't it amazing what they can do medically today? And thank God they can, or I wouldn't be here,' Paula murmured.

'Modern miracles,' Shane murmured, and then clearing his throat he went on slowly, carefully, 'Listen to me, Paula, you're doing very well, very well indeed. But many people don't, so I'm told. Some patients who survive a brain haemorrhage develop memory loss, blurred vision or speech problems. So far so good, my darling, as far as you're concerned, but you *are* going to have to take it easy.'

'Yes, I know. But when can I come home, Shane? Have the doctors told you?'

'You do have to stay a bit longer, darling. Just until you get your strength back. You've had a major operation, don't forget. The doctor told me it will be at the end of next week, *providing* you do as well as you have so far.'

'Oh, Shane, that's days away! Such a long time . . .' Her voice trailed off helplessly. She was disappointed she wasn't leaving with him today.

'No, not long at all, under the circumstances,' Shane responded. 'A week is not so very long to wait, considering you might not have been coming home at all. And I might have had to spend the rest of my life without you.'

Paula squeezed his hand, and murmured lovingly, 'I know what you mean, darling. I can have visitors, can't I? I want to see the children. Oh, Shane, I forgot, what about Jean-Claude?'

He shook his head sadly. 'No news, none at all, actually. As far as seeing the children is concerned, I'm sure you can, but they mustn't tire you.'

The smile on her face was beatific as he bent down to kiss her.

'Miss Paula! Whatever are you doing at that there desk? You're not supposed to be working, you're supposed to be in bed!'

'I'm not working, Margaret, I'm just sitting here.' Paula grimaced, shaking her head. 'I got up to make a few notes and I can't. My brain seems unable to work the way it did. I sincerely hope that's not a permanent thing.'

'Oh, it won't be, it won't be,' Margaret clucked, her mother-hen manner in place today. Wanting to reassure Paula, she continued, 'You're bound to be tired, all you've been through. I've brought you up a nice cup of tea. Where do you want it? Here or in bed?'

'I think I'd better go back to bed,' Paula replied, knowing that this was the best place for her. The effort of going from the bed to the desk earlier this morning had exhausted her, and she, who had thought her recovery would be fast, had discovered it was quite slow. She had been out of the hospital almost two weeks now, yet doing small, normal things even seemed too much at times. Simple tasks taxed her or left her reeling.

Taking her arm, the housekeeper helped Paula across the upstairs parlour and into the adjoining bedroom. Once she was in bed, Margaret plumped the pillows, straightened the coverlet, and then hurried across the room to retrieve the tray with the cup of tea on it.

A moment later, placing the cup and saucer on the bedside table, Margaret asked, 'Is there any news of Tessa's fiancé?'

'No, nothing, and it's been over four weeks now. She's distraught.'

'Oh, I'm sorry, it's awful, it is that. Is she coming for the weekend?'

'Yes, Margaret, she is, and bringing Adele and Elvira. Linnet's also coming with Julian, and there's a possibility Mrs Hughes will come, too.'

'A houseful, eh?' Margaret smiled happily. 'But I knows you like it that way, Miss Paula, and so do I. It's a bit lonely, this here big house is, when there's nobody else running around in it but us oldies.'

'Speak for yourself!' Paula exclaimed, and reaching for the cup she took a sip of the tea.

'Will Tessa be doing any cooking? Or isn't she going to be up to it?' Margaret asked.

'I don't know, I didn't think to ask her.'

'Shall I give Priscilla a tinkle? Or is *she* still in your bad books?'

'You know very well she's never been in my bad books! It's just that . . . well, frankly, Margaret, most of the family are cross with her. They think she told that nasty cousin of mine too much.'

'I know very well what they think, but *I* don't think she's a bad woman, you knows.'

'Let's find out who's coming altogether, when Mr Shane gets home tonight, then we'll make a decision. Is that all right?'

'Oh, yes, it is indeed. Well, I'll trot off to the kitchen. I'm making you a nice piece of plaice for lunch, and a baked apple. You've always loved baked apples since you were a child.'

'Thank you, Margaret,' Paula murmured and sank back into the pillows. She was exhausted again, but then Margaret could be trying at times.

Half an hour later the phone jangling on the bedside table brought Paula out of a doze. 'Hello?' she said as she picked up the receiver.

'It's Emily, Paula dear. How are you?'

'Back in bed. I felt very tired.'

'Oh, I'm sorry. Have you been doing too much?'

'No. I guess this kind of sudden tiredness goes with the territory.'

'I thought of popping over for lunch. I came up to Yorkshire last night. But perhaps you're not up to it?'

''Course I am, and I'd love that, Dumpling.'

'You cannot possibly call a woman in her fifties Dumpling. You *must* please *stop*.'

Paula laughed. 'See you soon.'

'Sooner than you think.'

A few minutes later Emily was walking across the upstairs parlour and into the bedroom. Paula was taken aback. 'How did you get here so quickly?'

'I called you on my cell from the terrace.'

'Emily! You should have said you were here!'

'I didn't want you to feel obliged to invite me to lunch, if you were exhausted.'

'I'm fine—'

Paula stopped as Emily's mobile, still in her hand, began to ring. 'Emily Harte here. Oh, hello, Great-Aunt Edwina! How're you?'

Walking over to a chair, Emily sat down, listened attentively, and then said, 'Oh dear, I am sorry, so very sorry. How sad. Yes, yes, I'll tell her, and I'll get back to you in a few moments.' Emily clicked off the phone, looked across at Paula and said quietly, in a saddened voice, 'That was Great-Aunt Edwina, as you heard.' There was a moment's pause, and then Emily went on softly, 'Uncle Robin has just been found dead.'

Paula sat bolt upright in the bed, gaping at Emily, her face turning extremely white. '*Where?*'

'At Lackland Priory. By Bolton, just a few minutes ago. Apparently he'd been out for a walk, Uncle Robin I mean, and when he came back he asked Bolton for a cup of coffee. Bolton took it to him in the library ten minutes later, and he found Uncle

Robin sitting in his wing chair near the fire. Stone-cold dead. Obviously Bolton is dreadfully upset, not only because Robin's dead, but of the way he found him sitting there. It was so unexpected.'

'How terrible for Bolton. However, sad as I am, what a wonderful way to die. Robin never suffered an illness . . .' Paula's voice faltered and tears came into her eyes. She brushed them away, confided, 'I grew to like Robin so much in these last years or so.'

'So did I. Paula, isn't it a pity the twins haven't been born yet . . . He never got to see his great-grandsons, or hold them in his arms. He so wanted that.'

'At least he met Evan, got to know his only grandchild, was aware that she was happy with Gideon. And he also knew he was going to have great-grandsons to carry on his line,' Paula pointed out, resting her head against the pillows.

'That's true,' Emily answered and a deep sigh escaped her. 'My mother is going to be grief-stricken. He was her twin.'

'Poor Aunt Elizabeth, she *will* take it hard, and so will Edwina.'

A small silence fell between them as they sat thinking their own thoughts about Robin's sisters.

It was Emily who suddenly exclaimed after a moment or two, 'Paula, I've just had the most terrible thought! Does this mean that Jonathan Ainsley will be coming to Yorkshire? Will he be coming to Uncle Robin's funeral?'

'I don't know the answer to that, darling. Presumably he *will*. After all, Robin *is* his father.'

Emily said, 'I'd better phone Great-Aunt Edwina back, she wants to know what to do about the funeral. When Bolton phoned her he said he hadn't wanted to bother you with it.'

'I'm just not up to dealing with this death, the funeral, Emily. I'm so sorry, but I'm not. I'm not back to normal, not by a long way.'

'I know that. I'll take over for you. Or help Edwina, whichever she wants. Shall I tell her it's her decision?'

'That's fine, but let's not forget she's ninety-five.'

Emily's phone jangled again, and clicking it on she said, 'Hello?'

'Mother, it's me.'

'Hello, Gideon. Listen, I have some news—'

'Let me give you mine first,' he cut in excitedly. 'Evan went into labour earlier this morning. I didn't phone you because she thought it might be a false alarm. She's not due for a few days. Anyway, you're a grandmother! You've got two bouncing baby grandsons. And there's no mistaking they're Hartes. They both have bright auburn fluff on top of their heads.'

'Oh, Gideon! *Congratulations*. How wonderful, and Evan is all right, I'm presuming?'

'She's great, Mother, but very tired.'

'I'm sorry I'm here in Yorkshire, Gid. I'd come up to town but I've a problem here.'

'Don't worry, Ma. Marietta is already at the hospital, and Dad's on his way there. Listen, I've got to go—'

'Gideon, wait a minute. I started to tell you I had

some news, and a problem. It's rather upsetting I'm afraid. I'm here with Paula, and we just heard that Uncle Robin died this morning. Peacefully, at home, sitting in his chair by the fire.'

'I'm so sorry, Mother. How sad he never got to see the twins . . . he couldn't wait to hold them, he told me last week.'

'Are you going to tell Evan?' Emily asked, sounding suddenly concerned.

'I won't, not today. I think it'll upset her too much. What do you think?'

'Keep it to yourself at least for twenty-four hours, Gideon. At least, don't mention it to Evan today. But you'd better let your father know. Because of Robin's obituary for the papers.'

CHAPTER THIRTY-THREE

'Since I am the oldest person in this family, the most senior, I think it's only appropriate that I take charge of Robin's funeral,' Great-Aunt Edwina said, looking from Paula to Emily. 'However, I shall certainly need your help, Emily, since I'm not as swift as I was.'

'You have it,' Emily responded, leaning forward, picking up the silver teapot, pouring herself another cup of tea. She couldn't help thinking that Edwina was swifter than most people she knew. 'My main concern has been Jonathan Ainsley. What do we do about *him*?'

'I have all the information we need, Emily. His telephone numbers around the world, the name of his solicitors.' Reaching for her handbag, she opened it and took out an envelope, handed it to Emily, who was seated next to her. She explained, 'Robin gave me this several weeks ago, I have a feeling my brother knew he was going to die soon.'

'It's funny you should say that, Great-Aunt Edwina, but I think he did, too,' Paula murmured, staring at

Edwina across the coffee table. She was stretched out on the other sofa, covered with a light quilt and propped up against many pillows which supported her back, neck and head. 'In fact, only a few weeks ago, just before I had my brain surgery, I went over to see him. We discussed various matters regarding his will.'

'Oh, yes, he told me all about it,' Edwina murmured, giving her a knowing look. 'Now, Emily, getting back to Jonathan, I think we should just go ahead and plan the funeral without consulting him. He's never here, and he's never been here for Robin. Not only that, they were at loggerheads lately. So, where shall we have it? Here at Pennistone village church or at Fairley Church?'

'Gosh, I hadn't even thought of Fairley!' Emily exclaimed, throwing Paula a quick look.

'Grandy's buried there,' Paula explained in answer to her questioning look. 'And her brothers and her parents. As well as a lot of Fairleys.'

'Oh, that doesn't matter, about the Fairleys, I mean. Robin wasn't one. Only I,' Edwina pointed out, as if they didn't know. That was all she had ever talked about at one point in her life, as Paula and Emily were well aware. It had driven Emma crazy, this preoccupation with her lineage.

Paula closed her eyes, realizing that she was suddenly having trouble dealing with all this, and for a moment she couldn't think straight. In fact, unexpectedly she was baffled, her mind overloaded.

Emily announced, 'If convenience is a consideration, I think Uncle Robin should be buried here in the graveyard next to Pennistone Royal church. Do we really want to trek across the moors at this time of year?'

'Very well put, Emily!' Edwina took a sip of tea, sat back and straightened the skirt of her dark-purple wool dress. 'What time of day should the funeral be, do you think? I prefer the morning, so we can have a small gathering afterwards, buffet lunch, nothing fancy, just for the family.' Raising a brow, she looked at Emily intently.

'If we arrange the funeral for ten o'clock it will be over in an hour,' Emily asserted, pushing a strand of hair away from her face. 'So we could have lunch at twelve-thirty, or thereabouts. Do you agree?'

'That sounds about right,' Edwina replied, and put a finger to her lips as she glanced at Paula.

Emily followed the direction of Edwina's gaze and nodded. Paula was dozing. 'So now we should inform Jonathan Ainsley of our plans and invite him to come to his father's funeral, then let the rest of the family know the details.'

'Do you think you can do that, Emily dear?' Edwina asked, then added quickly, 'Speak to the rest of the family?'

'Of course, and Jonathan as well. I'll also—'

'Oh, no, no,' Edwina cut in. 'I wish to make that particular phone call.'

'Very well. I understand. Now, Great-Aunt, when should we have the funeral? Next week? Monday, Tuesday or Wednesday?'

'Since it's Friday today, Monday's far too soon to make all the arrangements in time. I think we

486

had better speak to the vicar here in Pennistone, and ask which day is the best for him. Tuesday or Wednesday? Probably we should aim for Wednesday, since I'm sure Anthony and Sally will come from Clonloughlin and other family members have to travel here.'

'That's true. Great-Aunt Edwina—' Emily cut herself off, staring at her aunt, her mother's sister and best friend.

'What is it?' Edwina asked, noticing the odd look on her niece's face. 'Is there something you want to tell me?'

Nodding her head, Emily said, 'It's the most bizarre thing, Paula and I both agree on that. Just after you phoned me this morning, I had another call. From Gideon. Evan gave birth to the twins at about eleven o'clock . . . Everyone's doing fine, and the boys have bright red fluff on their heads, according to their excited father, but don't you think it's a most curious coincidence?'

Edwina sat back against the pillows, shaking her head, her expression contemplative. 'How extraordinary. Just as Robin died, his great-grandsons were coming into this world. Well, I never. You're right, it is bizarre, and perhaps prophetic . . . signals of something wonderful. Maybe they will inherit all of his talents and gifts – and none of his faults. But then none of us is perfect.'

'Yes,' Emily agreed.

'And Evan is all right, you said?' Edwina's brow lifted, her expression questioning.

'She's doing splendidly. We'd better be in touch

with her father, Owen Hughes, just in case he wants to come to the funeral?'

'Perhaps he won't want to come. Personally, I detest funerals. A long time ago I promised myself I would only ever go to weddings and christenings. Naturally, this funeral is a bit different, because Robin was my brother and he was always my favourite. But I never go to my friends' funerals these days. Too many of them to begin with, and secondly, they go against the grain. I'm for life, Emily my dear, not death.'

Emily couldn't help it. She burst out laughing.

Tessa Fairley sat in the back of the car, staring out of the window, her expression morose, her beautiful eyes dull and empty. Although there were hints of spring in the countryside as they drove towards Pennistone Royal, she did not notice the change. Her thoughts were elsewhere: they went from Jean-Claude, still missing and a source of extreme worry, to her mother, deeply affected by the brain haemorrhage, and the other source of constant worry.

There was nothing she could do about Jean-Claude, except pray he was safe; as far as her mother was concerned, she felt the need to protect her, cosset her, help her get well.

Whatever the others in the family thought, Tessa knew that her mother had had a traumatic few weeks. She had come home to Pennistone Royal from King's Hospital thinking she was perfectly normal, only to discover, much to her chagrin, that she was not. Paula had quickly realized that the smallest things, which she had done automatically all her life, now took her much longer; she had also admitted to Tessa that she was frequently baffled by all the information being thrown at her brain in the most normal way. She couldn't process things, or fathom them out, and she became exhausted easily.

There was another troubling thing for Paula. There were no bandages on her head, because they were not needed, and so most people saw the woman they had always known, and didn't understand that she had had a major brain injury. 'They think I'm just the same,' Paula had complained to Tessa only a week ago. 'And I'm not. I'm still suffering. I haven't recovered completely yet. It's funny, you know, if I had a plaster on my leg or my arm in a sling they'd recognize I'd been hurt. As it is, they don't.'

Naturally, close members of the family, such as Shane, Linnet, Lorne, Emsie and Desmond, and the staff at Pennistone Royal, understood everything, but Tessa had decided on the drive from London that she would remind everybody again this weekend, just to be sure.

Adele began to stir.

Tessa looked down at her daughter on the seat, and at Elvira, who was soothing Adele, stroking her hair. 'I think she had a bad dream,' Elvira murmured. 'But we'll soon be there, and she can have—'

Elvira broke off as Tessa's mobile phone buzzed. Grabbing it from her carry-all, Tessa clicked it on, said, 'Hello?'

'Tessa?'

'Yes.'

'It's Philippe. I have fantastic news!'

Tessa gripped the phone all that much tighter and held her breath. 'Yes, yes, tell me.'

He seemed to fade away for a moment, and then he was back. 'Did you hear me?'

'No, I didn't.'

'My father is now in Kabul. With the American forces. They found him. Wounded in some make-shift hospital. Somewhere. He is coming home, Tessa!'

'Oh my God! Philippe, this is wonderful news,' Tessa shouted down the phone, afraid of losing him. Tears were rolling down her face, and she could barely get the words out. 'When is he coming back to Paris?'

'I do not know. I'll phone you as soon as I have news.'

He hung up before she could tell him she would be at Pennistone Royal for the weekend, and to call her on the landline.

Looking over at Elvira, she cried excitedly, 'Mr Deléon is safe.'

'That's wonderful news, Mrs Fairley.'

'Why are you crying, Mumma?' Adele asked, sitting up, touching Tessa's wet face.

'Because I'm happy, darling, very very happy!'

Adele stared at her, looking nonplussed.

A moment later the driver was pulling up outside the front façade of Pennistone Royal.

As Tessa opened the car door, she saw Great-Aunt Edwina and Emily standing on the doorstep, and she leapt out of the car, ran towards them waving her hand, and shouting, 'He's safe! Jean-Claude is safe! He's coming home.'

Emily ran to meet her and they embraced, and Tessa started crying again. So did Emily. After a moment they managed to compose themselves and walked back to Edwina, who was beaming at them.

'Tessa, my darling Tessa, this is wonderful news. And I think we all deserve a drink. I was going home, but I think we must now go back inside the house and pop a cork, or at least have a lovely glass of sherry.'

'What a good idea, Great-Aunt Edwina. And hopefully we can have it in the upstairs parlour with Mummy,' Tessa answered.

Adele came running to Great-Aunt Edwina, stood staring up at her, a smile on her face. Then she said, 'Mumma told me you're my great great great great aunt.'

Edwina looked down at this exquisite blonde child, a true Fairley if ever there was one, she thought, and said, 'Not so many greats, my darling. I'm not *that* old.'

'How many greats then?'

'Just *one*, Adele . . . I'm Great-Aunt Edwina, that's what you must call me.'

Adele laughed and allowed the nanny to guide her inside. Elvira took Adele to her room to freshen up, and Tessa helped Edwina to climb the stairs, followed closely by Emily.

As they walked into the upstairs parlour, Paula glanced across at the door, and asked, 'Where were you?' Then spotting Tessa, her face lit up, and she exclaimed, 'There you are, darling.'

'Mummy! Wonderful news! Jean-Claude is safe.' Once again Tessa began to cry, and so did Paula, as they embraced.

Emily said, 'Whilst you mop yourselves up, I'm going down to the kitchen for a bottle of bubbly. We've got to toast Jean-Claude.'

During the time that Emily was gone, Tessa told her mother about Philippe's phone call, and then explained, 'I'll go back to London over the weekend, and fly to Paris on Monday. He's bound to be on his way by then.'

Paula was silent for a moment, and then she said quietly, 'We have news here, too, darling. Rather sad. Uncle Robin died today.'

'Oh, Mummy, I'm so sorry, what happened?'

'He just died, peacefully.'

Edwina said, 'We're planning his funeral for Wednesday.'

Tessa's face fell. 'Oh, dear . . .'

She got no further. Edwina exclaimed, 'But there's absolutely no reason for *you* to be there. You're better off going to Paris to look after that darling fiancé of yours, tend to his needs. Robin won't mind if you're not there when we bury him. *He* was a true romantic, if ever there was one. Look at the way he carried on with Glynnis. And for fifty years!'

Tessa stared at Paula, biting her lip.

Paula nodded. 'Edwina's right, darling.'

Within minutes Emily returned with a bottle of champagne in an ice bucket, followed by Margaret with a tray of glasses. 'It's luvely news, Tessa,' she said. 'I'm glad he's safe and sound.'

'Thanks, Margaret.'

Emily poured the Pol Roger and passed the flutes around. 'Here's to Jean-Claude! And to the two new Hartes.'

Tessa gaped at Emily. 'Evan's had the babies!'

'Exactly,' Emily responded, smiling. 'A couple of redheads, too, according to their delighted father.'

'True Hartes then,' Tessa said. Looking at Edwina once again, she asked in a low voice, 'Are you sure I don't have to come to the funeral, Great-Aunt Edwina?'

'Absolutely. I've *banned* you!'

The four women laughed, and Paula thought, What a day. And thank God I haven't had a difficult time dealing with all of this. Two happy events. One sad one. Somehow the balance is right.

CHAPTER THIRTY-FOUR

Jack Figg stood with Linnet and Julian near the lych-gate of Pennistone Royal church, waiting for members of the family to arrive.

There was security everywhere, and there had been guards around the church for several days. Jack and his security staff had also used bomb-sniffing dogs and metal-detectors in the church itself, not wanting a repeat of the explosion which had happened on the day of Evan's and Gideon's wedding. The wall had been skilfully repaired and cleverly restored.

Jack had taken all these precautions because, as he knew only too well, it was impossible to predict what might happen in any given situation, especially with Jonathan Ainsley in the picture. And yet, deep down, Jack knew instinctively that Jonathan would come to the funeral of his father . . . and therefore nothing would happen to the church or its occupants.

As if reading his mind, Linnet suddenly turned to him and said, 'I bet Ainsley comes to the funeral, so nothing's going to happen to any of us. Bad things only happen to the Hartes when he's far away.'

Jack chuckled and exclaimed, 'You just read my mind, Beauty.'

Julian said, 'Yes, she's developed a bad habit of doing that lately. I've started to think she's a witch.'

'I'm glad Dad persuaded Mummy not to come, Jack, aren't you?' Linnet said, swiftly changing the subject.

'I am, yes. She's really not up to it yet.' Jack lifted his eyes, glanced at the sky, pale blue and blameless, filled with early morning sunlight. 'It's a grand spring day, but there's a cold wind blowing down from the moors. In fact, it's going to be very nippy in the cemetery. That's why I'm pleased Evan won't be here either. A funeral is always very draining on everyone: she's better looking after herself.'

Linnet nodded. 'Tessa won't be here either, you know that, don't you?'

'Your father told me,' Jack replied. 'I understand Great-Aunt Edwina forbade her to come, sent her packing off to Paris to wait for Jean-Claude.'

'Yes, she did, she apparently *banned* her. And Edwina was right, let's face it. As Mummy said to me this morning, life is for the living. Anyway, she left Adele and Elvira at Pennistone Royal, which we all agreed was the best thing for her to do. She'll have her hands full in Paris.'

'I hear she's pregnant,' Jack murmured, gazing at Linnet, his eyes narrowing. 'I suppose that means you're going to be the boss lady after all?'

'You bet!' Julian exclaimed.

'Only until Mummy can come back to work,' Linnet immediately interjected. 'She's not *retiring*. And anyway, one never knows with Tessa. She might easily decide to commute from Paris, after the baby's born: she's always believed she's the Dauphine.'

'Linnet will be going it alone, Jack, for the time being anyway. *Solo*, so to speak,' Julian explained. 'Evan's out on maternity leave, Tessa's preoccupied with matters in Paris and her baby, and India's got to cope with Dusty and his problems as well as the northern stores. But I've no doubts about my girl. She'll do a fine job.'

'I second that,' Jack exclaimed, and then asked Linnet, 'When *will* your mother be well enough to go back to Harte's? Another month or so?'

'Oh, no, Jack! The neurologists have told her she has to take it really easy for at least six months. They said she can go back to living her normal life, if she's comfortable doing that, but she can't even contemplate returning to work for six to eight months, perhaps longer. Yesterday Daddy confided that he plans to take her to Villa Faviola in the summer. He thinks the South of France will do her good.'

'I always trust your father's judgement,' Jack remarked, and pulled out a sheet of paper, looked down at it. 'Emily gave me this list of names last night. Can I just read it off to you, Linnet, so you can tell me if there are any changes?'

'Of course, and I think there might be some, Jack. The phone's been ringing this morning.'

Jack gave her a quick glance. 'Let's start with the Hughes family. Owen, Marietta and Elayne. They will all be here, I imagine.'

'Only Marietta, unfortunately. She arrived at Pennistone Royal very late last night, and this morning at breakfast she told me that Owen and Elayne didn't come over from the States as planned after all.'

Jack exclaimed, 'Really! That's surprising. She told me two days ago that Owen had agreed to come and was bringing Elayne with him.'

'Obviously he changed his mind. She wasn't very forthcoming earlier, but I think she's embarrassed that Owen is staying away from his father's funeral. You know Evan can't come. She's exhausted, Jack, after the birth of the twins. Also, there's some minor complication. Anyway, she's still in Queen Charlotte's, and her doctor won't let her leave the hospital until the end of this week.'

'She's all right, though?' Jack asked, concerned.

'Oh yes, she'll be fine in a couple of days. It's just rest she needs.'

'Okay,' Jack muttered, crossing out more names. 'Only Marietta from the Hughes family. Now to the Clonloughlin lot. Emily has a big question mark against all of these names. What do you know? Are they coming?'

'No. Edwina told them not to. She decided she wanted to keep the burial low-key. She thought it silly to drag Anthony and Sally and the family over from Ireland. Especially since she's planning a big memorial for Robin in London in a few months.'

Jack put lines through the Dunvales and their two sons, and said, 'So it's only India, then, representing her parents and brothers?'

'That's right,' Linnet answered. 'But Dusty's coming with her.'

'So I see. Robin's other sisters are coming, aren't they, Linnet? Your grandmother Daisy and Elizabeth, Robin's twin.'

'*Absolutely*. Grandma's staying with us, and Elizabeth is with Emily at Allington Hall. Oh, and don't forget Elizabeth's husband, Marc Deboyne. I'm sure Emily listed him, since he's her stepfather.'

'She did. But Amanda and Francesca are not mentioned.'

'Amanda's in China: you know she does all the buying for Harte Enterprises. Emily thought it ridiculous to pull her back here. As for her twin, Francesca is on holiday in Thailand. Again, Emily made the decision to let Francesca and her family finish their holiday in peace.'

Jack nodded his understanding and went on, 'As Hartes go, I have Emily, Winston, Toby, Gideon and Natalie. I know they're all going to be here. Then there's you and Julian, your father, Grandfather Bryan, and Emsie. Your mother's not coming, but what about your brother? Desmond's not on the list.'

'Dad decided not to take him out of boarding school for a funeral of one hour, and Mummy agreed. She said it was silly.'

'My father is definitely coming,' Julian murmured. 'I'm sure he's been included.'

'He has indeed, Jules. Well, I guess that's it.'

Linnet shivered and exclaimed, 'I think it's getting colder out here. Can we go up to the church?'

Leaving the lych-gate, Julian and Jack followed Linnet up to the porch, where they stood waiting, sheltered from the cold wind.

Within minutes, the procession of funeral cars rolled down the hill into the village, and the family, dressed in mourning black, alighted, began to file into the church.

And at last came the hearse bearing Robin Ainsley's body. His pall-bearers were Winston, Toby and Gideon Harte, Michael Kallinski and Shane O'Neill.

After shouldering the coffin, the five men, representing the three clans, walked up the path and into the church in measured steps.

The church was filled with masses and masses of flowers. Sunlight poured in through the beautiful, stained-glass windows and organ music soared to the rafters as the pall-bearers brought Robin's coffin down the aisle to the altar steps.

As Linnet slid closer to Julian in the pew, she recognized the strains of William Blake's *Jerusalem*, her own favourite hymn.

It was when the choirboys began to sing the words that a lump came into her throat and she discovered her eyes were moist. She thought of Evan, and the conversation they had had yesterday. Evan had so wanted to be here, to pay her last respects to the grandfather she had only known for just over a year but had grown to love so much.

The funeral service began with prayers and hymns, and then the vicar, the Reverend Henry Thorpe, spoke beautifully about Robin Ainsley, and all that he had been as a man, a politician and a parishioner. When the vicar had finished, Robin's three sisters came to the lectern together.

It was Edwina, the first-born child of Emma Harte, who was the first speaker, as the eldest. Her words about her brother Robin were eloquent, and she touched on his many kindnesses to all of his sisters, of his genuine brotherly love and his enduring friendship to each one of them until his death.

Elizabeth, Robin's twin, spoke of their closeness, and then went on to enumerate in a faltering voice his many acts of courage during the Second World War. At that time he had been a fighter pilot in the R.A.F., and very brave.

And lastly, Daisy, Emma's daughter by Paul McGill, talked about Robin's acts of kindness to his R.A.F. comrades. He had brought warmth and comfort to them during the Battle of Britain, she said lovingly, by making them part of his family, bringing them home to be spoiled by his mother, Emma Harte, and by his sisters. He had always been true blue, she finished.

Finally, it was Winston Harte who went up to eulogize his uncle, speaking about Robin's brilliant career as a Member of Parliament, expounding the major differences he had made in the country through the bills he had introduced, his many triumphs in the House, the things he had accomplished during his long and successful political life.

At one moment Linnet turned her head and spotted Jonathan Ainsley standing at the back of the church, as the funeral service was coming to an end. She grabbed Jack's arm and whispered to him, but when Jack looked behind him Ainsley was no longer visible. He had disappeared.

Outside in the cemetery there was no sight of him either, but during the burial Jack suddenly noticed him standing apart from them, near a copse of trees.

It was only at the very end that Ainsley came closer, finally showed himself to the rest of the family. He did not acknowledge them in any way, nor did they acknowledge him.

He bent down, picked up a handful of earth and threw it into the grave, as the vicar was intoning, 'Ashes to ashes, dust to dust.'

And then without a word or a glance, Jonathan Ainsley swung around and strode away, a tall, sombre figure in black.

The ringing of her mobile phone brought Marietta out of a deep sleep. Sitting up in bed, slightly disorientated, she reached for the phone, pressed it on. 'Hello?'

'I hope it's not too late to call, Mother,' Angharad said. 'I hope you're not mad.'

Startled to hear from the daughter who had so nonchalantly disappeared from her life without so much as a goodbye, Marietta exclaimed, 'Well, yes, as a matter of fact I am. Don't you think it's kind of rude? Not calling me for weeks and then ringing up at eleven at night.'

'Oh, come on, Mom, don't stand on your high horse. I just wanted to say hi. Listen, I heard you were at that funeral today . . . I suppose you're staying there at Pennistone Royal with Paula?'

Marietta took a deep breath. 'Why are you calling me, Angharad?'

'Just to say hello. How's Paula doing after her brain haemorrhage? Does she have . . . bats in the belfry?'

'Don't be so stupid!' Marietta snapped. 'I'm going to hang up.'

'No, don't, Mom. Listen, I'm engaged. Did you know that?'

'No, I didn't,' Marietta lied.

'I am. I've got the most gorgeous diamond you've ever seen. What's that saying? A diamond as big as the Ritz. Well, mine is! I'm going to marry Jonathan, you know. He's crazy for me . . . because I drive him crazy in bed.'

'I don't want to hear any of this nonsense, Angharad.'

'Dad didn't come to the funeral, did he? Why is that?'

'Angharad, it's very late. I have to hang up.'

'I'd like to see you, Mom. When you come back to London, I mean. I'm not up there in Yorkshire. Jonathan is, he went to his father's funeral. He's going to be even richer, bet you didn't know that.

He's getting everything. Nothing for little Evan. And how's she doing? Had the baby elephants yet?'

'Good night.'

'Mom, don't click me off. I'll be in London all week. I want you to see me, meet me for tea at the Ritz.' She started to laugh, sounding shrill.

'I don't know whether I can. I'll call you.'

'I'm leaving on Monday, Mom. Back to Paris we go. So call me before then, okay?'

'Very well.'

'You won't recognize me, I'm very chic these days, that's what everyone says, even Jonathan.' The laughter echoed down the phone once more, as Angharad continued, 'I'll be richer than Evan . . . much, much richer. You see, I am going to be Mrs Ainsley.'

'Good night, Angharad,' Marietta said and turned the phone off.

Sleep eluded Marietta for a while, her mind preoccupied with Angharad and what she had said. Thank God she had not given anything away about Paula, or the twins being born.

Should she meet her daughter for tea later this week? She wasn't sure. She would have to ask Evan what she thought and, perhaps more importantly, Linnet. Maybe they would want her to have tea with Angharad just to find out whatever she could.

CHAPTER THIRTY-FIVE

And so it began. The most relentless, driven, back-breaking work schedule ever conceived by anybody – except Emma Harte.

Many many years before, Emma had set out to accumulate money and power. And she had succeeded, reaching heights she herself had not dreamed of achieving. She had done it through sheer will-power, discipline, self-sacrifice and stamina. She had been seventeen years old when she had embarked upon this extraordinary journey to the top; her great-granddaughter Linnet was almost ten years older, and her aim was not to acquire money or power. What she was aiming to do was bring the great emporium Emma had founded into the Twenty-First Century. And faster and better than any of the rival stores could do – rivals who sought the same customers, were attempting the same thing, and had the same goals.

Linnet, more than any other member of the family, was blessed with those characteristics which had been Emma's stock in trade: that unique drive, stamina, and penchant for hard work, and, most importantly, the sheer will-power to push herself beyond endurance. And there was also the talent and intelligence which underscored those traits, and which Emma had bequeathed to her.

Aside from these very special characteristics, Linnet had been gifted with Emma's understanding of retailing and her enormous vision. Linnet's mother Paula had succeeded very well over the years, running the stores as Emma had run them, never deviating very much from Emma's rules. She had been trained by the founder, and revered her, and she steered the ship well.

Whilst she was an astute businesswoman, with lots of flair, Paula had never had the vision which had set Emma Harte apart, and way above her competitors. Neither did Tessa, India or Evan, Emma's three great-granddaughters. It was Linnet who had inherited this very special gift.

The vision made her aware of what could go wrong, as well as what could go right. Many a day, especially lately, she had muttered to herself, 'I know exactly what will go right. What I need to calculate is all those things which could easily go wrong.'

It was almost as if Linnet had a demon telling her things. She could sit in her office, staring into space, and see into the future . . . imagine all those things that could bring her and Harte's tumbling down. Or fulfil her dreams to give the store a dazzling future.

Although she had free rein at the moment to

run the company, Paula having made her Creative Director and Manager, Linnet knew very well she had a board to answer to, should there ever be a problem. Harte's was a public company, trading its shares on the London Stock Exchange, and even though her mother and the family owned the majority of the shares, she nevertheless knew that she had to watch her p's and q's. Her father had warned her of that, several days after the funeral, when he had come in to see her at the store in Knightsbridge. And so had Emily, who with Paula, Winston, and the ever-absent Amanda Linde, ran all of the Harte companies, and were on the board of the stores.

And so she was watching her step, as her grandfather had instructed her to do, and at the same time going at it hammer and tongs, working around the clock, pushing forward, her plans underway. The Tranquillity Spa was finished; the bridal floor was totally revamped and decorated, and was only waiting for basic merchandise so that it could open; she had started to design an area for luxury goods, even though her mother had not told her she could do this. Nevertheless, Linnet knew it was essential.

In order to cover as much ground as possible, in a very short time span, Linnet had hired two new assistants and two new secretaries. Jonelle was holding the fort in the executive suite, and Linnet was finding her invaluable.

Although her schedule was brutal, she was managing to hold to it, mostly by sacrificing all of her social life at the moment. And also thanks to her husband. Julian Kallinski had grown up with her, had similar responsibilities, and would one day inherit the vast international conglomerate, Kallinski Industries, from his father Michael, who had inherited it from his father, Sir Ronald Kallinski, who had inherited from *his* father, David Kallinski, the founder of their clan. And so, better than any other man, Julian knew exactly *what* she was doing and *why* she was doing it, and he applauded her for it.

Basically, Linnet wanted to bring something wonderful but just a bit old-world into the future, thereby saving its life.

Today, more than ever, Harte's had a lot of competition in London – not only the big department stores, but boutiques, ateliers, and small shops, all of them vying for the fashion-conscious pretty woman . . . and the older more sophisticated woman as well. Julian supported her, cheered her on, and never doubted for one moment that she would win. His Linnet was a winner all the way.

And so together they formulated a plan.

Every morning, Linnet leapt out of bed at four-thirty, and so did Julian. She went to the shower first; he put on the coffee pot. Within minutes he was in the shower, she was doing her make-up; he went to shave as she made the toast. Minutes later, in their robes, they sat together in the kitchen enjoying a light breakfast, then they dressed for the day and left the apartment.

Their driver dropped Linnet at the store first, then took Julian on to Kallinski House. She was behind her desk at five forty-five, he was at his office at six.

Every night, at seven o'clock, Julian picked her up at the store, and the driver either took them home for a cosy supper in front of the fire, or they dropped in at a favourite restaurant for dinner.

Because Linnet needed to work Saturdays, he did the same. At the end of the first month it had become a well-oiled routine; they were enjoying it because they were both, in their different ways, seeing their intense work come to fruition.

Now, on this lovely spring morning in May, Linnet went out onto the fashion floor, holding her breath and crossing her fingers. Today was the day.

The Tranquillity Spa would be opening its doors for the first time, and the floor now named BRIDES would be proudly showing off its fabulous gowns and every type of other bridal merchandise. Even the luxury goods area was finished, and would open to the public today.

Just as exciting, as far as Linnet was concerned, was her total revamping of the fashion floors. She had rushed to Paris for three days, just after Robin's funeral, had gone on a marathon buying spree, selecting clothes from all of the prêt-à-porter lines produced by the top fashion houses. She had also bought merchandise at Valentino, Ungaro, Chanel, and some of the lesser houses, determined to bring her fashion floors up to par.

The handbag and shoe departments had been given the same revamp, and her new assistant,

Phyllis Peters, had filled both boutiques with the most delectable, glamorous and sexy merchandise she had ever seen.

Looking at her watch, Linnet saw that it was only eight, and there was no one around at this hour. But as she tried the handle on the door of the spa it opened, and she came face to face with Sophie Forrester, the manager.

'Good morning, Linnet,' Sophie said, opening the door wider. 'Do you want to come in and look around again?'

'I'd love to, Sophie.'

Together the manager and Linnet toured the spa, and once more Linnet was struck by the absolute tranquillity of the space. The lighting was subdued, perfumed candles flickered everywhere, and there was the sound of tinkling water falling over stones. The overall décor had an Oriental flavour, with beautiful but spare floral arrangements, Japanese in style, whilst the treatment cubicles had the feeling of pagodas. The sense of restfulness and peace was underscored by the gentle music playing in the background.

'I wouldn't mind lying down and having a treatment myself,' Linnet said, smiling at Sophie. 'And what an apt name Tranquillity is . . . *perfect*.' As she left the spa, Linnet added, 'Thanks for the tour, and lots of luck today.'

'Thanks, Linnet.'

Walking across the floor, Linnet now stopped and surveyed the luxury goods corner, created diagonally opposite the spa for obvious reasons. She had named it LUXURY, and the boutique featured beautiful evening bags, pashminas, antique silk shawls, rare bead necklaces and earrings, exotic sandals, cashmere jackets and bathrobes, hand-embroidered, and all manner of exclusive items. Fingers crossed, she muttered under her breath as she moved on, heading for the escalators.

There were no two ways about it, BRIDES was one of the most well-designed boutiques in the store. Thanks to Bobbi Snyder, Linnet thought now as she walked through, gazing at the exquisite and elegant wedding gowns displayed on mannequins. Even her own wedding dress was on show in the boutique within BRIDES, which Linnet had named, very simply, *Evan Harte Couture*. Her own dress was there because the seamstresses had only been able to finish five gowns in the time allotted to them, and Bobbi wanted a sixth wedding dress to make a real showing. All of the Evan Harte gowns were couture, and made to measure; Evan had promised to keep on designing even though she had now extended her maternity leave to six months.

There were beautiful veils; tiaras made of pearl or diamanté; wreaths of flowers; bridesmaids' dresses; flower girl dresses; velvet and satin suits for the little page-boys. Shoes and sandals, lingerie, and other decorative items were beautifully arranged and set out, and Linnet was filled with positive thoughts as she left and went down on the escalator.

There was a lovely feeling evocative of spring on the fashion floors, which had always been under her aegis, and she was as thrilled with the way the clothes were mounted and displayed as she had been yesterday. The dresses and suits, all designed for spring, were in pretty pastel colours, made of silk, chiffons and light wools. And the banks of potted azaleas and hydrangeas furthered the sense of spring and summer everywhere.

Returning to the executive suite some twenty minutes later, Linnet felt a rush of gratitude towards the people she had hired, who had made such a tremendous effort to meet her deadline for the revamping of the various areas in Harte's.

Her mobile phone rang a few minutes later, and it was India on the line. 'I wanted to wish you lots of luck, Linny,' India said. 'I know the store must look beautiful, doesn't it?'

'*Fabulous*. There's a real spring-like feeling here today, what with all the pastel clothes and the flowers. The store-designers have done a wonderful job on all the floors, India. Oh, and the spa is . . . *tranquil*!'

'I can't wait to see it. I'll be coming up later in the week. I have my last fitting for my wedding gown.'

'Shall we have lunch or dinner?'

'Both if you can,' India laughed. 'I really miss you. And the store, as well.'

'I miss you, too, and Evan.'

'Do we have any special news from Tessa?'

'Only that Jean-Claude is making very good progress. He has really bad wounds in one leg: he was shot. But she sounded cheerful, so Mummy said.'

'I spoke to Paula yesterday, and I was a bit disappointed when she said she might not be feeling well enough to come to my wedding.'

'I knew you would be. Daddy mentioned it to me . . . he just thinks everything that requires real effort still exhausts her. Let's wait and see how she feels closer to the date, but you can count on me being there, with bells on.'

'You'd better be, and Evan and Tessa . . . you're my three matrons of honour. How's Evan doing, by the way?'

'She's well, very happy, and the babies are adorable. They have auburn fluff for hair, as Gideon calls it, and green eyes. Right proper Hartes, Uncle Winston tells everyone.' Linnet hesitated, and then confided, 'Evan's taking a longer maternity leave, India: six months altogether. I felt a bit down in the dumps about that, but it's her choice.'

'God, I can imagine! I wish I could be there in Knightsbridge more often, but I've a lot to do up here, especially without Tessa.' Now it was India's turn to hesitate for a moment, and then she asked, 'What's Tessa going to *do* finally, do we know yet?'

'Not really, but she spends most of her time in Paris, and I doubt that's going to change.'

'I agree, but listen, talking of Paris, have you heard anything more about Angharad?' India probed, curiosity getting the better of her.

'Mummy gets bits of information from Sarah. She's definitely engaged to Jonathan – well, according to Sarah. Marietta had tea with Angharad a few weeks ago, and all she did was boast about her acquisitions, according to Marietta.'

'Ill-gotten gains, you mean,' India shot back acidly.

Linnet laughed. 'Only too true. But listen, she's seemingly keeping him occupied, very busy. The devil finds work for idle hands. Perhaps he'll continue to lay off us since he's preoccupied with his fiancée.'

'I hope so. My father told me that Jack's been over to Ireland, to check the security at Clonloughlin. I'm glad of that, and glad he's coming to the wedding as a guest. He's sort of . . . like my favourite uncle.'

'Mine, too, India. I'd better go, I want to do another walk around the store.'

It had not worked.

By the end of the week Linnet was aware that business had been flat in all departments, and there were few bookings at the day spa.

The sales figures for Fashion were low; only two gowns had been ordered from BRIDES; not one item from the Luxury boutique had been bought.

Now, on this Saturday morning, Linnet was at her wits' end and filled with gloom. Her judgement had obviously been totally wrong. She had believed that jazzing up the store was the way to pull Harte's into the Twenty-First Century. Obviously she had blundered.

The great emporium's new look, the latest, up-to-date merchandise, the extraordinary Tranquillity Day Spa . . . none of these innovations had made a dent, had not brought in any new customers. As far as she knew.

The Food Halls had been busy, but then they always were. She cringed when she thought of the way she had fought her mother about creating snack bars there, and instantly pushed the memory of their quarrel to one side. And there was something truly weird . . . Mattresses, relegated to the basement, had had record sales this past week. She wondered why and had no answer for herself.

As she sat at the desk, her head in her hands, tears came into her eyes and Linnet began to weep. *Failure.* That was what she was facing, something she had never even considered. And she had a board to answer to, as well as her mother. The mere thought of this made her shiver, and she sat there for a long time, as though paralysed, unable to think let alone move.

The problem was she had no one to talk to, no one to turn to for advice. India had cancelled her trip to London, but even if she had been here, what could her cousin have said? Linnet knew *she* was supposed to be the smart one in the family when it came to retailing. But as far as she was concerned, at the moment she was a total failure.

Too much chutzpa, she thought, that's what Julian would say. And she could hear her mother saying, '*Pride comes before a fall.*' The tears suddenly spurted again and she put her head down on the desk and wept as if her heart would break.

'Crying's not going to get you anywhere,' the voice said, echoing around the large office.

Startled, Linnet sat up with a jolt, looked from side to side. Of course there was no one there. It was seven o'clock on Saturday morning, and there was hardly anyone in the store yet, especially at this hour. Sitting back in the chair, Linnet wiped the tears from her face with her fingers and found a tissue in her pocket. After blowing her nose, she got up and went to the adjoining bathroom, stared at herself in the mirror. Her face was streaked with mascara, and she had chewed most of her lipstick off. After splashing her face with cold water and patting it dry, she went back to the desk, took out a compact and patted her face with powder, freshened her lipstick.

Walking across to the door, she went out and hurried to the long corridor, came to a standstill in front of the portrait of Emma. 'It was you, wasn't it, Grandy?' Linnet said, staring at that famous face. 'You were talking to me, weren't you?' Obviously there was no answer. A portrait couldn't speak, couldn't give you advice, however much you wanted it to do so. But, nonetheless, Linnet went on talking to the painting. 'How did you do it alone?' she asked, staring into those green eyes so like her own. 'How did you cope? Who guided you? Who did you turn to when things were tough?'

Linnet knew the answers to her questions. Emma Harte had not had anyone to help her or guide her. She had done it all by herself.

Solo.

And *she* was solo now. Just as Grandy had been for most of her life. Leaning closer to the portrait,

Linnet whispered, 'You're right, crying won't get me anywhere. I'm not going to cry anymore. I'm going to solve the problem. Just as you solved your problems, Emma.'

As she always did, Linnet smiled at Emma's portrait, touched her great-grandmother's face, and then hurried back to her mother's office, which she had used off and on these last few weeks.

Linnet knew that everyone would think her fanciful if they knew she believed Emma Harte spoke to her, and that was why Julian had always warned her not to tell anyone. Certainly they would think she was crazy, if they knew she was actually talking to the portrait.

Fanciful or crazy, what did it matter? Linnet felt better when she sat down behind the desk, picked up a pen and began to make notes. She had done all the right things, she was sure of that. She had done plenty of clever advertising in the newspapers, so customers knew about the Tranquillity Day Spa and fashion innovations; she had hired new window-dressers and designers, and had even brought Perry Jones over from the New York store to lend a creative hand. Advertising and windows had been taken care of properly. So what had she missed? What had escaped her? Bad weather? It had rained during the week . . .

Impatient, Linnet thought, the word popping into her head. I haven't given it enough time . . . Yes, perhaps that's it . . . She remained at the desk making notes until eleven o'clock; then she went down to the ground floor and outside to look at the windows.

Staring at them as objectively as possible, Linnet began to realize they were too busy. It was true she had asked the designers to create a spring-summer feeling, but wasn't there just too much décor and not enough fashion here?

As she moved on, went around to the side street, to look at the window containing new handbags, she heard two women talking. One of them said, 'You can't see the wood for the trees here. But there's the Cholly Chello bag, the one I told you about. Do you see it, that red one? It's the only bag in the world that every woman wants. I wish I could afford it.'

The woman was right, there were too many bags in the window, Linnet recognized this at once. But what struck her most was that phrase about the Cholly Chello being the only bag in the world, and she dashed back to her office, her busy mind working overtime.

The side window of Harte's was stark, had a plain cream backdrop. On a simple wooden packing crate stood the red Cholly Chello handbag, and, to one side of the crate, a large yellow board hung down from the ceiling. Written in bold black letters were the words THE ONLY BAG IN THE WORLD THAT EVERY WOMAN WANTS.

'It's perfect, Perry,' Linnet said to the American window-designer whom she had brought over to London weeks ago to revamp their windows. 'You'll see, it's going to do the trick.'

'From your mouth to God's ears,' Perry answered,

and taking hold of Linnet's arm he led her to the front windows of Harte's, facing Knightsbridge. 'Now, what do you think? We finished them about half an hour ago, and I sincerely hope they do the trick, too.'

The large front windows were as stark as the other one on the side street, and Linnet could see the clothes were no longer overwhelmed by the décor. 'Oh, Perry, they're great! You've done a terrific job!' she exclaimed, her eyes on the pale-blue sky filled with puffy white clouds. The sky, a white picket fence with three yellow daisies growing next to it composed the backdrop for the clothes. And only two dresses were displayed in each window, so that they had breathing space.

'Less is more,' Linnet murmured. 'And thank you for working such long hours to re-do the windows, Perry. I really appreciate it.'

'It's my pleasure; and by the way, that was a great slogan you came up with about the bag. Actually, I've never heard of the Cholly Chello.'

'Neither have I,' Linnet admitted with a laugh. 'But my handbag-buyer says it's the up-and-coming item for the fashionistas.'

Perry laughed with her as they went back into Harte's, the greatest emporium in the world.

'It's the Cholly Chello that's bringing them into the store in droves,' Linnet said to India two weeks later. 'We can't keep it in stock, and the manufacturer can't make it fast enough. They've never had such success with a bag. *Ever*.'

'It's strange,' India answered, giving Linnet an odd look. 'But I've never heard of it before, have you?'

'No. Still, it *is* a big hit.'

'You know what, it's the slogan you thought up,' India suddenly asserted, pushing the fish around on her plate. 'You created a market for the bag with your slogan.'

'Oh, really, India, come on, I'm not that clever.'

'Listen, Hermès did it with the Kelly and the Birkin. They cleverly created a market by not producing so many. These days people have to put their names on a waiting list to get either bag, and they wait years.'

Linnet chuckled. 'We've got waiting lists, too, for the Cholly Chello. And when these smart young women are putting their names on our list for the bag, they notice the Tranquillity Day Spa and wander in, become entranced. And they're also very taken with my Luxury boutique, not to mention the fashion floors. But I've got to admit, this upswing in traffic in the store is happening because of that darn bag.'

The two cousins were sitting in the Bird Cage having lunch, and catching up. It was a relief for Linnet to see India, to have someone to talk to about work. Evan was preoccupied with the twins, Tessa was still in Paris, and her father did not want Paula disturbed. During the hour they were together Linnet went over her plans for the store with India, and they agreed that she would come to London more often. The Leeds and Harrogate stores were now running well, and Dusty's problems regarding the Caldwells and Molly's will were all in the past.

'What he has to look forward to now is our wedding in Ireland,' India murmured as they left the restaurant. 'As you know, Atlanta is going to be a flower girl along with Adele, and she's very excited about that.'

'I'm so happy for you, India, and thankful that everything worked out for you and Dusty in the end. And I can't wait to come to Clonloughlin in June for your marriage.'

CHAPTER THIRTY-SIX

S he had come here to Ireland as a young bride over seventy years ago, the wife of Jeremy Standish, Earl of Dunvale, and it had all been like a dream. Here in this beautiful Georgian house in Clonloughlin she had spent the happiest days of her life.

She wished now that he was here today to see this other bride of Clonloughlin, their exquisite granddaughter India Standish, only daughter of their son Anthony. She's a mixture of all that's best and bright, Edwina thought: part Dunvale, part Harte, part Fairley. Oh yes, India has inherited a lot in *her* genes.

Edwina sat at a table in the ballroom of Clonloughlin House on a glorious Saturday in the middle of June, and she was, as was her way, surveying the assemblage. The guests were mostly family, but there were a few friends present, about fifty people in all. The house here had been a whirl of activity for several weeks, but the wedding was not the splashy event it had been meant to be, for a number of reasons – good taste, death and security. Bowing to what they deemed her better judgement, knowing she was correct, Anthony and Sally had agreed to her suggestion of keeping it simple. And so had India and Dusty, who were totally on her side. Robin had died only a few months before, and then there had been the upsetting deaths of Molly Caldwell and her daughter. 'Such poor taste, such bad form to have a big splashy fancy affair,' Edwina had intoned weeks ago. 'Let's be correct, proper about this.'

The deaths aside, there was also the matter of security, plus the spectre of the deadly Jonathan Ainsley overshadowing everything. He was Anthony's first cousin and they had quarrelled badly years ago. Since then, Ainsley had been vindictive and threatening, and especially so after Anthony took Paula's side in the great débâcle some years before.

It was a lovely gathering, nonetheless.

Edwina had caught her breath in delight and pride when India had walked down the aisle in the little church on the estate, holding on to the arm of her father.

Edwina looked across at her now, standing with her parents, talking to Winston, her mother's brother. What a gorgeous young woman, she thought, there's no other word to use. The pale-ivory taffeta wedding gown, designed by Evan, had big puff sleeves, a scooped-out neckline and a huge crinoline skirt that floated around her like a puffy cloud. She had removed her veil but the antique diamond tiara was back in place on her shining silver-gilt hair. Adele

Fairley's tiara, Edwina mused, smiling, thinking of their lineage, India's and hers.

India was a dreamlike creature on this, her wedding day, and looked out of this world. And the bridegroom was standing there, darkly handsome, and so proud of his wife. It showed on his face, that pride. A genuine man, honest and true, a dependable man, and oh, what a talent he possessed.

She would never forget the look on Dusty's face as India had glided towards him and his best man Gideon, who were waiting at the altar in the little church. It had been one of pure love, pure joy.

After the marriage vows, they had all come back here to Clonloughlin House for cocktails in the main drawing room, where many photographs had been taken by the professional photographer. Two hours later, at six-thirty, they had settled in the large formal dining room for supper. All of the antique Georgian furniture had been removed, the room filled with circular skirted tables partnered with gilded ballroom chairs. Edwina had been pleased with the effect. Almost everything was white, from the organza tablecloths to the flower arrangements. The women in their lovely gowns introduced a splash of colour, and as she had looked around she couldn't help admiring the glittering Waterford crystal chandeliers she had chosen years before, which hung down from the high-flung ceiling.

After the supper, where many speeches were given, many toasts made, they had moved in here to dance and enjoy the rest of the evening. There was a trio at one end of the room, and now, much to her pleasure, came the bride and groom. They walked onto the dance floor for their first dance together as man and wife. When the strains of *True Love* filled the air, Dusty took India in his arms and led her into the middle of the floor.

'Are you all right, Great-Aunt Edwina?' Linnet asked, sitting down with her.

'I'm in great form, Linnet, great form.' Peering at her intently, Edwina continued in a low but vibrant voice, 'My goodness, in your pale-blue gown and those emerald earrings, you have such a look tonight, the look of my mother.'

'So Grandfather Bryan said earlier.' Staring at the couple on the dance floor, Linnet exclaimed, 'Oh, Great-Aunt Edwina, isn't India the most perfect bride you've ever seen?'

'She is indeed, but you three girls look wonderful, too. Everyone does in fact: the women in all their elegance, the men in their morning suits. It's just sad for me that Paula and Shane aren't here.'

'Daddy is very protective of Mummy. He thought the strain of travel, the excitement of the wedding would be too much.'

'But she's looking so well, I thought.'

'She gets mixed up a lot, and can't always fathom things out the way she used to,' Linnet explained.

'But she isn't ill?' Edwina pressed, giving Linnet a keen look.

'No, no, she's not. It's all part of the recovery, so I understand.'

'And you're holding the fort, so to speak?' Edwina asked.

Linnet smiled a little wryly. 'Trying to, and I must admit, it's tough at times, especially without India, Tessa and Evan. And I'm lonely.'

'It *is* lonely at the top. Always. I know what my mother went through.'

'Can I ask you something, Edwina?'

'Anything you wish, my dear.'

'Once, you said you heard your mother's voice talking to you. Did you mean really *heard* it, or was it simply an echo from the past in your head?'

'An echo mostly, I'm sure,' Edwina responded thoughtfully. 'But sometimes I thought I did really hear her . . . Perhaps I was simply remembering . . . it could have been memories coming back to me. Why do you ask?'

'Because I hear her voice . . . hear her telling me things. Do you think I'm daft in the head?'

'No. *Imaginative.*'

Linnet was silent, studying her aunt.

Edwina leaned forward, pinning her eyes on Linnet. 'You've been told all of your life that you look like her, sound like her, act like her. You've grown up believing you've inherited her strength, stamina, intelligence and business acumen. She's been all around you since the day you were born. She is part of you, just as you are part of her, and you do have her genes. So when you're stressed and worried and feel utterly *alone*, you think she comes to your aid.'

'Yes, yes, I do, that's true!'

'It's all in your head, in your mind, Linnet. Don't fret about it, my dear, because if it helps you, so

what? No harm done. However, don't tell anyone else!'

Linnet smiled, and leaning closer to Edwina, she
whispered, 'That's what Julian says. I suppose he's
worried people will think I'm crazy.'

'Perhaps they would. On the other hand, why
should you care what the world thinks of you?
You are your own woman, and that's what you
must always be, Linnet. Then you really will be
the new Emma Harte.'

India and Dusty were suddenly standing at the
table, beaming at Linnet and Edwina.

'May I have the honour of this dance, Edwina?'
Dusty asked, bowing slightly.

'It will be my pleasure, Dusty. And did I say it
before . . . ? Welcome to my family.'

'You did say it, but you can keep repeating it as
much as you want,' Dusty responded, leading her
onto the dance floor with a show of gallantry.

India put her arm through Linnet's, and murmured sadly, 'I miss Paula and Shane not being
here.'

'So do I, but it's better Mummy stays quiet.'

'Is she getting back to normal, though?' India
asked softly.

'Yes.' Linnet nodded her head.

'So when is she coming back to the store?'

'I don't know. Dad's taking her to Villa Faviola
at the end of June, for July and August. Also, Tessa
told her the other day that she and Jean-Claude
want to get married the first week of September.
In Yorkshire. So there'll be another wedding.'

'I'm glad, I'm happy for her,' India remarked, meaning every word, and glanced around. 'Look at her, Linnet, over there. She's so in love with her lovely Frenchman.'

'I know. What a difference there is between him and the horrible Mark Longden!'

'Has Tessa mentioned what she'll do after she's married?'

'I don't think she'll work in London, India. Still, Mummy gave me the impression that Tessa wants to keep her hand in by doing our fashion-buying in Paris.'

'That might work out well for us all,' India exclaimed.

'I hope so. India, just look at your grandmother and Dusty! She's having a rare old time out there, a regular Ginger Rogers.'

'And she's a rare old bird, don't you think?'

'There's no one like her . . . She's the jewel in the crown.'

The two of them sat watching Edwina waltzing past with Dusty. Regal and elegant in purple chiffon and diamonds, and truly a miracle at ninety-five.

A short while later Dusty brought Edwina back to the table, and danced off with India; then Julian came to claim Linnet. Suddenly Edwina was alone, watching the festivities, a smile on her face. Within seconds, Gideon and Evan joined her, followed by Grandfather Bryan, Emsie and Desmond. A moment later Jean-Claude and Tessa arrived, and sat down with them, and so did Lorne. Edwina was suddenly surrounded by those she loved, and this pleased her enormously.

Touching her arm, Grandfather Bryan remarked, 'Well, well, just look over there, Edwina. Marietta Hughes dancing with Jack Figg. They make a grand couple, mavourneen, don't you agree?'

'Sure I do, Bryan, my lad,' Edwina said, adopting a soft Irish lilt. 'I'm all for romance.'

Bryan laughed, and so did the rest of the table.

Edwina, at one moment, glanced around, and her wise old eyes settled on each one of them and she thought: most of them are the progeny of Emma Harte. And they are absolutely . . . the very best. Emma would be so proud of them all . . . because they do her proud every day of their lives. And Edwina's heart was full and she felt happy, so glad to have witnessed this day.

A week later Linnet was working late at Harte's in Knightsbridge, and she glanced up when her mobile phone rang. Picking it up, she said, 'Hello? Linnet O'Neill.'

'It's India,' her cousin said.

'Hi, darling, how's the honeymoon going? Is Dusty enjoying being at Clonloughlin?'

'Oh yes, he's fallen in love with the place. Linnet?'

'Yes, what is it? You sound odd.'

'Grandma died.'

'Oh, no, not Edwina!' Linnet cried, her eyes filling up. Her throat instantly became tight, but she managed to say, 'I can't believe it, she was going strong at your wedding.'

'She *was* ninety-five, you know.'

'Everyone thought she'd live to be a hundred, that was her goal, she told me. Oh, India, it's just awful that she's gone . . . the whole family's going to miss her terribly.' Linnet reached for a tissue, wiped her eyes.

India began to cry. Through her tears she managed to say, 'I found her, Linnet. I thought she was dozing on the sofa in her bedroom, but she was gone. And in her hands she had a photograph of herself and Emma when she was a little girl, and she was clinging to her mother's hand. She must have been thinking of Emma when she died.'

'I have to put the phone down a minute,' Linnet said, tears rolling down her face.

'It's all right.' India was weeping herself, her eyes streaming.

A moment later, after blowing her nose and getting hold of her swimming senses, Linnet finally said, 'When is the funeral, India?'

'We've buried her,' India replied, also sounding less tearful. 'This morning, actually, in the cemetery on the estate. That's the way she wanted it. She told my father recently that her funeral should be totally private, that she didn't want the whole family dragging themselves over to Ireland.' India paused, took a deep breath. 'She said she didn't believe in funerals, only weddings and christenings.'

'I would have liked to be there,' Linnet remarked. 'And I bet *everyone* would have come.'

'You'd all just left, after the wedding. Dad thought it wiser to abide by his mother's wishes.' There was a pause, and India began to laugh through her tears. 'Grandma did say she wanted a memorial service, though. A big one.'

After India had hung up, Linnet sat for a while staring into the distance, her mind on Edwina, thinking of her and all that she had been as a woman. How odd that she had been holding a picture of Emma and herself when she was small. But no, perhaps it wasn't. After all, she had loved her mother.

For a split second Linnet thought of going down the corridor to tell the portrait of Emma that her first-born child was dead. But she didn't.

Instead she wrote a letter to Anthony, telling her uncle what a remarkable woman his mother had been, speaking of her own sorrow at this loss, and sending him her condolences.

It seemed to Linnet later, when she looked back, that this particular summer had just slid by.

She and Julian kept to their routine, working hard at their jobs. Much to her relief, the innovations she had made at Harte's in Knightsbridge had proved to be successful. There was heavy traffic right through June, July, and August, with customers flocking to the Tranquillity Day Spa, invading the fashion floors, and making the Luxury boutique their favourite place to buy the most expensive merchandise in the store. BRIDES had finally taken off, and, in particular, bridal gowns designed by Evan Harte were the pick of the summer season.

Every day Linnet prayed that her luck would hold.

And it did. The store acquired a lot of new, younger customers, and also provided better choices to the old core customer who had patronized Harte's for years. And everyone remarked on the fresh look, the updated merchandise, and the spectacular displays on every floor.

Linnet knew she had managed to pull Harte's of Knightsbridge into the Twenty-First Century; she was also aware that her work had only just begun. She had to keep improving on everything, launching new ideas to titillate the taste buds of the customers, whilst making sure that the other stores, her rivals, didn't outsmart her.

India came up to London twice a month, and the two cousins enjoyed being together. Linnet was fully aware how much she needed India running the northern stores; many a time she asked herself how her great-grandmother had run all three stores when it took her all of her time to cope with just one.

If there were occasions when she panicked, felt alone, stressed and even a little afraid, there were many more times when she experienced the thrill of satisfaction, knowing she had pulled off yet another little coup. This might be the new Cholly Chello bag, called Cholly Baby, a smart little evening bag that had not walked, but run, out of the stores in London, Leeds and Harrogate. Or it might be success with a beauty product or a spa treatment.

And so the days went by.

* * *

Late one afternoon, towards the end of August, Jack Figg buzzed her. 'It's me, Beauty,' he announced when she answered her private line. 'Do you have a minute? Can I come up and see you?'

'Of course. Is there a problem, Jack?'

'No. I wouldn't call it that. Be there in a jiffy.'

Linnet stood up when Jonelle showed him in a few minutes later, and went around the desk to embrace him. Then she led him to a circular table at one end of her mother's office and indicated the chairs. 'Let's sit here, Jack, I much prefer it to those dumpy sofas over there.'

He laughed. 'So do I.'

'Do you want a cup of tea?'

'Why not . . . but only if you are,' he replied, sitting down.

Nodding, Linnet went to the phone, spoke to Jonelle on the intercom and returned to the table, took a chair opposite Jack.

'How's your mother?' he asked.

'Great. The South of France is doing her good, according to Dad. Julian and I have been trying to get down there off and on for ages, but we're just too busy right now.'

'I know your routine. It's twenty-four seven, these days, isn't it, Linny?'

She laughed, and looked at the door as Jonelle came in carrying a tea tray.

Once they were alone again, Linnet poured the tea and asked, 'So Jack, if it's not a problem, what is it? Why did you want to see me?'

After taking a sip of his tea, Jack put the cup back

in the saucer, and said, 'Emma used to say to me that everyone got their just rewards in life, got what they deserved in the end. And your great-grandmother was right.'

'Do you mean we all reap what we sow?'

'Sort of, yes . . .' Settling back in the chair, Jack gave her a long look through narrowed eyes. 'One of my operatives in France just gave me some extraordinary news. About Jonathan Ainsley.'

'What is it?' Linnet asked, staring back at him with great intensity. 'You sound solemn.'

'Ainsley has been in a terrible car crash. Just outside Paris, so I understand. He's in the American Hospital in Paris, has sustained horrific injuries, according to my chap.'

'He's not dead then?' Linnet asked.

'No. But he's not expected to live.'

'What happened? Do you know?'

'A head-on car crash with a lorry.'

'What about Angharad? Was she with him? Is she injured?'

'It seems she was not in the car.' Jack's mobile warbled, and he took it out of his pocket. 'Jack Figg here.' He listened attentively, and after a few seconds, he said, 'Keep in touch. And thanks, Pierre.' Clicking off the phone, he went on, 'My operative, who's at the hospital, told me that Jonathan Ainsley has just lapsed into a coma, and is not expected to live.'

'Oh, my God! I can't believe it!' Linnet shouted, grabbing Jack's arms. 'We're free of him at last! Free of his evil and wickedness!'

'Just rewards, as Emma always said,' Jack murmured, smiling at her. 'Jonathan Ainsley got his just rewards.'

'I can't wait to tell everybody,' Linnet cried. 'There's going to be a mass celebration throughout the family.'

And there was.

Late one morning, at the end of that same week, Linnet had a surprise visitor. She was studying the overall sales figures for the previous month, when a soft voice said, 'Hello, darling.'

Swinging her head, a look of astonishment crossing her face, Linnet saw her mother standing in the doorway.

'Mummy!' she cried, jumping up, rushing to her. 'I didn't know you were back from the South of France.'

'We got back last night.' Paula embraced her daughter, holding her close. 'I've missed you, Linny.'

'And I've missed you, too, Mummy. Come on, come and sit down. Better still, come and sit at the desk. It's yours, you know, I've only been borrowing it.'

'No, no, I haven't come to work,' Paula answered, and, spotting the circular table, she headed over to it, saying, 'This is a good idea. Better than those awful sofas.'

Linnet laughed, following her mother, thrilled to see her looking so well. 'You're your old self, Mums.'

'Not quite, not yet, but I'm getting there.'

Sitting down with her mother, Linnet asked, 'Do you want a cup of coffee or tea? Anything?'

'No, not really, darling, but thank you. The store looks beautiful,' Paula began, and paused. Reaching out, she patted Linnet's hand. 'You've done a wonderful job. And you've certainly introduced a fresh, modern look without destroying all of those traditional things our customers love. Your innovations have been successful . . . *Congratulations.*'

'Thanks, Mummy. It was a bit tough at times, and I never stopped wanting to ring you up, but Daddy was adamant: he didn't want me to bother you. He told me to do the best I could.'

'Oh, yes, he told me all about that, Linny, and I longed to talk to *you*, too. I kept worrying about you, knowing how tough it is here sometimes. But I restrained myself.'

'Let me sink or swim, was that it?' she asked, her green eyes sparkling.

'Sort of, darling.'

'Anyway, Mummy, welcome back. It's wonderful to see you. I'll clean my stuff out of the office this afternoon. I never moved very much in, actually.'

'No, no, you don't have to do that, Linnet.'

'What do you mean?'

'This is *your* office.'

Again Linnet looked baffled. 'I don't understand.'

'I'm not coming back to work.' Paula sat back in the chair, and gazed at her daughter for the longest moment, and then in a strong, steady voice, she explained, 'Long ago, my grandmother told me that there comes a time in everybody's life when it's appropriate to step aside, to let younger voices be heard, greater visions be perceived . . . This was said when she was eighty years old. It was at the birthday party we gave for her. She wasn't saying those words only to me, Linnet, she was saying it to everyone, and especially my generation, her grandchildren. It was the night she retired.'

Linnet gazed back at her mother, transfixed. 'Mummy, I don't understand . . .'

'I'm retiring, Linnet. It's your turn now, your turn to run the Harte stores, to be the boss lady, as you've always called me.'

'But—'

'No buts,' Paula cut in firmly. 'All those years ago, Emma said to me: "I charge you to hold my dream." And I did. Linnet, I charge you to hold Emma's dream and my dream. All this . . . It's yours now. I know you love the stores as she did, as I do. I know our dreams are safe in your small but very capable hands.'

Epilogue

The woman was tall, slender, and elegantly dressed. She stood by the window in the dimly-lit room, looking out at the mountains, snowcapped, glittering in the bright afternoon sunshine. She liked Zurich: it was a beautiful place. She hoped she would be living here. She swung around as the door opened and the man walked in, holding out his hand.

Hurrying towards him, she shook his outstretched hand, and looked at him intently. 'What are the results?' she asked in a low, well-modulated voice.

'I am happy to say that the X-rays told us a great deal more than we expected. The problem is not as terrible as you have been led to believe. You were right to come to us, and yes, we can help you . . . there will be recovery, I am certain of that. It will be slow. But in the end it is worthwhile, is it not? If everything can be restored to normal? As, in fact, we believe it can.'

'Yes, you're right, it *is* worth the time and effort. And money. I am going to trust you. I will put myself in your hands.'

The man inclined his head graciously.

'Please give me a moment, and then I will come to your office to go over the details.'

'Of course, madame,' he said and slipped out of the room.

The woman walked over to the corner, looked down at the bandaged head and face, the almost lifeless body which was prone on the narrow bed.

She reached out, put her hand on one shoulder. 'It's going to be all right,' she whispered. 'You'll be all right.'

There was no response, no sound, no movement. Nothing.

She knew he was alive. The doctors here had confirmed that. And now she knew they would make him better, get him back for her. The director of the clinic had just told her so.

Bending down, she kissed the bandaged cheek and stepped away. She did not want to leave him, but she knew she must. 'You'll get better, darling,' she murmured, and walked across the room to the door.

He had to get better. She was carrying his child. That longed-for child . . . And he would be called Jonathan Ainsley, just as his father was. Angharad Hughes Ainsley smiled to herself.

They would win in the end. Because they were winners. Jonathan had told her *that* the day he had married her.